MW01182133

WAKING THE BEAST

D Hall Books LLC.

All rights reserved, including the right to reproduce this book in its entirety or any portions thereof in any form whatsoever.

Cover illustration image by: Anoldent
Cover illustration title: "Old Home Place 1985"
Cover illustration copyright: © June 2007

2002 © Copyright by: Dustin Hall
Cover design by: Jessica Hall
Interior design layout by: Dustin Hall
ISBN-13: 978-1502511676
ISBN-10: 1502511673

For more information please visit:
dhallbooks.com

This book is a work of fiction. Any references to historical events, real people or real places are used fictitiously. All other names, places and events are products of the authors imagination and any resemblance to actual person, places or events dead or alive is entirely coincidental.

Table of contents

PROLOGUE

May 9, 1944, Munich, Germany

World War II was at its peak. Chaos and mass destruction were everywhere. For three years the allied forces dropped tons of artillery over German occupied territory. Towns and cities alike were turned into boundless piles of rubble. The Third Reich had been hit hard, suffering heavy casualties. Jews and undesirables were arrested daily and forced into segregation camps by the thousands. They had no choice other then to leave their possessions and loved ones behind. Some of whom, were thrown to the front line to combat their oppressor who also happened to be their own flesh and blood. They resisted and fought furiously at every opportunity, but they were no match for their nemesis.

The United States' onslaught brought Germany to its knees. Frustrated and shocked from the briefing of his top aides, Hitler was more determined then ever to rebuild his rapidly depleting Nazi army. In desperation, he turned to his team of renowned scientists to find a solution, hoping one was available. Germany had already invested an enormous amount of time and resources in the field of medical science. Nevertheless, as they tried to produce a hybrid vigor, progress was minimal at best. Disgruntled by the results, Hitler issued an executive order summoning all scientists to meet with Germany's defense team.

Memos were also distributed to all top ranking officers and two weeks later a meeting was held at an undisclosed location. Top of the agenda was to intensify every effort in the search for a genetic enhancement. A designated team specializing in Deoxyribonucleic Acid (DNA) was selected to secretly perform tests of genetic composition in both animals and humans.

The project involved the alteration of the nucleotide sequence of the DNA coding. By changing the physical arrangement of chromosomes, they could create a new trait of the human species. If successful, the new species would replace the Third Reich soldiers at the battlefront. If this wild card panned out, Hitler would be able to defeat the allied forces and conquer the world.

August 1, 1944, Joshua Tree, California

Despite the war escalating in Europe, Joshua Tree was celebrating its third year since declaring itself as a township. The vast terrain had slowly developed into an industrial town. The economic growth attracted new settlers from all the neighboring counties. Within the last three years alone the population had nearly doubled. Housing and construction sights were in view as far as the eye could see, rapidly changing the natural wilderness into a prospering town.

Although the community was thriving and enjoying its good fortune, their enthusiasm came to an abrupt halt as a series of disappearances suddenly plagued this once quiet residence. Frustration soon turned into outrage and the townsfolk were in frenzy. Finger pointing and reproach became random. No one was immune to the accusations of their neighbors and everyone was a suspect. The number of missing persons had climbed to sixteen within a month's time. Everyone was astonished and couldn't understand how or why all of these people were vanishing without a trace, leaving behind all their belongings and loved ones with no explanation or reason.

Concerned about the possibility that the town's violence might escalate, the sheriff called a town meeting to be held at the Sacred Heart Church on August 3rd. All of the locals attended, expressing their growing fears. They wanted resolve, justice and an immediate explanation for this madness that was complicating their peaceful lives.

Sheriff Jim Jenson, the person responsible for assembling the vigil, was just as baffled by the mysterious disappearances. In an attempt to calm the crowd, Jenson assured everyone in the audience that he would make every effort to locate the missing persons. He tried to rationalize with everyone in attendance and suggested that they form a neighborhood watch until he could come up with something solid. Not satisfied with his response, the crowd became restless and began to exit the church more frustrated then when they had arrived.

August 3, 1944

It was a typical hot summer day in Joshua Tree where the cooler air of night was about to fall. As the sun set, the skies changed from a dark blue to a vibrant orange yellow color. There was not a single cloud in the sky that evening and the slight cooling breeze was a relief to everyone. Aimee Edge, a nineteen-year-old waitress at the local diner had been engaged to Rob Drolet. Rob was the latest victim of this mysterious vanishing that plagued the community. Finally, on this cool summer night, Aimee and her friend Billy decided to take a walk to the outskirts of the town. Billy Pasco was twenty years of age, a good friend of Aimee's and Rob's best friend in the world.

As they were taking their stroll, they heard a sudden sound echoing out to them from the woods. Startled, Aimee leapt into Billy's arms. Shaken and frightened, she began to cry. When Billy asked her what was wrong, she just shrugged her shoulders as tears rolled down her cheeks.

"Are you still thinking about what Sheriff Jenson said?" Billy asked calmly.

She nodded her head in agreement and whimpered, "Yes."

"I don't like what's going on either, but I'm sure we're gonna find Rob soon," he reassured her, trying to make her feel as if it was a promise. But she knew that even if it was, it was one he could not possibly keep.

"I certainly hope so, I miss him," she replied trying to sound confident.

"Me too, but I'll keep you safe while we sort this mess out and look for him," Billy replied as he lifted up the tail of his shirt exposing the weapon at his side.

Not sure of what his answer would be, she asked, "You don't think that he'd just leave because," she paused briefly, "well, because he just got fed up with everything and left?"

"Na, I know Rob," Billy tried to reassure her, "he loved you too much and would never do something like that, at least not without telling me first. Besides, who are we kidding, he'd never leave you."

Rob Drolet was tall and extremely handsome with a medium build. He was two years older then she and he helped take care of his three younger siblings. It had been almost a year since his father had died; Lieutenant Adam Drolet was killed during a routine flight. Rob loved his father and when the news of his father's death hit the town, everyone was shocked. That's when Rob first started to close himself off emotionally, quite often he would tell Aimee that he just wanted to go away and forget everything. She knew that the only thing that kept him here in this small town was his love for her.

Completely unaware of the time that passed, they walked for miles through the woods on the outskirts of town, each drifting in their own thoughts when finally Billy broke the silence, "He must've been in a hurry, for him to leave like this," he said out loud, trying to convince himself more then Aimee. But before she could respond he added, "Do you know 'bout the old man that recently moved out here?" She nodded, but he just went on talking as if she wasn't even there. "I heard he lives in a cabin out here along these trails."

"Yeah, I heard that too, what about him?" she asked.

"Well, he seems awful strange to me. You never see him with anyone, he's always by himself. It's like he doesn't have even one friend."

She arched her head back and looked up to the heavens trying to gather her thoughts. The glow of the evening's stars reflected off her soft baby blue eyes causing them to sparkle. She finally broke her endless gaze upon the stars and stated, "You know, now that you mention it, I've noticed that myself." Billy nodded his head in agreement, Aimee continued, "Do you think he has something to do with Rob's disappearance?"

"That's not what I'm saying. I just think that there's something about him that just doesn't seem right." In a tone bearing the sudden excitement in her voice, she said, "Oh, let me tell you this! The other day when I was working at the restaurant, he walked in, had a look around, then he left without buying or saying anything to anyone." Every muscle and tendon in Billy's face tightened up as Aimee was finishing her sentence.

Ever since the disappearances started, Billy kept to himself. Out of nowhere, he got a sudden gut feeling telling him there was something odd about this quiet man that strolled into their town only six months ago.

His name was Eric Aben. None of the locals really knew who he was or where he came from. All they knew was, one day he walked into the town looking for a place to stay. He rented an apartment for a short time while he worked on building some cabin in the woods. Since he had moved out to the cabin, he had only been spotted in town occasionally buying canned goods and other little necessities. After purchasing the items, he would leave without ever saying a word. Eric Aben seemed to enjoy his privacy and never said more than necessary.

"You know what?" Billy asked, "I've actually been wondering where that cabin was at, no one has ever seen it, ya know? I'll bet it's this way."

"I don't," hesitating for a second as if trying desperately to find the right words, she continued, "I just don't think we should. After all, he just doesn't seem like the type who would do something like this. He might seem strange, but I'm sure that's because we don't know him."

"Look," Billy pleaded, "we don't have to go in. All I'm saying is that we should go out there and have a look around." Still trying to persuade her he added, "What harm is there if we're just going to look around? We just might find something out there. And I'm not gonna pass up on anything that might help us find Rob."

"It'll still feel like we're trespassing," Aimee insisted. "I'm sure he lives out here because he doesn't want to be bothered."

"Look," Billy said aggressively with a smirk on his face. Trying to ease her uncertainty, he patted his hand on the piece at his side and said, "I promise, nothing will happen to you, I will protect you."

"Is that why you brought that with you?" She asked curiously.

"Na," Billy sighed as he tried to lighten the seriousness of her question, "but you've got to admit, that with all these people going missing, you can't be too careful."

"So we're just gonna go out there and have a look around, that's it, right?"

"Yeah, I promise," Billy replied.

As the two continued to walk for a little while longer, they reminisced over all the good times the three of them shared together. As Aimee realized that they were heading into the area where this man's home was supposedly located, she once again brought up the subject of her discontent, but finally gave in to his relentless pursuit.

Treading their way through rugged trails, they wandered aimlessly through the night in pursuit of a cabin that refused to be found. Before they knew it, two more hours had passed. Exhausted from their search, Aimee insisted that they call it a night. She had worked all morning, then right after the town meeting turned sour, they had started on this seemingly endless journey through the woods. All of the walking had tired her out. She wanted nothing more then to be back at home, asleep in her bed. When she turned her head to face Billy, he was actually walking a little ways behind her.

Something had caught her attention. Forcefully, she closed her eyes briefly in an attempt to force them back into focus. When she reopened them, she still couldn't make out the image through the darkness that she was looking at. By now, Billy too was trying to see what she was looking at. When their vision finally adjusted, they could see a clearing just ahead with a large rustic log cabin sitting in the center.

It was surrounded by full-grown evergreens, which almost completely concealed its whereabouts. From this distance combined with the cover of nightfall, it was barely visible to the naked eye. In fact, it would have gone completely undetected if they hadn't been standing in this exact spot. Overwhelmed by the sudden adrenaline rush, Billy let out a sigh of relief and began to quietly repeat, "There it is! Look! There it is!" His voice slowly escalating as he pointed to the mysterious cabin.

Drifting away in her thoughts, Aimee began to wonder what really lay up ahead. She disposed of that thought just as quickly as it had entered her mind. There were other, more disturbing thoughts beginning to haunt her. She began to think about her darling Rob and wondered, what if they discovered his body out in the woods? What if they found him alive? What fate would befall them?

"Aimee, Aimee! Are you all right?" a voice called out. Startled by the unfamiliar sound, she was slowly becoming aware of her surroundings, but everything around her had turned into one big blur and she found herself lying on the ground. She blinked her eyes again as she shook her head back and forth, hoping to regain control of her senses. There was something towering over her, but she was unable to identify it. Confused by what was happening around her, she attempted to lift herself off of the ground, as a comforting hand reached out and gently held her down. "Just lay there for a few moments," Billy whispered to her.

"What happened," were the only words she was able to mutter out from her mouth. Embarrassed by the awkwardness of the position she found herself in, again she tried to get back up, but Billy stopped her.

"Just lay there for a few minutes," he insisted.

"What happened?" she asked softly as she slowly regained the ability to think.

"You passed out," then he repeated the same question again, "are you all right?" showing minimal compassion.

"Yeah, I'm fine, just a little dizzy, that's all. How long

was I passed out for?"

He had lost all sense of time and could think of nothing except going to search that cabin. "Let's get going!" he suggested, totally disregarding her questions. "It's getting late, let's just have a look around and see what we find. Then we can go home."

The last sentence was all she was able to process, it was like music to her ears. It was as if he'd been reading her mind, because that was all she could think about. She just wanted to get this over with and go home.

After helping her up to her feet, they proceeded toward the cabin. They now came to realize their one last hurdle they would be forced to overcome before they would reach their desired destination.

Suddenly, they found themselves standing before an antiquated bridge. Much to their dismay, it appeared to be the only visible passage connecting the two sides of this enormous ravine. Looking to either side, the rift stretched as far as the eye could see. The valley itself wound like a serpent through the wilderness, with the narrowest point connected by the bridge.

The gorge was enormous, seventy five feet deep and fifty feet across. The whole scene looked as if something had grabbed each side and tore a large fissure right through the middle of the forest, eliminating any other possible ways to cross. The bridge itself was scariest of all. Looking home made, it was constructed of old ropes and misshapen wood planks that looked as if they'd been cut by hand from whatever was lying around. The ropes that sustained its massive frame were fastened to iron stakes wedged into the exposed bedrock, two on each side of the canyon.

In order to get to the cabin, they had to travel over this old flimsy death trap. When they reached the edge of the cliff,

Aimee took a step backwards, away from the canyon and made her objection known. Under no circumstance was she going to cross this bridge with him and nothing in the world was going to convince her otherwise. Outside of her fear of heights, the bridge itself appeared frail and unstable. Just standing there by the edge made her feel nauseous, she was ready to vomit and the discoloration of her skin had confirmed it.

Billy observed her symptoms, but actuality, he didn't care. Determined to continue with this journey at all costs, he was going to let nothing get in his way, not even a friend he knew he was obligated to protect. From this moment on, his demeanor took on a whole new twist for the worst. He became rude, obnoxious and was not willing to listen to reason. Surely no phobia of hers would prevent him from crossing this bridge to find out what secrets this cabin was hiding.

Upon noticing the change in his personality, tears began to form in her eyes and she began to sob uncontrollably. Her apparent pain had no affect on him, but made him seem more odious. Persistent as ever and using a different approach, Billy began to manipulate the situation by attacking her where she was most vulnerable. After the disappearance, Aimee became extremely sensitive whenever Rob's name was mentioned. Aware of this, he exclaimed, "Look Aimee, I know that you're scared of heights." As if it mattered, he went on, "If you have any hopes that we might find him alive, we've got to go there and we have to start by crossing this bridge."

Her whole face turned beet red as she snapped back at him, "Look! Don't even try to use that guilt trip shit on me!" Knowing instantly that she would later regret this, her gut feeling told her that she was going with him to this cabin.

"Look," Billy pleaded, "I'm sorry, honestly I never intended for it to come out like that. All I'm saying is, this is our only chance to find out what happened to," Billy never got a chance to finish the sentence. He took off running, as he suddenly found himself having to chase after Aimee. Trying to catch up with her, he could barely see her through the darkness, slowly inching her way across the rickety bridge one step at a time. She had made it all the way across before he had even made it half way. When he finally reached the other side, Aimee was stopped, trying to catch her breath as if she hadn't breathed the entire way across.

Looking directly into her eyes, Billy said proudly, "You see. It wasn't all that bad." She gave him an evil look before they resumed their journey toward the cabin without saying a word.

From its outer appearance, the cabin was built to look rustic, yet it was still in mint condition as if it had just been built. Common enough for this area, the location still seemed a bit odd to them. The exterior walls were rich in texture and cut out of the surrounding redwood and evergreen trees. The roof was made of light colored cedar shake shingles. To the rear of the cabin, a tall chimney stood upright, constructed out of small pieces of limestone and other small boulders from the surrounding area. Most peculiar, was the one and only visible window. It faced the northern part of the field from which they approached and was the only apparent clear path to the mysterious cabin.

Precipitously aware of their intrusion onto the property, they slowly began scouting the yard directly encompassing the cabin. Apprehensive about the possibility of being seen, they ever so quietly inched their way closer and closer toward the cabin. Hearts and minds alike, racing uncontrollably. They eagerly hoped they'd find something, even a single clue, anything that could resolve the mystery of Rob's disappearance. Much to their dismay, they found nothing more than their own heightened paranoia sneaking up on them. Billy suggested they move on and head up toward the cabin.

Shaking her head in disbelief, Aimee closed her eyes and took in a deep breath of fresh air. "All right," she hesitantly exhaled.

They resumed walking, it wasn't long before they stopped, realizing their close proximity to this man's home. Vexing the guilt of their trespass, they continued, attempting to get closer without being detected. Crouching down, they stepped onto the porch and quietly crept up to the windows ledge and paused for a moment. Leaning onto the windowsill, they slowly perked up their heads to peer through the glass.

Disconcerted with the lack of viability, they could not see a thing. The unfortunate result of bad lighting and a dust covered pane left them frustrated. As a measure of last resort, they slowly tilted their heads and cupped their ears to the glass. Patiently waiting, they intently listened for the slightest sound. They heard nothing, there was virtually no sign of life inside or outside the cabin. With the exception of their presence, the whole area seemed virtually lifeless and abandoned.

Coveting the secrets that lie in wait beyond this door, what ensued, remained a mystery. With his moral compass shattered, Billy dubiously began doing the unthinkable. He was crossing a line neither imagined they'd ever cross.

They were breaking the law, committing a home invasion. Against Aimee's better judgment, Billy seemed to be oblivious to this fact, including any consequences that may follow. He was clearly an object in motion. His heart was racing, the rush of adrenaline and uncertainty was more than he could sustain, relinquishing now was no longer an option.

The abrupt fear of being left all alone overwhelmed her body and senses. Simple lack of options forced her to follow as he led the way toward the door. Aimee vocally asseverated her feelings and vigorously protested the idea. Nevertheless, Billy's persistence prevailed.

Once inside the cabin, they noticed an array of wild game trophies, ranging from lions bear, to squirrels rabbits, with their heads mounted precariously on the living room wall. A three-foot stack of logs had been neatly stacked in front of the catalytic style pass through fireplace. In the center of the room, a couch and love seat sat facing one another. The upholstery on the furniture looked hand sewn, black leather, possibly made from the skin of the animals hanging on the wall.

A long wooden coffee table was awkwardly positioned between the two appurtenance. The placement seemed odd, obviously disregarding the pleasant view offered by the window, this arrangement seemed to better suit conversations. They both silently wondered who would venture this far into the boscage.

The anxiety and duress over their moral laps in judgment was starting to fade. Confident they were alone, they suddenly became all too aware of a nauseating stench permeating the entire cabin. They tried desperately to locate the source of this awful smell, but their efforts were to no avail. After a brief and futile glancing search, they reached a conclusion. They determined the disgusting odor could only be derived from the vicious creatures hanging on the walls. More likely, the remnants of the carcasses were decomposing undisturbed somewhere nearby.

They began to regain their composure and Billy resumed the lead. Trying to remain silent, they slowly crept toward the coffee table. Upon arrival, Aimee startled Billy when she started hyperventilating. She'd been overcome with dread and angst when she noticed the town's daily newspaper sitting right in front of them. Much to their dismay, the date on the paper read August 3rd 1944.

"Look, this is today's paper," she excitedly whispered.

"So what?" Billy replied in a lewd tone, "you can get one when we get back."

Frustrated by his ignorance, she glared at him resentfully and said, "No! It's today's date! That means someone was here today!" She was totally oblivious to the ascending tone of her voice.

By this point in time, Billy wasn't paying much attention to her rant and just resumed what he was doing. Getting very little sympathy, she tried to hasten the search and helped rummage through the area.

Without warning, the room began to tremble and shake as a loud rampant trampling sound began echoing from somewhere nearby. Someone, or something, was racing up the stairs from the basement and was approaching rapidly. With too little time to even process a thought, there was no possible chance to make an escape.

Fortuitously, he was standing in front of the fireplace, leering at them through thick rimmed glasses as he savagely brandished a 9mm Luger. An elderly man in his late fifty's, unshaven, with his hair long and wild, towered in the shadows. Yellow stains emanated from his teeth, accentuating the heinous grimace augmenting his face. Wearing a white lab coat with rage conspicuously visible in his eyes, he started clamoring boisterously in a frenzy, "Holen Sie sich die Hölle aus hier, ich habe eine Waffe!" speaking only in German.

This quandary was not ideal for introductions and exchanging pleasantries. The situation had went sour fast.

Before they had a chance to attempt explaining why they were there, he unleashed two shots from his pistol.

The projectiles whizzed by, barely missing Billy's head. The echo of gunfire reverberated throughout the cabins interior with a deafening cacophony, causing an intense ringing in everyone's ears. Everything was happening so fast, they were mortified by the events unfolding around them to which there seemed no escape.

Billy's adrenaline was pumping so intensely that everything appeared to be happening in slow motion. Advantageous as it was, he noticed that Aimee had frozen in her tracks, standing motionless, paralyzed and unable to control the movements of her body. Billy knew she would soon be the target of this mans fury. Without giving it a second thought Billy rushed to her aid. Diving through the air he grabbed Aimee by the arm, tackling her as he yanked her to the ground.

Billy laid there with his body on top of hers in a desperate attempt to shield her from the sudden onslaught of gunfire. In one fluid action, he simultaneously drew the weapon from his side, aimed and fired a single shot. The round was a direct hit, catching the assailant in the cavity of his chest. The blunt force of the shot sent him staggering backwards, hitting his head against the wall. Arms flailing wildly, he began grasping randomly in a futile attempt to maintain his balance. Losing intermittent control of his legs, he dropped to his knees. The weapon he was holding slowly slipped through his fingers and fell to the ground.

Instantly, Aimee became hysterical from the gruesome sight of blood splatter and the wounded man. She stumbled, barely keeping her footing as she took off running out of the cabin into the field. Still overwhelmed, in a state of shock from what transpired, Billy followed her lead and took off running after her. He slammed the door shut behind him as he exited, hoping this gave them a few extra seconds toward making a successful escape. Still trying to grasp the reality of the situation, he realized he was catching up, trailing close behind her. About a hundred yards from the cabin, they finally reached the treeline. With the cover of the thicket separating them from the cabin, they started to gain confidence they had reached a safe distance, finally coming to a stop. Both gasping for air, they tried frantically to catch their breath.

The gun had no more than hit the floor when Dr. Aben buckled over forward in agonizing pain. Knowing he would soon pass out and bleed to death if he didn't find a way to stop the blood. He lifted up his head and was relieved to see the intruders had left. He placed his hand on his chest in an attempt to slow the outflow of blood. Having little success, he slowly began to crawl across the floor. Paying for every inch of floor he covered in blood loss, he managed to successfully make his way through several rooms before he pulled himself up into a chair and sat behind his desk. Still bleeding profusely, he pulled a journal out of his desk drawer, grabbed a pencil and raised his hand to jot something down. He took in a deep breath before his head suddenly fell over limp as he died.

Aimee's face was trembling with fear. She screamed at Billy at the top of her lungs for everyone to hear, "You bastard, this is entirely your fault, you killed him!"

Trying to calm her, he pulled her into his arms and embraced her firmly to his massive barrel chest. Trying to keep his composure, he said, "I didn't mean to shoot him, we're not even sure if he's dead," Billy tried to rationalize.

"I didn't even wanna come out here and now," her voice trailed off into the night.

"I know," Billy replied. "I panicked after he fired at

us." Trying to select the right words to calm her down, he finished the sentence, "We'd have been killed if I hadn't fired back."

"I didn't want to come out here," he repeated. "I knew that you would do something stupid."

"Just calm down!" Billy shouted. "You have to promise me that you'll never tell a soul what happened out here tonight, or else we're both gonna wind up in jail for the rest of our lives."

"Oh my god," she cried out, with the sudden realization that they might both wind up going to jail over this.

Billy reaffirmed his grip on her shoulders and repeated, "Just promise me you won't say a thing."

Shrugging herself free from his grip, she reluctantly nodded her head in agreement and said, "I promise."

Now sworn to secrecy, they headed back into the dark woods as they began their journey back toward the town. They were confident in each other that no one would ever hear of what happened out at this cabin tonight.

CHAPTER ONE
FIFTY YEARS LATER

Before the arrival of the outsiders, as they were called by the locals, the small town was a large close knit family. There was a wholesome feeling throughout the community and when faced with diversity every one pulled together. A great majority of the town was middle class, most of the people were hard working blue-collar laborers. Their pay was not all that it should be, but few ever minded. This peaceful little town of theirs provided a decent life and was more than their fathers ever had.

Fifty years after WWII came to a halt, the town of Joshua Tree had expanded and flourished at the rapid pace of any boom town. The once peaceful town had drastically changed. The population had increased from 2300 to 3500 in the first year alone. The county had vast natural resources, especially oil. After the war, the town continued to grow into the industrial town it is today with more than 30,000 residents now calling it home.

Joshua Tree prided itself on its friendly folks, wild forests and mountain resorts. Most of all, they cherished their independence and their self reliance. The winter months transformed this tranquil town into a haven for tourists. Its mountain slopes were an exemplary attraction for avid skiers of all ages and skill levels. The back country stretched for miles, plentiful with wild game, it lured hunters from other nearby areas to their quaint town.

Petroleum drilling was something new in the area and had only started changing the town on a large scale in the last ten years. In a short period of time, derricks sprung up like weeds on the horizon and many of the locals gained an abundance of wealth from their oil rich fields. Before the flood of new money from the oil wells started rolling in. Lumber from the logging industry was the main source of income to most of the residents and would always be a strong part of the town's rich history.

The one thing haunting the town's peaceful image was the legendary myth from fifty years ago. It is said that during the months of July and August of 1944, while Eastern Europe endured the wrath of Adolph Hitler, seventeen people had vanished without a trace. The last was a newcomer by the name of Dr. Eric Aben.

For five decades, this story was told, changing as often as it was repeated. The most famous of all is the tale of a drifter. It is said that a man would come out late at night, kidnap the children and take them to his cabin where he would mutilate them. According to the legend, it was said that he would someday return to finish what he started. After an investigation was launched, both he and the cabin vanished without a trace never to be found.

The discrepancies in the tale made it extremely difficult to know what actually happened on those dreadful nights. With nothing ever officially confirmed, no one can truly claim to have all the answers. Some of the elders refused to even discuss the subject and if mentioned they would simply walk away. They feared that if word got out about the truthfulness of these stories, they would lose much of the income the outsiders and tourists brought into the town.

The younger generation on the other hand exploited this misfortune, taking full advantage of this opportunity. They used the repulsive twisted tale to draw business into their novelty shops. From wall to wall, assortments of tee-shirts and other memorabilia were advertised inside their establishments.

PART TWO

The Stevens & Healy Families

When drilling for oil had begun, it sent a shock wave through the region. People migrated by the hundreds with the hopes of earning a better living. Some people relocated to Joshua County because their jobs required them to do so. Since the mad rush to discover oil on one's land, the locals were no longer as polite to the outsiders. In fact, many of them were disgruntled by their arrival.

The locals felt that these people were invading their town and taking money out of their pockets. Factions were soon formed and feuds occasionally broke out between the locals and outsiders. But for the most part, Joshua Tree accommodated all of their needs.

The temperature for the past summer had risen to record-setting highs. Everyone was relieved when the heat wave finally came to an end. It was mid-afternoon and a typical day in August of 1994. The sky was clear and a cool autumn breeze had made its way in from the western shores. The scenery was beautiful and serene. The faint rays of the sun gently touched the treetops, causing the foliage to dance, displaying vibrant colors of red, yellow and orange.

Fourteen year old David Healy was five feet, ten inches tall, with sparkling blue eyes and shoulder length blonde hair. He had a fair complexion and his thin mustache made him appear older than he actually was. Living the simple life suited Dave just fine.

Dave was an honor roll student, who loved biking and other sports. Up until a year ago, he was on the school's baseball, gymnastics and football teams. He was extremely talented, with his athletic abilities really excelling in football. To prove his toughness, he often showed off his battle-scared body to anyone that would listen.

Shortly after his father's death, Dave had to give up on playing sports. He was needed more often around the house to help take care of his younger brother, Jeff Healy, while their mother was at work. Dave's father, John Healy, was killed on the job in a lumberyard accident. Dave loved his father very much, taking the news of his death extremely hard. Becoming depressed, he started smoking cigarettes and acting out in school.

After graduating from the eighth grade, Dave began attending Rosemont High School. It was his freshman year at the school and there were plenty of new faces he had never saw before. All of the strangers were a part of the big migration stemming from the recent oil discoveries all over the valley. Dave was not popular with them, like he'd been with all of the old town's native students. Whenever the outsiders came around, he would withdraw himself from the crowd, keeping to himself. As far as he was concerned, these people were strangers to him and that made him uncomfortable.

The Stevens family moved in from San Gabriel and had been residents of Joshua Tree for only the past eighteen months. The Stevens household was a family of four, Mike and Patricia and their two sons, Allen and Raun, who was the youngest. The family had moved in about seven months prior to the biggest part of the migration. Mr. Stevens was an executive for the Shell Oil Corporation. He was transferred to this region when the company he worked for decided to set up an oil pumping operation here. He was promoted and placed in charge of all the oil drilling fields in the region. His annual average salary was well over the six figure mark and their lavish lifestyle said they were living the American dream.

It was difficult for both Allen and Raun to adjust to

their new way of life in this new environment. Unlike the big city life they were so accustomed to, there was nothing here that they were really interested in. To them, this little old town was boring. They missed their friends back home and not knowing any children here their own age made matters even worse. Their father tried to break the monotony by taking them hunting on his days off, but even that didn't work.

Allen soon started getting into mischief and his father had to repeatedly reprimand him. He was only thirteen when they first came into town. He attended junior high school and it is there where he met Dave Healy.

Allen was a month older than Dave. In middle school, they were both forced to compete for the same positions on the football team. When Dave beat out Allen for the spot, it started a rivalry in everything they did. From that point on, they tested each others limits in every thing they did, all the way to the point when one of them would submit and admit that the other one was better. In the process of always competing, they became good friends. Both being new to the high school, they formed an alliance, soon becoming inseparable, even though it started more out of convenience than admiration.

Dave and Allen's friendship continued to grow as time progressed and few people knew they hadn't known each other their entire lives. After school they would go out riding their bikes on the trails. On rain days, they would seek shelter at the bowling alley in town. For the most part, they would spend all of their free time out exploring the foot trails of Mt. Anthony with their younger brothers in tow.

It was five after three and the school bell had just sounded. The children exited the school building with their books and stationary strapped to their shoulders inside their backpacks. Some were holding hands while others made plans to hang out for the evening. When Dave exited the gymnasium he headed directly toward the bike rack where Allen was already waiting for him. Shorter than Dave, Allen stood only about five feet, eight inches, kind of stocky, with shoulder length black hair, green eyes and a thin mustache. Before Dave had even reached the bike rack Allen started talking, "Are you and Jeff going out to the trails today?"

At first Dave evaded the question, walked past Allen, pulled his pack of Marlboros out of his shirt pocket, removed one from the pack and lit it, then proceeded to unchain his bike from the apparatus. As he wrapped the chain around the seat of his bike he finally said, "Yeah, I just gotta go home and check the answering machine first."

"Why are you such a wus?" Allen asked, knowing that this remark would get under Dave's skin.

"Why do you always have to be such a jerk?" Dave quickly came back with a remark of his own, smirking as he finished his statement, "I have to go home to see what time my mom will be home, plus I gotta wait for Jeff."

When they straddled their bikes, Allen stated, "My dad wants us to cut the grass, but I think we can get out of it until this weekend," referring to himself and his brother Raun.

Dave sat there for a moment with a blank look on his face when suddenly, he came up with a plan. "Hey! I'll bet if we can get in and out of there before your dad gets home, your mom will let us go riding."

"Yeah, that's gotta work, she won't even realize I'm trying to ditch out of it." Allen always tried to manipulate his way out of helping with the chores, more often than not he got away with it because his mother had spoiled him rotten, always side stepping their fathers orders.

"Lets hurry then," Dave suggested. "What time does your dad get home?"

"Four thirty," Allen replied.

Finally pulling away from the bike rack and school property, they headed toward their houses discussing their plan in more detail. Shortly after they turned down Beaverland Street, Allen made a right turn and pulled up his driveway yelling, "I'll see ya in a little bit."

Dave nodded his head without slowing down as he shouted, "I'll be back in a half an hour. Be ready!"

The street that they both lived on, Beaverland, was a long, narrow, dead end gravel road. The huge pine trees on both sides of the street kept most of the houses hidden from plain view.

Dave peddled even faster as he headed toward the end of the dead end street where he lived. When he got within ten yards of his house, he swerved to the side of the street, launching his bike off the small hill in front of his neighbors house. He landed on the lawn, almost losing his balance and getting thrown from his seat. He struggled, but luckily was able to regaining control of his bike. He peddled fiercely, trying to pick up his speed as he crossed the lawn before he hit the pavement of his driveway.

Pulling up to the house, he leapt off his seat and gently laid his bike along side of the porch. Without breaking a stride, he ran around to the side of the house, hurdled over the railing and landed at the side door. Standing at the side entrance, he fumbled for his keys. The telephone was ringing as he tried to insert the key into the lock. Fearing he'd miss the call, the door finally popped open. He rushed over to the kitchen table, lunged forward and grabbed the receiver off its cradle. Letting off a heavy sigh, he placed the phone to his mouth, "Hello."

"Hi Davie," a woman's voice responded on the other end of the phone.

Still trying to catch his breath he said, “Ma, don’t call me that, you know I hate it.”

“I’m sorry Hun, what took you so long to answer the phone and why are you breathing so hard?”

“I just walked through the door,” he replied, totally disregarding the second question.

“So what took you so long to get home?” Her question was more to make conversation than one of concern. She went on to say, “Are the other kids giving you a hard time again?”

“Na, I was just messing around with Allen, we must’ve took longer than we realized.”

“I guess I called a little early, I really shouldn’t worry so much.”

“No you shouldn’t,” Dave interrupted.

“I know, just make sure that you’re there when Jeff gets home. You know that I still haven’t given him a key.”

Jeff was her little baby, she'd always been over protective of him while relying heavily on Dave for his supervision. Not giving a key to Jeff was deliberately designed. This forced Dave to come home after school, tending to keep him out of trouble. Additionally, having him at the house to let his brother in ensured that he'd be looked after without the added cost of hiring a babysitter.

Growing impatient with his mother, he grumbled, “I know ma, I always am.” Raising his brow and exhaling a deep breath loud enough for her to hear, hoping she'd realize he was getting bored and annoyed.

Not letting on that she'd heard his overly dramatic reaction, she shrugged it off after a long pause and calmly said, “Anyway, I have to work late tonight, Caroline went home sick and I have to close again.”

Ann Healy attended community college on the outskirts of town. Studying hard, she only had about a year left before graduating and becoming a registered nurse. A heartbreaking turn of events suddenly changed her life completely when her husband died abruptly in a tragic workplace accident. The life insurance they received was beyond inadequate, barely paying off the mortgage on their modest home.

As if the loss wasn't hard enough, it left an income gap she alone was left trying to fill. Desperate to make ends meet, she was forced to cut back on some of her classes, taking on an evening job at the Railway Company as a receptionist. The pay was exceptional, but she was really limited on the hours she could work between trying to finish school and caring for her two children. It seemed like there was never enough time or money, yet somehow, they always manged to make it work.

"What time is that?" Dave asked without any emotion. He had gotten used to her working late.

"I should be home a little after nine, so make some sandwiches for you and your brother, alright?"

"Yeah," Dave agreed, "then were going riding in the trails." It was more of a statement than a question.

"Alright, but do your homework first and make sure you take Jeff with you."

"I don't have any and I will," at this point Dave was getting frustrated, ready to slam down the receiver.

"Why is it that you never have homework anymore?" She was getting overwhelmed with concern because Mr. Kenny, Dave's principal, had recently called to tell her that he was failing because his grades were dropping drastically.

"I do it in school, ma," he calmly replied, lying to his mother.

"Then when do you do your schoolwork?" she asked out of frustration. "Oh, never mind, are Allen and Raun going with you guys?" She didn't really approve of him hanging out with Allen. She had noticed that ever since they had first started hanging out, Dave was becoming more and more defiant of her and all authority.

"Yeah, we're supposed to meet at their house when Jeff gets home."

"Alright then, you boys be careful and make sure that your home before nine."

"Okay, we will," he said in a nasty tone.

She just ignored his snark attitude and said, "Well, I have to get back to work. I'll see ya guys when I get home, I love ya baby. And hey, make sure ya take care of your brother." She knew she was really starting to get under his skin so she decided to leave him alone for now and end their discussion on a good note.

"Love ya too, good bye," Dave replied and hung up the phone before allowing her to say another word.

Turning around, he looked out of the living room window to find Jeff flying across the lawn on his bike. Dave rushed to hide behind the front door, trying to conceal himself. Standing there motionless, he waited for his brother to enter the house. Dave listened intently for the sound of his brother's footsteps as he stared at the doorknob, watching and waiting for it to move. Dave's whole body tensed up as the handle slowly started to turn. When the door finally popped open, Dave jumped out in front of him and screamed, "Boo!" then began laughing uncontrollably at the priceless expression on his brother's face.

All of the blood flushed from his brother's face and he looked white as a ghost. As his skin slowly returned to its normal color, he punched Dave in the stomach with all that he had and asked, "Why do you always do that?"

Finally regaining his composure after having the wind knocked out of him, he gave Jeff a quick one handed push on the shoulder, snickered and said, "Because you always fall for it, you goof." Chuckling, he resumed holding his abdomen .

Jeff, in a child like voice replied, "It's not funny!"

"Since I'm the oldest, tormenting you is my privilege and duty," Dave stated. "Besides, it's fun and I enjoy it."

It wasn't just Dave who did this, all of the kids in the town did it, especially when it came to taunting their younger siblings with the story of the drifter to get a good scare out of them. Some even went as far as dressing up in rags and dark clothes, sneaking up on them in the night and chasing them around the town until their parents finally made them stop.

"I'm telling mom," Jeff insisted.

"Just go up to your room and get dressed, I already talked to ma and told her were going out to the trails. She said that we gotta be home by nine, so hurry up."

Jeff's face lit up with excitement. He loved going out to the trails riding with his older brother. In fact, despite their little squabbles, they were quite close. Jeff actually adored him and thought highly of him as a role model, Dave knew this, taking full advantage of the situation at times. When push came to shove, he was utterly protective, guarding Jeff from everyone and everything. Reserving the right for himself to intimidate and torture him in every possible way.

Jeff had blue eyes, brunette hair and inherited his father's chiseled jaw line and features. He was only eleven years of age and hadn't fully developed for the most part. Standing only five foot, three inches tall, weighing approximately ninety-five pounds, he was small for his age.

Dave told him, "There's only one problem." Jeff froze in his tracks mid stride at the bedroom door. Dave continued, "We have to go and rescue Allen and Raun and we gotta do it now, before their dad gets home and makes them cut that million acre lawn," Dave exaggerated, using his arms as he explained the scenario.

Knowing they were in a race against time, Jeff hurried up in getting dressed, learning of this new, possible dilemma that could hinder their afternoon plans. When he returned, he was wearing a faded black jogging suit that fit loosely on his small frame. It was one of Dave's old hand-me-down outfits, but it was still in good condition. Jeff actually liked it, but he would never admit that fact to anyone.

"I'm ready," Jeff exclaimed, all excited.

"We won't see 'em for days if we don't get them out of there," Dave suggested.

"You're right," Jeff agreed, "unless we want to help them." Jeff was even willing to help them, so long as they went riding in the trails afterward.

"No way," Dave replied, "they ain't tricking me into that again, it took forever last time. Let's just get over there before their dad gets home."

"Will their mom let them go?" Jeff curiously asked, praying that the answer was yes.

"I don't know," Dave replied, toying with his arm a little bit. He knew that Jeff desperately wanted to go out to the trails. After the sustained moment of suspense, he added, "I'm pretty sure she will, but we'll know soon enough."

"Come on, let's hurry then," Jeff demanded, wanting desperately to leave.

As Dave pulled the door shut behind them, "Oh shit!" He said with a frustrated look on his face.

Drawing a confused look from his brother, Jeff asked, "What now?"

"I forgot to check the answering machine and I think I left my cigarettes on the table."

"Damn, mom would kill you if she found them again," Jeff suggested.

"Ya think?" Dave agreed sarcastically as he ran back into the house, momentarily closing the door behind him.

"Did anyone call?" Jeff asked.

"Damn!" Dave shouted, showing that he once again forgot to check the machine.

Jeff was ready to go and wasn't willing to waste another second with Dave's antics. "You said that mom called already, so let's just go," he insisted.

"Oh yeah, she called as soon as I walked through the door," Dave agreed.

"Then don't bother," Jeff suggested, "the only people that call us is her, Allen and Raun. You talked to mom, right?" Dave just nodded his head. Jeff continued, "And we're on our way over to Raun and Allen's?"

"I guess it'll be alright, lets get going," Dave conceded.

Jeff was the first one out of the driveway and started racing down the street. Dave started peddling fast as he aggressively tried to catch up. It didn't take long before Jeff was falling behind since Dave was faster than he was.

As they pulled up to the Stevens' they laid their bikes down on the lawn and headed up to the porch. The front door was open and they peered inside through the screen. Dave raised his arm, trying to get noticed without being impolite, he knocked gently. Jeff saw Mrs. Stevens as she stepped out of the kitchen past the front hallway with an apron clad around her neck.

Pat Stevens was a tall and slender girl, with short dark hair that curled in around her cheekbones. She had soft, milky skin with animated emerald eyes. She had an elegant walk that displayed an aura of confidence.

Knowing in advance where this was ending, she stood there directly in front of Dave and Jeff, with a thin smile she said, "Come on in boys."

Dave pulled open the screen door and the two of them entered into the parlor. Once the entryway closed behind them, the three of them turned their heads to the loud trampling sound of footsteps and found Allen stopped in his tracks, halfway down the staircase. As soon as Jeff's eyes made eye contact with Allen's, he asked, "Can you go?"

"Well I kind of haven't even asked yet," Allen softly replied, making his way down the remainder of the stairs. When he reached the bottom, he turned to face his mother only to find her with a dumbfounded look on her face. She was now positive this was a preplanned episode, but she really didn't mind. She stared hopelessly at the three of them with a blank look of amazement frozen onto her face. The silence was more than Allen could bear and he earnestly started pleading with her, "Well, can we go ma?"

Jeff quickly added, "Yeah, Mrs. Stevens, Pleeeazze, can they come?"

Pat first looked at Jeff, then back at Allen and said, "I don't know Allen, your father wants you and Raun to cut the lawn."

"Mom, come on, please!" Allen begged.

With six sad puppy dog eyes staring at her, she could hardly say no. Willpower broken, she explained, "I guess I can let you slide, but only if you get out of here before," The three of them began to cheer, not allowing her to complete her sentence.

While in the midst of their ecstatic celebration, she interjected and said, "Now you boys listen here, as I was saying, you gotta get out of here before Mike gets home from work. Allen, you have to promise me that you'll mow the lawn this weekend."

"I will," Allen agreed, grinning from ear to ear.

"I mean it. The yard has to look perfect, all of your fathers executive friends are coming over this Sunday."

Allen gave his word that he'd have it done and then he yelled up the stairs to Raun. Totally unaware of anything that was going on downstairs, Raun was nonchalantly strolling out of his room when Allen called out to him. Approaching the balcony, he heard the commotion downstairs and headed over to the railing, bent his head over and saw everyone standing there ready to go.

"Come on, we're going out to the trails!" the kids all eagerly shouted out to him.

Virtually expressionless, Raun made a u-turn and staggered back to his alcove to change into his riding clothes. The whole time he was getting dressed, he pondered the agitation of never being in the loop until the plan was well in the works, but he'd gotten used to that by now. Still not showing any emotion, Raun came darting down the steps. When he made it to the bottom, Jeff extended his arm up in the air, anticipating the high five and Raun accommodated him.

Raun was a year older than Jeff and stood almost three inches taller than him. He loved biking just as much as the rest of them, but had unusual serene qualities, where nothing else seemed to bother him. He kept his head closely shaved because it was easier than dealing with his naturally curly hair. His eyes were such a dark shade of brown that they almost seemed black and the rest of the kids sometimes gave him a hard time, because quite often they flashed a brief red tint if the light caught them at the right angle. He was academically inclined and received straight A's in school, with his only weak subject being gym class. Having nothing to do with his athletic abilities, it was mainly because he was not a big fan of competitive sports outside of bike riding.

As they were leaving the house, Pat reminded them to be careful. She gave her two sons a quick peck on the cheek, embarrassing them as usual, then the four of them marched out of the house, jumped on their bikes and off they went.

"Be home by dark, it's a school night and stay out of trouble," she shouted as they took off flying down the street. Allen raised his right hand from his handlebars in acknowledgment to indicate that he had heard her decree. When they all knew that they were far enough down the road that she wouldn't be able to see them, Allen directed his bike into the middle of the road and the rest of the kids followed.

PART THREE
The Trails

All four of them thought of themselves as expert free stylists on their BMX's. Whenever a curb came into sight, the leading man would accelerate his speed before launching his bike into the air. The rest would follow suit, each trying to launch higher and farther, doing a more spectacular stunt than the previous man. These events were common place between them, occurring on any surface even vaguely resembling a ramp. They had a whole routine of favorite hills and ramps on the way to the trails. Already, with no sense of time whatsoever, a half-hour had passed and they had made it all the way uptown.

The main strip through the small town was Warren Road. Just south of Beaverland Street, the business section was only four city blocks long. There were approximately ten restaurants, a tavern, a gas station and a typical variety of small mom and pop stores. In the center of the town, near the three schools, was the civic center, a newly constructed, moderate sized bowling alley right next door to the recently remodeled hotel and ski resort. The sheriff's office and the library were right across from the high school where Allen and Dave went. Joshua Tree, anticipating another large migration, built a new hospital near the edge of town only a year ago.

The boys tinkered around uptown for a brief time before they headed down the dirt road at the edge of town leading toward the trails. They headed west down Warwick Street, passing the entrance to Hickory Estates, a large subdivision built to house all of the people that had recently flocked to this booming town. The custom homes were large and beautiful with scenic views in every direction. Most of the townsfolk were envious, possibly even jealous they couldn't afford to live in this ritzy sub. Some flat out resented that a neighborhood of this design was forced upon this once quaint family orientated rural town.

As soon as they had ridden their bikes passed the fancy gated second entrance to the subdivision, the road turned back into the gravel path it had always been. When the boys reached this part of the journey, they knew the trails were close by. They raced all the way to Whitlock, another dirt road that crossed Warwick. This ungraded pot marked road would take them to their favorite set of bike trails located in the foothills of Mt. Anthony.

They made their way through the entrance leading to the path. Jeff was peddling with his legs faster than he thought possible, strictly concentrating on being the first one to enter the trails he shouted, “Last one there is a chicken shit.” Hearing nothing in return he turned his head to glance behind him. Suddenly, he noticed everyone else had slammed on their brakes and stopped about a hundred yards back. They were all laughing at him for not noticing that he was the only one involved in the race. Embarrassed, the only thing he was able do was laugh along with them as he turned around and headed back to where they'd all stopped. They waited for him to arrive at the detour before they resumed proceeding toward the trails.

The trails split off in all different directions and each path had its own unique and innate obstacle course. There were ramps, steep turns, natural half pipes of all-different shapes and sizes throughout the many hills and valleys. It seemed to them, that nature had designed these trails for one purpose only, to test the individual limits and capabilities of each of them. Simultaneously gratifying their need for the ultimate thrill from each and every path they dared encounter.

Once the boys made it into the heart of the foothills, they separated, each taking on a different trail to let loose and go hog wild. They raced around the tracks several times, experimenting with different tricks, while pushing themselves almost beyond their limits. After a short period of time, Dave stopped to light a cigarette. He looked to his left and on top of one of the larger hills, he noticed that Allen had stopped and appeared to be staring off at something in the distance intensely.

Transfixed by what he was witnessing, Allen tried to focus his eyes to gain a better look into the woods and at what he was observing directly in front of him. Allen's trance and empty gaze was finally broken hearing the sound of Dave's voice yelling up to him, "Hey Allen, what 'cha doing?"

Allen gestured with his arm frantically for them to come up to the top of the hill where he was paused, perched on his bike. One by one they started making their way toward him. Dave was the first to arrive. "What the hell is your problem, dude?" Dave asked.

"Have you guys ever seen this before?" Allen reiterated, pointing at what he had just encountered. Simultaneously, they looked at one another, turned their palms right side up to the skies while shrugging their shoulders and drooping their upper lips perplexed. "No, never," Raun agreed.

Allen had discovered a new set of trails similar to the others they knew all so well, yet they had never explored them or even noticed their existence. How could this possibly be they wondered, contemplating how they'd never noticed this path before, especially as often as they came here. Even more disturbing, they could swear that they had been in this exact same spot just yesterday and they were positive this passage wasn't here. Pondering the confusion, they curiously contemplated to themselves, could this trail just have materialized out of nowhere?

Behind the semi-tall grass was a rusty chain blocking the path to all intruders that might wish to wander into the area. To hold up the massive weight of this colossal antique, each end was bolted to itself, wrapped around a large evergreen. The trees trunk had grown undisturbed for so long, it grew right through the chain's tight grip and was being absorbed into the trees mammoth core. Hanging in the center of the old rusted chain, a sign dangled, barely legible due to weathering, but clearly once read "KEEP OUT" in bold red letters.

Flailing his arms and jerking his head to the side several times, motioning for them to follow, "Let's go and check it out," Allen suggested.

Dave replied apprehensively, "I don't know, dude, the sign says that we should keep out and I'm sure its there for a reason. Besides it looks kinda dark and spooky."

Dave's tentative response drew a laugh from the rest of them as Raun asked, "What do you mean it looks spooky? It's the woods. You're not scared of the woods are you?"

"No, I ain't scared of the woods! It just looks, well, creepy and dark," Dave barked back, trying to defend his logic.

Allen had to bite his tongue, trying hard not to laugh long enough to ask one of his usual sarcastic questions, "What are you scared of, the drifter?"

They all busted out laughing again at Dave's expense. As Raun chimed in on the mocking, Dave lost control and shouted, "You'd better shut your mouth before I get off my bike and beat your ass!"

The thought of Dave losing his temper quieted them down real fast. Dave stood there breathing heavily, with the look of fire in his eyes. Allen tried to calm him down by rationalizing with him, "Come on man, lets just go and check it out real quick."

Still not persuaded, Dave had started regaining his composure, but still stood by his original thoughts as he repeated, "I just don't think that it's a good idea."

"Come on, no one will ever know," Jeff said, siding with the other two.

"Yeah," Raun added, "and the reason that it looks darker is because the trees are thicker on top and block out more of the light."

With everyone wanting to go except for Dave, he tried desperately to think of a valid excuse that would compel the others to change their minds, but came up empty-handed. It was three against one and he knew he was stuck in a no win situation. Even if he found a way to stay behind with some logical reason, he knew they'd never let him live it down. He resorted to making one desperate final plea before proceeding to do something he suspected they'd all later regret. When his attempt failed, he tried to restore some dignity to himself as he submitted to their will, making one last suggestion, "I think we should leave our bikes here and walk through the trails first." When asked why, Dave searched for an acceptable answer and all he was able to muster was, "We've never been down these trails before and it looks like it gets really dark up ahead."

Much to Dave's surprise Jeff actually agreed. "It might be a good idea, the grass looks a little taller out there… just look, you can see it," he reaffirmed as he pointed down the newly discovered trail at the large over-grown patches of grass swaying blissfully in the wind.

Redundantly, Dave again tried to save face. "I mean come on, the sign says 'keep out'. I just don't want us to accidentally ride off a cliff or something. Besides, what if someone chases us out of there, ain't it easier to get away on foot, especially if we're not familiar with the area?"

Frustrated, Allen shook his head repeatedly in disbelief and sarcastically said, "We could have went and been back by now if you wouldn't have sat here and cried about it for so long."

"I ain't crying 'bout shit!" Dave protested, "I just don't want to get myself killed or all busted up on your account."

"Fine, we'll do it your way if it will make you happy." Allen let Dave have his way before adding another cocky remark, "I guess you're kinda right in your own chicken shit frame of mind."

Like so many times before, another power struggle was initiated between the two. Pissed, Dave jumped off his bike with his chest puffed out, both fists tightly clenched and ready to go. He walked over to Allen, slowly managing to regain some control of his anger, but still, he felt the need to be the one getting in the last word. "I don't need any lip out of you!" he shouted, poking his index finger into Allen's chest. Taking in a deep breath, in a calmer voice, he sarcastically added, "And if I decide I want any, I'll definitely fatten it up first." Allen had really gotten on his last nerve.

"Temper, temper, who dropped a house on your sister," Allen said, achieving a laugh out of Raun as he mocked the Wizard of Oz. Opting not to join in, Jeff just shook his head from side to side.

"Listen, you might be a little older and from the big city, but out here we don't care 'bout any of that and I'll beat your ass," Dave spouted, blowing off some excess steam that had been accumulating from Allen's incessant pushing of his buttons.

"What? You and your brother gonna jump me?" Allen asked, as if he knew that even together they wouldn't be able to pull it off.

"Hey! Why you gotta bring me into this?" Jeff interrupted. He smiled as he tried to break the tension in the group. "Besides, In a couple of years I'm gonna beat both of your asses anyway."

Patiently waiting and rapidly tiring of watching everyone argue, Raun finally decided to intervene, "Come on guys, what's up? Are we gonna have an all out rumble or go and check this shit out?"

The whole situation was really eating away at Dave's nerves, out of sheer frustration he abruptly snapped at Raun, "What's it to you?"

Raun was always quick with the lip, although rarely did it ever go farther than that. He was mainly just an instigator, loving every minute of it. "I'm getting bored watching you three bitch and moan, so either someone takes a swing or let's put our bikes behind these," pointing at some rose bushes next to the rusty link chain, "and get going," Raun explained.

Surprised by Raun's sudden assertiveness, Jeff chimed in, "He's right, let's do something, this sucks."

With everyone finally calming down, Dave was happy that he at least sold his idea of leaving the bikes behind while they went on their escapade. As they scouted the immediate area for a suitable spot to stash their valued possessions, the rose bushes were the only reasonable spot they could all come to agree on. Allen and Dave were silent as they placed the bikes in the back of the bushes. They used the extra twigs that Raun and Jeff gave them to aid in their camouflaging attempt. When all was said and done, they stopped to look at one another, as if to congratulate themselves on their proud achievement. In all actuality, the concealment was poor, but they did exhibit a valiant effort and managed to accomplish what they had set out to do.

When the amusement of stashing their bikes wore off, Allen didn't utter a word as he ducked under the chain and proceeded to head down the rustic path. With the others trailing close behind, they eagerly followed his lead with the exception of Dave, steadfastly believing this was a bad idea.

Everything appeared normal for the first hundred yards, but all of that slowly began to change as they continued to advance into the unknown. The further they progressed away from the familiar territory, the harsher the environment became. There was an aura of unusual stillness enveloping their surroundings as the thickening canopy of forest gradually consumed the sunlight. Soon the path they were following began to twist, tilt and curve. At times, it reached arduous angles that seemed impossible to climb. Before long, the packed soil beneath their feet started turning into loose gravel and crumble beneath them. The whole ordeal was difficult, causing an unpleasant feeling in their legs and it made walking, the simplest of tasks, difficult to perform. The boys were determined to keep moving forward and nothing was going to impede their progress, no matter how big of a hurdle they would encounter. It was as if their journey was somehow predestined, with some foreign object or supernatural force beckoning them closer. They were subconsciously oblivious to this force drawing them in and blissfully unaware, they unwittingly continued forward.

Attentive as ever, Dave detected any and all of the slightest changes in his surrounding environment. The same question continued to boggle his mind, he just couldn't figure out why these trails differed so much from the rest of them. He pondered on this thought momentarily when suddenly it all made sense. The trails had nothing to do with the way he was feeling. His conscience was bothering him because he knew they were trespassing and that it was wrong. Once again he began to second guess himself, maybe Raun was right and he really was scared? He tried desperately to pull himself back together because he knew that worrying about it wouldn’t solve the problem. By now they'd traversed quite a ways into the woods and turning back was no longer an option, so he continued to follow the pack.

As they continued the rest of the boys began to notice that as the distance they covered grew, the more extreme the darkness was becoming. Soon it was pitch black and with the exception of their heavy breathing and footsteps, there was total silence surrounding them.

Dave was the first to notice a bright light up ahead, shaped like a giant pear. It seemed as if they were nearing the end of a dark tunnel. As they headed in the direction of the light, the forest finally gave way to the light and they were temporarily blinded. Their eyes had to readjust, they attempted to aid this process by shielding their eyes with their hands. Almost an entire minute had passed before they were finally able to see and regain focus on their well-lit surroundings.

As their vision returned to normal, they stood there momentarily in awe. None of them had ever been in this part of the woods until now. What they saw, simply amazed them. It was a canyon that stretched out for miles on end and oddly enough was formed in the shape of a snake. Deep in its vast belly was total desolation with the exception of large boulders and several patches of tall weeds which appeared to be random and the only life it sustained. An even more amazing sight towered about seventy-five feet above the canyons floor and right in front of them.

An old wooden plank bridge stood there in front of them, appearing to have been built ages ago. The bridge itself drew quite an astounded reaction from the boys, the fact that it was still standing and hadn't yet fallen to the canyon's floor simply amazed them. They couldn't even imagine all of the punishment the harsh California weather had lashed out at it since its creation.

The ropes that were sustaining the bridge were anchored to iron stakes, appearing to be rotting away in place. The blistering sun had caused the ropes to wither and fray. The bridge itself was made from oak boards, roughly thirty-six inches in length, with approximately a two inch space between each plank. The extreme weather and blistering sun had caused the wooden planks to dry out and start deteriorating. Decay had set in on the bridge with full force and its image alone projected its vulnerability to the elements or to any sudden movements that might be inflicted by anyone attempting to cross its dry rotted skeleton. The section the bridge crossed was fifty feet across and seventy-five feet to the canyon floor. The kids stood there in awe, knowing that one good gust of wind could very easily send them and this rickety contraption crashing to their death on the rocky canyon floor.

"What now?" Raun asked.

"We're going across. We have to see if the trails continue on the other side," Allen wondered.

Immediately Dave's gut feeling told him the others were going to want to cross the bridge and that he would be forced to join them. He knew that he had to act fast, making up a reason that would prevent them from doing something stupid. "See! I told you that it wasn't a good idea to bring our bikes. We'd have rode right off this cliff if it had been dark out," Dave said, trying to stall for some more time until he could come up with something more concrete to detour the crossing of this bridge.

Allen threw both of his arms up in the air and bowed down at his torso three times as he said sarcastically, “Alright, you were right, hail King David. But don’t get used to it, because it don’t happen very often.”

On a hot streak, Dave pressed his luck and went for two in a row, “Look guys, this thing is a death trap. We should turn around and go back.”

“Are you gonna start that shit again?” Jeff wondered out loud.

Still upset for letting himself get dragged out here, Dave’s only choice was to let Allen have his way for now. He also promised himself that he would deal with Jeff later for going against him and siding with Allen, planning intently on beating him down as soon as they got home.

Although he was reluctant to cross the bridge, Dave knew that it was inevitable. Whether he followed or stayed behind, the rest were going across, it was a no win situation. He didn’t want to be left behind, but if he continued to speak out against the idea, he knew that Allen would continue to embarrass him in front of their little brothers again. It was either now or forty-five minutes from now, but the results would surely end up the same. To prevent another confrontation or any more of Allen’s abuse, Dave decided the only way he could get out of this while still maintaining his dignity was to take the bull by the horns. “Come on,” Dave suggested as he waved his arm and started walking out onto the bridge. As he was walking, he turned back to see if the others were following his lead. Jeff, Raun and Allen were just staring at him as if he was possessed. Dave now wondered if he had initiated something that could have actually been avoided. If so, he knew that it was too late, he had sealed their fate. Their destiny was uncertain with the exception that they were now all crossing this bridge.

Shocked by what had just transpired, Allen slowly caught up to Dave, rested his right hand on Dave's shoulder and said, "Now you're talking, I'm glad that you're not a total chicken-shit. There might be some hope for you yet."

The bridge was barely wide enough for them to walk single file. They felt like the man from the circus trying to perform the high wire act as they slowly inched their way across. Trying not to reveal any signs of weakness to the others, they continued marching forward without uttering a sound. A gentle breeze on the cliff's edge felt like a hurricane as their feat was progressing. The bridge was shifting from side to side and was beginning to bounce and reverberate with every step they took. The ropes and planks beneath their feet were squeaking as if they were crying out not to be stepped on. Ignoring the clamoring they continued with their hearts beating so fast and loudly they believed everyone else could hear them. Struggling with fear and uncertainty, they were barely able to breathe through the enormous lump in their throats. No one dared glance down, afraid that at any second this dilapidated contraption would soon send them plummeting to the rocky bottom below where they would surely meet their death.

When they arrived on the other side of the canyon, they all but jumped for joy and kissed the ground. They were proud that they had made it across, however, deep down inside they were all trembling with fear, knowing this obstacle will once again stand in their way on the return trip. Regardless, for now, they continued to move on and entered the second section of the trail. Although it was still daylight, not even a single beam of light was able to penetrate through the dense branches of pine, redwood and cedar trees. It was dark to the extent they could barely identify the person standing right next to them. Dave, aware of his surroundings made a mental note, but didn't share his observation with anyone. He was concerned that if he said something, the rest would mistake his alertness for paranoia, or worse yet, they would think he was losing his mind. The more he listened, the eerier the silence became. Even the sounds of crickets, beetles and birds were absent in this part of the woods.

Further into the trails, their curiosity began to wander as things they were noticing were starting to intrigue them. The trail they'd discovered seemed endless, but somehow they knew this path would inevitably lead them somewhere, but where? They'd walked about a hundred yards from the bridge and into the secondary part of the trails. Suddenly, as they finished making their way around a sharp curve in the trail, they found themselves standing in a large open field of weeds that were as tall as their waist in some spots. As the path emptied out into this open meadow, Allen shouted out in excitement, "Yes! I knew there was a reason that I wanted to come all this way."

Momentarily standing there in an acute state of shock, they were simply amazed by the sight of this log cabin standing before them. It appeared frozen in time and reminded them of looking into a snow globe at something abstruse. Scary, captivating and yet strangely inviting, they couldn't believe their eyes. Perplexed, they wondered, could this really be the mysterious cabin that plagued their town for ages.

Standing in the clearing at the edge of the tree line, the field itself looked as if it hadn't been passed through in years and consisted of nothing except overgrown weeds. Not a single tree was left standing within the circular patch of wild overgrowth and brush. It was as if the trees had been cleared out of this field and used to construct a large portion of this cabin.

This place had apparently been built around the same time as the degrading bridge, possibly by the same builder and they couldn't believe that either were still standing. The whole place looked as if it had been abandoned for at least a hundred years. The chimney was starting to crumble and break away from the roof and green mold had infested large sections of the outer walls. Standing in front they could only see one visible window which was to the right of the front door and the fact that the glass was still intact simply amazed them. The stairs leading up to the long front porch looked deadly deteriorated and the railings were rotting away from absolute neglect.

Allen looked at the others and finally broke the silence, "Come on guys, let's go and check it out."

A cold chill passed through Dave's body, he shook his head back and fourth and said, "I don't think that this is a good idea, besides, what if someone is home?" Not taking into account the age and condition of the cabin.

Frustrated, Allen threw his arms up in the air, as he pointed to the cabin he said, "Look around moron! Ain't no one been home in years!"

"I guess you're right," Dave agreed, again trying to save a little face, "but we'd better not stay long, as soon as the sun falls behind those trees, it's gonna get dark real quick and we probably won't be able to find our way home."

Dave wasn't only using this as an excuse, he was sincerely concerned about it getting totally dark while they were still out in this unfamiliar part of the woods.

"Alright, we'll hurry," Allen agreed.

Allen led the pack as they headed through the patch of wild growth toward the cabin. As they got closer, they were starting to get a better visual of this rustic cabin. The stairs and porch were covered with a large wooden awning that too was rotting away, possibly ready to cave in and collapse at any time. One by one they walked up the steps and onto the porch. Standing there, a chill suddenly passed through Dave's body, giving him goose bumps. He instantly froze in his tracks and could not build up the nerve to take another step. "Hey, I don't think this is a good idea, I've got a bad feeling," Dave stated, addressing his concerns to Allen.

In one swift motion, Allen turned around and stood toe to toe with Dave, looking straight into his eyes Allen stated, "You don't have a bad feeling! You're a coward! I'll tell you what, if you admit that you're a chicken-shit, we'll leave right now." Allen had just humiliated Dave in front of their little brothers again and his face was beet red.

"I'm not a coward, chump! But what if this is that old crazy drifter's house and what if he's still here?" This was Dave's abstract way of defending his honor.

"Come on you chicken-shit," Allen said. "If he was here, he'd be a hundred years old and I don't think he'd be that much of a threat."

"Yeah," Dave softly replied. "What about all those people that came up missing? I don't want to end up like them, or even find them for that matter."

"No wonder you're such a wus," Allen stated the facts. "We don't even know if those stories are true and now we have a chance to find out."

"And prove them," Jeff added.

Raun moved in a little closer and cut in, "Come on Dave, has anyone even ever admitted those stories are true?"

"No," Dave replied, "But everyone knows what happened, they just won't admit to it."

Despite Dave's discontent, Jeff continued to side with Allen and Raun, "Yeah, they're just old folk tales that give the tourists something to remember our hole in the wall town for."

Raun was the first to break the circle as he walked over to the window, the rest of them followed suit. They made a tremendous effort trying to keep quiet, but it seemed the lighter they treaded, the louder the boards creaked, echoing throughout and breaking the deafening silence surrounding them. Raun stuck his face to the window, cupping his hands to his forehead as he attempted to peer through the glass to no avail. There was a thick build up of dust and grime coating both sides of the window pane making it virtually impossible to see anything through it. As Raun pried his straining eyes away from the window he looked at everyone and stated, "I can't see a damn thing."

"Get out of the way," Allen said, shoving Raun out from in front of the window to have a look for himself, but that turned out to be more of a waste of time. Frustrated, he wasn't able to see anything either, he pulled his head away from the window, walked over to the door, turned the knob and yelled back over to the others, "Hey, come on, it's unlocked."

Stunned by Allen's forward attempt to check this place out, they couldn't do anything but look at Allen with surprise in their eyes. Dave managed to fight the lump in his throat and said, "Now, I know that this isn't a good idea, in fact, it's illegal."

"Come on, look at this place, it's creepy and been abandoned for centuries," Allen persisted.

"That doesn't mean its okay to break in just because they haven't been home in a couple of decades," Dave said, trying to be the voice of reason.

"Well, if you want to be a wus all of your life that's your call and you can stay out here but I'll bet they'll go. Little as they are, they're the ones that should be acting like scared little babies," Allen said, pointing at Raun and Jeff.

Jeff stepped in front of Allen and repeatedly poked his index finger into his chest as he said, "We'll go, but if you call me a baby one more time you can count on coming up missing yourself." Jeff looked over to Raun as if to say, I can put him in his place.

Raun patiently waited for his turn to speak, "So, are you coming, or what?"

"Yeah, I guess. Something just tells me we're going to regret this," Dave reluctantly conceded to their persistence. He knew that there was something about this place that just wasn't right, but he couldn't put his finger on it.

"You worry way to much, come on, it'll be alright, no one will ever know," Allen assured him.

With the decision made he slowly pushed the door open, the hinges made an awful screeching sound, as if they hadn't been oiled in ages. Slowly, they stepped inside one by one, batting their way through massive cobwebs that had taken over the living room long ago. The whole interior was covered from wall to wall and from the size and quantity, they figured the spiders that spun them must have been just as large. The webs looked virtually undisturbed and content with living alone in this abandoned cabin. With the exception of the dust that coated the furniture and cobwebs the place appeared to be as perfectly preserved in time since the day it was first abandoned.

On the right side of the room there were full-bodied stuffed mountain lions at each end of the sofa and mounted animal trophies throughout the cabin on every wall. Everything inside looked ancient, projecting the image that whoever used to live here was an antique collector in addition to being an avid hunter. Everyone spread out in different directions searching for whatever they might be able to find.

The light filtering inside was dim, making it difficult to see anything. As Dave and Allen searched the left side of the room by the fireplace, Jeff called over to them from next to the sofa, "Hey guys, come 'ere and check this out real quick."

As they all made their way over to him, Dave asked with panic inflecting in his voice, "What! What is it?"

They carefully inspected the item Jeff was holding in his hand. It was an old town newspaper dated August 4th, 1944. The paper was in great condition other then turning slightly brownish in color. Dave abruptly snatched the paper out of Jeff's hands and walked over to the dimly lit window in an attempt to read it further. The only print he was able to make out was the headline which read; "**SUSPECTED MADMAN UNAVAILABLE FOR QUESTIONING.**" In a slightly smaller print just beneath the headline but still legible, the sub heading stated, "Bringing the total missing persons to 17."

Raun, being the observant one of the bunch stated, "That's today's date! And that paper is fifty years old!" Dave, thinking with his wallet, folded the paper carefully in half and stuffed it into his back pocket, proclaiming, "This could be worth a lot of money."

"Yeah and when you collect it, don't forget who was with you when you found it," Allen said, stating his interest in his cut.

Dave pretended to ignore Allen's remark and said, "Alright, at least we know the old tale is true." As Dave actually heard himself saying that, he continued, "Do you guys think this is where he brought them and killed them?"

"If it is, I don't wanna find out." Jeff was shaken and scared by the thought of being in the same cabin where the murders might have taken place.

"Yeah, this doesn't seem fun anymore," Raun added.

"No one has ever been able to find this place. Let's get out of here before we find something that we don't wanna." Dave was not ready, willing or able to find out what hidden secrets this cabin might be holding.

On the other hand, Allen was much more daring and eager to learn the truth about what tales the inside of this cabin would tell. "Come on Dave, you're such a drag. We're already here, so let's just have a look around for a few secs and then we'll leave."

"That way we might become famous for solving the mystery of your town," Raun said, being more of a wise guy than actually being serious.

"Fine, whatever, let's just make it quick and get the hell out of here. This place gives me the creeps." Dave was incensed about their lack of concern.

When all was said and done, the four of them walked through the archway in the center of the living room, entering into the dining room. Since there were no other windows in sight allowing the sunlight to penetrate, this room was poorly lit in comparison to the previous one. Barely recognizable, was an eighteen foot oak dining room table which sat square in the center of the room. Directly above the table, hanging from the ceiling, was a six-candle chandelier made of tarnished silver. Fourteen chairs were neatly arranged around the edges of the table. The legs and backrests of the chairs had some type of abstract design on them that appeared to have been hand carved. A matching oak hutch stocked with fine crystal, covered with dust and cobwebs, rested in the far right corner of the room. Next to that was an old wooden ice chest. There was a large wood burning stove with its smoke stack tied right to the chimney through the catalytic style, two-sided pass through fireplace.

There were various other mounted animal trophies

throughout the dining room. On the far wall just on the other side of the large table was a Dutch double door. Each door was made from solid mahogany, approximately nine foot tall and three feet wide. They looked extremely out of place for being in this old rustic cabin.

Stunned by the remarkable size of these doors, Allen walked around the table to the other side of the room. He extended both of his arms, grabbed the brass handles and with his thumbs he pressed down, having no luck. The doors were locked shut. Allen found this to be strange. He was curious and wondered why these doors were locked when even the front door wasn't. He turned around to face the others and stated, "It's either locked or rusted shut, but it don't wanna open."

"I don't know what's behind that door and frankly, I don't think I wanna," Dave reaffirmed, still apprehensive about invading someones home.

Much to Dave's surprise, on this occasion Jeff leaned more to his brother's side as he suggested, "We really should get going, it's gonna get dark soon and the smell of this place is making me sick."

Allen finally caved in to being out numbered but stipulated they will only leave under one condition, "Alright, but were coming out here right after school tomorrow to get a better look around."

They all agreed to his demand. Dave gladly led the way as they headed for the exit. Suddenly they heard a loud crashing noise echoing from behind them.

PART FOUR
The Diner

It was getting late and within the last hour alone, the weather had begun to make a drastic change for the worse. Dark thunder heads hovered in the sky and the gorgeous day had turned into the beginning of a gloomy night. The weather bureau had issued a severe thunderstorm warning for Josiah Tree and all of the surrounding towns. The winds had picked up several notches and everyone was hurrying home for shelter, trying to beat the unexpected storm unfolding right above them.

Except for the cook, a waitress and a few of the last stragglers who were finishing up their meals, the diner was virtually empty. Donna, the evening waitress, was wiping off the tables and was glad that the dinner rush was finally over. Donna had long blonde hair with baby blue eyes and thin-lined pink lips. Everyone in town enjoyed eating at Tiffany's Steakhouse. The diner was well known for its good food and reasonable prices. People came from near and far because of Tiffany's good nature and friendly personality. Often the younger generation dined there just to watch Tiffany's sensual walk, not to mention some of the other girls that worked there. Tiffany especially enjoyed the attention and got a kick out of teasing the children by saying she was going to tell their mothers that they were hitting on her, but she never did.

That evening the boys strolled through the front entrance after chaining their bikes to the light post just outside. They looked around, checking out the entire area, bewildered by the approaching storm. As they walked inside, they headed over to the corner booth where they always sat and settled in. Tiffany saw them before they had even sat down and she proceeded over to their table to take their order.

When she arrived at their table she asked, "What are you boys doing out, can't you see there's a storm blowing in?"

Before they could even answer she glanced down at Raun's arm and noticed that he was injured and bleeding pretty heavily. Concerned, she asked what happened. Raun started to explain, but under the table Allen kicked him square in the shin to shut him up. Tiffany detected their awkward behavior, gave them a curious look, took their orders and left for the kitchen.

"Are you stupid?" Allen snapped at Raun as Tiffany walked away. Taking a long pause to let his words sink in, he continued, "You...we can't say a word to anyone 'bout this."

Sympathetic toward Raun's injury and obvious pain, Dave defended his little buddy, "Why don't you just leave him alone already?"

"Yeah!" Jeff cut him off, not allowing Dave to finish his sentence.

Dave glared at Jeff with a look to kill for interrupting and then went on to finish what he was saying, "He's bleeding pretty bad, maybe we should go home and have your mom take a look at it."

"All I'm saying is we can't discuss this with anyone until we find out what is up there," Allen demanded, showing that he was more concerned with the cabin than his own little brother's welfare.

"I don't know," hesitant, Dave let his words trail off while he gathered his thoughts, a few seconds later, "Something about that cabin gives me the creeps. I mean come on, look what happened to Raun already."

Simultaneously, they all suddenly fell quiet as Tiffany returned with their two orders of onion rings and four large drinks. She set everything down on the table and once more asked Raun if he was all right? Raun did not respond, instead, he looked over to Allen, waiting for him to respond to the question for him. Before he could even say a word, Tiffany knew she wasn't going to get the truth, so all she added was, "You boys look like you've been up to no good tonight." Then she glared at them with her "I'm gonna tell your parents" look in her eye. Allen quickly thought of a lie, trying to convince Tiffany not to tell their parents. Of course, he was sure his attempt was in vain, she wasn't buying the old 'he fell off his bike' story.

The rest of them had a hard time with not busting out in laughter as Allen tried to sell her on this farce of a story. When In all actuality, as they were exiting the cabin, Raun suddenly got spooked as he realized he was about to be the last one out. As a temporary hysteria shuddered over his body he panicked and picked up the pace. Not watching where he was going, he managed to trip over the head of a bear skin rug lying on the floor. Losing his footing he came crashing down on the coffee table in the living room, breaking something glass and sustaining a deep gash to his elbow.

His sweatshirt was ripped and soaked in blood. Tiffany could tell from their behavior alone that there was more to this story then they were letting on, but for now she knew that her only choice was to leave it alone and wait to mention it to their parents. She gave them one more suspicious look before leaving to tend to another customer.

Once she reached a distance where they knew they could talk without her being able to over hear them, Allen said, "What happened there tonight was all because this klutz tripped and hurt himself. But think about it, we might find something that will help us solve the town legend of the disappearances. We can be the first ones to know exactly what it was that happened fifty years ago."

"I gotta go," Raun replied.

"That's what I'm talking about, a sense of adventure." Allen turned to face his brother and smiled.

"No! I need to go to the bathroom and clean this up." Raising his arm to flaunt his injury in the hopes of reminding his brother that he was slowly bleeding to death.

"It'll be alright," Allen suggested as Dave stepped aside to let Raun head to the bathroom, giving him just enough room to squeeze between himself and the table.

"You'd better hurry! Or I'm gonna eat all of your onion rings," Jeff said sarcastically, attempting to cheer Raun up a little.

"You better not even think about it!" Raun replied, without breaking a stride while on the way to the bathroom to rinse off his wound.

Meanwhile, at the table Dave asked Allen bluntly, "Why are you so obsessed with going back out there?"

"Something's out there and I just know that it'll make me crazy if I don't go and check it out myself," Allen said with a look of confusion burned into his face as if he didn't understand why either.

"It's just an abandoned cabin, why do you care?" Jeff asked, putting his two cents in while chewing on an onion ring.

Allen slammed his drink down on the table and insisted, "But it's not, what if it's more then just a run down cabin? We gotta find out."

"I just don't like the place, it's kinda spooky," Raun interjected as he sat back down at the table.

"You guys have to look at the big picture, there's something out there." Allen was getting goose bumps just thinking about it.

As Jeff grabbed the last onion ring off one of the plates, he curiously asked, "What's that?"

"What the hell is wrong with you?" Allen was almost shouting. "Haven't you heard a word I've been saying? We can actually be the first to know what really happened way back then."

Dave replied, "I don't really care all that much, besides, why can't we just send your uncle out there to check it out?"

Allen and Raun's uncle, Nick Balden, was the sheriff in their rapidly growing small town. He was a detective in Los Angeles, California before he moved to Joshua Tree to be with his sister, not to mention he was tiring of all of the problems that came with the big city. He didn't mind the pay cut, to him the reduced workload was a nice break after being in law enforcement for ten years.

"Listen nitwits! We all..." Allen stopped briefly, as Tiffany passed by their table, there was total silence. From across the room, she gave them a dirty look as she was clearing off another table. As soon as she was out of the proximity of their voices, he continued quietly, "We all agreed that we would go back out there and that we weren't going to say anything, to anyone!"

"I still don't think this is a good idea," Dave persisted.

With Raun back from the restroom, Allen turned to face him and said, "Look at this, can you believe how scared these two are?" He downed the rest of his drink through the straw before slamming his empty glass on the table again.

"To tell you the truth, I'm not so sure I want to go back out there," Raun tried to express his thoughts without offending his older brother.

Frustrated and filled with rage, Allen slammed his fists down on the table, "What is with you cowards? I swear, I hang out with a bunch of whiny bitches!"

Irritated by Allen's outburst, Dave raised his voice

slightly and said, “What makes you think that you get to make all of the decisions around here?” Dave was really getting tired of being pushed around by Allen. Allen knew it, but seemed to get off on pushing Dave’s buttons.

Feeling frustrated and stonewalled from the pack, Allen stated, “Well, I’m going back out there. The three of you can stay home and play with your Barbies, but I’m going back, I have to know whats out there.” More persistent than he'd ever been before, he continued to unleash his verbal assault, “I just can’t believe you pussies are scared of an empty cabin.”

“I’m not a pussy, I’ll go with you,” Raun grudgingly surrendered to Allen’s relentless reverse psychology.

Allen once again turned his head to face Raun, “I don’t know who suggested you had a choice, you were coming regardless.”

“Come on Jeff, it’ll be fun,” Raun pleaded, now aware he would be making this trip with or without the strength of his friends.

“I’ll go if Dave’s going,” Jeff said, praying that Dave would say no.

With three sets of eyes staring at him intently, Dave knew that he'd regret this decision later. “Fine, but for the record, I still say this is pointless and a bad idea,” he reiterated, looking steadfastly at Allen as he finished his sentence.

Now that they'd finally came to an agreement, Allen outlined some of their plan that was to take effect on the following day. They finished up at the diner and paid Tiffany for their meal. Nervous, anxious and excited, they exited the building, unlocked their bikes and proceeded off into the stormy night.

PART FIVE
The Lecture

The boys raced home trying to beat the brunt of the storm and make it in time to abide by their curfew. As soon as they reached Beaverland, Allen and Raun swerved sharply to the right, turning down their driveway. They all shouted goodnight to each other as Dave and Jeff continued racing down the street toward their house at the end of the block.

Mrs. Stevens was sitting on the leather sofa knitting a sweater for her husband. Their fifteenth wedding anniversary was rapidly approaching and this was the present she intended on giving him, she'd been working on it fiercely for weeks.

She heard the sound of the front door opening, lifted her head and watched as Allen stepped through the front door with Raun closely in tow. The boys thought they were slick and positioned themselves in a manner that shielded Raun's injury from her line of sight. Trying not to act too obvious, Raun headed for the staircase using Allen to hinder her vision, but before he was able to make a clean getaway, Pat caught a glimpse of the blood soaked sweatshirt he was wearing. She immediately dropped her project onto the sofa, jumped to her feet and summoned him back into the living room.

"What happened?' She sincerely asked with a frightened expression on her face. "Are you alright?"

"I fell off of my bike on the way home," Raun said, trying to minimize the seriousness of his injury. He looked over to Allen for his approval on the lie he just told to their mother. Allen was shocked, but proud of Jeff's instinctive and quick response.

"Let me have a look at that," she said, carefully grabbing Raun by the arm.

"See, it's not that bad, I just need to clean off the dried

blood."

Her voice was still slightly trembling, "Alright, it looks like you'll live, now you guys go wash up and get ready for bed." They both started to walk away when she once again called out to them, "Allen, your father would like to see you before you head up to bed." She barely finished her sentence and Raun was already halfway up the stairs. She added one last request to Raun as Allen headed into the kitchen to see his father, "And make sure that you clean that cut out with peroxide. It's in the medicine cabinet."

Allen walked into the kitchen and pulled out a jar of Jiffy peanut butter and a loaf of Taystee bread. Picking up a spoon, he scooped a large portion out of the container and began spreading it out on the bread. After using the jelly, he took a nice sized bite out of the sandwich, turned to the left and saw his father leering at him from behind his newspaper, with a pipe dangling from his mouth the whole time he fashioned his sandwich. "Allen, can you come in here for a moment, I want to speak with you if you're finished," Mike said in a calm, yet very serious tone.

Allen nodded his head in acknowledgment as he inhaled the rest of his sandwich. As he was walking, he downed the better part of the glass of milk he'd poured for himself. He stepped down the single step into the den and sank his body into the chair next to his dad's recliner.

Mike Stevens was very elegant, keeping himself well groomed and he always wore a suit and tie. He was five foot, nine inches tall, with short dark hair. Mike graduated from the University of Southern California and landed a job with Shell Oil Corporation at a young age. He worked his way up the company ladder and within two years time he already made it to the executive level. When Mike learned he was going to be reassigned to Joshua Tree, he figured that it was better to relocate here than to make the daily two hour long commute each way. His wife Pat had came into town several times to look at a few houses in an attempt to find a suitable home, After an extensive hunt, they settled for the house on Beaverland, mainly because of the large vacant lot adjacent to their property line. They felt this lot gave them lots of potential to build on in order to accommodate the ritzy lifestyle they had grown so accustomed to.

Relaxing to the soothing sound of orchestra music, Mike pressed the mute button on the remote when Allen sat down. In one of his best theatrical performances, Mike placed the remote on the armrest, took a long drag off of his pipe and shook his head from side to side. Dramatizing his displeasure Mike said, "You guys," he paused to allow his words to sink in, "you talked your mother into letting you go ridding today after I explicitly asked you to mow the lawn." Mike took another drag off his pipe, bent his head back and exhaled, filling the room with smoke.

"Dad," Allen began to explain, "I promise, it's gonna get done this weekend."

"I realize that your mother is lenient on you and she loves you both very much," pausing again to emphasize the rest of his sentence, "but you know that I needed this done and how important it is."

Humiliated by the chastising he was receiving, Allen mumbled, "I promise, it'll get done."

Mike cut him off and stressed, "We're having very important guests from out of town this Sunday. I need the lawn mowed and the place picked up, everything has to be perfect when they arrive."

"I promised mom that we'd do it on Saturday," Allen pleaded, hanging his head in shame, trying intently to avoid looking directly into his fathers piercing eyes.

"I know, she informed me, I just don't want any excuses from you on Saturday." Mike was stern and wanted to make his point crystal clear to Allen.

"Alright dad, I'll make sure it gets done right," Allen said sheepishly.

"You sound as if you're going to be supervising the job by the way you said that."

"No, I don't do that dad," Allen replied, trying hard not to burst out laughing.

"Good, I don't want you thinking we brought your brother into this world for you to have a personal slave to do your chores for you." Lately, Allen had been getting out of his share of the responsibilities around the house by reallocating the bulk of the tasks to Raun and Mike was well aware of this.

"I know. I don't." By this point in time, Allen was fidgeting, anxiously waiting to be excused.

"One more thing," Mike added, disappointed by his son's behavior. "What is this that I'm hearing about you shooting at the cat with your BB gun? Your mother said it looked as if you did this for amusement?" he asked with a puzzled look on his face.

"It was accidental dad, I swear," Allen insisted.

"I know that you're not going to sit here in front of me and lie, are you?"

"I'm sorry," Allen apologized, but not sincerely.

"Now, I want to start taking you to the shooting range more often, but this cruelty towards animals, it has got to stop."

"I won't do it anymore," Allen agreed, trying his hardest to sound genuinely remorseful.

"All right then," Mike said with a deep tone in his voice, "when you start behaving more civilized, we won't have to keep having these awkward little discussions."

"I know," Allen agreed, asking permission to be excused, Mike consented by nodding his head as he took another drag off his pipe. Allen stood up, said goodnight and headed upstairs. On his way to the bathroom, he passed by Raun's room and noticed the door was closed. When Allen had finished up in the restroom, he headed to his own room, set the alarm clock and climbed into bed. Exhausted, as soon as he laid down and shut his eyes, he was out like a light.

Although Raun went to bed a half-hour earlier, he was not quite as fortunate. He laid there for the longest time, tossing and turning repeatedly before he was finally able to fall asleep.

It was ten after nine when Dave and Jeff walked in. Ann Healy was unpacking some groceries she had picked up on the way home. In one hand she had a box of Captain Crunch cereal and a bag of flour in the other. Ann had both arms extended in the air, carefully placing the items in the kitchen cabinet.

Mrs. Healy was short and a little on the pudgy side, but nevertheless, very attractive. She was only five foot, two inches tall. With long bleached blonde hair, she was a hard working widow with a heart of gold and two young mouths to feed. As she finished putting the groceries away, she pivoted sideways and said, "Hi guys, how was your day?"

"We went out to the trails and raced around the tracks, that's all." Without thinking, Jeff almost told her about their excursion when he suddenly clammed up, remembering Allen's egotistic warning.

"That's nice, though you guys are a little late." Ann really didn't mind, so long as her boys came home safe at the end of the night.

"We know ma, we lost track of time," Dave stated, also conveniently leaving out any mention of the cabin.

"That's alright hun, long as you guys enjoyed yourselves and stayed out of trouble," she insisted.

"We did." They synchronously chirped, feeling slightly guilty over dodging the second part of her sentence.

"That's good. I'm very proud of you and it really helps me out knowing that you two can take care of yourselves while I'm at work."

Ever since John's untimely death it seemed Ann's time was spread thin and extremely limited, either being at work or in school. She felt as if she was neglecting her children because she wasn't able to spend more of her precious time at home. Ann had been promising them a vacation, providing she was able to save up enough money for a trip. However, Dave and Jeff realized their mom was overwhelmed with bills and never took her offer seriously.

"Did you guys eat yet?" she curiously asked.

"Yeah, we stopped at Tiff's and had some onion rings," Dave answered for the both of them.

"Okay then, you two go wash up and get ready for bed, you have school in the morning you know."

Dave and Jeff went about their normal routine. They washed up and brushed their teeth and somehow still had a half-hour before bedtime. They went to their shared bedroom, switched on the TV and watched the end of a X-files rerun before falling asleep.

PART SIX
The Double Doors

Raun found himself standing under the living room archway. He remembered the smell, which had contaminated the whole cabin with a nauseating foul odor. He covered his nostrils with the palms of his hands, eyes were watering from breathing the toxic air. It was dark, but Raun noticed that it was lighter than before. He turned around to look out the window behind him, but there too, was total darkness. Curious, Raun proceeded forward, hoping to locate the source from which a glimmer of light derived. When he could not find its origin, Raun started heading back toward the front door.

Tired and confused he reached out for the handle, but before he could make his exit, a hollow deep voice called out his name softly. He was alarmed by the abrupt realization that someone else was in here with him. Quickly, he turned back around and began scanning the entire room through the darkness. Using only his head he looked to the right, then to the left, even checking the ceiling and the floor, but found no one, anywhere. Knowing this was not just a figment of his imagination, Raun shouted aimlessly into the darkness, "Hello, is someone here?"

Frightened, Raun stood motionless in the silence of the desolate cabin, wondering why this was happening. Cautiously he watched and listened in all directions for even the slightest sound or movement. Consumed by darkness and fear, Raun waited a few more seconds before he heard the chilling voice call out to him once again. Rather than respond, Raun listened for the audible sound and followed the reverberation with his eyes to the giant wooden double doors in the dining room. Slowly he made his way over to them, cautiously he extended his arms and grabbed the two brass handles on the mahogany doors towering in front of him. Using only his thumbs, he pressed down on the button latches firmly and the lock released.

Unsure of what he was doing, or even the reason he was doing it, Raun carefully began pushing the doors open. Nothing could have prepared him for what he was about to see. When the door opened wide enough for him to step inside, he was mystified by what he was looking at. The size of this room was incredible in comparison to the rest of the cabin. The walls, ceiling and floor were all painted jet black and without a window it appeared even darker.

That dim eerie light, with no visible origin, again blanketed the room. As Raun inched his way into the room, he noticed that the room was virtually empty. There were no other exits, the only visible object in the room was a silver table. It appeared to be some sort of shrine that had been set up in the center of the room. The shrine consisted of two triangular shapes which rested one on top of the other. The one that formed the base was eighteen inches thick, and the sides were twenty-four inches equidistant. The triangle on top was identical in thickness, but its surface diameter was of a larger dimension. Because it was three feet long from point to point, it caused the top surface to overlap the one on the bottom by six inches on every side. In the center of the table was a single black candlestick resting inside an oxidized copper candle holder. The corner shaped angle of the table was perfectly aligned with the red pentagram drawing which was painted on the black floor. The pentagram was centered between the door and the peculiar shrine, its diameter was approximately five feet across.

Raun seemed to be drawn to the charm of this magnificent object, he was almost in a trance like state as he continued inching his way closer. He was half way there, when suddenly the double doors he had entered through slammed shut behind him. Startled, Raun abruptly made a complete circle as he surveyed the entire room, only to find no one there. He took in a deep breath and continued stealthy as he walked toward the shrine. When he reached the perimeter of the object, he bent down on one knee to examine this awesome sight. He reached out to the table and as soon as his fingertips grazed the shrines surface, the candle in the center ignited. The entire room kindled from the flickering of the flame.

With the glow of the candle Raun was able to see three figures engraved into the table's surface, one in each corner. As he sat there in awe, he didn't understand how the three images he was looking at tied together. One was of some type of bird, another a serpent and the last was an image of a man. The candle sat directly in the center of the three images.

The triangular altar appeared to be at least a thousand years old, it was unlike anything he had ever seen before. In this cabin it seemed oddly out of place, it looked far older and didn't match the decor of anything else in the room.

Raun slowly stood up when a voice called out to him, "You must turn the key!"

Trembling with fear, Raun replied, "What key? Why don't you show yourself?"

"You must help set me free!" The hollow voice echoed.

"Where are you?" Raun asked, talking into thin air and thinking he was losing his mind.

"Together we can make everything the way it was meant to be."

"What do you mean? What's wrong with the way things are? Who are you?" Raun continued shouting into the empty space.

Suddenly a hand reached over and grabbed him by the shoulder. "Raun!" the voice said. Drenched in sweat, Raun opened his eyes and jumped out of bed. It was Allen, standing next to the bed, staring down at him perplexed.

"What's your problem? It's seven o'clock! Get your ass up and get ready for school," Allen forcefully suggested.

Abruptly, Raun jumped up in bed, wiped the sweat from his brow and the sleep from his eyes as he sat there momentarily confounded in silence. Perplexed by the bizarre dream that had been impetuously cut short, he sat there dumbfounded. Before he could utter a word, Allen turned around and exited the room to finish getting ready for school. Still trying to make sense of it all, Raun got up, gathered his thoughts and walked over to the bathroom. Standing there seemingly frozen in place, he stared blankly at Allen without saying a word. Puzzled by his brother's awkward behavior, Allen scratched his head slightly confused and went on about his daily ritual in preparation for the day, thinking nothing more of the strange behavior. Shortly thereafter, Raun reappeared in Allen's doorway and asked, "Are we going back out to the cabin today?"

"Dude, what's wrong with you this morning? You knew that yesterday." Allen was just baffled by his brother's bizarre behavior at this early hour of the morning.

"Just checking," Raun replied. "What time are we going?"

After putting on his socks, Allen got off his bed, walked over to his dresser and pulled out his attire for the day. "After school, I'll come home and grab some flashlights and supplies, then we'll meet you and Jeff over at the library." Allen would be able to return home and still make it back to the library before Raun and Jeff got out of school because they got out half an hour before them.

"What about our bikes? I don't want to stash them in the woods again," Raun said, worried about the bikes getting stolen, since there was virtually no way to secure them in the trails.

Allen answered, "Just lock them up with ours at the school. They'll be safe there and then we'll just walk to the cabin."

By now Raun was finally able to get a grip on himself and put the nightmare behind him. "Alright then, I'll see you after school," he said.

Allen replied, "That's what I'm talking about, now your acting like a Stevens."

"What's that supposed to mean?" Raun asked, unsure about the statement.

"I was starting to think that all that hanging around with Jeff was starting to rub off on you. I'd hate for you to turn into a big wus like they are," Allen explained.

Wanting to be accepted by his brother for his toughness, Raun said with a smile, "Not a chance, you know me, all balls, no brains."

"Get out of here you goof, you're gonna make me late," Allen said feeling proud of his brother's bravado. Raun retreated back to his room while Allen finished getting ready for school. Shortly afterward they left at their usual times, unaware of what mysteries today might bring.

PART SEVEN
Final Warning

On school days, Mrs. Healy would get up at five in the morning, take a shower and wake up her two boys as she was heading out the door. On this particular day, Dave and Jeff were both already awake and getting dressed. "Oh, it's a surprise to see both of you up so early," she said with a smile, adding, "I'll be home tonight about eight thirty. Make sure you're home before dark." They acknowledged her and she gave each of them a peck on the cheek, even though Dave tried to resist. "Now don't you guys be late for school and that especially goes for you," she said, pointing at Dave.

Ever since her husband's death, Ann felt as if she was losing touch with Dave, she truly felt helpless because she thought there was nothing she could do about it. She noticed the change in his behavior when Dave started to spend more of his free time away from home. To top it all off he was becoming more of a reckless teenager, defiant of her and all forms of authority. There used to be a time when Dave was responsible, obedient and kept out of trouble. Dave was also becoming more particular about his appearance, to a degree that it had almost became an obsession. Sometimes the kids even teased him about his compulsion for neatness, calling him names such as 'mommy's boy' and 'freak.'

All of that changed during the course of time since he started hanging out with Allen Stevens. His grades dropped drastically and last year he almost failed his math class. It seemed that he had just stopped caring and often went to school just to hang out with his friends. On several occasions, his mother tried discussing this with him, she decided that all she could do was hope it was just a phase and that he would soon return to his old self once he got over the loss of his father.

"Don't forget to lock the door," Ann said on her way out. As she walked outside, she closed the door behind her, climbed into her Dodge Caravan and drove off to work.

Trying to avoid being late for school again, Dave ran out of the house, not even finishing the bowl of cereal he'd just poured moments ago. If he hurried, Dave thought, he would be able to make it just before the bell rang. Jeff stepped into the bedroom just as Dave was getting ready to go and asked, "Are we going back out there today?"

"I really don't wanna, but we both know they probably stayed up all night planning it," Dave stated indicating Raun and Allen.

"I don't either," Jeff said, "I guess we'll just have to wait and see if they bring it up."

Dave agreed and added, "But if we don't go, or at least act like we wanna go, we'll never hear the end of it."

"I know that's the truth," said Jeff, "Allen talks too much shit. I don't understand why you don't just punch him in that big fat mouth of his."

Unwilling to admit his fear of Allen to his younger brother, Dave simply replied, "I really should, but I don't think that it'd make a difference."

"Let's just hope that they forgot about it," Jeff suggested optimistically.

"Yeah right, I doubt that much very seriously. Something just tells me that they've already got it all planned and we're gonna end up out there right after school," Dave said, showing his lack of enthusiasm. He grabbed his pack of Marlboro's out of the sock drawer, removed one from the pack and lit it before he placed the smokes and matches in the pocket of his flannel shirt.

"Your probably right. I'll see ya after school."

Bothered by the smell, Jeff waved the cloud of smoke out of his face.

"Alright," Dave said, "now get out of here! You're gonna make me late for school again." Ignoring the last part of Dave's sentence, Jeff moseyed his way into the bathroom to finish getting ready for school.

It was ten minutes to eight when Dave finally made his way out of the house. He grabbed his bike from the side of the house and headed toward Allen's house on his way to school. When he made it to the top of his street he tried to spot Allen's bike at the Stevens' home, but it was gone. Allen had already left for school. He started peddling faster as he shook his head from side to side knowing that now he would most likely be late.

The conductor pulled the cord three times, giving warning to all passersby. The whistle was loud and could be heard for miles. This week alone, this same train had caught Dave every day. Growing frustrated, Dave refused to allow this train to make him late once again. He started to peddle faster in his dangerous attempt to race the train. He was only a little more then a block away when he saw the red lights start to flash and the red and white guard rails started coming down to block the road. The conductor pulled the cord several more times as the train was approaching the intersection. The loud whistle was deafening and sounded its last warning to discourage anyone who might be in a rush to cross its path.

With their trajectory and speed already set, Dave and the locomotive seemed predestined for a violent head on collision. Committed to reaching this intersection of the tracks and his path first, Dave's legs were circling out of control with no intention or desire to use the brakes, delaying the inevitable.

There was only fifty yards between them, twenty, ten,

he could feel the tremendous vibrations coming from the giant roaring engine. His adrenaline was flowing so intensely that it felt as if his heart was going to explode at any second. "I got to make it, I'm gonna make it," were the only thoughts going through his head. He was nearing the apex of the approach hill the tracks passed over, accelerating even faster than he could have thought possible. Reaching the highest point of the approach hill, his bike was suddenly airborne, successfully launching it across the tracks.

Missing him by no more than several inches, the train whooshed by him as he landed safely on the other side of the hill. Dave turned his head to look at the passing train that he'd finally beaten, only to see the conductor raising his fist and shaking it as he shouted some obscenities at him. Excited and feeling victorious, Dave shouted, "Yea!" He looked back at the engineer once more, smiled and gave him the middle finger before continuing on his way to school.

The school was just beyond the tracks, as Dave pulled up to the bike rack, he glanced up at the clock located just above the gymnasium door which indicated it was two minutes to eight. Upset with himself, Dave said out loud, "Damn! I can't win for losing." The bell rang before he even finished locking up his bike.

As Dave was finishing up, he noticed that Allen's bike was already chained to the rack. He snapped the clasp shut, stood up and walked across the lawn to the main entrance located right next to the school's office.

In order to get into class, Dave needed a pass from the principals office. He waited patiently while the secretary finished attending to her phone call. When she placed the receiver back in its cradle, she saw Dave sitting in the chair. She paced herself as she walked over to the counter and said, "Mr. Kenny would like to see you in his office." Dave was well known by all of the office staff, due mostly in part to his persistent trouble with making it to school on time.

Mr. Rick Kenny was sitting behind his large intimidating desk, reading the papers he clutched in his hand. He was a big man, with thick glasses and a receding hairline. He had been the principal at Rosemont High School for ten years. He was a well-respected man and a pillar of the community.

Wanting to get this over with as quickly as possible, Dave took a deep breath and softly tapped on the principals partially opened door. Mr. Kenny waved his hand without even glancing up from his paperwork, motioning for whoever dared to interrupt his work to step inside. Finally, Mr. Kenny glanced up over the papers that had sustained his interest so diligently, only to find Dave standing there in front of him once again. He set the pile of papers down in front of him on his desk and said, "Mr. Healy! What are we going to do with you? Your tardiness has become a real problem lately." Frustrated, the principal repeatedly tapped his fingers on his desk, patiently awaiting a response.

Dave was quietly thinking to himself, 'If he only knew what I had to go through this morning in a failed attempt to make it here on time.' As he thought about that for a second, he realized telling him that story probably wouldn't be such a good idea. In fact he decided that it would most likely get him into bigger trouble than he was already in. As Dave sat there silently in the chair, he tried desperately to figure out an acceptable reason for his excessive tardiness. Before he was able to come up with one, Mr. Kenny said, "I'll tell you what Mr. Healy!" Taking in a deep breath, he momentarily paused as he leaned back in his chair and placed both of his hands on top of his balding head. He forced himself to calm down and added, "I'll give you another pass today, but this is your final warning. If you even think about coming in late next week, even once, you will be suspended. I don't care if the whole world is coming to an end, breaks in half, trapping you on the wrong side, you will find a way to get here, and on time. Now, do we understand one another?"

"Yes sir, Mr. Kenny," were the only words Dave could utter.

Mr. Kenny added, "I really don't think your mother will appreciate it very much if I were to suspend you, now would she?"

"No sir, she wouldn't be very happy with me," Dave softly replied as he graciously accepted the pass and strolled out of the principals office.

His first hour class was almost entirely over by now. However, he did arrive in time to participate in the last fifteen minutes and catch the weekend homework assignment. When he handed the teacher the pass and proceeded to his seat in the back of the classroom, he spent the remainder of the math class trying to figure out the logic of the way the rules were set up. To him, no matter how he looked at it, they made no sense. In a nutshell, if you were late or skipped school you would get suspended and sent home, which is where you obviously wanted to be in the first place. He had pondered over this on several occasions but was never able to come to any type of reasonable conclusion.

It took until lunchtime for Dave and Allen's paths to finally cross. Allen was already sitting at their regular table, he was used to beating Dave into the lunchroom, or everywhere for that matter. Lately it appeared to Allen that Dave had lost the ability to tell time all together.

Dave made his way through the long line to receive his rations of slop. The menu read pizza with fries and jello for desert, but the main coarse resembled something more like ketchup spread on a piece of cardboard. He paid the lady at the counter and proceeded to the far corner table of the lunchroom where they usually sat. They ate their lunch there in the same seats where they had sat for as long as they had hung out together. No one ever sat at the same table with them. Most of the students were intimidated by Allen's attitude and the crude remarks he often made didn't encourage anyone to try initiating a conversation with any of them. At times Dave himself wondered how and why he put up with Allen's sarcastic personality, but somehow he had gotten used to it. However on this particular morning the privacy was somewhat of a blessing that no one was in earshot. They could carry on freely with this private conversation without the worry about someone listening in.

They were sitting directly across from each other as they began shoveling down their meals, at times, it seemed they were swallowing their food without even chewing it. Allen was the one to break the silence and initiate the dreaded conversation, "I'm surprised to even see you here today."

Dave swallowed the reminder of food he had in his mouth, then he washed it down with a giant swig of his chocolate milk before asking, "Why is that?"

Allen replied, "I left late myself this morning and saw you were still at your house."

Shocked to hear a different response then he had anticipated, Dave explained, "Yeah, I was late again, Mr. Kenny wanted to see me and told me I'm dead meat if it happens again."

"I really just didn't think that you were going to show up today," Allen stated as he finished his juice container.

"Why?" Dave asked reluctantly, well aware of where this answer would lead.

"I just figured you'd chicken out and have your ma

call in sick or something, that way you wouldn't have to go back out to the cabin with me," Allen said, sincerely surprised that Dave even showed up at school.

The teasing and shit talking was inevitable and Dave knew that Allen's civilized mannerism was too good to last. "Just because I actually think before I go and do something, it don't mean that I'm scared, I just ain't stupid," Dave said, defending himself while trying to articulate his words in a manner that wouldn't offend Allen.

Confused by the meaning of Dave's response, Allen asked, "What's that supposed to mean?"

"I'm just saying that sometimes you do dumb ass things without thinking about the consequences," Dave explained.

Agitated, Allen stood up from the lunch table with his veins visibly about to explode as they pulsated out of the sides of his temples. He walked around the table and got right up in Dave's face and asked, "So, are you going or what?"

"Yeah, relax a little, I'm going," Dave said, trying to calm Allen down a little before he made any more of a scene. "What's the plan? I'm sure you've got one," Dave asked.

"After school," Allen started to say as he sat back down next to Dave, in a much quieter voice he continued, "we're all going to meet at the library. I told Raun to bring Jeff with him and to lock their bikes up with ours, this way we don't have to stash them in the woods again."

"That's the smartest thing I've heard you say in a long time. But we're gonna need some flashlights or something ya know?" Dave stated.

"I know," Allen replied. "I'm gonna run home and grab 'em right after school while you wait for them guys at the library. I should be back before they get out, that way we'll all meet up about the same time," Allen confidently explained.

"I don't know why I doubted myself, I knew you already had this all figured out," Dave said trying to lighten the tension a little.

When the bell rang, the rest of the students in the cafeteria got up, disposed of their leftovers and headed to their respective classes. As Dave and Allen parted ways, they headed off in different directions, as they didn't share any of the same classes this semester. Dave had social studies for fourth hour and walked to the rear of the building. The whole way to class he couldn't stop thinking about what he'd gotten himself into, but he knew it was too late to back out now, his destiny was written in stone. He was committed to a return trip to the cabin, even though in his heart he knew it was a bad idea.

At Lamphere Elementary, Raun wasted the entire day reminiscing about his nightmare from the night before. The dream must have had some kind of significant meaning. If only he had stayed asleep just a few moments longer, maybe then he could understand what it was that his subconscious was trying to tell him. Still trying to make some sense of it all, the bell rang and the school day was over. Raun raced outside to meet up with Jeff at the bike rack located in the front of the school. As soon as he exited the building, Raun saw Jeff already straddling his bike. As Raun headed over to the bike rack, he called out to Jeff, "How the hell do you get out here so fast?"

"We have gym at the end of the day and Ms. Rose always lets us go and change early, by the time the bell rings we're all waiting by the door ready to go," Jeff explained.

"Must be nice, I don't ever get a break. Mr. Siwicky talks our ears off. He'd still be talking now if he thought he could get away with it," Raun said, trying to explain a little about his teacher.

Mr. Siwicky was a teacher at Lamphere Elementary and he taught with great enthusiasm. Many of the students thought he was weird, mainly because of the way that he over-pronounced every word when he spoke. "I'm glad that I didn't get stuck in that class," Jeff rubbed it in by laughing at Raun and the troublesome teacher whom the students referred to as the cockatoo for his never-ending, seemingly pointless speeches.

As Raun was unlocking his bike, Jeff asked, "Where were you at this morning? Your bike was on the side of the house, but no-one answered the door."

"Oh, I went with my mom and picked out a bike she's gonna get for Allen's birthday," Raun explained.

Shocked, Jeff asked, "She let you skip class?"

"Yeah, it was the only time she could take me with her without Allen knowing. She figured if he doesn't think I know, he won't ask me what he's getting."

"Is it a nice one?"

"Yeah, it's bad as hell." After maneuvering his bike out of the rack he asked, "You're coming out to the cabin with us, right?"

Uncertain of how to respond to Raun bringing up the dreaded subject Jeff said, "Yeah, I guess, but I have to go home and check in with Dave first."

"Allen already took care of that," Raun stated, "we're supposed to meet them at the library."

"Do you think they're there already?" Jeff asked, desperately trying to think of a reason not to go, but he remembered what his brother had told him this morning.

"Dave should be, Allen had to go home and grab some flashlights and stuff," Raun replied.

"Hold up a sec, let me run this back inside," he said, holding up his backpack, "I didn't know we weren't going home first."

"Hurry up!" Raun shouted, as Jeff took off running back into the school. Only a few moments had passed before Jeff returned, they jumped on their bikes and started heading up the street toward the library. As they road down Warren Road they passed the sheriffs' department, which was only a block away from Rosemont Middle School. At the bike rack they noticed Dave's bike, but Allen's wasn't there yet. When they pulled up at the rack and locked up their bikes, they were the only three bikes there.

"Hey, check out your arm," Jeff said as they headed toward the library.

Uncertain about what Jeff was implying, Raun asked, "What?"

Jeff grabbed Raun's wrist, gently twisting his arm, exposing the cut he obtained at the cabin yesterday. With the exception of the discoloration, the elbow was almost entirely healed. The dark purple and black bruise was the only remaining trace of any injury ever being present.

Standing on the curb while waiting to cross the street, Raun lifted his head after examining his elbow and said, "I guess it wasn't as bad as I thought? All that blood must've just made it look way worse."

"Wow you got lucky, I thought you'd need stitches for sure." As an afterthought Jeff added, "I wonder why it didn't even scab up?"

"I know, it was bleeding pretty bad yesterday, but I did put some peroxide on it when I got home," Raun justified.

"Does it still hurt?" Jeff asked.

Raun tapped on his elbow several times to test it for pain and said, "Not really. To tell you the truth, I actually forgot all about it until you said something."

The traffic light had changed to green and they both

took off running, halfway down the street they saw Dave sitting on the steps of the library smoking a cigarette. Dave stood up and waved at them with the hopes of catching their attention. He shouted several times before they acknowledged him, "Hey, over here!"

They started to walk toward each other, meeting in the parking lot of the library. They happened to notice Allen to their left, he had just made it back to the bike rack at the school with a black Nike gym bag. When he finished locking up his bike with the others, he too headed across the street. As soon as he felt that he was within earshot, Allen asked, "Are you guys ready?" Unlike the youngest two of the bunch showing some level of excitement, Dave just reluctantly nodded his head in agreement.

CHAPTER TWO
THE RETURN TO THE CABIN

The people that were out and about around the town were few and far between. Most everyone sought shelter in the comfort of their homes and the streets were practically deserted on this lazy, dreary afternoon. The severe thunderstorm warning was still in effect from the previous night. The clouds lingered just overhead, threatening a downpour without a moment's notice. At times the wind gusts blew with such fierceness that fallen tree limbs were scattered all around the town. When they made it to the edge of town and closer to the trails, the strong wind gusts blew fiercely, kicking up dust from the dirt roads, making it difficult to see at times. Despite the hazardous conditions and poor visibility, the boys marched on toward the cabin without uttering so much as a word to each other.

The awkward silence between them was eerie, strange, and something of a rare oddity between this restless bunch of boisterous kids. Usually the boys were extremely talkative and playful with each other. The horseplay could even become a bit intense at times, but on this particular afternoon the boys had only one thing on their mind, what possibly awaited them on their return trip to the cabin. Three of them were filled mostly with fear. Allen was apparently on some kind of personal mission, he was being obtuse and totally unwilling to compromise or let anything stand in his way before reaching his destiny. To him this cabin was exactly what he needed from this small town. It gave him a new purpose in life that had quickly became an obsession. He was determined to learn the truth about the myth that sent shock waves throughout this growing community fifty years ago. He ate, drank and slept thinking about what he'd find there. The more he let his thoughts wander, the more he just had to know what hidden secrets the place would reveal.

The anxiety that came with making this return trip into the woods caused knots in all their stomachs that might have deterred a less determined group, but they all knew there was no turning back. They all kept their fears hidden from each other, knowing that showing any sign of fear to the others only revealed a weakness that would make them vulnerable and subject to further ridicule.

With not much more then a word spoken, they'd made it all the way to the chain barricade. As they stood there before it, they paused for a moment, trying to suppress their gut feeling that this would be the last time they'd ever see this place. After taking in their surroundings they started to proceeded forward. They perceived everything from a new perspective and suddenly life itself had taken on a whole new meaning. Subconsciously, they began to take notice of even the slightest changes being displayed before their eyes. For as long as they could remember, none of them recalled their surroundings ever being so different. It must just be this restricted part of the trails, they assumed to themselves. To their right they could see the imprints their bikes had left from the prior day.

Briefly, Allen looked each of them in the eyes, then without a spoken word he ducked under the chain barricade and made his way onto the trail. One by one, the others followed suit until they were all heading down the newly discovered path. Dave was hoping the trails somehow vanished just as quickly as they mysteriously appeared, but there was no such luck. His mind raced ahead to the cryptic thought of that old wooden bridge, still standing in the way of their destination. A few seconds later, his gut started to churn as fears quietly started to resurface, knowing he couldn't say anything, he resentfully continued on their perilous journey.

Further up ahead Dave's thoughts reverted back to the present as he broke the silence, blurting out, "Hey! Listen!" The others suddenly turned their attention and stared at him, each with a peculiar look in their eyes. Silently, they were all wondering if Dave's next statement would be the one revealing he had officially lost his mind. "No, really, listen for a sec, what do you guys hear?" Dave asked curiously.

Glancing over their surroundings, Jeff tightly squinted his eyes, leaving the opening no more than the thickness of a dime. He did this as if it would enhance his ability to see, hear and fine tune his senses. "What is it?" he impatiently asked.

Raising both of his arms in the air out of sheer frustration, Dave began spinning around in a circle as he pointed his hands in every direction. He shouted, "The woods! I thought it was weird yesterday, but since I wasn't sure I didn't say anything."

Aggravated by Dave's dubious shenanigans, Allen sarcastically asked, "Exactly what is it that I'm listening for?"

"The woods," Dave said. "They're alive right now, the birds, the bugs, all of the sounds that you normally hear in the woods, they are here!"

"So what is your point?" Raun wondered aloud.

"Look, I know you guys all think I'm going crazy, but if you take the time to listen, you'll see, you won't hear any of these sounds in a little bit." Furious and stymied, his anger was so intense that he was actually shaking and stuttering, trying tirelessly to get his point across. He continued on, "I'm not sure of exactly where it stops, but I know the closer we get to the cabin, more and more of the sounds disappear and it ain't right. Just listen, I'm not crazy."

Allen had heard enough of this nonsense and was quickly getting fed up with Dave antics. He was so angry, the vein on the right side of his forehead was protruding out as if it was about to rupture and explode. He shouted, “Are you out of your rabid ass mind? Do you have any idea how insane that sounds? Your ma must've dropped you a lot when you were little or something, because you sure ain’t right!”

“Or recently,” Raun said, adding fuel to the fire.

“Really man, you sure have been acting funny today,” Allen said.

Rather than trying to defend himself, Dave kept his composure, dropped it and decided to just prove it to them. “Maybe then these idiots will see what I’m talking about,” Dave mumbled to himself.

Regardless of what everyone was thinking, Dave was positive that he wasn’t going insane. To him, the most devastating part of the whole scenario was the fact that his own flesh and blood brother sided with the Stevens yet again, but that was a matter for another time. For now, Dave just couldn’t get over how they could be so stubborn and oblivious to what seemed so obvious to him. What irked him the most was their complete refusal to even consider the idea as remotely possible. He knew the only way he could prove he wasn’t going batty or looking for an excuse not to go was to prove it, even if it meant going toe to toe with Allen once and for all.

With the tension so thick it could be sliced with a knife, they continued perilously down the trail. As the clearing ahead slowly became visible, Dave’s last hope of reprieve was shattered. The ancient bridge had survived the night and made it one more day. How this bridge still existed remained to baffle him, but the fact remained the same, they were going to cross it once again, destined to end up back inside the abandoned cabin.

For reasons known only to Dave, he took charge and

headed to the front of the pack. Stopping abruptly in front of the bridge, he cut everyone off before they were able to step onto it. Pausing for a moment, he struck a match and lit a cigarette. Everyone stood there confused as he took two long drags without saying a word. “All right, lets go,” he finally suggested as he turned around and stepped onto the bridge. Proceeding forward, he was followed by Allen, Jeff and finally Raun.

The bridge creaked beneath their feet with every step that they took. A strong gust of wind was howling in their ears as it ripped through the canyon, causing their passageway to rock and sway from side to side like a baby’s cradle. Dave couldn’t figure out for the life of him how this contraption had endured all the years, especially with the weather conditions as they were.

Approaching the halfway mark of the bridge, Dave noticed something odd. He stopped and began unconsciously scratching his scalp with his fingers. Puzzled by what he was observing, Dave crouched down on one knee and brushed his right hand against the mysterious object. Dead in the center of the bridge was a freshly cut wooden plank that stood out from the rest. When they'd passed through here yesterday, he was sure it wasn’t here, or was it? Is it possible that he'd missed it, blinded by the fear of crossing the bridge? The thought was absolutely ridiculous, surely he would have noticed something so strange and out of place. Things were really starting to get weird and Dave didn’t like it one bit.

Stuck midway on the bridge, the rest of the boys had enough and were really getting fed up with Dave’s unpredictable antics. They all wanted off the bridge and they wanted off now. “Hey! What's the hold up, what the hell is your problem?” Raun anxiously yelled from the back of the pack.

"Really, what the hell are you looking at?" Jeff added.

Dave turned his head to face them and said, "Hold up a sec...and you'd better shut your mouth," mainly speaking to his little brother.

Allen was directly behind Dave. Inching his way closer, he leaned over Dave's shoulder trying to see what all of the fuss was about and replied sarcastically, "It's a two by four and it used to be part of a tree."

"A board? You're holding us up because of a freaking board!" Raun shouted from behind, adding, "Come on, let's get going."

"It just seems out of place, I mean come on, it's the only part of the bridge that don't look older than us," Dave said. Still confused by the fact that he didn't notice it yesterday. He pondered the thought that within the last twenty-four hours someone had come out and replaced that one board. Why would they do that? Why only that one board? That wouldn't make any sense, especially when the whole bridge needed to be replaced, or removed altogether. Dave's mind continued to wander as they continued their epic journey the rest of the way across the bridge.

As Jeff passed over the out of place board, he glanced down at it briefly and then stated to Dave, "I'm glad that you quit messing with that board, it looks like it might be the only thing holding this death trap together."

When they finally reached the other side of the cliff Raun said, "You're right, I don't hear anything on this side of the canyon."

Once again Jeff decided to speak without thinking about what he was about to say first, making himself sound stupid, "He's right, the animals must be scared to come over here."

"You moron," Raun said, as he pushed Jeff by the

shoulder, "animals don't have to cross the bridge, they're everywhere."

"Damn Dave, for the first time in your life, you're right," Allen said, hating to admit it.

For Dave, just hearing those words come out of Allen's mouth meant more to him than all of the money in the world. Dave was trying to enjoy the moment without rubbing it in Allen's face too badly. He knelt down to tie his shoe and suggested, "I don't know 'bout you guys but I'll bet this place is haunted." He was giving it all he had in a last attempt to persuade the others that coming out here again was a bad idea. But again, his repeated cries fell upon deaf ears.

"I'm going. I don't care what you pussy's do, but I'm definitely gonna go and see what's out there. All this shit about the place being haunted is crazy," Allen said, showing his dominance and determination.

Over time as they walked, Raun had carefully positioned himself to be directly behind Dave. All of a sudden he grabbed Dave by the hips and shouted in his ear. "Boo!" Startled, Dave nearly jumped out of his shoes, immediately he began chasing after Raun who was running around the group in circles trying to avoid being caught. Raun finally stopped as he shielded himself behind Allen, hoping he would help in stopping Dave. Carrying about, they were all laughing hysterically with the exception of Dave, who was beet red with rage from being made a fool of so easily. "It was a ghost," Raun said, feeling a little cocky standing behind Allen.

Dave was furious, but he turned his attention away from Raun and said to Allen, "I just knew you guys were gonna act stupid. Come on, look around, this don't seem the slightest bit creepy to you?" Dave asked, still pleading his case.

Raun forced himself to stop laughing long enough to utter out, "Of course it does, but this is our chance to figure it all out. Think about it, we're gonna be the first ones to know what really happened."

"Yeah, we might get a reward and become famous or something if we solve it," Jeff added, "and they'll talk about us forever just like they do about all those missing people."

"Why don't we just go tell your uncle?" Dave asked.

"Before we can go and tell him anything, we gotta find out something first. That way we won't look like a bunch of idiots," Allen took it upon himself to respond.

"Are we going or what?" Jeff impatiently asked.

"Yeah, so what's it going to be?" Allen insisted as an awkward silence befell the group with everyone looking to Dave for an answer.

Dave paused, sighed heavily and mumbled under his breath, "I guess we go and be hero's or get ourselves killed?"

With the matter at hand finally resolved, they started back on the path of the dark twisty trails. As they continued they soon found themselves entering a heavy fog, which blocked out the remainder of dim light that had been lighting their way. The strange silence throughout the woods along with the density of the fog, had them all feeling slightly uneasy, yet no one dared mention a word about it. Further down the trail the fog began to slowly dissipate and it was only now they noticed the physical change in their surroundings. They made two important observations, first, they noticed the return of the light the tall evergreens had been shielding, even after it forced its way through the thick gloomy overcast hovering just above the tree line. Next, they realized the tall evergreens were starting to transition, rapidly becoming replaced with a closely condensed bunch of giant oak, cedar and redwood trees. At first glance the changes were nominal and gradual, but it didn't take long before finding themselves surrounded by the new variety of trees. As they progressed down the trail, the remnants of fog continued to gradually dissipate and in some spots, the faint light from above was once again able to fully penetrate to the forest floor, giving them some semblance of daylight.

It seemed like they'd entered into another dimension and they really had no idea of exactly where they were. Lost in the growing darkness and unable to locate the cabin, the boys formed a huddle in an attempt to figure out what to do next. They glanced over their surroundings hoping to recognize something from the prior day that indicated they were on the right track, but the fog had thrown them off. As they stood there taking in their surroundings they were suddenly spooked when a fierce, piercing sound ripped through their ears sending a chill through their bodies. It was the angry roar of a mountain lion ready to strike. Startled by its abruptness, they all took off running in the opposite direction from which they assumed it came. They continued running aimlessly until they became winded. As their pace slowly diminished to a trot, they finally came to a complete stop once they felt certain they'd put enough distance between the hungry predator and themselves.

"Why did we take off running? Those cats are more scared of us than we are of them," Allen rushed his sentence, hunched over, greedily gasping for more oxygen to enter his lungs.

Dumbfounded by Allen's idiotic question, Dave looked around once more for the sake of precaution. When he felt sure the mountain lion was no longer around he answered, "I don't know. Reflexes, it caught me off guard. Why are you asking me? You ran too."

"When you guys took off, I thought you must have

seen the cat or something," Allen stated, trying to reinforce his macho attitude and justify his joining in on the run.

"Hey look! There it is," Jeff said, pointing at the cabin.

"Shit, I thought you meant the cat," Dave said in a quick panic.

Until this moment they didn't even notice it was there, lying just behind the tree line. They all paused momentarily and just took in the intriguing sight. They all had their own mixed feelings about the cabin. Over all, they were kind of surprised it was still there and they were able to find it.

They started making their way toward the cabin through their path of trampled grass from previous day. Dave began thinking about the savage roar they'd heard as they continued walking. They hadn't heard a single sound since they'd passed over the bridge and it really bothered him that the only sound making itself known came from a ferocious mountain lion.

When they made it across the open field and approached the entrance to the cabin, the boys cautiously crept up the steps. Momentarily standing there motionless, each patiently waited for someone else to initiate the next move. Allen set down his bag on the wooden porch and unzipped it. Pulling out four heavy-duty metal flashlights, he handed one to each of them. Dave accepted the weapon graciously, when attempting to turn it on, he realized why he regarded it as that. It barely worked as a light, but was heavy enough to incapacitate anything in the path of a full on swing. Dave was tempted, but contained himself from sharing the choice words that he'd selected for Allen. He just deemed him as a babbling fool for bringing faulty flashlights that really weren't worth carrying all the way here.

Leading the way Raun reached out for the doorknob,

twisted it to the right and slowly pushed the door open.

"Did you guys hear the door squeak?" Dave suspiciously asked.

"We must've busted the rust loose yesterday," Allen justified.

Apprehensive about invading the premises for the second time, Dave took one last glance out over the large unkempt field, turned on the dim flashlight and stepped inside closing the door behind him.

PART TWO

The Image and The Light

The disrupted spider webs from the previous days excursion had been carefully woven back together with fine silk, looking as if they'd never been disturbed. The interior of this abandoned shack truly was an incredible sight. Every detail was critiqued and designed to give off the appearance of a model showroom in a furniture store. The furnishings were nicely set up as if they were intended to be looked in on and not to be tampered with.

Armed with their flashlights and no darkness to obstruct their view, the boys spread out across the living room and began randomly searching the area. Their flashlights illuminated the room and made it possible for them to see their way around. Not knowing what they were looking for, they aimlessly moved about from one location to the next. Nothing about this place made any sense and they'd all but given up on finding any type of clue when Allen called out to them from the dining room. With excitement vibrant in his voice, Allen shouted out. "Hey guys, come here and check this out."

The rest of the boys rushed into the dining room to see what the commotion was all about. Much to their surprise, Allen was standing there brandishing a weapon. "Wow! Where did you get that?" Jeff asked.

"Is it real?" Raun curiously asked.

"I think so," Allen replied, standing there inspecting the gun and wiping the dust off of it. "Yeah, it's real." The gun was a German 9mm with the eagle holding a swastika on the handle. The gun had seven bullets in the clip with one already loaded into the chamber.

"Does it work?" Raun asked.

"I don't know. It looks like it's in good enough shape," Allen remarked stuffing the gun into his waistband.

Infuriated by this bizarre behavior, Dave said, protesting, "What do you intend to do with that?"

"I'm going to keep it, you know, just in case," Allen defended.

"In case what, do you actually think the old dude is still here, alive?"

"Maybe, hell, I don't know," Allen tried to justify as he once again tried adjusting the gun for comfort. The explanation Allen gave to harness the gun was ridiculous and absurd. This escapade was getting way out of control and Dave knew he had to do something to put everything back into perspective before things got any worse.

"You said yourself that he'd be at least a hundred," Dave reminded Allen.

Still trying to justify his actions, thus enabling him to carry the weapon, he replied, "Who knows, what if someone else comes in? Or that cat attacks us?"

Dave laughed sarcastically, "That's a good scenario, you can accidentally shoot yourself in the foot and save the cat the trouble of chasing you down and making the kill!"

Raun and Jeff snickered mischievously as Allen snapped back, "Bite me!" Pushing Dave out of his face and pointing the gun at Dave from a range nobody could miss from, he added, "I know how to use it, my dad takes me to the range all the time."

"Don't point that damn thing at me!" Dave furiously demanded.

Before lowering the firearm, he lunged forward aggressively stating, "That's right, you know damn well that I know how to use it."

"You've only been there one time," Dave contested,

"and that certainly don't qualify you as an expert! And if you ever point another gun at me, you'd better use it. Or I'm gonna take it from you and shove it up your ass!"

"Relax a little, we probably won't even need it," Allen said as he holstered the gun back into the waistband of his jeans.

Jeff was frightened this situation could continue to escalate and that the gun could accidentally go off next time. He suggested, "Why don't you two just settle down? None of this is necessary."

"Don't worry, I know what I'm doing," Allen replied, temporarily turning his attention away from Dave.

Meanwhile, Raun managed to step in between Allen and Dave, trying to prevent the two wannabe gladiators from continuing their power struggle and said, "Forget about the damn gun, let's just see what we can find and get the hell out of here."

"He's right," Jeff agreed.

"Fine," Allen conceded as he adjusted his belt to accommodate for the gun. Satisfied with the results, he headed for the large double doors. Tensions still high, the rest of them silently followed his lead.

Allen struggled with the double doors for a moment to no avail, it didn't budge, even an inch. They appeared to be locked or rusted shut, barring them from entry. Everyone watched as Allen had no luck in freeing the jammed passageway. In a trance like state, Raun moved in closer, pushing Allen aside as he gazed up into his eyes. Startled by the empty stare in his brother's eyes, he felt the awkwardness of this whole situation intensifying by the second. Not knowing what to do, he found that he'd subconsciously stepped to the side allowing Raun access to the door without saying a word.

It was like he was possessed, effortlessly extending his arms to the brass handles and simultaneously pressing down on the two thumb latches. Without any resistance, there was a click as the locks gave way and the door opened ever so slightly. Instantly, there was a loud hissing sound that filled the room as the pressure equalized. It sounded like they'd broken an air tight seal on a giant glass jar. Like an abrupt smack in the face, they were suddenly overwhelmed by the foul odor of rotting flesh seeping out from the partially opened doorway. They assumed the source of the awful smell permeating throughout the cabin was located just beyond this entryway.

Ignoring the overpowering foul odor, Allen asked, "How the hell did you do that?"

Raun had snapped out of his trance-like, still slightly dazed and confused, "What?" Raun asked as if he really had no idea of what Allen was referring to.

"How did you do that?" Allen repeated, pointing at the now opened doors.

"I don't know, but never mind that, let's check it out, and get out of here, this place stinks." Raun replied.

"Literally" Jeff added.

The event that just transpired before their eyes was hard to believe. How Raun was able to open the doors so effortlessly was inconceivable to Allen, especially since he had exerted all of his strength and energy in a failed attempt to accomplish the same task. Perplexed, Allen gave Raun a suspicious look before briefly looking over to Dave and Jeff for any clue to what just happened.

Raun was the first to enter the room, the rest of them followed, exercising extreme caution as they proceeded. They were only a several feet inside the room when the doors behind them suddenly slammed shut without any help or warning. Panicked, they all nearly jumped out of their shoes with the exception of Raun, who Allen happened to be starring at still. Dave turned around immediately and ran toward the doors trying desperately to yank them open with no success.

Jeff cried out, "Who did that?"

"Who's there?" Dave added.

Realizing they were trapped and there was nothing they could do, the boys returned to scanning the room with their dimly lit flashlights. In unison, the three boys standing at the jammed door noticed Raun standing in the center of the room gazing down upon a table. Puzzled, they started making their way over to him. Still trying to regain their composer, Raun suddenly spoke out, "This is it! This is it!" Repeating to himself, overwhelmed with excitement.

"What are you talking about?" Dave curiously asked.

"This room, I was here last night, in my dream!" Raun tried to explain.

Allen forcefully grabbed Raun by the shoulders and spun him around so they were facing each other. "What dream? You never said anything 'bout no dream!" Allen screamed at Raun.

Raun took a step backwards shrugging himself loose from Allen's tight grip. Furious, he said, "You never asked. Besides, you wouldn't have believed me anyway."

"Show them you're arm," Jeff interrupted as he reached for and grabbed Raun's wrist. "Look at it!" Jeff demanded.

"What's up with that? Yesterday that cut was pretty bad. I thought that cut was real bad and deep," Dave remarked.

"Now it's almost totally healed," Jeff insisted.

"It's fine! It wasn't that bad, really," Raun said as he

yanked his arm back and out of their hands.

"Forget the arm, what else did you see in your dream?" Dave desperately wanted to know.

Raun was getting frustrated, feeling like he was being interrogated. Blowing it off, he took his attention away from the table and started to glance around the room and said, "This is really weird, it's exactly the way I remember it in my dream! This red drawing, the black walls, the table, everything." As he returned to the silver table he began to trace his fingers over the engravings. Overcome with the feeling of deja vu, Raun continued thinking out loud, "It's all the same, except I was here all by myself, and, the voice! Shit! There was this evil sounding voice! But I couldn't see where it was coming from," Raun nervously finished his sentence and began to wipe the beads of sweat off of his brow with sleeve of his shirt.

Overwhelmed with anxiety, Dave frightfully asked, "What was it saying?"

"It kept telling me that I must turn the key or something, I don't know, I didn't understand it, it was a dream. I really don't know what it was trying to tell me," Raun finished stuttering.

"Is that why you were looking all stupid this morning when I woke you up?" Allen asked.

"Yeah, but it was only a dream, besides, would it have made a difference? We would have still came out here, I know you," Raun defended.

"He's got a point Allen," Dave agreed.

Jeff knelt down by the table next to Raun, "Hey guys, check out these engravings."

Trying to remain alert to their surroundings, Dave and Allen stepped closer to this odd object that had captured all of their imaginations. Raun and Jeff spread out a little to allow room for their older brothers to move in closer and inspect the strange object. Dave gently grazed his hand across the silver shrine. When he lifted the candle in the center of the table, he noticed a fourth engraving chiseled into the center of the triangular table. It looked to be some kind of symbolic image that appeared to represent the earth. Dave placed the candle back in its original location and turned to Allen asking, "What do you think these all mean?"

"I don't know," Allen replied as they both stood up. Dave bumped into Jeff, he'd been standing too close, hovering over his shoulder. As they stood there, they turned around to scan the room once again when Allen abruptly interjected, "Where's Raun?"

"Quit goofing around asshole," Dave remarked. Jeff had no idea what they were talking about until he too gazed around the room. Raun was nowhere to be found.

They scoured the room with their dimming lights, repeatedly calling out to him but receiving no response in return. In a frenzy of panic, the boys ran to the doors and began to pounding frantically, jerking desperately on the handles in the hopes of getting the door to open or intercepting some kind of signal from Raun they assumed was on the other side. All three of them tried pulling on the door simultaneously for added strength. They even tried it together on a three count, but the doors were jammed shut and wouldn't give even an inch. Frantic hysteria had begun to set in.

Dave took several steps backwards and told the others to move out of the way. He forcefully ran toward the door at full speed, leapt into the air and gave the door a flying drop kick just above the handles. To their dismay, the door didn't budge. Adding to the disappointment, Dave landed on his ankle and it had twisted in the wrong direction. With the force of his kick and the weight of his bad landing, his ankle began to bruise and swell up immediately. He screamed out in pain as he grabbed his foot in agony. Allen extended his hand to Dave and helped him to his feet.

"Stand back," Allen suggested as he pulled out the pistol from his waistband. He aimed it at the keyhole and squeezed the trigger. "Click!" was the only sound it rendered.

Humiliated Allen looked over to Dave briefly before focusing his attention back to the gun. After all, he did make such a big fuss about how he knew so much about guns. But now that the time had come for him to show off of his skills, he'd made a fool of himself. He toyed with it for a few more seconds and then insisted, "It must be jammed."

"Ha!" Dave laughed sarcastically, "I told you that you don't know shit 'bout guns! I'm glad you weren't shooting at that cat, or anything else that thought we were its lunch."

"Look, I don't need your shit right now. The rust must have built up inside of it. I forgot to check it," Allen tried to explain.

"You'd forget your head if it wasn't attached to your neck," Jeff joined in on harassing Allen.

"Both of you shut the hell up. Let's quit worrying about me and find Raun," Allen said, still trying to figure out what the malfunction with the gun entailed.

"Why don't you try loading a round into the chamber?" Dave suggested, since the amusement of watching Allen struggle was wearing off.

"I knew that, I just thought I did it already," Allen replied, trying to cover for his incompetence.

"Whatever," Jeff added.

The boys were forced to turn around as they suddenly noticed a white beam of light shooting up to the ceiling from the surface of the shrine. The light was confined to the same shape as the triangular table. The intense wattage was blinding to look directly at, but it was restrained to the beams shape only, it didn't shed a drop of light into the room outside of the triangular shape extending from the tables surface all the way to the ceiling.

The giant pentagram painted on the floor was faintly glowing in a red hue. It wasn't until now that they realized it was there. Glancing back to the light protruding from the table's surface, they noticed a mysterious holographic image began floating in the center of the beam. It appeared to be of human form, clad head to toe in a long black hooded robe. The bottom of the robe appeared to be dangling several inches above the table's surface. It was obvious the creature was levitating in the beam of light. The sleeves covered its entire arms, with the exception of the distinct claws barely protruding from the ends. The shadow had one arm embraced tightly to its chest holding a plain black book with what appeared to be silver pages. Where the face should have been there was only an extreme hollow darkness revealing no features at all with the exception of two fiery red beads they assumed were its eyes.

The boys stood motionless in a state of total dismay, wondering what this creature was and what its intentions were. "Where's my brother?" Allen shouted, breaking the deafening silence that eerily filled the room.

The hologram turned its head to face Allen, in a deep audible voice the shadow forcefully answered, "I am he and he is now me."

Although his eyes gleamed brighter with every word that he spoke, they still weren't able to illuminate the dark mask that shielded his face. Confused by his response, the boys looked at each other momentarily before turning their attention back to the hovering shadow.

“You are not my brother! What did you do with my brother?” Allen demanded.

“He’s here, safe with me. He'll complete what I’ve started,” the eerie voice replied.

“I don’t understand, where is he? What have you done with him?” Allen pleaded, as tears began streaming down his cheeks.

“You shall be reunited in due time, but only if you conform to what is long overdue.”

“What do you mean? We don’t understand,” Dave interjected.

“I will show you the way. When you complete the task, I shall release him...and he may go,” the shadow replied, vanishing into thin air, leaving only the concentrated beam of light behind.

PART THREE

The Serpent

As the image inside the light disappeared, the triangular beam remained the same as it had been, but something strange began to happen. The shrine began to spin counterclockwise while the beam of light rotated in the opposite direction. Both objects revolved in their opposite directions, allowing the beam of light to penetrate all the way to the floor as the two objects spun in unison out of alignment. When they both completed one full cycle they came to a complete stop, the light disappeared and the latch on the door gave off a loud click, allowing the door to pop open slightly. The boys were baffled. Frozen in their tracks, they looked at each other and each waited for someone to show some initiative and take charge.

"Did you guys see that?" Allen asked, unsure of the fact that this was really happening.

"Yeah, but what the hell was it? And what does he want us to do?" Jeff asked panicked, with the pitch in his voice slightly elevated.

"The doors were locked," Dave stated. "Where the hell did that thing come from and where the hell did Raun go? There ain't other ways out of here."

"I don't know, but we're not leaving here until we find him, that's for sure," Allen stated, showing his determination.

Trying to comfort Allen, Dave placed his hand on his shoulder and assured him, "Don't worry, we're definitely gonna find him."

"This just doesn't make any sense. How could he have just vanished into thin air, he never made a sound," Allen was mumbling to himself. The others could tell Allen was truly distraught by the sudden disappearance of his younger brother. He was pacing aimlessly before wandering over to the far wall, he paused briefly, then started slamming his fists in anger against it yelling into the empty void of the room. "Raun, where are you?" he started sobbing. Jeff and Dave stood there momentarily silent, allowing Allen a few seconds to vent and grieve.

"Where could he have gone? There's nowhere to go," Jeff sympathetically whispered to Dave.

"I don't know, he could be anywhere!" Dave replied.

"Come on guys, we'd better get started," Allen strongly suggested, as he had apparently regained his composer and walked back over to where they were standing.

"Yeah, but we'd better stay close together, that way we don't end up vanish..." Jeff stopped himself short before finishing his sentence.

"I'm not so sure he wanted all of us. If he did, why didn't he just take us or kill us when he had us trapped in this room?" Dave suggested hopefully.

"What the hell does he want from us?" Allen said, showing his frustration.

"He wants us to help him," Jeff replied without thinking first or realizing Allen was really talking to himself.

"When did you get so smart? I swear, you act like you know everything and you don't know shit!" Allen snapped at Jeff more out of anxiety than anger. In an act of desperation, Allen began spinning around aimlessly as he resumed yelling into the empty space of the room, "What do you want from us?"

Again in a soothing voice, Dave tried to comfort Allen, "Come on bro, just settle down, I'm sure he didn't go far. Yelling into an empty room ain't gonna accomplish anything. That thing said that he's gonna show us what he wants us to do. Then we'll get Raun back and get the hell out of here."

Allen began pacing back and fourth and it wasn't long before he once again lost his temper. He stormed over to the table in the center of the room and gave it a good forceful kick. He actually hurt his toe quite badly, but his anger and outrage shielded his senses from registering the pain. Totally oblivious to the possible broken toe the solid silver table had inflicted, he shouted, "I should have shot that freak when I had the chance!"

"Then why didn't you?" Dave curiously asked.

"Come on guys, he's the problem, not us," Jeff interrupted before Allen had a chance to react.

Both Dave and Allen looked over to Jeff. "Every once in a while you do have something intelligent to say," Dave said. Turning his attention back to Allen he continued, "You're absolutely right, you should have emptied the gun into that freak and turned him into Swiss cheese."

"I would have, but it was like I was paralyzed or something. I totally forgot I even had the gun until the light shut off and by then it was too late," Allen said, explaining his actions, or lack of.

"I guess I'll let you slide this time for chickening out on me," Dave said, trying to ease the tension.

Allen became defensive and said, "Oh, like you weren't scared."

"Of course I was, kinda. But the whole thing wasn't all that scary. It was more hypnotic than anything else," Dave suggested.

"I know what you mean, I don't think I could have ran out of there, even if there was a way out," Allen concurred.

"Are you two done reminiscing because we're wasting time! Let's get going and find out what this freak wants from us, get Raun back and get the hell out of here,"

Jeff forcefully interjected.

"He's right," Dave agreed.

Just as they turned around and were about to exit the room, for a split second, the light from the table flickered back on in its full brightness. Strangely, just as quickly as it appeared, it was gone. The boys quickly turned back around giving their undivided attention as they anticipated the return of the shadow, but that was not the case.

"Hey guys, look over here!" Allen said, pointing his flashlight onto the surface of the shrine. He had noticed something sitting there but was unable to make it out from this distance.

"What is it?" Jeff curiously asked.

The silence and perpetual darkness throughout the cabin was unreal. The only distinguished audible sounds they were able to hear were the beating of their hearts and their own erratic breathing. Both sounds appeared to be amplified, mostly because of the stone silence permeating throughout the cabin. After a few awkward moments the boys finally built up the courage to make their way over to the strange table. As they inched closer they were able make out the mysterious object lying on it. It was the black book the shadowy creature was holding onto with his claw. Allen held his light fixated on the book while Dave and Jeff diligently scanned over the entire room expecting the unexpected. Feeling confident they were alone in the room, the boys marveled over the black book with the silver pages lying centered on the shrine.

"Wow! Where did that come from?" Jeff asked, immediately knowing how stupid and redundant his question sounded.

"I think that he wants us to have it," Dave humbly suggested, turning to face Allen he added, "go ahead, grab it."

For the first time in his life Allen felt insecure about

the actions that were expected of him as the leader of their group. He looked over to Dave for reassurance and then ever so slowly he started to extend out his arms and reach for the book. Just before he was able to grab a hold of it, Dave grabbed his arm by the wrist and yanked him back from the table. A split second after pulling him to a safe distance the rest of them noticed the reason for Dave's sudden and swift action.

Hidden underneath the triangular table was a ten foot long king cobra. Its body was coiled up with only its head lifted and visibly poised in attack mode. It was gently swaying from side to side as it started to hiss a warning at them, apparently waiting to strike. They'd all taken several steps carefully backing away from the table trying to increase the gap between them and the giant snake. The serpent hissed and expanded its thick neck to form its flattened head while exposing huge venomous fangs dripping with poisonous saliva. "Holy shit! Look at the size of that thing!" Dave awed.

"It's a king cobra! It almost got you," Jeff said, pointing out the obvious to Allen.

"What do we do now?" Dave asked, as he lifted up his arms holding Jeff and Allen behind the barrier he formed.

"We gotta get that book," Allen insisted.

"How," Jeff asked, "That thing wants to eat us."

"No way am I grabbing it," Dave declared, lowered his arms. "You get it, or at least get rid of that snake somehow."

"Man, that thing is huge," Jeff said, taking several steps to the side hoping to get a better view of it in its entirety.

"Get back away from that thing," Dave ordered Jeff, "it's gonna bite you!"

"Hold up a minute," Allen said, forcing himself to overcome his fear of the serpent, "I'm gonna shoot the damn thing, then you can grab the book."

"Don't forget to load the gun this time," Dave nervously said.

"Bite me! I'm gonna kill it and you just grab the book," Allen suggested, taking aim as he started inching his way closer to the snake. As Allen closed in on the serpent's territorial space, it again started to hiss, following his every movement. Allen felt secure being just out of range of its striking distance when he paused, steadied his arm and took aim at the snake. Allen inhaled a deep breath, holding it in as he slowly squeezed the trigger. "Bang!" the loud shot exploded, echoing throughout the cabin with a violent deafening ring. The shot was a direct hit, blood and snake skin splattered all over the side of the silver shrine. It's head exploded on impact and its lifeless body fell limply to the floor. It twitched for several seconds as it bled out the last few drops of life through the gaping hole where its head used to be.

"Nice shot," Jeff congratulated Allen.

"Thanks!" Allen said, with a big proud grin on his face.

"Don't let it go to your head," Dave said as he kicked the snake's dead carcass with the tip of his shoe several times, making sure it was actually dead.

Jeff was fascinated with snakes, he found this action to be quite amusing so he joined in on examining the carcass. His motives were of a slightly different intent, he was trying to straighten out the snake's enervated body to see how big it was. Jeff kept himself occupied messing with the dead snake while Dave leaned over the table and reached out for the book. He had it in his hand for only a second when he suddenly realized it was much heavier than he had expected.

The cover of the book wasn't only jet black with no

writing on it, but it was made out of a soft strange feeling leather. The tome itself was only made to look like a book at a quick glance. What appeared to be silver pages was actually a solid block of silver. Even that did not particularly amaze them as much as what they discovered next. When Dave opened the thick cover, they learned it was a tablet of some sort. It had the same four engravings etched inside that the triangular shrine had carved onto its surface. On the tablet, each of the engravings were placed symmetrically in one of the four corners of the thick silver blocks surface. In the upper left corner was the same image of the earth that was engraved into the table, to the right of it was the bird with its wings fully extended as if it was already in flight. The lower left side was the image of the serpent and to its right was the image of a man. In the center space between these identical images there were six holes cut deep into the slab of silver.

The holes were all set one inch apart and formed a visible pentagram. Five of the holes were triangular in shape with their points all facing away from the middle, each side measuring one inch in length. In the center of the star was the sixth hole, this one was shaped differently, it was round and wide on top and inverted to a point at the base of the book, like a cone. It was also larger than the other holes, approximately two inches across. There were also two thin lines engraved into the book, they were circular, one slightly larger than the other, both of which could have formed perfect circles had they not been broken up by the slots cut into the tablet. Upon closer examination they realized the design matched perfectly to the red circle and pentagram painted on the floor.

“What do you think all these holes in this book are for?” Allen curiously asked.

“Hey, check this out guys!” Jeff shouted as he stood

up from playing with the dead snake's body.

"What! What the hell is that?" Allen asked.

"Where the hell did you get that?" Dave added without giving Jeff a chance to answer.

"I found it when I moved the snake's body, it was laying on top of it." Jeff was holding in his hand a red triangular shaped stone that resembled a ruby.

"Let me see that," Allen demanded practically yanking it out of his hand.

Under protest, Jeff relinquished the stone to Allen and the three of them began to examine it more closely. They marveled at this odd looking stone. "I think it goes in one of these holes," Dave suggested, breaking the silence.

"I think so. It has to," Allen said, adding, "that might be why he didn't snatch all of us up like he did..." unable to complete his sentence, Allen's words trailed off. He couldn't bear the thought of his brother still being missing.

"He must need us to find these stones for him. Then he'll give us Raun back," Dave assumed out loud trying to ease Allen's grief.

"But why did he take Raun?" Jeff asked with a confused look on his face.

"He's probably got him for an insurance policy or something. That way we have to cooperate. It's the only way we'll get Raun back. You see his logic?"

"It's working," Jeff agreed.

"God, I hope he's not hurt." Allen said.

"Me too," Dave seconded, "but I don't think it's God that were up against."

"Do you think the rest of these stones will be this easy to find?" Allen wondered aloud.

"I hope so. I think him putting that snake there was his

sick way of showing us where the stone was," Dave replied. "I mean, think about it, how come we didn't see that big ass snake earlier? He obviously wants us to find the stones," Dave was mainly talking out loud to himself reciting the facts.

"Do you think that we're supposed to put the stones into these slots?" Jeff asked.

"I think so. Why else did he give us the book?" Dave replied.

"So which hole does it go in?" Allen asked.

"I'm not sure," Dave stated, staring at the tablet intensely as he tried to figure out which hole to place the stone in.

"Just try one! They all look the same anyway, except for the middle one, I'm sure it doesn't go there," Allen anxiously said. "It doesn't take a rocket scientist to figure that one out."

Being trapped inside this madness was taking its toll on all of them and the tension was getting thick. "I'm really not in the mood for your shit!" Dave shouted back at him. "Coming out here was your damn idea, even after I told you it was stupid!"

"You didn't have to come!" Allen barked back.

"Yeah, but you would have came with or without me. Then you'd have been all by yourself right now," Dave stated.

"Come on guys, let's just get Raun back and go home," Jeff interrupted, trying to defuse their anger before it escalated any further.

Both Dave and Allen were taken aback by Jeff's sudden outburst. They'd never heard him speak to them in such a forceful tone. Allen looked over to Dave and apologized once again. "I really hate it when you're right," Dave said to his younger brother Jeff.

"Yeah, I know what you mean," Allen added, "If it

wasn't for him, I'd probably have killed you by now."

"Let's get started," Dave suggested, "there's no telling how long this is gonna take. We don't even know if that freak has some kind of time limit on us to find the rest of these stones."

"Yeah, let's just get them so we can save my brother," Allen earnestly pleaded with Dave.

PART FOUR
Calling For Help

They all stepped back a few paces from the table in the center of the room and took in a deep breath. Standing there motionless and silent, Allen was about to drop the stone into one of the slots as Dave held the book open in his hands. With only two fingers and his thumb he held the stone directly over the hole, exhaled and let go. As soon as the stone fell into place the gem flashed bright red, illuminating the entire room for a split second. Dave struggled not to drop the tablet out of sheer surprise. They were shocked when during the split second the tablet came alive with the glowing stone, they were able to hear Raun's voice.

"That was Raun! I heard him!" Jeff shouted as raw adrenalin pumped through his veins.

All of them heard Raun's voice clear as day, he cried out, "Help!" The boys were unable to locate him or to even tell where the voice had come from.

Dave slammed the cover of the book shut in a panicked clapping motion and they all scattered about the room desperately calling out, "Raun, Raun, where are you?"

Several moments had passed by when they finally came to the conclusion that they weren't going to get any response. They all somehow found themselves standing in front of the mysterious table once again. Panic stricken and aimlessly shining their dimming lights around the empty room Jeff cried out, "His voice! I heard his voice, right here, in this room!"

"I know," Dave compassionately replied, "I heard it too."

"Try taking the stone out and putting it back in again to see if we can hear his voice again?" Allen suggested.

"Good idea," Dave agreed. He opened the cover of the book again and placed it on the floor, he tried everything imaginable but there was nothing he could do to remove the stone. "I can't get a hold of it," Dave pleaded to the others.

"Try hitting it from the back of the book," Jeff suggested.

Dave tried hitting the back of the tablet with his palm like Jeff suggested, he even tried hitting the corner of it on the floor, but that also proved to be ineffective. When Dave realized he was getting nowhere fast, he collapsed to the floor with a tear in his eye and began to repeatedly hit his forehead on the closed cover of the book. Wanting to help, Jeff put a comforting hand on his brother's shoulder. This managed to stop him from slamming his head on the floor, but it also reinstated the eerie silence echoing throughout the room. It was only now they realized they weren't going to be able to find Raun or even hear the soothing sound of his voice again until they complied with the shadow's game and retrieved all of the stones.

"Don't worry Jeff," Dave calmly whispered.

"Were gonna find him," Allen added, trying to reassure the group.

"But now what are we supposed to do?" Dave curiously asked as they finally quit scanning the room with their flashlights in hopes of finding Raun.

No sooner had they stopped when Jeff sighed, "Uh-oh guys, I think that we have another problem."

"What's that?" Allen asked hastily as he and Dave both turned to face Jeff, suddenly noticing what had caught his undivided attention.

"Where the hell did the door go?" Dave asked as they stood there staring at the suddenly barren wall where the fancy double doors used to be located.

"It was right there!" Jeff insisted, pointing his light at the wall.

"It was there," Dave reaffirmed.

Confused and rapidly losing any semblance of hope, they continued aimlessly shining their dim lights around the room. The double doors were nowhere to be found. Making another sudden observation, Jeff blurted out, "Hey! Wasn't that red star thing right in front of the door when we came in?"

"Yeah, it was, I remember!" Allen said, showing his excitement.

"Now it's on the other side of the room," Jeff went on stating his point.

Dave asked, "Even if we did get turned around in all of the commotion, where did this door come from? There weren't any other doors in here, and where the hell did the other one go?"

Allen suggested, "The shadow said he was going to show us the way, maybe this is what he meant by that?"

"I hope that's what he's doing," Dave mumbled under his breath, "but I'll tell you guys this, I don't like where this is going one bit. When we get out of here, I'm gonna beat your ass!" Poking his finger firmly into Allen s chest as he finished his sentence.

"Exactly how was I supposed to know?" Allen conceded. For the first time in his life, he was well aware that the majority of this situation was his fault.

"Because I told you it was a bad idea from jump street you dip shit!" Dave gloated.

"Fine, I'll let you beat my ass later. Let's just get Raun back and get the hell out of this nut house," Allen said, trying to sound sure that everything will be alright.

With a partial grasp on what was required of them,

they slowly headed toward the strange new door, quietly wondering where it would lead and what was behind it. With the gun locked and loaded, Allen semi confidently led the way. He was carrying the gym bag in one hand and the gun in the other. Jeff and Dave followed closely in tow, with Dave carefully holding the mysterious tablet tight to his chest.

As their flashlights continued growing dimmer by the second, they stood in front of the door with their minds and hearts racing a mile per minute. When they finally agreed it was time to proceed, Allen closed his eyes and turned the handle. Cautiously pushing the door inward, it slowly gave way. The hinges let out a loud creaking cry as if the door itself was physically in pain. With the door now all the way open, Allen stepped to the side allowing Dave the lead. Carefully, they walked back into the dining room.

As they stood there glancing over the room, they could see it was almost identical to when they had been in here before. The first noticeable difference was the door they just walked through didn't exist previously and the fancy double doors that should be directly in front of them were gone. The archway that should have led them back into the living room vanished without a trace. They could only imagine any of the smaller changes they had yet to notice. Intrigued by the shape shifting room, they slowly began walking around the large dining room table and chairs. Just past the wood burning stove and fireplace they found themselves standing where the large archway used to be. Jeff reached out and touched the new wall only to learn it was rock solid. Oddly enough, the wood trim looked as ancient as the rest of the cabin. Allen continued to walk through the dining room, past the mounted wolf statue and ice chest over to where the double doors used to be, that wall too appeared to be impenetrable.

Puzzled, Allen turned around to face Dave and Jeff and asked, “What’s going on in here? How are we supposed to get out?”

“I don’t know,” Dave hesitantly replied, “but it’s not looking like he’s gonna just let us leave, is it?”

“He’s making us help him!” Jeff snapped, “He’s not gonna let us leave! Were trapped!”

“Yes he will,” Dave insisted, “he told us that he’d let us go once we helped him. Why would he tell us that if he wasn’t gonna do it?”

“I ain’t doing it!” Jeff shouted. “I'm leaving! You guys can stay here if you want, but I want the hell out of here!”

“Exactly how do you plan on doing that?” Allen curiously asked.

“The fireplace,” Jeff abruptly suggested, remembering the fireplace was an early style catalytic fireplace. “It has two fronts, the opening leads to the living room right?” Finishing his sentence as he raced around the table toward it. Dave and Allen doubted the opening would still be there but they followed behind Jeff to satisfy their own curiosity. They wondered if the shadow would have left them an option for escape.

“Come on Jeff,” Dave pleaded, “Raun wouldn’t have given up on you.”

“He ain’t going anywhere anyway. Look, it doesn’t even go all the way through anymore! He’s just as trapped as us,” Allen said, stating the facts.

“Damn it!” Jeff screamed out in frustration as he kicked the fireplace so hard that he lost his balance and fell on his back side. Embarrassed by his futile attempt to knock the bricks through the wall, he finally came to the realization that he too was trapped. With leaving the cabin no longer an option, he climbed back to his feet and humbly apologized,

"I'm sorry guys, I just don't wanna be here anymore."

Standing there momentarily serene, they tried perilously to regain some type of control over their peculiar situation. Unintentionally, Jeff found himself leaning against the mammoth stone fireplace, as he innocuously adjusted his position for comfort, one of the large stones behind him suddenly gave way. His shoulder blade had been resting against it, when he shifted his weight, it slightly recessed into the face of the structure. When the stone reached the back of the hole it had been pushed into, there was a clicking sound, as Jeff suddenly fell to the floor.

The sandstone burn plate in front of the fireplace had given way beneath his feet, knocking him off balance. When the stone was pushed into the wall, it must have released some kind of hidden switch or door handle, revealing a hidden staircase. Jeff was lucky he fell forward rather than backwards, this was better than the alternative of falling down the stairs. Fortunate as this was, he did manage to give himself a nice sized lump on his forehead from where he smacked into a leg on one of the dining room chairs.

"Hey! Look at that!" Allen blurted out as Jeff lay on the floor holding his head. He looked as if he was trying to prevent it from breaking into two halves. He struggled as he painstakingly returned to his feet, desperately wanting to see what had captured their attention.

Dave turned around and finished helping Jeff to his feet, asking sincerely, "Are you alright?"

"Yeah, I'm fine. We're not going down there, are we?" Jeff hesitantly asked as he looked down the dark staircase.

"I don't think we really have much choice, I don't see any other way out of here. Look, the door we came in through is gone," Allen pointed out, noticing the latest change in the room.

"This cabin's nucking futs! We're never gonna find our way out of here if the way changes every time we leave the room," Jeff said, sounding as if he'd lost all hope.

Dave looked at them both and shook his head as he held his light aimed down the cavernous stairwell. "It's the only way out. He's making us play by his rules."

"Why did I know that you were gonna say that?" Jeff asked, voice crackling and sounding like he wanted to cry.

"I was just stating the twisted obvious," Dave said, letting his frustration get the better of him. He was tiring of his younger brothers willingness to throw in the towel. He was trying real hard not to lose anymore control of the situation than they already had.

"I'll go first, I've got the gun," Allen suggested, unclear of why he volunteered rather than trying to trade Dave the gun for the book. Dave knew Allen regretted it even before he finished saying it, but it was to late. He felt obligated because he was the one carrying the gun, which Dave didn't think was very reassuring in the first place. In his head he compared the whole scenario of Allen with the gun, to going through all the trouble of putting on a bullet proof vest and then accidentally shooting yourself in the face. Much to Dave's surprise, Allen actually made good of his word and slowly began making his way down the rickety stairwell toward the second door. When Allen made it to the bottom, he reached for the door handle, turned the knob and gently pushed the door opened.

PART FIVE
The Water Stone

They were almost knocked over by the foul odor seeping intently through the partial opening in the door. Quickly, Allen yanked the door shut again and tried to make the seal even tighter by holding onto the handle with every ounce of his strength. Jeff was puking off to the side, only a few steps above them. Dave and Allen had their shirts covering their faces, trying frantically to avoid the overpowering smell of rotted flesh and decomposed bodies. When they looked up and saw Jeff puking, it took everything they had to avoid getting sick themselves.

Trying to talk through his shirt and hands, Allen remarked, “Smells like a million people died in there.”

“I know,” Dave agreed, “I can’t believe a spot in this house actually stands out worse than the rest.”

After a couple of minutes of voiding everything in his stomach, Jeff was finally able to pull himself back together and announced he was ready to go on. With that said, they all took one last deep breath from the better of two bad air supplies. They readjusted the necks of their shirts so they could cover their noses in a vain attempt at reducing the smell. Awful as it was, this had to be sufficient until they could adjust to the level of the rank scent lingering throughout.

By now they had done all the preparing they could manage. Allen closed his eyelids briefly and forced himself to push the door open once again. As they walked inside, each of them continued holding their breath for as long as they could, failing to realize they would eventually have to resume breathing again.

They shined their lights around the room and

immediately noticed this room was far different from any of the other rooms they had been in so far. It looked like a scene stolen and frozen in time right out of a Frankenstein movie. In the center of the room was an extremely long and narrow wooden table stretching almost the entire length of the room.

At the end of the table nearest to them, there were rows of racks containing test tubes of all different shapes and sizes. The center area of the table had a large body located on it, unlike anything they had seen before. They weren't sure exactly what it was, but it didn't look like it made it through the last operation.

This whole section of the room was almost entirely covered with stainless steel, presumably for the ease of cleaning any messes made from the blood of whatever was being worked on down here. Even the flooring was made with metal sheeting and the counters had large drip trays connected to the edges to control the flow and run off of blood.

There were jars scattered throughout the room, some appeared to be empty, but most of them contained either a red, yellow or clear fluid. Whatever the preserving liquid was seemed to be necessary for storing the disgusting contents of the jars. They weren't sure of what the contents actually were yet, but they were sure they were likely body parts and organs. The boys had no idea of whether the body parts and organs belonged to animals or humans, but they didn't belong in those jars. The walls on either side of the table were lined up from one end to the other with animal cages stacked three high. The cages on the bottom row were the biggest and progressed to the smallest ones on top. Almost all of the cages contained skeletal structures of a wide variety of animals, most of which they weren't able to identify.

The boys again found themselves inadvertently wandering away from each other as they searched the room.

As they spread out they couldn't help looking at the skeletons in the cages, it was like being trapped in some type of cryptic fun house, although all of the fun had been sucked out of this trip. They didn't know what most of the creatures used to be, but it didn't detour their curiosity. They picked up on the fact that some of these creatures had never existed in nature, it was clearly obvious that these beasts had been genetically altered. They weren't sure if any of these creatures had ever lived like this or if the previous owner of the cabin was trying to connect different animal bodies to each other after they died. Either way, they were now starting to get a grasp of how twisted the whole existence of this cabin actually was. Some of the alterations were so obvious and hideous that it was sick and twisted just to have attempted it. There were creatures with wings that had no business having them, some with two heads and others with arms and legs you could tell came from another animal.

They were now sure of what the rancid odor in this cabin was caused from and why it was so strong. The cabin had no air circulation whatsoever and there had to be seventy-five dead animal bodies in this room alone. Not to mention the rats and roaches they could only imagine had taken over the interior of the walls for generations.

Dave made his thoughts known. "It looks like when whatever went wrong here happened, all of these animals were suddenly left to starve to death. Just look," he said, aiming his flashlight into a cage in the middle row, housing a raccoon's body with the wings of a hawk that had both of its legs chewed off.

"Do you think he was trying to create some new kind of animal?" Allen curiously asked.

"Yeah and it looks like he was successful, but why?" Dave replied.

"What about all of those people that came up missing?" Jeff asked.

Allen replied, "We don't even know if there is any truth to those stories, although I'm a believer."

They were all in a state of shock as they stood there looking at the wide variety of twisted bones belonging to these would-be fictitious animals. After a few moments of silence passed between them, Dave could no longer hold back his thoughts and they became words of total disbelief. "It's all wrong! None of this makes any sense! We can't even tell what's real anymore."

Allen responded with a question of his own out of guilt, "Why Raun? Why did he have to take Raun and not me?"

"Maybe it had something to do with that dream he had?" Jeff suggested, adding the question, "How the hell do you have a dream about a place you have never been?"

Dave was frustrated and confused and he found himself lashing out at them. "Why do you guys keep asking me? How the hell am I supposed to know? None of this makes any sense!"

Allen had to bite his tongue trying hard not to respond to Dave's momentary loss of composure, then he suddenly made an important realization, "Wait! Hold up a sec! What about yesterday, when Raun cut himself in here?"

"Yeah, that's gotta be it," Dave shuddered in agreement. "Maybe it's Raun's blood that somehow brought this spirit to life?"

Jeff added, "Maybe that's why that deep ass cut on his arm healed over night...and turned black."

"Damn!" Dave said, beginning to pace. "We just don't have any answers and this cabin just keeps getting weirder and weirder."

They now consciously decided to spread out a little and begin searching the room from top to bottom and front to back. They knew searching this room could take forever since it was so big, especially since they had to open each and every cage to check around the bodies for the relatively small gems. Their senses finally adjusted to the foul smell as much as humanly possible, but they didn't think they could ever get used to handling the massive amount of skeletal bones that belonged to creatures that didn't even exist in the wild.

Jeff made a good point, "Once we give him all the stones, what if he won't give us Raun back? Or let us go?"

Dave looked over to Jeff like that thought had never entered his mind until this very moment. Dave replied with the only response he was able to muster, "That's a good question, but right now we don't really have much of a choice, do we?"

"This sucks!" Jeff stated.

"The only thing we can do is give him the stones and hope he keeps his end of the deal. Besides, I don't have a clue as to how we get out of here," Dave continued, "or how long we have been here?""

Allen interrupted, "No shit! I've totally lost track of time and none of us are wearing a watch."

"I haven't seen a window since we got here and I know that was hours ago," Dave said.

"At least," Allen added.

"And I gotta take a piss," Jeff interjected.

"Just go in one of those empty jars," Allen suggested. "That's what I did."

Finally able to relieve himself, a glimmer of hope returned to his eyes and Jeff suggested, "Maybe our parents will come looking for us?"

Allen threw his arms up in the air and forcefully

stomped his foot on the floor. “Ah shit! We didn’t even bring our bikes. Without our bikes they might not even check the trails.”

Dave tried adding a remote chance of hope to their situation. “You took all of your dad’s flashlights, so maybe they’ll know we’re into something we ain’t supposed to be? Or at least know we’re in the woods somewhere?”

“My dad?” Allen asked. “My dad wouldn’t know a truck was coming if it ran right into him. Besides, he’s so unobservant he probably won’t even notice the flashlights are gone until he needs one.”

“Well, at least there is some kind of hope of us getting rescued,” Jeff reminded them as he screwed the cap back onto the jar he'd just filled with urine.

“Yeah, but for now we’re on our own so we’d better get started,” Dave stated. “What else did you bring in that bag?”

Allen replied, “Just some bottled water, chips, a couple candy bars and some Duct tape.”

“Duct tape?” Dave asked curiously.

“It's great, you can fix anything with it,” Jeff chimed in. “Give me a water and some chips.”

Allen obliged Jeff's request and passed out some rations to the group. They took a few minute break before they resumed searching the lab for the stones. Allen started off in the back corner of the lab to search the most obvious places first. It wasn’t long before he came across a large cabinet. Shining his light, he opened the cabinet doors, finding mostly surgical tools and other miscellaneous supplies, but on the lower shelf there was another newspaper in its entirety. Curious, he reached in and grabbed the paper, took it out and placed it on top of the cabinet. As he read the headline across the front page, he was immediately sure that he had discovered something of major importance.

"Dave, Jeff!" Allen called out in an excited tone, "come here, quick!"

"Did you find the stone?" Jeff calmly asked as they headed over toward him.

"No," Allen replied as Dave and Jeff were now both standing next to him reading the headline over his shoulder.

The papers headline read; "**ANCIENT TABLET STOLEN FROM TOMB**." They each began reading the article. "On the morning of May 19th 1939, a hidden entrance into the tomb of King Austin was located in Cairo, Egypt. The discovery was pure luck and was only made because a team of archaeologists were studying the anatomical procedure from the ancient art of mummification was derived. Their study was nearing its end when Dr. Eric Aben stumbled onto a secret entrance allowing them into a hidden room where this mysterious silver tablet was discovered. Continued on page 7-a."

When the rest of them caught up to where Allen had finished the paragraph, carefully he thumbed his way through the brittle browning newspaper for where the article continued. It didn't take much effort and before long they were on their way right from where they had left off. "The tablet was stolen before they had a chance to authenticate it's origin. Scientists feared the strange hieroglyphics on it would never be possible to translate with any type of accuracy by memory alone, especially since they feared the artifact would never be recovered. The heist was well planned and financed. The getaway was virtually flawless, as it happened during one of the worst sandstorms in almost twenty years. With the loss of the known artifact, Egyptologists fear that other priceless pieces of their heritage may have also been stripped away from the homeland and who's to say these weren't the missing pieces of history that could have completed the absent links telling the complete history of the Egyptian people."

"So that's where this tablet came from," Dave suggested.

"But the article didn't really tell us anything," Jeff stated.

"Well at least we know where it came from," Allen remarked.

"That helps us how?" Jeff asked sarcastically.

"I don't know, but we know more than we used to about it," Allen stated with a confused look on his face.

"Lets just get this over with, I really wanna go home," Jeff pleaded.

"Good idea, we're wasting time," Dave agreed.

They resumed searching the room and still couldn't help themselves from looking at the grotesque looking creatures in the cages. It seemed the farther they made it toward the other end, the stranger the corpses were getting. Dave found himself stopped in the center of the room staring onto the autopsy table. His stomach was churning as he suddenly realized exactly what it was he was looking at. He was looking at the decomposed upper body and skull of a mountain lion, but the torso and legs were that of a human being. The mere sight of this baffled his imagination, but he could tell this operation was at least in part successful because the spinal column and all of the smaller bones appeared to be correctly fastened together and not just laid out to look the part.

Allen and Jeff both happened to notice Dave's paralyzed gaze and they started heading over toward him. Dave didn't even notice their approach until Jeff brushed up against him, "Ahh shit!" Dave screamed, nearly jumping out of his shoes.

"What is it? Did you find the stone?" Jeff quickly rattled off two questions.

As Allen and Jeff stood there trying to locate the exact object that had captured Dave's attention, the big picture came into focus and they too saw what he was looking at. Transfixed from the sheer size and ferocious potential a living version of this creature could cause, all they could do was stand there in shock as if they were gazing down at their own death.

"What, is, that?" Jeff asked in slow motion with his words barely finding their way off his tongue.

"I hope the only one," was all Allen was able to mutter out of his mouth.

"Somehow I just knew we were gonna find something like this," Dave added, speaking softly, as if trying not to wake the strange creature.

Ever since the discovery of this malevolent cabin, things had rapidly gone from bad to worse. It was at this point in time when they suddenly realized the flagrant truth. The disappearances in the town's dark past were indisputably linked to the madness that now held them captive.

Just by the insidious way this creature lay on the operating table, there wasn't a shred of doubt in their minds that every one of these freaks of nature were once alive for a brief period of time if nothing else. With that sudden cryptic realization, their thumping hearts echoed loudly in this subterranean prison, skipping beats in an erratic rhythm and causing an actual physical pain deep in the cavity of their chests. With their minds racing, they quickly lost any remaining hope that these beasts were only assembled like this after their death in some type of morbid exhibit.

As creepy as it was, it was the only sick, plausible explanation that made any type of sense in this twisted aversion. The only conclusion they could even fathom at this point in time was, when this madman's experiments began proving successful using the animals, he started to incorporate human beings into the equation, creating these ungodly abominations. The elusive question of why it all ended so abruptly still lay beyond their comprehension.

Subconsciously backing away from the table, they made another morbid discovery they preferred not notice at all. Their theory about the subject laying on the operating table being one of a kind swiftly evaporated from their thoughts as they gazed down at the frighting sight of a slightly larger one. It had almost evaded their detection as its massive body was mostly hidden underneath the large table in a slide out tray. From the look of it, this one must have been alive at the time when this place suddenly became abandoned. Since this was the only creature not on the operating table or in a cage, they figured this one must have been some type of pet or his watch dog.

"I wonder why it just crawled under the table and died, especially since it's part human?" Jeff asked curiously.

Dave tried answering the question to the best of his ability, especially since he was just guessing himself, "Probably because only parts of its body were human, its head and brain belonged to the mountain lion."

"Really?" Jeff asked, knowing Dave was just guessing.

"Yeah, it probably couldn't figure out how to get out of this room, or even how to get the other cages open to prolong its life a little bit," Dave continued.

"This place is whacked," Allen said, shaking his head. "And why haven't we heard from that freak in the robe again?"

"I don't know?" Dave replied, "but I kind of like it

that way."

"Me too!" Jeff said, seconding that thought, "that thing gives me the creeps."

Dave turned around, setting the book down on the table. Curiosity getting the better of him, he picked up one of the small blue notepads that were laying on the table. "Hey guys, check this out."

"What? What did you find?" Allen asked, as he walked over to where Dave was standing so he could see the inside of the notepad.

"I don't know, it looks like a journal or a diary, I can't tell, it's all written in German or something," Dave replied, as he thumbed through the pages.

"I think you're right," Jeff said. "That definitely ain't American."

"What do you mean American?" Dave said with a dumbfounded look on his face. Realizing how moronic his brother sounded, he slapped him in the back of the head with an open hand as he corrected him, "English, we speak English in this country, you goof!"

"That's what I said," Jeff insisted, taking the defensive. "But look, he wrote the time and date next to each, oh wait, that can't be the time, there ain't any 16:35."

Dave and Allen both briefly chuckled at Jeff, trying to teach the concept of military time. Explaining how they use the different methods to avoid any confusion and preventing a mix up between a.m. and p.m.

"I wish we could understand what it says. I bet it'd be helpful?" Jeff insisted.

"We can't! So don't worry about it. Let's just find these stupid stones and get the hell out of here," Allen said showing his frustration.

Dave set the journal back down on the table and the

three of them took a few steps backwards, stepping away from the disfigured skeleton lying at their feet under the table. Once again they resumed rummaging through the clutter in this cryptic lab. They were already on edge from the insanity of the whole situation, but inside this lab, the awkward feeling felt multiplied a hundred fold. They couldn't get over the feeling of being watched. It felt as if all of the twisted creatures in this room still had their eyes and were intently watching every move they made from their immortalized positions within their cages.

Much to their surprise, it didn't take long after they resumed their search before they were pleasantly rewarded. Dave was the fortunate one that by chance spotted the next elusive stone. It was only because of the shifting beam from Raun's flashlight illuminating the jar that Dave caught a glimpse of the stone lying on the bottom of one of those morbid jars. The container this stone was located in was surrounded by a half dozen other jars containing organs and other miscellaneous small body parts. That alone made Dave question how he had even noticed it since he was trying hard to forget those disgusting jars were even there. Everything in this surreal lab was so strange that nothing stood out from anything else as being out of the ordinary, especially the jars with their red, yellow or clear fluids.

"Hey guys! Quick, over here," Dave demanded from the center of the room.

"What?" Allen retorted as Dave had abruptly caught his attention.

"Did you find it?" Jeff asked as they both started quickly walking over to where Dave was. He was standing on his tip toes trying intently to extend his reach across the extremely wide table, enabling him to grab the jar containing the stone. "What's that jar full of?" Jeff curiously asked.

"Water, I hope?" Dave calmly replied, suddenly realizing the probability of this substance being water was slim to none at best.

"If it's water why didn't it all evaporate?" Jeff curiously asked, reassuring Dave that his hopes of this substance being water were nil.

"I don't know," Dave replied, struggling to open the jar while simultaneously trying not to spill it or worry about what the contents was.

"Why can't you get it open?" Allen asked one of his rhetorical questions that never seemed worth asking since the answer was so obvious.

"Probably because the lid is on tight as hell and the damn thing is rusted shut," Dave replied, still fighting a losing battle with the jar.

"Give me the jar!" Allen demanded, snatching it out of Dave's hand.

Allen too was having a hard time getting the jar opened for a few seconds when Dave could no longer bite his tongue and had to say "See! That bitch is on there tight as hell."

"Want me to show you how to get it?" Jeff asked, immediately striking a nerve with Dave and Allen.

"Yeah right," Allen replied, "If we can't get it open, what makes you think you can get it?"

"Just watch the master," Jeff remarked as Allen reluctantly handed over jar with his mind filled with doubt. With the jar in hand, Jeff paused momentarily and glanced it over, then added, "Now this is how it's done." Jeff turned around, cocked his arm back and slammed the glass container onto the floor. The glass shattered, the mystery fluid went flying everywhere and the stone now lay in a puddle on the floor.

"We could have done that," Allen remarked with a dumbfounded look on his face.

"But you didn't," Jeff replied sarcastically as he bent down to pick up the stone.

Jeff anxiously handed the stone over to Dave as he set the book down on a clearing at the edge of the table. He carefully opened the black leather cover revealing the silver tablet.

"Are you guys ready?" Dave asked.

"Yeah," Allen and Jeff both agreed.

"And this time we've gotta listen carefully," Dave suggested. "Hopefully we can figure out where his voice is coming from."

"Or at least hear what he's trying to say," Jeff added.

"Then here goes nothing," Dave said as he leaned forward, dropping the stone into place. They didn't even notice it themselves, but subconsciously, they had each taken several steps backwards trying to put some distance between themselves and the mysterious tablet.

As soon as the stone had fallen into place it flashed bright red for a split second, illuminating the entire room. As soon as it went dormant, the first stone they found repeated the exact same routine. During the brief second the stones were completing their cycle, they were again able to hear Raun's voice crying out in the distance, coming from nowhere in particular.

"Stop, don't!" Raun's bodiless voice echoed through the room before it was abruptly cut off, as the second stone returned to its original dormant state. The boys regained their frustrations as they were once again unable to tell where Raun's voice was coming from. This whole ordeal was making them crazy because it appeared to be coming from nowhere and everywhere at the same time.

"That's his voice again!" Jeff shouted, stating the obvious.

"Yeah," Dave agreed, "I just wish I could hear what he's trying to tell us?"

"It sounds like he's being tortured," Jeff said.

"I hope he's okay," Dave said to himself, not realizing he said it loud enough for the others to hear.

"Don't worry, we won't let him down," Allen added, resting his hand on Dave's shoulder. "Come on, I think once we find the rest of these stones we'll be able to get Raun back."

"Or at least hear what he's trying to say," Dave added.

"He's probably right," Jeff agreed, "it seems like the more stones we find, the longer we are able to hear his voice."

"I think the book needs all of the stones so it has enough power to bring him back."

"That makes sense, "Dave replied, "but we won't know for sure until we find the rest of the them. I just wish we could hear what he's trying to tell say."

A brief silence fell between them before Jeff finally cut in asking the question they were all trying not to think about. "What if he won't let us go once we find all of the stones?"

"He should," Allen replied, "especially since he's claiming to be trapped. We don't like it and we know he doesn't."

A tear started to roll down Jeff's cheek as he began to sob, "I miss Raun, I just want him to come back so we can all go home."

Dave struggled for a moment as he tried to find the right words, but all he was able to mutter out of his mouth was, "We will, soon, I hope."

Once again they found themselves engulfed by the

eerie silence that surrounded them. They stood there wondering where they were supposed to go next. They had no clue as this was the first time they had been in a room where the doors weren't vanishing and reappearing somewhere else, leading them into a new room they didn't even know existed. The impossible question of where to go next soon answered itself. They suddenly heard a loud crashing noise, immediately followed by the sound of something large running across the floor above them.

As they all looked up to the ceiling, Dave was sure that all of them had completely forgotten they were even in the basement. Without giving it a single thought, they all took off running across the lab and back towards the door that gave entry to the rickety staircase. The whole time they were running they continued calling out to Raun, thinking that the noise they heard could have been caused by him. Just before they started heading up the stairs Dave turned to the others and asked, "What if that isn't Raun up there?"

"Yeah, I just thought of that too," Jeff stated.

"Who else could it be?" Allen asked.

Dave was totally astonished by his stupid question. He turned to face him and asked, "What are you, some type of idiot? Have you forgotten all of the weird shit that's happened since we got here? Not to mention, the insanity of this whole place in general."

"I guess your right," Allen agreed, slowly coming to his senses. "It could be anything up there."

Dave hated saying it, but he managed to make his thoughts turn into words, "Well, we gotta go up there. That's obviously where we're gonna find the next stone."

"Not to mention that it seems to be the only way out lab that I'm aware of," Allen added.

Jeff looked over to Dave with intense fear in his eyes

and let out a soft whimper, "What if it's still up there?"

Frustrated, Dave threw his arms up in the air as he snapped at Jeff, "How the hell am I supposed to answer that? Especially when I don't even know what 'It' is that's up there!"

The uncertainty that awaited them upstairs rekindled their fear to the highest levels imaginable. Allen tried to restore their confidence a little and retracted the gun from his waistband once again. He stepped between them and the staircase and said, "I'll lead the way since I've got the gun."

Dave and Jeff stepped to the side and freely allowed Allen to lead the way. As they slowly followed behind him, Dave made a comment in a sarcastic voice, "And you having that gun makes me feel so much better. I don't know why you didn't shoot that freak when you had the chance."

Dave was right behind Allen as he turned around and crammed the nose of the gun into his chest and barked back at Dave, "Don't start with me again or else you ain't gonna hold your fluids very well."

"Fine, just point that thing somewhere else," Dave replied as he pushed Allen's arm to the side and added, "You're gonna quit pointing that gun at me and I mean it! Let's get Raun back and get the hell out of here."

"You're right, I'm just a little on edge with this freak taking my brother, but you gotta quit pushing my buttons."

"I know, I understand," Dave agreed with Allen.

Jeff took in another deep breath, knowing it was only a matter of time before Allen and Dave would throw blows if they didn't escape the craziness of this cabin soon.

As they started climbing up the rickety stairwell it sounded as if the stairs were crying out in pain, shifting and creaking with each step that fell upon them. When they reached the top Allen poked his head through the opening and began shining his light randomly around the room, “Whoa guys, this is getting stranger.”

In a quiet and panic stricken voice Dave whispered up to him, “What? What is it? What do you see?”

“It’s hard to explain,” Allen replied.

“Try,” Dave demanded.

“Well the fireplace is gone, in fact, so is the whole damn dining room,” Allen tried to answer, not fully understanding it himself.

“What do you mean the dining room is gone? What the hell is up there?” Dave asked, feeling frustrated enough to rip all of his hairs out one by one.

“It’s the room with the silver table, but I don’t see what could have made all that noise.”

“Move out of my way then, I want the hell off these steps,” Jeff insisted in an aggressive tone as he pushed his way past them.

PART SIX

The Earth Stone

The three of them finished climbing out of the hidden stairwell and they now found themselves in a familiar location, yet they were still lost in this labyrinth of a cabin. They were caught totally off guard as they were once again standing in the black room with the silver table and the red pentagram painted on the floor. Momentarily confused, they continued aimlessly shining their dim lights around as they scanned the room. For reasons unbeknownst to themselves they appeared to be unable to retain focus on anything but the silver table in the center of the room. Worse yet, it seemed to be drawing them in to the table whether they wanted to or not.

The room was virtually the same, but there were some subtle changes they noticed. The double doors they originally came in through were still gone. Another door was located on the wall behind them as they faced the table. They were positive this wasn't the door they were forced to exit through last time, even if it were, they knew it would no longer lead them to the same place as before. They were starting to get used to doors vanishing and reappearing out of nowhere. What intrigued them the most was the small copper candlestick holder now located in the center of the mysterious table, holding a single black candle.

"I think we're supposed to light the candle. Do you still have your matches?" Allen suggested.

"Yeah," Dave replied. "I just wish I had another cigarette to go with it. I smoked my last one on the way here and that was ages ago." Dave reached into his pockets in search of the matches and pulled them out. He opened the pack and ripped out the second to last match, closed the cover and struck it on the back.

As the match ignited it gave off a bright glow of light for a moment, illuminating the whole room. As the sulfur burned down, the room returned to being only dimly lit by the faint light from their flashlights. With the match now burning by the paper alone, he reached across the table and touched the flame to the wick of the candle. When the wick ignited, he quickly retracted his arm and extinguished the match, throwing the burnt stick on the floor, returning the rest of the pack into his front pocket.

With the candle flickering and burning, they found themselves backing away from the table. As they stood there motionless staring at the candle a chill ran through all of their bodies, causing their hair to stand on end over their entire bodies. This continued in silence for several seconds until they felt a cool breeze pass through the room. This was particularly odd, being there was nowhere for a draft to originate from. As soon as the candle stopped flickering from the sudden draft, Allen asked, "Did you guys feel that?"

"Yeah, but where did it come from?" Dave asked, baffled by the strange draft with no visible source.

"Well, now what do we do?" Jeff asked.

"I'm not sure," Dave whispered. "There's really nowhere in here to search." As Dave finished his sentence, he began walking around the table in hopes of finding the next stone or anything that might help to make some sense out of the peculiar situation they now found themselves in.

"We can try the other door," Jeff suggested.

"Good idea," Dave said, "if he wants us in this room, I'm sure the door will be locked and we'll be trapped in here."

"We can always go back down the...ah, never mind that." Allen stopped himself as he looked to the floor only to learn the stairway had disappeared. Dave and Jeff instantly knew the stairs had vanished by Allen's fading words alone, but they curiously looked anyway.

"We can scrap that idea," Dave remarked.

"Damn! This cabin sucks!" Allen said. "You can't even blink your eyes in here. Every time you do shit disappears and reappears out of nowhere."

"That's how we lost Raun," Jeff quickly added, immediately realizing that he should have probably just kept that thought inside rather than saying it. Stating the obvious wasn't necessary, the dirty looks that both Dave and Allen gave to him said more than a mouthful. "I'm sorry," Jeff quickly apologized, "I was just thinking out loud."

"Don't worry 'bout it," Allen insisted, much to Jeff's surprise. "I know what you meant."

"Yeah," Dave agreed, "right now we've got bigger problems, like figuring out what the hell were supposed to do next."

"Well, should we try the door?" Jeff suggested, pointing at the door.

"What about the candle?" Allen asked. "He must've put it there for a reason."

"I can't think of one, I'll put it out," Dave replied.

"That's probably a good idea, we shouldn't leave a candle burning in a cabin we've got no idea how to get out of," Jeff stated, showing some semblance of common sense.

"Good point," Dave agreed as he walked over to the table, bent down and blew out the wick on the candle. Before he was even able to resume standing back upright, the wick on the candle reignited of its own free will. Dave leaned back over the table, thinking it must not have been extinguished all the way and blew it out once again. The flame again reignited on its own.

"Okay," Allen said, ever so slowly, "I guess we'll leave it lit."

"I don't think we have a choice," Dave said, perplexed by the sheer determination of this candle. Abandoning the idea of blowing out the candle, they started proceeding over toward the enigmatic door. When they arrived at the door, they were stunned by the fact that it remained there and it was actually unlocked. Allen gently pushed the door open and peered inside with the gun and flashlight in hand.

"It's empty," Allen whispered back to them as he looked into the empty void laying just beyond this room. Regaining his confidence, he slowly pushed the door open the remainder of the way and they cautiously entered the strange emptiness.

This room was extremely strange to them. They knew they were still inside the cabin, they could tell that by the fact that they were still surrounded by walls and the open rafter ceiling. Strangely, instead of having a wooden or tiled floor, it was raw earth, for some reason they couldn't get over their sensation of somehow being outside. The ground was hilly and the surface was nothing more then loose gravel and dirt sliding away beneath their feet. "What the hell kind of room is this?" Jeff asked curiously.

"You got me," puzzled Allen replied. "What are we supposed to do, sift through all these loose rocks?"

"Dig," Dave suggested shining his flashlight on an old minors pickaxe leaning up against the wall in the corner of the room. They started making their way over to the pickaxe when they also noticed two shovels lying on the ground. They were overlapped, forming the shape of an x, presumably marking the spot they were supposed to dig. What intrigued them was that in the opposite corner of the room was about a twenty foot length of three quarter inch braided rope. They were surprised they even noticed it due to the uneven ground.

"Dig where?" Allen asked.

"On the x would probably be a good place to start," Dave sarcastically suggested, mocking Allen's intelligence.

"How deep?" Jeff asked, unaware that Dave had just pissed Allen off.

"Hell, I don't know. Why do you guys seem to think I have all of the answers? Maybe we'll get lucky and accidentally dig a hole leading out of here," Dave snapped at them.

"I don't see that happening," Allen replied.

"Alright," Jeff said, trying to gain their attention. "I understand the shovels and digging, but what's the rope for?" He finished, with a look of confusion etched into his face.

"No clue," Dave replied. "But I'm sure it has some type of purpose. Why don't you try to find something to tie it off to in case we have to dig real deep?"

Dave and Allen started to dig the hole where the shovels were lying crossed. Meanwhile, Jeff wandered aimlessly around the room in search of anything sufficient enough to tie the rope to, but he was having no luck. "There's nothing to tie it to!" Jeff shouted from across the room.

"Just find something to tie it to, damn it," Allen shouted as they continued to dig.

Jeff conformed to Allen's request while the two of them continued digging the hole in the corner of the room. As Allen slammed the shovel into the ground once again, it felt as if he'd hit a large rock or something hard. He then placed the tip of the shovel on the object, raised up his foot and stomped down on the top of the shovel. As his foot connected to the shovel with all his might, he felt it penetrate clear through whatever it had been stuck on. Instantly both Dave and Allen's legs felt as if they had suddenly turned to Jello as the earth underneath them started to crumble away into the unseen abyss below. It was all happening so fast, it felt as if someone had ripped out the whole undercarriage of whatever this room had been built over.

Jeff immediately turned around to face them as he heard the sudden frightened screams of Dave and Allen, combined with the strange sound of the earth caving in beneath their feet. "Dave! Allen!" Jeff cried out as he quickly but cautiously made his way over to the giant hole that had just collapsed in front of him, consuming his brother and Allen right before his eyes.

"Jeff!" Dave yelled up to his brother in a panic.

"Down here," Allen added.

"Are you guys alright?" Jeff replied.

"Yeah, were fine," they both answered.

Allen added, "And we know what the rope is for."

"You do?" Jeff asked.

"Yeah," Allen replied, amazed by the stupidity of Jeff's question. "It's to get us out of here! Now get the damn rope!"

"Oh yeah," Jeff suddenly realized the stupidity of his question, but still managed to utter another one, "What is that place down there?"

"I don't know," Dave hollered back up to him. "We need your flashlight, we've lost the book, the gun and both of our flashlights."

"Is there anything that you didn't loose?" Jeff asked.

"Yeah, gravity, now drop down your light," Allen shouted.

"And the rope too," Dave added.

"And don't throw down the whole rope! Be sure to keep one end up there with you," Allen stated what should be the obvious.

"No shit Sherlock," Jeff yelled back down the hole,

"I'm not as dumb as you look."

"You'd better watch it," Allen tried making a threat.

"Or what? I'm not the one in the hole," Jeff asked, knowing he had the upper hand for the time being. "Without me you guys can't even get out."

"Just give us the light," Dave demanded.

Jeff inched his way over to the edge of where the hole caved in and tossed down the light. Much to Dave's surprise, he actually managed to catch the flashlight. As he caught it, his thumb pushed the button forward, turning it on for a brief second before it cut out. Dave adjusted the light in his hand and pushed the button all the way forward, luckily it still worked.

"What do you see?" Jeff asked impatiently.

"Hold on a minute," Dave yelled back up to Jeff as they started brushing the dust and dirt off themselves. They quickly realized that their attempt to dust themselves off was hopeless. Changing plans, they began shining the light around the cavity of this hole they found themselves trapped inside of.

"What the hell is this place?" Allen asked Dave.

"I don't know, it looks like some kind of massive graveyard," Dave replied, suddenly realizing they were standing atop of an unfathomable pile of remains, containing loose bones and partial skeletons that appeared to belong to both animals and humans. The actual size of this horrible pile was left mostly to their imagination due to the fact that most of it was covered by all of the dirt, rocks and broken boards that came crashing down on the pile when the floor suddenly gave way, revealing this hidden tomb below the dirt covered floorboards. Jeff wasn't close enough to the edge to realize what had captured Dave and Allen's attention so fully.

The two of them were completely transfixed as they

stood there in awe looking at the scattered remains lying all over the floor of this burial chamber. They couldn't believe that a hole this large had been dug out for the sole purpose of filling it with dead bodies. What intrigued them even more was that the hole was then covered with a sub floor to conceal the fact this room even existed.

As time progressed, the dirt and gravel were probably scattered over the floor to reduce the rank odor of decomposing bodies. There was no specific order or noticeable system to which the bones were laid out, but they could plainly see that some of the bones had obviously been cut with a saw. They could only imagine the morbid experiments that went on in this cabin, which only these victims ever know.

"This place is totally gross," Allen said as he continued gazing around the room before adding, "why would he have wanted us to find this place?"

"Right there," Dave softly whispered as he was shining the light on the next stone. They began walking but were having a hard time trying to keep their footing as they weaved their way down the massive pile of debris they had landed on. When they made it all the way to the bottom of the hill, Dave leaned over a small pile of bones and picked up the small red stone out of the dirt.

With the stone in his hand, Dave paused for a moment, placing the stone into the front pocket of his jeans. Feeling confident he wasn't going to lose the gem, the two of them began to look for the rest of the stuff they had lost when they crashed into the hole. Surprisingly it didn't take them long before they were able to locate the pistol, book and one of the flashlights. Even armed with the other light, locating the other one seemed to be a lost cause, it probably wouldn't work anyway, so they abandoned their search. They yelled up to

Jeff and had him toss down one end of the rope. Dave grabbed the loose end of the rope and tied it into a slipknot, placed the book and gun through the loop and pulled the rope tight. Dave tugged on the line twice and hollered for Jeff to pull it up. Jeff pulled it up slowly trying not to let the items fall out of the loop, when the rope was all the way up, he loosened the knot, took out the book and gun, placing them on the ground near his feet. He threw the rope back down to them.

"Did you find anything to tie the rope off too?" Dave asked.

"No," Jeff replied, "there's nothing up here."

"Then I'll go first," Dave suggested to Allen.

"Why do you get to go first?" Allen asked, quite shaken by Dave's assumption.

"I don't weigh as much as you," Dave replied, "and to be honest, I don't think that Jeff can lift your fat ass."

"You'd better not leave me down here," Allen demanded, knowing he probably deserved it.

"I won't, I just know that Jeff can't hold the rope for you by himself."

"Alright, but hurry up. I don't like the idea of being down here by myself, all these bodies creep me out," Allen responded.

Dave finished tying the rope around his waist and he gave it another tug as he yelled up for Jeff to start pulling.

"I got cha!" Jeff replied as he started to back up and lift Dave up out of the hole. Dave was no more then a couple of inches off of the ground when he was suddenly dropped back down to the ground. He glanced up momentarily, only to watch, as the rest of the rope tumbled into the hole.

"You idiot," Allen yelled up to Jeff.

"Why did you let go?" Dave asked.

"Because if I didn't, I'd be down there with you

guys," Jeff replied.

"Well, good thinking then," Dave replied, "I'm gonna throw the rope back up to you."

Jeff agreed as Dave was coiling the rope back up. When he was finished, he gave it a good toss. Unfortunately his first attempt was to no avail. As the line was falling back down into the hole, Allen was fortunate enough to look up on time and move out of the way before it came crashing down on his head. Allen was pissed that he was almost hit with the rope, but Dave just ignored his whining as he recoiled it once again. As soon as he had it tied into a ball Allen snatched it out of his hand as he demanded, "Give me that."

Dave just stood there in shock realizing Allen had just taken the rope from him, insinuating he was incapable of throwing it all the way back up to Jeff. Dave hadn't even totally grasped what just transpired before Allen had tossed the rope back up to Jeff and made it. "Alright, I got it," Jeff hollered down to them as he caught the rope. He started to unwind it when he suddenly got an idea, "Hold on a minute, let me try something."

Dave and Allen were forced to wait in darkness and suspense as Jeff grabbed the pickaxe, rope and the flashlight before proceeding over to the open doorway. The long length of rope and the axe were quite heavy for someone of Jeff's build. He was only half way to the doorway when he began to fumble the objects in his hands and dropped them. "Oh shit!" He cried out before the worst even happened. The head of the pick landed right atop of the flashlight crushing the bulb and splitting open one of the batteries.

"What happened?" concerned, Dave yelled up from the bottom of the hole.

"I broke the light," Jeff replied.

"What a klutz," Allen said to Dave.

"Take it easy on him, he's trying his best to get us out of this hole."

"Great, so we're gonna be down here forever," Allen said, implying they were stuck in a hopeless situation. Dave and Allen continued to bicker with each other while it seemed they would be forever engulfed in this dark burial chamber.

Jeff was now aided only by the dim light from the flickering candle that seemed to be burning endlessly on the silver table. When Jeff made it to the open doorway, he set down the rope and axe, tying a slipknot around the top part of the blade. Once he felt the rope was tight and as secure as he could possibly get it, he laid the axe down on the floor and wedged it into the door frame so that it was stuck on both sides by the handle. He wasn't sure of whether or not this was going to work, but he knew he wouldn't be able to hold the rope without some kind of help. His mind raced, continuing to wonder about what the outcome of his ingenious idea would be, but it was the only reasonable option he could feasibly concoct in his desperate situation. Confident in his creation, he began walking out the rope as he headed toward the opening in the floor that held his brother and friend hostage.

"What the hell is taking you so long?" Allen hollered up to Jeff.

"You should feel lucky I even came back for you," Jeff yelled back down to Allen, "but the rope should hold you now."

Once again, Dave grabbed hold of the rope. Jeff was laughing, watching over the edge as his brother comically struggled with the rope. He was trying to tie it around his waist, but the way Jeff had it rigged now made it virtually impossible with majority of the rope sprawled across the floor above them, it was just too short.

"Just climb up it like we do in gym, I've got it tied off

to the door, it should be able to hold you," Jeff said, praying his knot in the rope wouldn't come undone, dropping his brother back down into the cavernous hole. Dave gave the rope a couple of quick tugs, checking the strength of the line, once he felt as confident as he could that the rope would hold, he began making his way up the steep incline of the cave in. At first he was making good progress, but as he neared the top, fatigue was starting to settle in on him. If Allen wouldn't have grabbed the bottom of the rope to stabilize it, he wouldn't have made it at all. Dave hadn't even caught his breath yet when Allen came crawling out of the broken floorboards behind him.

With all of them now standing safely back on the main level of the cabin, they paused momentarily trying to grasp the severity of what just happened. Temporarily relieved, they contemplated what they would have done if all of them had fallen into the hole together. Trying to put it behind them, they felt a little relieved and slightly proud they had overcome this latest deadly predicament, only to silently wonder to themselves what else was in store for them before, if ever, they found their way out of this nightmare.

Deciding it was time to move on Dave kicked the book over in front of himself with the side of his foot before reaching into his pocket and pulling out the next stone. As he leaned over to drop the stone into place, Jeff and Allen took several cautious steps backwards. Quickly, Dave dropped the stone into place and hopped backwards the distance deemed safe by the others. Dave was still in motion as the gems started their peculiar cycle.

One by one, the stones gave off their singular pulse of dominating red light for less than a fraction of a second. Simultaneously hearing Raun's voice cry out, "You won't!" before it was once again abruptly cut short of him finishing his sentence when the stones completed their short cycle, returning to their original dull red and dormant state.

"Did you guys see that?" Jeff frantically asked.

"See what?" Allen replied.

"An image," Jeff retorted, "it was like a dark spot in the middle of the red light on the ceiling, I think it came from the last stone, you guys didn't see that?"

"What? Are you sure? What did it look like?" Dave was rapidly firing off questions as he closed the book's cover and picked it up.

"I don't know. I only saw it for a split second and it was at the end," Jeff was pleading the fact that he didn't imagine this.

"You're out of your mind," Allen insisted.

"I'm serious, something was in the light," Jeff demanded.

"That's ridicules," Allen said, sticking to his story.

"And the rest of this is normal?" Dave asked.

"Well no, but," Allen stuttered.

"I saw something, I did," Jeff interrupted.

"He could have seen something," Dave agreed, siding with Jeff.

"I think he's full of shit," Allen said, speaking his mind, "and I know nothing was there because I would have seen it too," he continued as he poked Jeff in the forehead with his index finger.

"Just leave him alone," Dave said to Allen.

"Fine," Allen reluctantly agreed.

"We just need to get this figured out," Dave stated.

"But where do we start?" Jeff added.

"How about by imagining things?" Allen said.

"Knock it off," Dave snapped at him.

"I'm just giving him a hard time," Allen said as he patted Jeff on the shoulder. "So where do we go next in this stupid maze?"

"I guess we go back through that door," Dave suggested, pointing toward the open door with the pick axe wedged through the door frame.

"I don't see any other new options," Jeff added.

"Hell," Dave interrupted, "that's the longest I've seen any door in this place stay in the same spot."

"And lead back into the old room," Jeff again added to the obvious.

"Hold up a sec guys," Allen suggested.

"What now?" Dave asked, worry echoing in his voice.

"I think we should at least take the rope with us, you never know, we might need it again," Allen explained.

"Good idea," Dave agreed as Jeff shook his head with approval.

With that said, they began making their way over toward the doorway. Upon arrival, Allen leaned down and untied the rope from the axe, coiled it up and placed into in his gym bag. Once he finished they each had to step over the axe lying on the floor to head into the next room. Dave lead the way armed with their only remaining flashlight, Allen and Jeff followed close behind as they entered the room. They were no more than a full step inside when the doorway and the axe suddenly vanished right before their eyes. Generating an instant reaction out of Jeff, he turned around and began hopelessly beating on the spot where the doorway was just seconds ago but now it was gone. The wall standing firmly in its place seemed as solid as steel. Panicked, Allen abruptly checked his bag to see if the rope too had disappeared, to his surprise, it was still there.

PART SEVEN
The Fire Stone

"I can't take it, this place is driving me nuts!" Jeff shouted hopelessly at the wall.

"I know," Dave agreed, "nothing about this place has made any sense since we got here."

"Well, at least there is a new door in here now," Allen remarked.

"Oh and that's supposed to make me feel better, why?" Dave just had to ask.

"Look guys," Jeff insisted, pointing toward the candle sitting inauspiciously in the center of the table.

"What am I supposed to be looking at?" Allen asked.

"The candle," Jeff chirped, "it's been burning for a long time and it hasn't even started to melt yet."

"I don't even want to attempt trying to figure this place out," Dave insisted.

"Me neither, I was just making a point," Jeff said. "Do you guys have any idea of how long we've been in here?"

"No, not really," Allen took it upon himself to answer.

"It just feels like we've been in here forever," Jeff stated.

"He does have a point," Dave said, scratching his head with his index finger, "I've lost all sense of time since we got here."

"How long we've been here is irrelevant, were trapped!" Allen stated.

"He's right, we can't seem to find a way out of here regardless! And when was the last time either of you saw a window?" Dave questioned.

"Are you going somewhere with this?" Allen asked,

"because we really don't have time for this. I just want to find these stupid ass stones and get the hell out of here."

"Alright, we'll go, but with no windows or watches, we could have already been in here for days."

"We'll be out of here soon, trust me," Allen assured him.

They all proceeded to walking toward the door on the other side of the room. When they arrived, Jeff was the one who reached out to turn the knob. The door was unlocked. Very slowly, Jeff started pushing the door open, once again they couldn't believe the sight they were witnessing right before their eyes.

They no longer had any sense of where they actually stood in the layout of this cabin, but somchow they found themselves about to enter the dining room again. The biggest difference this time was immediately noticeable and didn't require them to enter the room to see it. The room felt as if it was two hundred degrees fahrenheit. Normally something this abstract would have deterred them, but they knew they had no other option and had to keep going forward. As expected, as soon as they stepped inside the room, the door behind them immediately vanished without a trace. The missing part of the wall materialized right before their eyes completely filling in the opening.

"Damn!" Jeff was sweating bullets. "Is the cabin on fire or what?" he asked wiping his brow with the back of his forearm and his shirt.

"I've got no idea, but I'm burning up," Dave replied.

"It seems to be coming from over here," Allen suggested as he wandered over toward the cast iron wood-burning stove. The others followed his lead.

"This thing is on," Dave couldn't believe what he was saying.

"Is someone in here with us?" Jeff asked, actually starting to wonder.

Without answering, Dave used the front of his shirt to grab a hold of the handle on the furnace door. As he pulled it open, they felt a huge blast of heat that seemed to surpass the already intolerable temperature of this room. With the door fully opened and the temperature of the room leveling out at what felt like five hundred degrees, they could finally see what was burning inside the furnace. The insides were glowing bright reddish orange as they radiated out its blazing heat. What shocked them was, not only was there no fire in the furnace, but there was nothing in it that would burn, the only thing inside of it was one of the small red stones, lying on a small pile of ashes.

"Hey, there's a stone in there," excited Jeff shouted.

"Give me something to grab it with, hurry," Dave demanded.

Allen grabbed a small furnace shovel that was lying next to the stove and handed it to him. Allen and Jeff were standing a few feet away from the blazing inferno, desperately trying to avoid the massive amount of heat it was producing. Armed with the shovel in hand, Dave squinted his eyes trying to shield them from the heat. He moved in a little closer and stuffed the head of the shovel into the furnace and scooped up the stone along with the pile of ashes it was lying on top of.

Their confusion intensified as he retracted the shovel from the belly of the stove, as soon as the stone was outside of the furnace the room's temperature dropped drastically. The wood-burning stove returned back to its original color of black, like it hadn't been used in ages, with no heat radiating from it whatsoever.

"What the hell is going on here?" Dave asked.

Jeff took several steps forward and made an attempt to

touch the furnace. Wondering if he was going to get burned, he started with the tip of one finger, followed by a quick tap and then his whole hand came to rest on it. "It's cold!" Jeff shouted, baffled.

"What?" Dave asked, quickly turning his head to face Jeff with an intense look of shock etched into his face. He dumped the stone and pile of ashes out onto the floor, bending down to pick it up in the same ritual Jeff had just performed, testing how hot it may or may not be. "It's cold too, how is that possible?" Dave asked perplexed, grabbing a hold of the stone. Crouched down, he held the stone loosely in his open hand with a blank look on his face as he glanced back and fourth between Jeff and Allen.

"Don't ask me," Jeff quickly replied.

"Really," Allen added, "I don't know anything more than you do."

"We gotta get out of here," Dave insisted as he shook his head. "This place is like a never ending mad circus with no hope for escape."

"Yeah, like the house of mirrors," Jeff added.

"Just put the stone in place, then we only have one more ta go," Allen strongly suggested.

"Alright," Dave agreed, wanting this perilous ordeal to just finally be over.

He set the book down on the dining room table and once again opened the leather cover. Holding the stone in his fingers, he reached over the tablet, dropped the stone into place and stepped a few feet away from the ominous tablet.

The first stone flashed, followed immediately by the second, third, then the fourth. The red pulses seemed to be getting brighter and stronger with each new stone they located. As each of the gems exploded with radiant bursts of light, they could actually hear the light making a slapping sound as it seemingly exploded out and connected with the ceiling.

"He's trying to..." Raun's voice cried out before once again trailing off as the book and stones went dormant.

"Did you see the images?" Jeff frantically asked.

"I saw something," Allen actually agreed, "but it could have just been a shadow in the light, I couldn't tell."

"I saw something, maybe it was nothing, I don't know, I couldn't tell either," Dave added his thoughts.

"But you did see something, right?" Jeff insisted, trying to reassure himself he wasn't hallucinating.

"Yeah, I guess," Allen replied.

"The hell with that b.s." Dave interrupted as he closed the tablets cover and picked it up off of the table, "we need to figure out what Raun is trying to tell us and not worry about some stupid reflection."

"But it doesn't make any sense," Allen retorted.

"He's trying to what, kill him, torture him?" Dave was rambling as he thought out loud trying to piece it all together. "It just doesn't make any sense."

"I don't know either Dave," Jeff felt his sympathetic input was needed.

"We're just going to have to wait until we get the last stone, then he can tell us when we leave this hell hole," Allen was forcing hopeful reasoning upon himself.

"And we need to figure out what those images in the red lights are," Jeff persisted, determined to prove himself.

"Another door! You gotta be kidding me," Dave blurted out. Caught off guard as another door materialized right before their eyes, opposite the wall they had came in through.

"I guess that's our cue," Allen smugly suggested as

they all started heading toward the new door. When they arrived, they paused momentarily, took in a deep breath and ever so cautiously, Allen pushed the door open.

PART EIGHT

The Skeleton Stone

They could tell right away they had entered some type of athenaeum. The farther they advanced, the more baffled they became. Everything they had observed so far paled in comparison to what they were witnessing now. The size correlation between the interior and exterior was perplexing. They thought they'd seen its entirety, but this boundless library alone was substantially larger than they had originally suspected the entire shape-shifting labyrinth to be.

Standing in the doorway was a remarkable sight. Massive amounts of fully stocked bookcases filled the room from wall to wall and floor to ceiling. There were wooden ladders attached to the cases, allowing for access to the high shelves. The boys stepped inside, almost immune to the fact the door behind them was about to vanish. As it did, they couldn't get over the sudden helpless feeling of being watched amidst this colossal maze of bookshelves.

Feeling slightly confident they had a grasp on what was required of them, to save on time, the three of them decided to split up. They continued to search for the stone but couldn't shake the eerie feeling they had about this room. They assumed the strange sensation was being caused by the unfortunate fact that they were surrounded by stuffed statues of the half man half creature they came across earlier. This time they weren't just bones lying there, they looked as if they were alive and waiting to attack. Just one quick glance at the strange creature sent bone-chilling feeling straight down their spine. But the remnants of these miss matched animals, frozen in time by a taxidermist, gave them their biggest clue as to what kind of twisted person the previous owner of this cabin actually was.

"Do you guys see all of these?" Jeff asked from the next isle over from the wall where Dave was searching.

"Yeah, I do, I don't wanna, but I do," Dave responded in a barely audible whisper. Allen was only a couple of isles away from Dave with Jeff in the middle when he heard Dave call out, "Hey guys, you need to come here and check this out." Jeff and Allen hurried to the end of the isle where they gained access to the corridor Dave was searching.

"What is it? Did you find the stone? What did you see?" Jeff curiously asked a rapid string of questions as they both now stood at his side. Dave aimed the remaining dim flashlight onto the wall, all six eyes followed the beam and were intently focused on the objects. There were several plaques hanging proudly on the wall, Dave began to read one of the awards out loud;

"**Scientific Medical Achievement Of The Year Award,**" just below that it read, "This award is being presented to Dr. Eric Aben on May 19, 1939 by the American Medical Association for his outstanding achievements in the genetics in medical science. It is because of him that we have made outstanding leaps towards understanding the molecular composition of all living things. We thank him for his hard work and the discovery of malignant neoplasms marked by the proliferation of anaplastic cells that normally tend to invade the surrounding tissues and metastasize to alternate body sights."

"And look at this one," Jeff added. "**Physician Of The Year**, 1936," he read out loud.

"This one is from Germany and it's signed by Hitler," Allen pointed out.

"Wow," Jeff stated. "No wonder everything in this cabin is so sick and twisted."

"Alright, I've had enough of trying to figure this place

out," Allen said, feeling like they were ending up with more questions than answers. "Let's just find this stupid stone and get out of here."

"Good idea," Dave agreed, as they resumed searching the library for the stone.

Each of them had utterly immersed themselves into the search. Allen was busy looking behind a variety of books on anatomy. He couldn't read them, as most of them were written in German. When he came to the end of the isle, he was so immersed in the search, he actually spooked himself as he turned the corner. He happened to glance up only to find the front legs, chest and head of a timber wolf snarling only inches away from his face. The rest of its body slowly faded into the giant reptilian that once would have been an eight foot long crocodile.

"How many of these things do you think this guy put together?" Allen asked.

"I think I have a better question," Jeff stated.

"What's that?" Dave asked.

"Are we going to stumble across any of those things that are still alive?" Jeff asked.

"I hope not, but somehow that just don't seem like it would surprise me, in the possibility sense anyway," Dave said, feeling discouraged that his words could soon end up being their frightening reality.

They all forced themselves to break free from these morbid fascinations these strange looking creatures induced. They started to regain their focus and resumed trying to locate the last remaining stone. This room was by far the most difficult to search, not only the endless possibilities of where the stone could be located, but the vivid mental anguish that any one of these extreme creatures could suddenly burst into life at any given second just to end theirs.

They were absolutely certain that without some type of sign or guidance from the shadow creature, this search was going to take all of eternity. Especially since the stones were so small and could be hidden anywhere. Jeff had almost given up on the isle he was searching when he rounded the corner. "AHH!" frightened, Jeff screamed. "I found it! I found it!"

Dave and Allen both instantly took off running toward Jeff. As they rounded the corner, they found Jeff frozen in a paralyzed trance. When they finally grasped what had Jeff's undivided attention, they too stood there for a moment transfixed in silence. They just couldn't believe where they finally happened to find this stone.

They found themselves standing in front of a human corpse sitting inauspiciously in a chair behind a large wooden desk. He was oddly wearing a long sleeved lab coat, jeans and a white butcher's apron covered with dried blood bearing an ominous bullet hole that had punched through the chest area.

The clothes no longer fit and now lay draped over the bare bones his body use to house before all of flesh, muscle and tissues decomposed and rotted away, leaving behind only an eerie skeleton. The body sat there with nothing more than a handful of white hairs lying on his lap and the remaining stone curiously implanted into his mouth resembling canine fangs. The strangest thing about this whole scenario was that it looked as if he had died suddenly and unexpectedly from the gunshot wound to the chest.

Loosely grasped between the remnants of his thin finger bones, he held onto a blue note pad and a fancy gold pen. It seemed that he'd taken his last breath trying to draft an entry into a journal as he bled out and died right here in his chair.

Suddenly, Dave burst out in an ear piercing scream, causing both Allen and Jeff to nearly jump out of their shoes.

The sudden torrent was initiated by a large gray rat the size of a large household cat running across his foot. As the large rat rapidly scurried away, disappearing behind one of the large bookshelves, they were finally able to turn their attention back to the grotesque skeleton bearing the final stone.

"Is this him?" Jeff curiously asked. "Is this the man behind all of the myths?"

"Only he knows the answer to that," Dave remarked, "but that is my guess."

"Grab the stone," Allen suggested to Jeff.

"Hell no," Jeff snapped back at Allen, "you grab it, I ain't touching that thing."

"Fine, I'll get it," Dave volunteered, "I really don't think he'll bite."

Dave handed the tablet over to Jeff, leaned forward and reached into the open mouth of the skeleton. With his thumb and index finger he grabbed hold of the stone and attempted to wiggle it free. Almost trampling Jeff and Allen in the process, he abruptly jumped backwards four feet, as the mandible fell open from its closed position. It was like it suddenly came to life, wanting a bite of Dave's finger. When the shock wore off, they found themselves standing there staring at the lower jaw bone as it now hung down in the open position resting against the bloodstained butchers apron.

"Here, let me try," Allen suggested, stepping up to the awful looking corpse. Smiling, he pulled the gun from his waistband.

With a confused look on his face, Dave asked, "What are you gonna do, rob the guy?"

"No," Allen replied.

"Good." Confident the corpse hadn't came back to life, Dave stepped forward once again and tried to break the stone free with his hands. Making no progress, he decided to give up before the head fell completely off the shoulders.

"I can't get it. It just won't budge," Dave stated.

Allen lightly pushed Dave to the side, "I don't think he's gonna give it to you."

"I already told ya, robbing him ain't gonna work," Dave responded.

Allen said, "No, moron! Just watch, you might learn something." With the gun firmly in his hand, he cocked his arm back and lashed out in a forward swing. Using every ounce of his strength, he smashed the butt of the gun into the top row of teeth. Upon contact, the back of the skull slammed into the wall from the sheer force of the sudden blow. The vertebrae holding the head connected to the body suddenly snapped, teeth rained down all over the floor along with the stone and was followed by the head. Allen had hit it with such immense force that it actually bounced off of the wall behind it, ricocheted forward, rolling down the body and across Allen's foot before settling into its new final resting place on the floor.

"That's gross," Jeff shouted at Allen.

Aggravated, Dave threw his arms up in the air, turned around and stormed off, walking aimlessly away from Allen and the freshly decapitated corpse. After only a few seconds, he turned back around to face him as he shouted, "That's really respectful! You're such an ass."

"What?" Allen asked showing no remorse.

"I hope that when I'm dead, some kids don't come by fifty years later, assault me, rob me and then disrespect my dead body."

Allen yelled back at Dave, "Don't give me your shit! I got the stone out, didn't I?"

"Yeah, you did," Dave reluctantly agreed, "but show a little tact next time, all that wasn't necessary and it's just rude"

"I didn't see you overflowing with bright ideas," Allen argued.

"Come on guys," Jeff pleaded with them, "let's just put this stone in place and get this over with."

Jeff bent down, plucking the stone out of the loose pile of teeth, handing it to Dave. They stepped away from the body, back toward the center of the room. "Alright," Dave said, trying to gain their full attention for what he was about to say next. Once he felt that he had their full attention he continued, "Now when I drop this stone into place, I want you guys to pay close attention and hopefully we can figure out what Raun is trying to tell us."

"What about those dark images in the light?" Jeff asked.

"We'll watch for that too," Dave agreed. "Even that might give us some kind of clue as to what the hell's going on around here."

"I can't seem to grasp it," Allen stated.

"Me neither, but we're gonna figure it out," Dave said, trying to boost their spirits a little before asking, "Are you guys ready?"

"Yeah," Allen replied.

"I'm about as ready as I'm going to get," Jeff added.

Dave set the book on the floor and once again opened up the soft leather cover revealing the cryptic engravings on the silver tablet. He crouched down, holding his hand over the last of the five small triangular holes surrounded the larger round hole in the center. He hesitated a little as he glanced over to Allen and Jeff. It was as if he was looking for their approval or some kind of sign he wasn't making a huge mistake by reuniting these long separated stones. No words were spoken. He closed his eyes momentarily and dropped the stone into place. As soon as the gem fell from his fingertips, he stood up, swiftly backing away as the tablet came to life and began performing its light show.

Much to their surprise, as the stones lit up, they all stayed lit long enough for them to see and identify the dark images they produced on the ceiling as the stones ran through their strange cycle. First was of a serpent, the next appeared to be of a tidal wave, then it was a symbol resembling the Earth, followed by an image of fire and the last one was a human body. Disappointingly, Raun's voice was no where to be heard during this cycle. After the flashing lights made there five solitary pulses, the book went dormant for a second or two, which felt like an eternity to them. Then in a sudden burst of light, all five gems flashed as one, each projecting their own distinct image on the ceiling for all to see. The lights then turned into darkness and the whole interior of the library and the doors vanished right before their eyes as they stood there. They suddenly found themselves standing back in the room where all of this chaos appeared to have started. The tablet that was lying on the floor had re-materialized and was now laying on the silver table next to the mysterious everlasting candle. The flame had some how extinguished itself, but the candle looked as if it had never been lit. For reasons unbeknownst to them, they happened to look down at their feet and noticed they were standing square in the middle of the giant red pentagram painted on the floor.

"Holy shit!" Dave cried out, breaking the paralyzed silence that had engulfed them. "What the hell just happened in here?"

"In here or do you mean in the library," Allen asked.

"It's the same damn room!" Dave shouted, not so much at Allen, but out of pure aggravation. "I know that much for sure, because we haven't moved an inch," he continued.

"I don't care where the hell we are," Jeff stated, "I just want the hell out of here!"

"He won't let us leave!" Dave cried out into the vast emptiness of the room.

"I'm tired of playing his stupid game." Allen added.

"Why is he doing this?" Jeff asked.

"What do you want from us? Show yourself!" Dave demanded, continuing to shout randomly into the room.

Receiving no response from the shadow creature, Dave stormed up to the table, grabbed the book, slammed the cover shut and picked it up off of the table. With the book in his right hand he began to spin around in circles with his arms extended out to his sides. "What the hell are we supposed to do now?" Dave asked to Allen. "There's no way out of this room!"

Neither Allen or Jeff answered Dave right away. They could both tell his fury was already at his boiling point. A few more moments of silence passed by before Allen suggested, "We can try lighting the candle again."

Dave reached into his pocket with his free hand. He pulled out the book, opened the cover and said, "One, Damn, I've only got one match left."

"Don't screw it up," Jeff softly suggested.

"Don't start with me," Dave quickly snapped at his brother as he walked over toward the table. He ripped the remaining match out and struck it across the back of the pack. Unfortunately, as the head of the match ignited, it broke off, separating from the rest of the match stick and fell to the floor where it went out. "Damn it! The match broke and it went out!" Dave retold what they had just witnessed as he kicked the table.

"Now what do we do?" Jeff asked curiously.

"This is hopeless," Allen stated. "Why won't this

freak show himself?"

All of a sudden the bright triangular white light from the tables surface flickered on and then abruptly disappeared right before their eyes. An all black pack of matches had materialized from thin air and was now laying on the table's surface. Dave reached out to the table and picked up the pack of matches. He opened up the cover and examined it. There was no writing on it at all. The pack was full. The only spot on the pack with any variation in color was the tips of the match heads which were a dull shade of red. "Are they real?" Jeff asked.

"I guess so," Dave replied as he ripped one out of the pack.

He then took the match that he had taken out of the pack and struck it across the back. The flame ignited, briefly and brightly illuminating the room. Dave reached across the table gently touching the flame to the candle. When the wick took, Dave shook out the match and threw it on the floor, placing the rest of the pack in his pocket.

They all cautiously stepped back away from the table as they waited ominously for whatever was supposed to happen next. Allen was growing impatient and shouted, "Show yourself you freak, I want my brother back!"

Allen had barely finished his sentence when the table once again came to life. The solid beam of light remained on, again confined to the triangular shape of the table from the surface to the ceiling. They couldn't see through the beam, it looked as if it was a solid piece of white plastic. It was so bright, they couldn't even tell if the candle remained in the middle of the table. No light was able to escape the beam and penetrate into the darkness of the room.

They stood there transfixed as the table and the beam of light began to rotate in opposite directions. The only time the light was able to escape its restricted area was as the two triangular shapes spun out of unison, allowing the protruding points to penetrate all the way to the floor. When they each had completed their opposite rotations, the light remained on and the shadow image suddenly reappeared.

Captivated by the return of the creature, they were frozen in disbelief as they stood there staring at the entity. Several seconds had passed when Allen sporadically shattered the eerie silence their fear had caused. "Where is my brother? We've gathered all your precious stones and now we want Raun back!" Allen demanded.

The shadow made no movement with the exception of its head, turning it ever so slightly to face Allen who had made the recent demand. Then in a low, deep-toned voice the creature spoke, "In time your friend will be returned to you, but you are not finished yet. There is yet another stone needed to complete the star. When it is in place, I shall set him free."

"Why should we believe you?" Jeff shouted at the creature.

"Perhaps you do not understand, this is not a choice. You will comply or your fate will be your death. And that is the only choice I will allow you to make." They could feel the anger rising in his voice.

"Once you have all of the stones you will set him free, right?" Dave blurted his way into the argument.

"That is correct," the creature responded in a slightly calmer tone.

The others could hear the disbelief in Allen's voice as he yelled, "What if we can't find our way out of here?"

"Your brother will know the way."

"Then where is the last stone at?" Allen demanded to know.

The shadow stood there motionless and silent for

several seconds., then with his free arm he pointed behind the boys with his claw like hand and said, "Behind you there are three doors." They all briefly turned around to look behind them, only to watch as three doors materialized on the wall. As they turned back around to face the entity, it resumed speaking, "One of these doors will lead you to your precious Raun, another will lead to the remaining stone. But if you choose the wrong door," the creature paused only to exhibit a short wicked laugh before continuing, "that one will lead you all to your death!"

"How do we know they all won't lead to our death?" Allen shouted in disbelief.

The shadow briefly chuckled, "Again, what choice do you have?"

"I'll show you a choice," Allen shouted as he drew the gun from his waistband. With the look of pure insanity and rage burning in his eyes, he screamed, "You're a lying son of a bitch!" The sentence was abruptly cut short as the loud echo of three shots rang out from the gun. Dave and Jeff were in shock as they made a late attempt to try covering their ears.

The shots either missed or went right through the entity and punctured a series of holes into the wall directly behind him. The creature was not amused. The fires that consumed his eyes turned into a raging inferno as he lifted his arm, aiming his claw at Allen.

Instantly, four intense bright blue bolts of electricity discharged, one from each of his claws. Dave and Jeff were paralyzed in fear as they watched Allen drop the gym bag as his body began absorbing the massive voltage being thrust into him. His body was shaking, his clothes and hair had both caught fire. Suddenly Allen's eyeballs exploded, all you could smell was burnt skin and singed hair. The shadow lowered his arm and Allen's charred, lifeless body fell limply to the floor as the flow of electricity stopped posthaste. A loud clanking sound rang out as the butt of the gun slammed into the ground, tightly fused in Allen's lifeless hand.

"No!" Jeff cried out as he broke out of the frozen state Allen's death had put them into. Still screaming in disbelief, he collapsed to the floor where he laid his head down on Allen's bare black, still smoking chest.

Dave also had started to cry as he began shouting at the creature, "Why! You didn't have to kill him! The shots didn't even hit you!"

As the shadow stood there virtually motionless, he began shaking his head back and fourth as he spoke in his deep agitated voice, "Your friend tried to destroy me so now he ceases to exist, which is what will happen to you all. So you will comply with what must be done."

Dave pointed at the entity with his index finger and shouted, "You will hold up to your end of the deal! Or we will find a way to kill you!" he threatened.

The shadow again started to laugh in his evil tone before saying, "Your efforts are vain against me, but you are free to try whatever you like. But now you are aware this is not some kind of game and that I have no use for any of you. So make your decisions wise ones, then maybe your fate won't be the same as your friends."

With that said, the image disappeared and the beam of light vanished as if someone had turned it off by a switch. The candle was back in the center of the table with the wick extinguished, looking as if it had never been lit.

PART NINE

Cryptic Choice

As Allen's dead body laid at Dave's feet charred to the bone, Jeff tried to force himself to stop crying as he stood up and embraced Dave in a tight bear hug. They were both struggling to retain control over their emotions when Jeff broke down and lost it. "Can't we just go home, I just wanna go home," he pleaded.

Dave pulled away from the bear hug and grabbed Jeff by the shoulders, slightly shaking him as he said, "We can't. We have to try to save Raun."

Jeff was mortally scared, letting fear flow out through his words. "He's probably already dead," he cried out, "we didn't even hear his voice with the last stone."

"I know, it's not a good sign, but we can't leave until we know for sure, he wouldn't leave us."

Jeff spun around to break free from Dave's tight grip on his shoulders, causing him to drop the book onto the floor. Jeff was trying to regain some type of control over this insane situation, but all he was able to do was turn his fear into a profound need for revenge. "You're right! We've gotta try. But if we can, let's find a way to kill that freak too. He's gotta pay for this," Jeff was on the brink of hyperventilating as he tried to own this second wind of courage.

"I agree, but for now we're forced to play the game by his rules," Dave reminded him.

"His rules suck!" Jeff stated, "that thing scares me, what about you?"

"I know," Dave mumbled, "me too."

They stood there for a moment, staring down at Allen's torched body when Jeff suddenly suggested, "I think we should bring the gun with us."

Dave questionably agreed, "You're probably right, but I'm not sure of how much good it'll do. We don't know if Allen missed, or if the shots just had no effect?"

Jeff tried to lighten the loss of their friend, reassuring Dave as well as himself, "This is Allen we're talking about, so we'll just assume that he missed."

"You're probably right," Dave agreed. "The gun itself didn't seem to be a problem until Allen decided to take a couple of shots at him."

Jeff felt a little better since his brother agreed with him, "I think I feel better just knowing we have it, even if it is useless."

With that decided, Dave bent down and pried the gun from Allen's scorched hand and picked up the gym bag. He then stood back up and embraced Jeff in another hug over the top of Allen's body. As they separated, Dave was trying to fight off his tears and said, "Well bro, just in case one or both of us don't make it through this, I love ya."

"I know, me too. We are gonna make it through this and kill that freak too."

"Enough worrying about the worst case scenario," Dave suggested. "Let's just get this last stone, get Raun back and get the hell out of here."

"Yeah," Jeff agreed. "Now all we have to do is choose a door. Got any ideas?"

"The middle one, definitely the middle on." Dave suggested, sounding as if he knew for sure.

"Why's that?" Jeff asked.

"Because to me it's the obvious choice."

"All right then," Jeff agreed. "Let's do this for Raun and Allen."

They both knelt down at Allen's side and had a final moment of silence over his charred remains to say their last goodbyes, knowing it was going to take more then a little luck for them not to be joining him shortly. When the moment was over, they both happened to raise their heads at the same time. They happened to make eye contact and could each see the intense fear reflecting in the others eyes.

Jeff grabbed the tablet off of the floor as he stood up. With their one remaining flashlight, they made their way around the shrine and headed for the center door. As they stood there in front of the door, Dave reached out for the handle but stopped upon contact. He had touched the handle with no more then a fingertip when they all of a sudden felt another cool draft blow through the room as the other two doors vanished simultaneously into thin air.

In a panicked voice Jeff asked, "Did you see that? Why did that happen?"

Dave shrugged his shoulders with the same confused look in his eyes, "I guess it means that we've made our choice and that it is final."

"That ain't fair! What if we change our minds? How does he know we wanted this door?"

"At least it's the door we wanted," Dave reminded Jeff, trying to offset his sudden hysteria.

"But what if we didn't?" Jeff asked. "It's like he's making up the rules as we go."

"I know," Dave agreed. "We can't trust him, but if you think about it, any door we'd have chosen would have led to the room he wants us in anyway."

"It still ain't right," Jeff insisted.

"Come on Jeff, let's just get going. This freak makes me sick."

Jeff was standing behind Dave as he slowly grabbed a hold of the handle. He gave it a twist and cautiously began to push the door open. Ever so carefully, they stepped into the room hoping they hadn't made the wrong choice. As they glanced around the room with their only flashlight, they began calling out to Raun.

With no reply from their friend, they realized they had chosen the room with the final stone and not the one that could lead them to their friend or death. The room itself was very similar to the one with the silver table in it. The walls, floor and ceiling were all painted jet black. This room was virtually empty. Similar yet was the fact that the main content of this room was only one object. This time, that one object wasn't a weird looking table, it was two separate cylinders, each about six inches in diameter. One hung down from the ceiling like a stalactite, the other protruded from the floor like a stalagmite. Each piece was approximately four feet long and stood aligned vertically to each other. A six inch gap separated the two cylindrical pipes from being one solid piece. To their amazement, the sixth stone floated effortlessly in the void gently spinning as it hovered in the vortex.

The tubes were hollow and the air flow coming from each of the cylinders was pulling in opposite directions. This system prevented the stone from falling down the lower shaft protruding from the floor, while simultaneously preventing it from being sucked into the upper chute hanging down from the ceiling.

They stood in the doorway, bewildered as they stared at the stone. The stone appeared to be a large, perfectly cut diamond with a clear bluish tint to it. The beauty of the gem was captivating as it seemed to harness and amplify what little light it was able to collect in the dark room. They couldn't get over their amazement of how this beautiful gem was floating ever so graciously between the two cylinders. Jeff looked over to Dave and suggested, "I'll grab it."

"Are you sure?" Dave asked.

"Yeah, I'll be fine," Jeff replied.

Dave decided to hold his ground and stand in the doorway. He hoped that if he was standing there the door wouldn't slam shut, vanish, or worse yet, re-materialize around him, in a sense, freezing him in carbonite like what happened to Han Solo in Star Wars. Dave was actually reconsidering this plan as Jeff was nearing the stone. Trying to take his mind off of his likely poor decision, he thought about how the diamond had to be the most flawless stone anyone had ever seen and that it was probably worth a fortune. With his brother now standing in front of it, he was stood there in awe as he watched it spinning freely as it graciously floated between the two cylinders. He paused for a moment to take in the marvel he was looking at.

Finally building up his courage, he reached out for the stone ever so slowly and then with one quick yank he grabbed it, removing it from the air flow it had been gracefully resting on. With the precious stone tightly clinched in his fist, he finally exhaled, completely unaware he had even been holding his breath. It was so loud, Dave was able to hear him exhale from all the way across the room.

Dave could tell Jeff was also surprised that something crazy didn't happen as soon as the stone was removed it from its suspended state. Jeff was still standing next to the cylinders as he examined the eccentric stone for a moment. Satisfied, he began walking over toward where Dave was still standing in the doorway, when he got there he sat down. Leaning against the wall, he told Dave to take a seat. Still paranoid the door could vanish, he sat down in the center of the doorway. Jeff inched his way a little closer toward Dave. Opening his hand, he exposed the stone enabling Dave to give it a closer look.

Dave plucked it from Jeff's hand and set the book down between them. He opened the cover, revealing the silver tablet and the five red gems, forming the shape of a star. The only remaining slot was a perfect match to this diamonds unique large shape. Neither of them could grasp how this stone could have been cut with such precision, especially for as old as it must be. It was crystal clear, flawless and shimmered blue if it caught the light correctly at certain angles. Instead of maintaining the traditional princess cut, the stones facet had a peculiar diamond shaped slot cut into the top that penetrated all the way through the stone. Because of this strange design, there were two separate points at the tip with a quarter inch gap separating them.

With the awkward shaped stone loosely rolling around in the palm of Dave's hand, Jeff asked, "What the hell is all this about?"

"I wish I knew," Dave replied, "all I know is it needs to end soon, I don't know how much more of this craziness I can take." They remained sitting there as Dave continued to examine the stone.

Jeff grabbed Dave's arm by the wrist and asked, "Do you think we're making a mistake? I mean, by giving him all of the stones."

"A mistake?" Dave replied. "Hell, I don't know. All I know is Allen's dead, Raun's missing and that shadow freak said he'd give us Raun back and let us go home if we gave him all of the stones."

"Do you think he'll do it?" Jeff asked, not wanting to think about the alternative.

"If not," Dave paused, "we're in a lot of trouble."

"I know, he'll have what he wanted and we'll have nothing left to bargain with."

Dave again began glancing over the empty room as he shined the light. Confused, shaking his head back and fourth he suggested, "But if he was going to kill us, he's had plenty of opportunities. I just don't understand any of this."

"I know, that's what doesn't make any sense," Jeff paused. "I guess all we can do now is hope he keeps his word and lets us go."

"I just wish we wouldn't have let Allen talk us into coming out here," Dave said, "And I should smack you a good one for siding with him."

"Trust me, I wish I would've taken your side now," Jeff proclaimed.

"Oh well, nothing we can do about it now," Dave answered, "but next time, you'll know..." Dave's voice trailed off, realizing there could never be a next time now that Allen had passed.

Sitting in silence, momentarily lost in their thoughts, Dave began to fidget hopelessly as he twirled the stone in the palm of his hand. When the moment had passed, he handed Jeff the flashlight and gym bag as they climbed to their feet. Placing the gun in his waistband, he precariously held the gem between his index finger and thumb with the sharp double point facing away from his palm.

With the tablet lying at their feet on the floor, they stood there feeling utterly defeated. Using his foot, he gently gave it a soft kick, nudging it slightly away from where they stood.

Frustrated and finally ready to get this ordeal over with, he bent down, leaned in slightly and was about to drop the gem in place, but as he stood there holding the remaining stone over the hole, he paused. His eyes rolled back, seeming to turn a dull shade of gray, before totally closing. Lost in thought, his mind began to wander. He couldn't get over the eerie feeling that he was about to do something they'd regret.

Perplexed, Jeff asked. "What's wrong?"

"Nothing," Dave replied as Jeff broke his empty train

of endless doubts, "my mind was just elsewhere."

"You sure you're OK?" Jeff asked.

"Yeah, I just wanna get this over with," Dave replied, forcing his fingers to let go, dropping the stone. As it fumbled into place Dave leaned back against the wall. They watched as the red stones began their seemingly routine light show. One by one they began to flash, this time being brighter than they had ever been before. This time the cycle didn't stop after each stone flashed once. They began flashing faster and faster until the star appeared to be spinning, now forming a solid ring of red light on both the tablet and on the ceiling. As the red stones went dormant, a sudden blast of blue light shot out from the center stone. There was an ear shattering sound that could only have came from the eight foot hole that abruptly ripped through the ceiling as the intense blast of light and raw power seared through it like a hot knife through butter.

The immense force of the explosion knocked Dave clear through the doorway he'd been leaning against and all the way into the next room. Jeff wasn't as fortunate, he wasn't standing in the doorway, so the brutal force of the blast slammed him violently right through the wall, creating a gaping hole and almost dislocating his shoulder. It was amazing that neither of them had been killed in the blast.

Presumably lighting up the entire area surrounding the cabin, the sudden immense blast of light was blinding as it illuminated both rooms in addition to pouring out into the night through the giant hole in the freshly decimated roof.

After being tossed when the book exploded through the wall and into the room with the table, Jeff struggled, trying to regain his composure as he slowly crawled to his feet and started looking for Dave. Barely able to see, his eyes were slowly starting to adjust now that he was facing away from the intense beam pouring in through the doorway.

Dave was also starting to climb back to his feet after being flung like a rag doll. “Are you alright?” Jeff asked him.

“Yeah,” winded, he replied, “what the hell was that?” Holding his head he narrowed his eyes, trying not to look directly into the doorway.

“I’m not sure, but I think the book blew up?” Jeff tried to explain.

“The book exploded?” Dave repeated. “Are you sure?”

Jeff finished helping Dave to his feet. Once he was standing on his own, he adjusted the gun in his waistband and was thankful it didn't go off, accidentally shooting himself. As their twisted reality started coming back into focus, he bent down and picked up the gym bag, he then handed it to Jeff in exchange for the flashlight. With the intense light radiating in from the other room he wasn’t even sure it was still working, much to his surprise, it was.

“Let’s go check it out,” Dave suggested, referring to the room they had just been thrown out of. As curiosity prevailed, they started making their way toward the door. The light coming from the room was so bright, it looked as if a thousand floodlights were all on inside that small confined area. Closing their eyes almost entirely, they were barely able to see the dark outline of the tablet as it lay on the floor where they had left it. Strangely, it looked as if hundreds of hands and claws were grasping at the floor, trying to climb out of it. The rest of the room was so intensely bright, it was impossible to try focusing on what they hoped they only imagined to be seeing.

“Very good,” the familiar low voice called out to them. They both nearly jumped out of their shoes as they recognized the eerie fact that the voice sounded as if the creature was standing right behind them.

CHAPTER THREE
THE RETURN

The silver shrine behind them had again turned itself on, revealing the triangular beam of light with the shadow creature standing motionless inside of it. They could barely even distinguish the beam as it was almost totally absorbed by the light coming in from the next room. Again like someone had flicked a switch, the intense glow coming from the room behind them yielded and dissipated as the table had now taken over their full attention. Once again they found themselves surrounded by darkness, the only exceptions were the triangular beam of light confined to the tables shape and the dimming light they were receiving from their only remaining flashlight.

As their eyes adjusted to yet another sudden change, they noticed the shadow was now wearing the stones from the book. The silver tablet was gone and the gems were now fashioned into a silver medallion that hung around his neck in the pentagram shape of an upside down star.

Jeff yelled at the creature, “Where’s Raun?”

“Yeah,” Dave added. “You said you’d release him and let us go once you had all of the stones!”

With the fires of hell raging in his eyes, the shadow responded, “I will return Raun to you and you could go home, but why would you want too? You have plainly seen all of my powers and I can make all of you more powerful than you could ever imagine.”

“You’re evil!” Jeff shouted.

“And you killed our friend!” Dave interrupted. “Just give us Raun back and let us go.”

“Fine,” the shadow replied, “but you've made the wrong decision.”

With that said, the light from the table slowly faded out, then it suddenly reignited for an additional fraction of a second, immediately followed by a loud "thump-thud" sound. Raun materialized out of the darkness that used to be the beam of light, falling forcefully onto the table's surface. With the cabin back to a state of semi reality, Dave curiously looked behind him into the other room. Shining the light through the open doorway, he confirmed the fact that the tablet had vanished and the stones the shadow wore around his neck were the ones they'd retrieved for him. Dave turned back around, following behind Jeff as he was helping Raun to his feet. He no more than stood up, shouting, "Do you idiots realize what you did?"

"Yeah, we saved you!" Davc quickly replied. Jeff had embraced Raun in a bear hug as he continued to protest to Dave's remark.

"No! You didn't, he tricked you."

"What do you mean?" Dave asked.

"I kept trying to warn you, you shouldn't have put all of those stones back together."

"Why?" Jeff asked, pulling away from the hug.

"Those stones form some kind of gateway to the dark underworld and he was trapped there," Raun tried to explain.

"What do you mean, was?" Dave asked, struggling to comprehend.

"But he was out already," Jeff insisted, failing to understand what Raun was trying to say.

"No!" Raun said raising his voice. "He wasn't, but now he is and he's free to roam the surface world now."

"I don't understand," Dave said in panicked tone.

"When I fell down and cut myself, that tablet was on the table," Raun started to explain, "somehow, my blood woke the beast and brought this evil cabin back to life, but that was the limit to his powers."

"A ghost?" Jeff implied.

"Yeah," Raun agreed, "but he's not just a ghost anymore, now he's a demon and he's loose."

"What's the difference?" Dave asked beginning to pace the floor.

"He's a lot stronger now and he is able to take on a physical form."

"What does that mean?" Jeff asked.

"Now he can take on the shape or body of all those grotesque looking creatures you've been finding throughout the cabin."

"So that's why we've only saw him as an image in the light," Dave mumbled, starting to grasp the insanity of the situation.

"Exactly," Raun agreed.

"How do we put him back?" Dave asked.

"Or better yet," Jeff interrupted, "how do we kill him?"

"Somewhere in this cabin there's a special dagger," Raun suggested.

Where's it at?" Dave asked curiously.

"I'm not exactly sure," Raun replied, "but it's in here somewhere."

"What if he won't let us find it?" Jeff asked.

"Really!" Dave agreed. "He might not even let us find the room it's in."

"We have to," Raun demanded. "It's the only way we can stop him. And we have to do it no matter how hard he makes it."

"Is this demon the man behind all of the myths of our town?" Dave had to ask.

"Yeah," Raun agreed, "all of those stories are horribly true and there is so much more that was either never known or forgotten as the years passed by."

"Like what?" Jeff asked.

"This guy was some kind of mad scientist back in the forties during WWII, he was an expert in the field of genetics. He was working hand and hand with the Germans trying to combine human and animal DNA patterns to create a hybrid killing machine."

"Why was he trying to do that?" Dave asked.

"Hitler knew he was losing the war and he needed a new way to replenish his depleting army. Not only that, but these mutants would have been trained to fight like humans with their loyalty and abilities to follow orders."

"That's nuts!" Jeff stated.

"Not to mention," Raun continued, "they would have had an added advantage from each of the different animal's DNA they were combined with. This would have enhanced their sight, speed, strength and other aspects of their hunting abilities."

"This guys whacked!" Jeff reaffirmed.

"I just knew all of these weird looking animals were once alive," Dave said, finding it hard to be surprised.

"You're right," Raun said, "He started off just using animals, but when that started working more often than not, he moved up to incorporating humans into the equation."

"So that's why we've been finding all of these strange looking trophy mounts and weird looking skeletons," Jeff stated.

"So he killed all of those people in the name of science," Dave suggested, disgusted by the twisted motivation for murder.

"He didn't start out with that in mind," Raun said, "at

first he was a legit geneticist, but he was promised massive amounts of fame and fortune if he could replenish Hitler's diminishing army with these morbid creatures."

"Did he succeed?" Dave asked.

"Yeah eventually, but before he was able to pass on the knowledge to anyone and start mass producing them he was killed," Raun explained.

"What's the deal with that tablet?" Jeff asked. "Is that the one from Egypt?"

"That's where this all began," Raun stated. "He was working with some archaeologists on a hidden tomb discovery. He was there to study early genetics and the ancient art of mummification. They had uncovered a mass burial filled with mummified remains of all types of animals. But the prize of their excavation was the discovery of this ancient tablet and a dagger."

"What about the stones?" Dave asked.

"When he discovered everything, he was alone. He put the stones into his pocket knowing they were probably worth a fortune," Raun replied.

"He took the tablet and dagger too, right?" Jeff asked, already knowing the answer to his question.

"That was how Hitler obtained his services. It was a down payment on the promise that he could produce an endless supply of a genetically enhanced army of soldiers."

"So these stones must've made all of this possible?" Dave assumed.

"Exactly," Raun agreed. "He could only partially translate the hieroglyphics at first, but when he figured them out he was able to make his creatures live."

"That's crazy," Jeff said.

"It cost him his soul and then he was murdered before he got the chance to cash in on disbursing the knowledge,"

Raun explained.

Dave walked back over to the table and began tracing his fingers over the engravings on the surface as he asked, "So what do you know about this gateway?" Raun and Jeff had followed Dave over to the table and were watching him as he continued to trace over the images, seemingly totally lost in his thoughts.

"Man, you guys really screwed up," Raun whispered, "I know that you did it accidentally, trying to save me, but I kept trying to warn you."

Dave turned his head to face Raun insisting, "We couldn't hear what you were trying to tell us."

"I know," Raun replied, shaking his head. "He only let you hear enough of my voice so that you'd still know I was alive. That way you'd keep looking for the stones."

"It seemed like with each stone we found, the longer we were able to hear your voice," Dave tried to explain.

"That's because with each surge of power, it became harder and harder for him to silence my words."

"Where the hell were you at?" Jeff curiously asked.

"I was trapped right here, in this room," Raun insisted. "Somehow he made me invisible, it was like I was paralyzed. I couldn't move, or speak."

"The whole time we've been looking for these stones?" Jeff asked, just baffled by the thought of it.

"After you guys left, he showed me what it was you were doing in the form of a hologram. It appeared in the light that came off of the table's surface, much like the image of himself that he presented to you."

"Then you know about Allen?" Dave asked as a tear formed in the corner of his eye.

Raun seemed to be holding back and hiding his emotions as he answered, "Yeah, I saw that too, that's why he totally silenced me from talking to you. He was starting to realize that I would never side with him and by that point in time, you had given him enough of the stones to make him powerful enough to totally cut me off."

"So before we started collecting the stones, he didn't have any powers?" Jeff wondered aloud.

"At first, his image and ability to keep changing the layout of the cabin was all in our minds for the most part."

Dave turned to face Raun with a confused look on his face, "You mean like a group hallucination?"

"Yeah," Raun agreed. "My blood gave him just enough strength to trick you into believing he was already powerful."

"But why did he snatch you up?" Jeff asked Raun.

"He had the most power over me because it was my blood that was waking the beast. That is what brought his spirit back to the surface world."

"And now he's free?" Dave mumbled to himself.

"With the blood alone, he was still bound by the chains of hell, but with each stone that you retrieved for him, the chains that bound him began to loosen their hold."

"So he needs your blood to survive?" Dave asked.

"No," Raun replied. "With each stone he became more powerful and less dependent on my blood for his survival."

"How come you didn't try to come after us?" Jeff asked Raun.

"As soon as you guys left the room my paralysis broke. But when I ran toward the door, it vanished."

Dave rolled his eyes back, slightly chuckling, "I know how you feel. I'm about tired of doors and stairs vanishing and appearing right before my eyes."

"I think if you wouldn't have given him all of the

stones, we'd have all been free as soon as my blood dried completely," Raun remarked, "I mean thanks for trying to save me, but now we messed up big time and we have to find a way to fix it."

Paranoid and growing suspicious, Dave asked, "How do you know so much anyway?"

Raun stalled for a moment as he quietly thought to himself, finally answering, "It's kind of like when Eric sold his soul to the devil. He tricked you into something similar. He agreed to release me and let me return home once you gave him the stones."

"What's your point?" Jeff asked.

"My point is," Raun snapped at Jeff, "he conveniently didn't say that we could all return home, just me."

"Oh great!" Jeff shouted into the room.

"But you're still here and we're still stuck in this cabin," Dave pointed out.

Raun turned to face the door, slowly pointing to it. "If we walk out that door, it won't be just another room. It'll be the front door. All he has to do to fulfill his end of the contract is to let me leave the cabin and he's already more powerful than you can even imagine."

Frustrated and still feeling paranoid, Dave walked over to Raun and gave him a push several feet backwards, shouting at him, "You still haven't told us how you know so much!" Pushing him again he added, "What 'cha guys do, sit down and shoot the shit over coffee?"

"No," Raun defended himself, "It's like he said when we first encountered him, he is I and I am he," Raun paused, "Remember?"

"Is that what he meant by that?" Dave asked, still confused and getting more frustrated by the moment.

"Yeah," Raun agreed, "but before he was mainly

limited just to having power over me. Now his only limitations are that of the contract, meaning the only thing he can't do is kill me and that's only until I've been home."

"At least you know that you're safe," Jeff said, showing his jealousy.

"Not really!" Raun replied. "I don't know whether that means my bed, my doorstep or just too far away from this cabin."

"What about us?" Dave proclaimed. "He's already killed Allen."

"He can kill either one of you, at any time. That's the way he worded the contract, I'm the only one he has to let leave and even that is only until I've been home."

"Well that shit just ain't right!" Dave protested. "We risked our asses to save you and all along, you were the only one that was safe."

"Really," Jeff added, "what a crock of shit!"

"But he knows if he kills you guys off, I will have no reason to return home," Raun said, trying to reassure them a little. "And if I don't go home, I really become a thorn in his side. Because if he can't kill me, he'll never have the full use of his powers."

"Why's that?" Jeff curiously asked.

"Since it was my blood that started this mess, I share in his powers and knowledge and he's greedy and wants it all. But like I said, that can't happen until I'm dead."

"Can we stop him?" Dave asked.

"I'm not sure," Raun hesitantly answered. "But we have to try, somehow, we have to get them stones back and separate them once and for all."

"Can't we all just go home and forget this ever happened?" Jeff begged.

"No!" Raun shouted. "He'll kill all of us! He plans on

finishing what he started years ago. But that can't happen until I'm dead. Then he'll become unstoppable and destroy the whole world."

With fear and doubt overpowering his words Dave mumbled, "Well, we just can't let that happen then, so what's the real deal, are you okay or what?" Satisfied with Raun's explanation for why he knew so much. He eagerly asked sincerely concerned about his well being.

"Pretty much so," Raun started to explain, "but I have been noticing a few small changes."

"Like what?" Jeff asked.

"Nothing real big," Raun said, trying to prepare them for what they were about to hear. "Just the fact that the skin on my legs, arms and back is slowly turning into the skin of a reptile."

"What?" Jeff asked, shocked by what he was hearing.

Raun continued, "And my head feels a little funny since his thoughts are intertwined with mine."

"What do you mean by that?" Dave asked, perplexed.

"I know a lot about his past and most of his plans for the future. The only thing I don't know is where this dagger is, that's how I knew so much about about his past."

"I was wondering about all that," Dave agreed, adding, "well, we're not getting anything accomplished just standing here, lets get moving."

Dave retracted the gun from his waistband as they all made their way over to the doorway. Grabbing the handle he slowly gave it a twist and slowly pushed the door open. Realizing that it did indeed lead them out onto the front porch, they were still baffled and slightly confused as they stepped outside. Much to their surprise, instead of being overwhelmed with fresh breathable air, the outside of the cabin had the same overpowering foul odor as the interior.

PART TWO
The Dagger

It was dark outside, there was a dark bluish gray overcast blanketing most of the sky. There was only one small break in the clouds revealing just a sliver of the moon with a single bright star shining just below and slightly offset to the right of the moon. The combination of the two gave off only slightly more light than what they had inside the cabin with the aid of their lone remaining flashlight. Standing on the porch, Jeff just happened to glance to the side and suddenly caught a glimpse of Raun's face out of the corner of his eye.

"Raun, your eyes, they're glowing red!" Jeff shouted with fear and surprise in his eyes.

"I know Jeff," Raun said calmly, "I can feel it. He must be up to something, but somehow he's blocking my thoughts and I can't tell what he's trying to do."

"Let's get back inside the cabin for a sec," Dave suggested. "If he's up to something, it's only because he knows that we're about to leave the cabin."

"You're right," Raun agreed, "and if we get too far away from the cabin, he'll be able to kill us all. For now, his powers are only limited to the immediate area surrounding the cabin."

"This just keeps getting weirder and weirder," Jeff stated.

"I know all of this sounds crazy, but it's true. The farther I get away from the cabin, the stronger he'll become," Raun explained.

With that said, they made up their minds. They had to go back into the cabin and find the way to destroy this entity they had accidentally released. They turned around and started heading back through the doorway. They had barely made it all the way through when they suddenly froze dead in their tracks, unable to believe their eyes. Somehow as they stepped back through the doorway that had just led them onto the front porch, they oddly once again found themselves standing on the front porch. Stunned and confused, they all turned around once again to peer through the still open doorway. Much to their dismay, it too, also still led to the front porch.

"What the shit!" Dave shouted, continuing to glance back and fourth between the two identical scenes. "Both sides of this door lead to the same exact spot."

"What the hell is going on here?" Jeff added. "How are we supposed to get back inside?"

Dave began to pace hopelessly back and fourth across the porch as he mumbled mainly to himself, "This just doesn't make any sense. We're standing on the front porch," he paused, stepping through the doorway before continuing, "and If we go through the door, we're still on the porch. How the hell are we supposed to get back inside if the inside don't even exist?" He was shouting as he completed his train of thought.

"He's trying to trick us," Raun explained, with the hint of the red hue still glimmering in his eyes. "He knows that I'm aware he can't kill me until I leave."

"So how are we supposed to find him and separate the stones if we can't even get back inside the cabin?" Jeff asked.

"Really, what are we supposed to do? Go back down the trail and start over?" Dave asked, lacking the ability to conger up a question that made any sense.

"No!" Raun shouted. Gaining their full attention, he continued, "We can't do that! If he's somehow tricks me into getting too far away from the cabin, he'll kill me. Then he'll be unstoppable and I don't even know exactly where my boundaries are."

"Somehow we've got to get back inside," Dave proclaimed. "Hold on, did you hear that?" he whispered, thinking he was hearing things.

"Shhh!" Jeff seconded. "I heard it too, but what the hell was it?"

Standing there, paralyzed in a trance like state, they continued glancing back and fourth between both identical versions of the front yard.

"It sounded like someone stepped on a stick or something," Raun suggested as they heard the snapping sound of yet another twig. This one sounded even closer, like what ever broke it was virtually right on top of them. Frightened, as they were unable to locate the cause of the sound. Suddenly breaking the eerie silence, a loud menacing roar of a mountain lion echoed through their bones. Immediately, they all turned their heads to face the left side of the porch they were standing on. With their eyes focused on the tall moving grass, they were finally able to catch a glimpse of the large carnivore stalking them.

It was everything they never wanted to imagine, half human, half mountain lion and the ultimate predator. The head, chest and front legs were that of the biggest mountain lion they had ever saw. From the waist down it was blatantly obvious that its hind legs once belonged to some unfortunate soul. The fact that its legs were covered entirely with thick light brown fur spoke volumes to the bestial genes dominating the genetic composition of this hellish creature.

Crouched down and poised to strike, it sat there motionless, trying to conceal itself under the dense cover of tall wispy grass. Looking perturbed it had been discovered before taking down its prey, it stared at them with solid black beady eyes and a look so cold and empty, it could freeze water with only a passing glimpse.

Luckily for them, they'd spotted it first. Overcome with fear, Raun quietly whispered, “Don’t move a muscle.”

Suddenly the cat creature let out another ferocious roar as it stood up on its hind legs and quickly took several giant strides toward them. It reached the edge of the porch and effortlessly leapt over the railing. They all began screaming out of control as they spun around in unison and dove back through the door. Raun was the last one to make it through the doorway and somehow managed to slam it shut on his way through.

Immediately following the loud sound of the door slamming shut, came the resounding crash made by the cat creature slamming thunderously into the door. They'd all dove through the doorway with such urgency and force that they nearly cleared the whole rickety porch. Landing in the tall grass of the mirrored image on the other side. The cat roared intently several times as it continued pawing at the door with hopes of forcing it open. Abruptly, everything around them became dead silent and it appeared that the cat had given up. Shaken to the core, the only thing they were able to hear was the beating of their own hearts as they slowly began climbing to their feet from where they had landed.

“Did you guys get a look at that thing?” Jeff asked hysterically.

“Hell yeah I saw that thing! I knew as soon as we started finding all of those weird looking skeletons we would eventually stumble across a living one! I just knew it!” Dave rattled off, still trying to catch his breath.

Frustration, fear and anger had taken over most of their emotions as they stood there on the porch trying to gather their thoughts. Feeling like they were starting to lose their minds, they came to accept the morbid fact they were rapidly losing what little control of the situation they assumed they had. “Damn it!” Dave shouted as he walked over to the door and slammed his fists forcefully against it. “How the hell are we supposed to get back inside?”

Jeff was standing only a few feet from Dave. They all seemed lost deep in their own thoughts when he suddenly realized there was a more eminent question deserving of their immediate and full consideration. “Hey guys,” he said, trying to garner what little attention they'd part with. “Can that cat thing be in this outside, or just the other one?”

Dave nearly jumped out of his shoes suddenly realizing the severity of what Jeff proposed. Quickly, he turned to face the tall grass and shined the light randomly about, scanning for that cat or anything else that might wish to see how they taste. With this new cryptic possibility in the forefront of their mind, they all started to make their way over to the door.

Dave was holding the gun tightly clinched in his fist as he began to slowly inch the door open just a sliver. Peering through the small crack, he wasn’t able to see anything out of the ordinary on the other version of this porch. Perplexed, he anxiously stood there momentarily as he continued canvassing the mirrored porch. He abruptly pulled the door shut as he suddenly had an epiphany and everything began to make sense. “He’s trying to trick us into leaving, right?” he blurted out, almost shouting.

“Yeah,” Raun agreed, shrugging his shoulders.

“Where are we right now?” Dave asked, sounding as if he had officially lost his mind. Jeff and Raun were just standing there with a forced look of confusion burned into their eyes.

“What's that supposed to mean?” Jeff asked, forcing himself to speak.

Sounding as crazy as he looked, Dave asked again,

"Are we inside or outside right now?"

Raun giggled a little as he stared at Dave, positive that he had totally lost his mind. "We're outside. You really should open your eyes and look around before you ask stupid questions."

It seemed that Dave had forgotten about their close encounter with the mountain lion creature and resumed pacing back and fourth across the porch and said, "No you guys, seriously. Look, we were in a room in the middle of the cabin. We walked through one door and wound up standing on the front porch."

"What are you trying to say?" Raun interrupted.

"Damn it, hold up a sec!" Dave demanded to finish his sentence. Trying to continue, "That cat thing, it scared us back through the same door we came out through and now we're on the front porch again. Think about it, in all actuality, we should still be in the room with the table in it, or even the library, but definitely not on the porch."

"He's right," Raun agreed. "We should be right where we started, this shits crazy."

"What are we gonna do?" Jeff asked.

"I think I can change the cabin back to its original layout. But his part of the power is a lot stronger than mine ever since you dip shits gave him all of the stones," Raun stated.

"How were we supposed to know?" Dave snapped at Raun.

"You couldn't have," Raun grudgingly agreed. "It's just that none of this would've ever happened off the strength of my blood alone," Raun briefly paused, "but it's too late for that now, he's got the stones."

"If I can help it, he won't have them long," Dave cut in, trying to boost everyone's spirits.

"Do you really think you can bring this place back to half ass normal?" Jeff asked with a glimmer of hope.

"I'm pretty sure, let me give it a try."

With that said, Raun dropped down to his knees and raised his arms straight up over his head. Reaching out as if he was trying to grab a piece of the sky, he leaned forward and rested his hands and forehead on the surface of the porch like someone using a prayer mat. Dave and Jeff stood there in silence as Raun appeared in a state of deep concentration. A few seconds had passed by when suddenly, right before their eyes, the whole area started to flash back and fourth between the porch and the room with the silver table where this all began. With a strobe light effect taking place all around them, it was hard for them to focus on any one thing in particular. With the scenery randomly flickering with the unstable images, it reminded them of a hologram losing its power.

After several awkward seconds, the unstable images leveled out and the porch finally returned to the dark room with the silver table in the center. Raun laid there on the floor for a few seconds longer as the cabin returned to what they could only assume was its original design. It wasn't too much longer before Raun slowly started climbing back to his feet, but his efforts fell short as he suddenly fainted, limply collapsing back to the floor with a thud. With no time to react, Dave and Jeff could only watch in horror as the whole ordeal appeared to happen in slow motion. Immediately, they ran to his side and Dave asked, "Are you alright?"

As he slowly came to, Raun lifted his head and looked Dave in the eyes with a look of pure exhaustion wearing thin on his face and replied, "Yeah, it's just taking a lot of my energy to hold the real image of this cabin rather than the one he wants us to see." Genuinely concerned, Dave helped Raun climb back to his feet as he continued, "I can actually feel him fighting my use of the powers right now."

"What do you mean, what's he doing?" Jeff asked.

"I don't know that," Raun paused briefly, "but I can tell you one thing for sure."

"What's that?" Dave asked impatiently.

"It's not going to be easy for us to get them stones back. He helped you find them before. But now that he has them, he's not gonna just give them back to you because you changed your mind."

"How are we even gonna know where to look?" Dave asked.

"I don't know," Raun replied, "but we have to find them if we're gonna stop him."

"We'd better get started then, there's no telling how long this is going to take," Dave paused, "and let's not get out if each others sight. We don't wanna get separated again."

Surprised to actually be looking at it, they all started making their way over to the double door they'd originally entered this room through. When they opened the door, they were even more amazed that it actually led them back into the dining room. They were almost overwhelmed by the fact that something in this cabin was where they knew it was supposed to be.

While they were ecstatic about this being the right room, everything was yet to return to the way they'd originally found it. Once again they found themselves unable to comprehend the correct layout of this cabin. The hidden stairwell in front of the fireplace was still open and where they had left it. But again, there was no other exit out of this room.

They all refused to let any of this bother them. They had grown virtually immune to rooms changing right before their eyes. They found they could tolerate dealing with that situation a lot easier than a two sided porch that they couldn't get off of. "Do you think the dagger is in here?" Dave asked Raun.

"I don't know," Raun paused, "he's blocking me out of his thoughts. That way I can't figure out where he hid it before he died."

"Then we've gotta search everything," Dave stated, he began to shake his head in doubt as he continued, "we don't even know what it looks like."

"We'll know it when we see it," Raun said confidently as they began searching the room. They searched everywhere they had looked before in their efforts to locate the stones. It didn't take long before they were running out of places to look. Their patience was wearing thin and the thought of never finding this dagger was starting to overpower their hopeful minds. By now they were certain they were not going to find the dagger in this room at all. It would be a miracle if they were going to find it anywhere, especially with Jeff carrying their only remaining flashlight.

"This is absolutely hopeless," Dave cried out. "It could be almost anywhere, if it's here at all?"

"It's here somewhere," Raun stated, trying to reassure him. "We can't give up, it's our only chance." He finished his sentence, reaffirming their dire situation.

"I know," Dave agreed. "I'm just getting frustrated, this whole situation is nuts!"

"Squawk, Squawk," A loud irritating bird like noise appeared to be echoing from the basement.

Frightened by the sudden outburst, their hearts all skipped a beat as Dave shouted, "What the hell was that?" They began spinning aimlessly around in a circle as they scanned over the room hoping they were not about to be attacked. They tried desperately, but were unable to locate the source of the loud ear piercing sound.

"I don't know," Jeff replied, "but I think it came from downstairs," pointing toward the wall with the hidden entrance through the fireplace.

Determined to locate the source of this loud obnoxious noise, they started making their way over to the stairwell. "Do you think we should go back down there?" Jeff asked, unsure of whether he liked the thought of that.

"It can't hurt," Raun replied. "We've already searched everywhere in here, maybe that's some kind of sign indicating we should move on?"

"Maybe it's a warning?" Jeff stated, before handing Dave the flashlight adding, "here, you go first."

Reluctantly, Dave accepted the flashlight and started leading them down the narrow rickety passageway into the basement. When they made it to the closed door at the bottom of the stairwell, they once again heard that loud squawking sound. Holding his breath, Dave forced himself to turn the handle. Ever so slowly, he began pushing the door open. As he began shining the light around the room, he recognized they were about to enter the strange cryptic lab. That was actually somewhat comforting because he didn't know how many more bizarre rooms he could tolerate. Although this room was the one he hated the most, it appeared to look the same as before. Intensely scanning over the room, he still wasn't able to locate the source of the eerie loud noise.

"Look. Over there!" Jeff shouted from behind him.

Panic and fear were running through Dave's veins as he struggled to find what had caught Jeff's full attention. "What, where?" he shouted, eagerly wanting to know.

"On top of that last cage, the one on the right," Jeff stated.

As Dave shined the dimming light into the area that

Jeff was indicating. The light was barely able to penetrate through the full length of the room. Fortunately, it was still bright enough to outline the large silhouette of what they were looking at. They couldn't believe what they were seeing, they were looking at an enormous jet black raven. The only variation in its color were its grayish beak and the dim light reflecting a faint red glimmer off its small beady black eyes.

"Squawk," the large bird demanded their attention.

Standing there admiring this awesome sight, they truly didn't know what to make of this monstrous raven. The bird began to flap its large wings as it took flight across the lab. It was heading right for them as they stood transfixed in the doorway. Flying full speed at them, the boys had to duck as the bird flew past, clearing them by no more than a few inches. Still in shock, they turned around to look behind them only to learn the bird had kept going and completely disappeared.

Once again they found themselves standing in the stone silence of this mysterious cabin. Confused, they didn't know what to make of the whole bizarre experience. Jeff was the fist to regain his ability to speak and said, "It's gotta be in here, why else would that big ass bird have wanted our attention?"

"Let's check over by the cage it was perched on," Raun suggested.

Figuring there was at least some kind of logic behind Raun's suggestion, they made their way over to the far corner of the lab. When they arrived at the site where the raven was perched, they stood there looking at a large cage containing a twisted skeleton of what looked like it used to be a rabbit with bat like appendages.

"What did it want us to do, follow it?" Jeff asked, not comprehending or seeing what it was trying to show them.

"I don't think so," Dave replied with a puzzled look on his face. "It seems like if that's what it wanted, it would have just appeared while we were upstairs."

Utterly confused, they all stood there in silence as Dave continued shining the dim light in the area surrounding the cage. Unable to figure out what this bird wanted them to see, they were starting to wonder if this raven even had anything to do with their situation. Regardless, they were desperate and reaching for anything, hoping this bird was helping them out. After all, it might have just been a stray bird that found itself trapped in this cabin, taking advantage of their providing it a way out.

"Look," Raun was almost shaking, shouting as he was pointed behind the cage, "I think this is what it was trying to show us!"

Jeff was standing closest to the cage, he reached over the top of it and slid his arm down the back. After struggling for a few seconds, he carefully retracted his arm. In his hand, he was holding the mysterious dagger they were supposedly looking for. They couldn't believe they didn't happen to find it earlier when they were in here looking for the stones. They presumed they missed it because it was wedged so far back between the cage and the wall.

The dagger was just over a foot long. Almost the entire dagger was made of solid silver, the only exception was the handle. The hilt was made of pewter and it looked as if it had been meticulously hand carved. There were three holes in the handle, one on each side of the handle and one through the butt of the dagger.

"This is it," Raun stated, showing his excitement in his voice. "This is what we need in order to kill him. But I think we have to find more stones?"

"Why?" Dave drably asked. "Why can't we just use

the dagger?"

"Look," Raun interjected, "all of the points on the dagger, something is missing and these holes, they look the similar to the ones in the book."

"How do you know that?" Jeff demanded to know. "You've never even seen the book."

Raun was shocked by Jeff's accusation and became defensive, "I saw it through the holographic images he was showing me as you guys discovered each stone."

"He's right Jeff," Dave said, trying to defend Raun and defuse the situation. "These holes are almost the same as the ones in the book, the only difference is that these ones are round."

"Then tell me this!" Jeff shouted at Dave. "How are we supposed to find these stones without the shadow helping us?"

"I don't know," Raun responded, "but he's definitely not going to make it easy for us."

"Crash, Bang, Smash." Suddenly the main floor of the cabin sounded like it was being ripped apart. A chill ran through their bodies as they clearly heard several loud noises echoing throughout, coming from the floor above. "What the hell was that?" Dave shouted.

"I don't know," Jeff replied, "but it sounds big as a," his words were cut short as they were suddenly drowned out by the loud ferocious roar of a mountain loin.

"That cat things back again!" Dave shouted.

Jeff was starting to hyperventilate as he asked, "What are we gonna do now? It's in the house!"

PART THREE
Sudden Attack

"Let's go check it out," Raun suggested.

"What?" Dave asked, shocked by Raun's suggestion. "Are you out of your rabid ass mind?"

"You still got the gun, right?" Raun said, trying to make his point that they had nothing to worry about.

"Yeah, but it didn't work on the shadow," Dave reminded him.

"That's because he's not human anymore," Raun stated.

"Neither are those half-breed cats!" Jeff added.

"True, very true," Raun replied, "but they're not spirits like he is, or like I can become if he kills me before he fulfills his end of the deal and lets me return home first."

"This is getting way too complicated," Dave said as he cut Raun off, rolled his eyes and started shaking his head.

Raun continued, "But he won't kill me, if he did, he'd never be able to achieve the full power of the star."

"You'd be a spirit like him?" Jeff asked.

"No! Not like him," Raun replied, "but we'd both share in the powers created by the star. But he's greedy and he wants it all, so he's going to do everything in his capabilities to make sure he succeeds."

"Then what happens?" Jeff asked.

"Then he'll be more powerful than you can even imagine and he'll be free to roam the whole world instead of just the area surrounding the cabin," Raun explained.

"Then no one would be able to stop him, would they?" Dave hated to ask.

Raun explained, "Right now he is already more

powerful than he's ever been before and that's just because of the stones. But for now, at least his powers are limited until he fulfills his end of the deal."

"That's comforting," Dave said sarcastically.

"In a way, it is," Raun started to remind them, "we have the upper hand right now, he's gotta do this at our pace. If I never give up, he never gets started."

More concerned with the problems in their immediate future, Jeff asked, "Are we going to be able to kill that cat thing?"

"I'm not sure," Raun hesitantly replied, "but since he can't kill me, why don't you hold onto the dagger." As he handed the dagger to Jeff, pointing to Dave he said, "And you keep the gun ready."

"What if he doesn't have any control over that cat or whatever is up there?" Dave asked, pondering Murphy's Law.

"If he's not controlling them, he definitely can't win, so I'm not worried about it yet," Raun said, stuttering with an awkward look on his face, seeming as if he was trying to convince himself.

Convinced they now had some sort of idea of what they had gotten themselves into, they slowly made their way across the lab and over to the door. With Dave leading the pack, he held the gun in one hand and the flashlight in the other. When they reached the top of the stairway, he carefully poked his head up through the opening in the floor. "Holy wild kingdom," Dave said loud enough for the others to hear, still standing at the bottom of the stairs.

"What's up there?" Jeff asked, standing between them.

Relentlessly shining the dim light, Dave was unable to locate the source of the chilling raucous in the enormous room. "Mounted animals," Dave mumbled, trying to comprehend what he was looking at. "There has to be hundreds of them."

"Do you see what made the noise?" Jeff asked.

"I can't see shit!" Dave explained. "There's so many trophies in here, whatever made it seems to blend right in."

"Come on, let us up and we'll help you look," Raun hollered up from the bottom of the shaft, Dave obliged. Ascending from the stairwell, he cautiously entered the room with Jeff and Raun following close behind. Baffled by the sheer enormity, this was easily the largest room they had discovered so far.

With everyone now nervously standing inside this huge trophy room, Dave asked, "What the hell's going on here? I thought you stopped him from switching the rooms around on us!" Dave was frustrated and practically yelling at Raun.

"How big is this place?" Jeff rudely interrupted before Raun was even able to respond to Dave's question.

"I'm just sick of these same doors always leading to different rooms, this is bullshit!" Dave continued complaining as they scoured the room in search of the mountain lion.

"For real! I can't keep track of whether I'm upstairs, downstairs, inside, outside or what! I thought you said you could make this place go back to normal?" Jeff demanded answers, aggressively getting in Raun's face.

"I tried," Raun insisted, trying to calm Jeff down. "His powers must be stronger than mine, that's the only reason I can think of."

With tension rapidly rising within the group, they knew they had to remain constantly vigilant. Anticipating a surprise attack at any possible moment, Jeff asked, "Is he trying to keep us from finding the stones or from finding a way out of here?"

"Who cares?" Dave shouted at both of them. "You

guys gotta be quiet! That cats gonna be impossible to find in here with all of these stuffed trophies."

"We knew this wasn't gonna be easy," Raun tried reminding them. "We just gotta keep our eyes open and be ready for anything."

"Alright, fine. Just keep your eyes peeled. I don't trust this freak," Dave reluctantly agreed, hoping they'd stop arguing and start paying closer attention to their surroundings. Content that he had successfully stopped their bickering for now, he resumed hoping they could find this cat before it found them.

Thinking they had safety in numbers, they tried to remain close together as they ventured into the museum like room. After searching the vast area for several intense minutes, they began growing frustrated as the cat maintained its elusiveness. With so many full size, life like animal mounts scattered throughout, they were quickly realizing the virtual impossibility of locating the stalking predator on their terms.

Aside from their own breathing, the room was filled with the same deafening silence that continued to echo throughout the cabin. That ghastly feeling caused an eerie sensation to permeate their bodies. As time continued passing by without incident or successfully being able to locate the creature, they started to gain confidence the beast had fled, leaving them alone in this vast museum like room.

Abruptly, Jeff dropped the dagger as he went tumbling forward to the floor. The giant cat had ran past them at full speed on its hind legs, slashing Jeff across the shoulder from behind as it passed by.

They never saw it coming and just as quickly as it appeared, the cat disappeared back into the darkness and the convenient camouflage of the room. Dave couldn't believe how it happened so fast he wasn't able to get a shot off at the disfigured humanoid-cat. Jeff was laying there on the floor bleeding profusely as he cried out in pain. Trying to cover the wound with his hand, the blood continued oozing out from in between his fingers and was rapidly soaking his whole shirt.

"Over there!" Raun shouted as he pointed to the right.

Frozen in its tracks, the cat appeared to be paralyzed mid-stride as it tried camouflaging itself within its unique surroundings. Dave just stood there, shining the flashlight directly toward it as he took steady aim with the gun. Crouching down on all fours, the creature appeared to be coldly staring back as it nervously contemplated a swift second attack. Exposing its long canine fangs, it snarled intently at them.

Still on the floor, Jeff was totally oblivious to the cold stare down Dave and Raun were immersed in with the cat as everything slowly came back into focus. When he realized what was going on he quickly noticed that all three of them appeared to be transfixed in a state of shock. "Shoot it!" Jeff demanded, trying to break the trance like pause.

With the cat still hypnotically held captive by the light, Dave pulled the trigger and a single shot echoed loudly throughout the room. It felt like they could actually watch the bullet travel since everything appeared to be happening in such an intense state of slow motion. The shot was a direct hit, piercing and shattering the top of the skull. Blood and brains splattered everywhere and the cat let out a final yelp as its limp body collapsed to the floor.

"Nice shot," Jeff complimented his brother as he sat on the floor immersed in a puddle of his own blood.

"Thanks, I wasn't sure if the gun would even work on those things. Are you alright?" Dave asked, with sincere concern for his younger brother's well being.

"Yeah, I'm fine," Jeff replied. "I'm bleeding a little,

but for the most part it just knocked me down. Then, when I hit the floor, it knocked the wind out of me."

Dave let out a sigh of relief, "That's good, I mean, that it didn't rip off your arm or something."

"Yeah," Raun agreed. "We're lucky that thing didn't kill one of us, we gotta be more careful if we're gonna make it through this."

"I agree," Dave said to Raun. Then as he looked over to Jeff he added, "Now lets get that bleeding stopped." He reached into the gym bag Raun was carrying and took out the roll of duct tape. Tearing off several strips of cloth from his shirt, he applied them to Jeff's shoulder and began taping them in place, eventually stopping the blood flow.

Once he was finished patching up his brother, he placed the tape back in the bag and handed it back to Raun. He then picked the gun up off the floor, stuffed it into his waistband and helped Jeff climb to his feet. As they stood there, they took a second glance over the room trying to reassure themselves there were no other cat creatures or anything else that might want to have them for a meal. They didn't want any more surprises and none of them, including Raun, knew the limits or capabilities of the shadow. Because of the vast amount of trophies in this room, there was no way to be sure they wouldn't be attacked again by some lab created hybrid. There was only one thing they were sure about, they knew they had to find this new set of stones and somehow this beast had to be dealt with before it killed them all and caused further destruction.

Suddenly, for no apparent reason, Raun collapsed to the floor. He was laying there in the fetal position with his knees tight to his chest. Holding his hands on top of his head as if he was trying to prevent it from splitting in half, he rocked back and fourth ever so slightly. As he lay there, he suddenly let out a loud scream. The ear piercing sound clearly indicated how intense and agonizing his pain was.

Panic stricken and surprised, Dave ran over to his side, hunched over and asked, “What's wrong?”

“I don’t know...Ahh!” he cried out in pain again. “Hold on a...Ahh!”

“What’s happening to him?” Jeff asked concerned.

Raun continued to lay there on his side. He was still rocking himself, but now he was also mumbling words neither of them could understand.

“What are you saying?” Dave asked, confused and wanting to help. “I can’t understand you.”

“I think the shadow is doing something. I’m not sure what it is but I know it won’t be to our advantage,” Raun’s voice was barely audible.

As Dave was hunched over trying desperately to hear what Raun was trying to say, he caught a glimpse of something out of the corner of his eye. He moved in closer to Raun trying to get a better look and almost went into shock as he suddenly realized what he was looking at. “Look!” Dave shouted, “your shoes have split in half and your hands, they’ve turned into claws! What the hell bro?”

They couldn't believe what they were seeing, in addition to Raun's shoes splitting, his shirt and pants had also ripped, falling away and revealing that parts of his skin were starting to transform into green scales, resembling that of a reptile.

Having no idea of how to react to this peculiar situation, Jeff just stood there dumbfounded. A few moments passed by in silence before Raun was able to finally sit up. Still holding his knees to his chest, he turned to face Dave and Jeff before saying, “It’s getting worse. Somehow, for some strange reason, I'm turning into a lizard or something.”

"It's the 'or something' that's freaking me out," Dave remarked, unsure of what to make of this new development.

"Are you alright?" Jeff asked, "does that hurt?"

"I think I'll be alright," Raun replied. "I'm just not used to having scales and claws. Although, I guess the claws could come in handy."

"Why's that?" Dave asked.

"All of these scales are starting to make me itch," Raun replied, holding up his claws, trying to make light of this insane situation.

Dave and Jeff both chuckled slightly. Then Dave reached out toward Raun, "Give me your claw, I'll help you up."

"I can use a hand," Raun agreed, "but somehow I'm just not in the mood for your sarcasm."

"You can joke but Dave can't?" Jeff curiously asked.

Raun ignored Jeff's remark deciding it better to just let the moment pass. As Dave finished helping him to his feet he apologized, "Alright, I'm sorry. I was just trying to ease the situation a little and it's just, well, you look kind of funny as a lizard with scales and claws." Trying hard to curb laughing at his face while delivering the apology.

"You'd look funny too if you were starting to look like this, so bite me! Let's just find these last few stones and get this over with," Raun snapped back at Dave feeling disrespected.

An awkward silence had fallen over them as a result of the rapidly building tension and fear of the unknown. As they resumed their search of this massive trophy room, they all managed to stay close together. Their nerves were shot as they slowly worked their way through the room. It was hard not to anticipate another attack, especially when every thing in this room seemed to be alive and waiting to jump out at them.

They continued to ransack the room for what seemed like an eternity. The only thing they had on their side was knowing the approximate size of the stones they were looking for. They had looked everywhere and done everything except to start breaking open every statue in the room. Having no luck at all, this was beginning to seem hopeless.

"I don't think there's a stone in here," Dave suggested as he was clearly losing his patience.

Raun stood up from the animal he was searching and began holding his head. Squeezing his temples with his claws, he began pacing around in a small circle. "It's gotta be here!" he demanded.

"Dave's right," Jeff calmly interrupted. "They could be anywhere in this damn cabin!"

"And who says they're even in here?" Dave suggested.

"We did find the first ones in the cabin, but he was helping us then and if anything, he's definitely working against us now," Jeff tried to side with Dave.

"I agree. it could be days before we find even one of them stones."

Showing his outrage with their propensity to give up, Raun raised his voice to an angry level and his eyes flashed red once again as he shouted, "There's one in here! I can feel it!" Dave and Jeff were both astonished by Raun's short temper.

When Raun stopped shouting, Dave humbly asked, "What do you mean you can feel it?"

Raun was struggling to regain control over his anger as he replied, "I don't know. It might be because of my blood, who knows, maybe it's because I'm turning into a damn lizard, but somehow I just know there's one in here."

"Maybe these stones give you power like the other

ones gave him his powers," Dave suggested.

"Yeah," Jeff agreed. "Maybe that's how you can sense where they're at?"

Dave let out a laugh that echoed with fear as he commented, "I just hope these stones don't make him any stronger. We already got tricked once and released him."

"That ain't even funny," Jeff exclaimed.

Dave was just standing there with a blank look on his face as the words he just said suddenly began to sink into his head. The hairs on his arms and the back of his neck were standing on end as a continuous chill ran up and down his spine. He shook off the chill and stated, "That's definitely something we need to be aware of. We need to put him back in his place, but we can't let ourselves fall for any more of his tricks."

Raun looked suddenly surprised by the thought of accidentally making him more powerful than he already was. Holding his claw to his chin, he spoke, "I don't think that's possible. The only way he'll get any stronger is by getting us out of here and killing me." He paused once more in deep thought, adding, "Why else would he be going through so much trouble trying to prevent us from finding them?"

"If he wanted them that bad," Jeff interrupted, "it seems like he would have made them a part of the original deal."

"I guess your right," Dave agreed. "So much weird shit has happened that I just keep expecting to wake up safe and sound, sweating in my bed. But this is the nightmare from hell and it just doesn't wanna end."

"Squawk, Squawk!"

"It's that raven again," Raun shouted.

"Over there," Jeff said, pointing his index finger at the bird. "It's pecking at that dead cat creatures head."

"I didn't even know that thing was still up here," Raun stated.

"Me neither," Dave agreed, "I forgot all about that damn bird."

"Where's it been hiding at?" Jeff curiously asked.

"I have no idea, but we've been in here a long time and I haven't seen it."

"Squawk, Squawk! Squawk!" The birds persistence was growing demanding.

"Come on," Raun suggested, "let's go see what it wants."

Not really wanting to, Dave and Jeff followed Raun's lead as they made their way over to the dead cat creature. They were half way to it when the raven began to flutter its wings and took flight. As it took off flying across the room, they thought it was going to crash right into the wall head first. The image of what happened next would never vanish from their minds. They followed the bird with their eyes, never blinking as it headed on its collision course with the wall.

When the bird made contact, instead of making a sound, the wall seemed to absorb it. At the penetration point the bird disappeared beneath the surface, sending out a series of circular ripples, like a pebble thrown into a still pond. They rolled out in a wave of motion toward the edges and disappeared as the wall returned to a solid state.

Immediately they all took off running across the trophy room toward the wall. When they arrived at the spot where the raven went through, they reached out and tried to force their way through it, but no matter what they did, every spot they tried was rock solid. "What the hell is up with that raven?" Dave was yelling randomly at no one in particular. "What's it trying to show us?"

"Obviously not the way out of here," Jeff stated, still trying to locate the exact spot where the raven went through the wall.

"It must have been trying to show us where the stone is, but this wall is impenetrable," Raun said as he too was scraping his claws all along the wall. "There's no openings leading to whatever is behind it," he added.

"Maybe there's a hidden entrance," Jeff suggested. "Like the hidden one that led us into the basement, through the fireplace, remember?"

With a confused look on his face, Raun stated, "No, it's in here somewhere," he paused momentarily, "what about that cat thing, did either of you check that thing out?"

"Nothing there," Dave stated. "I already checked it out. I even looked in its mouth just in case it had one of those stones for fangs like that skeleton we found."

Perplexed, they found themselves standing still, aimlessly shining their dying flashlight around the interior of the room. "Hey guys," Jeff was trying to get their attention since he thought he had noticed something they'd overlooked. "What about that?"

Dave asked, "What?" As they all found themselves looking at the grotesque dead cat again.

"That cat's shoulder ain't laying down flat. I think it fell on something when you shot it," Jeff tried explaining.

Raun agreed, "He's right." He knew that spot had to be where the stone was elusively hiding, they had already searched everywhere else in this room. "I knew we had to of missed something."

Simultaneously they all sprinted across the room over to where the cat's dead carcass was sprawled out. Without a word said, Dave grabbed hold of the cat's front limbs as Raun grabbed onto the hind legs. They counted down from three and then they rolled the cat's limp body over. As the cat flipped, the head suddenly shifted. A thick glob of blood and brains spurted out, splashing across the front of Dave's shirt. "Oh, gross!" Dave mumbled, smearing the blood on himself in a hopeless attempt to wipe it off. As soon as they looked to their feet, there it was. Jeff bent down and grabbed hold of a small beaver statue. They had found it, the first of the blue stones was located wedged in the mouth of a small trophy beaver statue. The stone itself was a small blue gem, about an inch and a half in diameter and only a half inch thick.

"I'll be a son of a beaver," Raun said sarcastically.

They both laughed a little as Jeff was trying to pry the stone out of the beaver's mouth. When the gem popped out, Jeff couldn't help taking the cheap shot that Raun had left himself wide opened for, "You look more like the son of a reptile."

"Just shut up and let me see the stone," Raun abruptly demanded. "If I didn't need your help so bad I'd kill you myself."

"Then do it you piece of shit!" Jeff shouted as he pushed Raun back several feet.

Immediately Dave jumped in between the two of them, trying to prevent the ensuing boxing match. "Come on you two! We have enough problems already, wouldn't you say? We don't need to be fighting each other too."

"Fine," Jeff shouted. Pointing the tip of the dagger at Raun, stating, "But whenever you're feeling like a frog, go ahead and leap!" He then lowered the dagger and started to pace around aimlessly in a circle.

Raun stood there motionless for a moment as he examined the stone. Standing there in silence, they suddenly found themselves looking to one another in fear .as that familiar cold chill once again fell over the room. In a group panic, they all began scanning over the room with their eyes and the one and only light. Unaware of what was about to happen, Dave drew the gun from his waistband, but they were unable to locate the shadow anywhere. With seemingly no point of origin, his eerie voice had taken over the deafening silence that had engulfed the room only moment ago.

"So you kids really think you'll be able to destroy me, I just can't see myself letting that happen. Since you've been wondering, the answer is yes, I'm going to kill you." They were all speechless, unable to utter a sound as the shadow continued to speak, "I just haven't made up my mind of how I want to do it yet, but I assure you, it won't be quick or painless."

Not knowing exactly where the ominous voice was coming from, Raun finally broke the trance like silence they'd been trapped inside of and started shouting randomly toward the ceiling as he spun around in a tight circle, "You can't kill me until I've been home!"

"Perhaps you're right," the voice replied, "but when you find all your precious little stones, you'll soon realize they will do nothing for you and eventually, you'll grow tired and leave."

Jeff shouted as he interrupted, "We won't leave until we kill you! You're gonna pay for killing my friend!"

"I'll pay for NOTHING!" The shadow said forcefully before adding, "I suggest you leave before I kill all of you like I did your worthless friend."

Then abruptly he was gone. The boys all knew it instantly as the same heavy cool draft returned, passing through the room with no plausible source. The temperature of the room returned back to normal and the only noise they could hear was the sound of their own beating hearts and erratic breathing. Still trying to piece together what had just happened, they couldn't believe how this whole situation just continued getting crazier and crazier right before their eyes. "Give me the dagger and the stone," Raun said.

Jeff willingly obliged, handing Raun the dagger and stone while reassuring himself aloud, "We're gonna get this freak! I don't care if it's the last thing we do, it's gotta get done."

Raun fumbled the stone around loosely in his hand, still not used to having claws. When he finally regained control of the stone, he placed it in the hole at the butt end of the dagger. With the stone in place, both of his eyes and the strange gem simultaneously flashed bright blue for a split second before returning to their normal state. "I can feel it!" Raun shouted. Then in a slightly calmer voice he added, "The dagger and these stones are what we need to destroy him."

"How are you so sure?" Dave curiously asked.

"As soon as I dropped the stone into place, I could feel a surge of energy building up like a fire inside me," Raun tried to explain. "As the energy ran through my body for that split second, I knew the answer to what seemed like every possible question in the universe, and then it was gone, now I can't even remember one of the thoughts I had during that fraction of a second. Come on guys, let's find these other two stones!"

They could just feel the excitement radiating out from Raun. Stunned, Jeff finally managed to mumble, "Do you think we'll be able to beat him?"

"Maybe," Raun said, trying to instill a little hope back into his comrades. "I don't feel like I can honestly answer that question until we find these other two stones, but hopefully."

Dave walked over to Raun, placed his hand gently on his shoulder and said, "We can do it, I know we can, we have to."

"He's right," Jeff added, "we let him out and now

we're gonna put him back in his place, wherever that may be?"

"Hell would be my guess." Dave answered, mumbling under his breath.

Startled, they nearly had a collective heart attack as they were suddenly spooked by the intense roar of another ferocious mountain lion.

"Shit, it's another one of those damn cats!" Dave shouted in a panic as they all started intently scanning the room. As Dave turned around, the cat leapt up at him and clamped down with its razor sharp teeth deep into his shoulder. He cried out in pain as he went crashing to the floor with the cat landing full force, with all of its weight directly on top of his chest.

PART FOUR

The Light & The Darkness

"No!" Jeff cried out as he frantically ran to Dave's aid and started relentlessly kicking the cat in its underbelly as it stood poised atop of his chest. When Jeff realized his kicks weren't doing anything except irritating the mutated cat, he took several steps backwards, then lunged forward and put all of his weight into one good solid kick. Much to his surprise, this actually proved effective in temporarily diverting the cat's attention away from trying to rip Dave to shreds.

The cat abruptly turned its head and fiercely snapped at Jeff. Angered, it snarled, showing its blood coated fangs. With its front paw, it took several quick swipes at him without losing its footing as it still stood on Dave's chest. On the third swipe, the cat caught a piece of him. As his blue jeans ripped and partially tore away, it revealed a large gash in his outer thigh where a huge chunk of flesh was now missing, causing a geyser of dark purple blood to erupt, spurting randomly in all directions.

Raun was standing on the other side of the cat. As Jeff collapsed to the floor, Raun stepped forward and plunged the dagger deep into the cat's exposed neck. It gave out a loud yelp as it turned its head the other way, taking a snap at Raun. Raun moved quickly, he thrust his hips backwards dodging the almost fatal bite. As he withdrew the dagger from the cats neck, he quickly dragged the blade backwards, slicing athwart the cat's throat like a hot knife through butter. Gallons of blood started pouring out of the gaping slash as the cat's lifeless body collapsed on top of Dave's chest. He tried bellowing out in pain, but only a soft whimper was audible. Everything suddenly fell silent, fading into blackness.

Raun slowly wiped the blood off the dagger onto what

remained of his tattered blue jeans. When he finished, he reached out with his free claw and helped Jeff climb back to his feet. Jeff could barely stand on his own since the cat had taken a palm sized chunk out of his upper thigh. He was bleeding profusely, but there was so much other blood from Dave and the cat that it was nearly impossible for them to tell whose blood was whose. Jeff was mostly leaning on Raun as they attempted to roll the dead cat off of Dave's chest. When it finally rolled off his chest, Dave let out another quiet shriek of intense pain as he lay there in a state of semi-consciousness Fearing the worst, Jeff collapsed forward, burying his head into his brothers chest as he started to cry.

Dave was lying there, soaked in blood as Jeff was desperately trying to keep his brother awake. He was fading in and out of consciousness and they weren't sure whether he was going to live or die. "Dave! Dave! Say something! Are you all right?" The only response they received in return were several quiet moans indicative of the intense pain controlling his body. As Jeff slowly lifted himself off his brother's chest he didn't utter a word. Wanting to help, Raun knelt down next to them and started to cut off the left sleeve of Dave's t-shirt with the dagger. Despite all of the blood, the wounds didn't look that bad once the shirt was removed. The teeth had made several deep puncture wounds, but the attack was cut short before the cat was able to start ripping and tearing at the wound. It wasn't until now that they realized most of the blood pooling on the floor belonged to the cat.

Realizing that Dave wasn't injured that bad, Jeff again started trying desperately in another failed attempt to wake up his brother. "Dave! Dave! Come on!" He continued crying out to his brother, but now he was totally unresponsive. Heartbroken and concerned, Jeff started feeling overwhelmed with panic, knowing there was nothing he could do. He leaned forward, placing his ear under Dave's nose to reaffirm that he was still breathing. "He's still breathing, he is!" Jeff cried out. "Barely, but he is!"

"That's good a good sign," Raun said. "How's your leg?"

"Not good," Jeff replied, "it feels like it's asleep and I feel cold. I think it's because I'm wet, soaked in blood."

"That ain't good, you're losing a lot of blood," Raun stated. "Come on, we gotta stop the bleeding."

Jeff paused for a moment, fearful as he looked down sorrowfully at his brother lying there unconscious.

Raun could clearly see that Jeff was more concerned about his brother than he was for his own well being. "He'll be alright for a minute," Raun tried reassuring him. "But you really look pale and if we don't stop that leg from bleeding you'll be worse off than him."

"Alright," Jeff hesitantly nodded in agreement.

Raun stepped over toward Jeff, allowing his shoulder to be used as a crutch. Guiding him, they took several steps away from Dave, enabling them to escape the pool of blood coating the floor. He helped Jeff to lie down on the floor as they carefully propped his leg up on the back of a wolf statue to slow down the flow of blood from his leg. Knowing they needed a tourniquet, Raun stood up and took off his belt. His pants fell to his ankles, but that didn't seem to matter much since his whole body, with the exception of his head, was now covered with reptilian scales.

"You look ridiculous!" Jeff commented, trying not to laugh as he held the gash on his leg in a vain attempt trying to stop the blood from continuing to drain out.

"You're in no position to be talking shit right now," Raun reminded him.

"I'm dying, not turning into a reptile," Jeff stated.

"We can laugh at each other later, now take your hand

off the damn cut," demanded Raun.

Jeff had to force himself to remove his hand from the cut. Somehow, it just seemed to not hurt as bad when he was holding onto it. Raun could tell that Jeff wouldn't be able to restrain himself for very long before putting his hands back in the way. In a hurry, Raun took the belt and wrapped it around his upper thigh just above the cut. Pulling the belt through the buckle, he pulled it as tight as he could in one swift motion. Jeff screamed out in pain, he couldn't imagine how this wasn't doing more harm than good. Holding the make shift tourniquet as tight as he could, Raun forced the latch to close as he punched a new hole through the leather.

"Ouch!" Jeff cried out. "Does it have to be so tight?"

"Yeah!" Raun shouted. "That's how it keeps the blood from draining out of your body. You gotta cut off the blood flow between your heart and the wound."

"I just hope I have enough blood left to make it," Jeff stated.

"Oh, I think you'll be fine," Raun tried reassuring him. "We've already stopped the bleeding and you're still conscious."

"Yeah, but I feel like," his words were abruptly cut short as Raun tripped over him and went tumbling forward. Neither of them saw it coming, another one of the cat creatures had jumped out at them, seeming to come out of nowhere, knocking Raun clear out of the way. As he now lay there tangled up in a pile of disrupted animal trophies, he blended in quite well with his reptilian color and scales. As he came to, he lifted his head and his eyes slowly came back into focus. In a vivid horrifying display, he could see the cat creature prominently standing on Jeff's chest. It was growling and thrashing about as it tore away large chunks of flesh from Jeff's throat.

He was stunned by the graphic sight in front of him, taking a few seconds before he was even able to register a response. He no more then jumped to his feet, when he heard three loud shots "Bang! Bang! Bang!" echoing throughout the cabin. He instantly froze in his tracks, unsure of where the shots came from. The cat suddenly collapsed, falling limply next to Jeff's body.

Raun looked to his right where they had left Dave lying on the floor. Sure enough, there he was, like an action poster frozen in time. Using his left hand to hold pressure on the right side of his rib cage, he sat on the floor, arm still extended as he aimed the gun steadfast at where the cat used to be.

Raun took off in a sprint. "Jeff! Jeff!" he was frantically calling out as he headed for the spot where Jeff's body lay on the floor. His sprint stopped several feet short as the remnants of Jeff's body came into plain view. He immediately knew it was too late. He couldn't get over the horror of looking at Jeff's lifeless body lying there in a pool of his own blood. As he got closer, he was now able to see the graphic extent of what that cat had done to him. His throat was ripped wide open and part of his face was hanging loosely off the side of his skull like a torn piece of leather.

Soaked in sweat and blood, Dave quickly climbed to his feet trying to ignore the intense pain radiating throughout his body. He started making his way as quickly as possible to where Raun was frozen in disbelief.

"Is he...?" Dave cried out, letting his words trail off. "Tell me he's alright! Tell me!" Dave continued to shout, getting no response from Raun.

Raun finally broke his rigid gaze from upon Jeff's body and turned his head, making eye contact with Dave. The empathetic look in Raun's eyes was enough to tell Dave that

Jeff was dead. Dave's movement slowed down to almost nothing at all as tears started rolling down his cheeks. Standing next to his body, Dave couldn't believe what they were looking at. He let himself collapse on top of Jeff's mangled body. His tears intensified as he started raising his head and banging it down on his brothers bloody chest. "Why? Why?" Dave cried out, pouring tears as he screamed out into the void. "I'm sorry, I should have gotten up sooner, it's all my fault."

Immersed in emotion and oblivious to his surroundings, Dave suddenly felt Raun place his claw on his shoulder as he whispered, "It's not your fault, there's nothing that either of us could have done, we're being hunted and we just have to be more careful."

Dave continued sitting there for a few more seconds in absolute silence. Tightly holding onto his brother's corpse, he tried hard to regain some semblance of control over his thoughts. After what felt like an eternity for Raun, Dave finally leaned back. Sitting on his knees, he said, "I know. It's just that, I hate this. I feel freaking helpless, it's like we're trying to fight a battle we can't possibly win."

A chill ran down their spines as that all too familiar cool draft passed over the room, dropping the temperature by fifteen degrees. They both started scanning the room as Dave shined the flashlight back and fourth. Again, they weren't able to see the shadow, but they could feel his eerie presence radiating out from everywhere. "Is this what you had planned to accomplish?" The dark voice reverberated as it called out to them, sounding as if it was coming from everywhere. "Two of you are dead, one is injured and the other is trapped inside a life he couldn't begin to fathom."

As they stood there glancing around the room, They were trying desperately to locate where the voice was coming from, but it was impossible to tell. Dave wiped the tears from his eyes and started screaming out into the vast room, “Where are you? Why don’t you show yourself? I’m gonna send you to hell!”

“Hell is here now!” the shadow replied, shouting back at Dave. “This is where I’m going to keep you, forever my prisoner. So why don’t you just bow down and serve me. Maybe I'll kill you quickly and painlessly.”

“I’m going to kill you myself,” Dave retorted.

“You couldn’t even find me if I was standing right in front of you,” the shadow sarcastically replied.

As the shadow’s voice stopped, an unseen force sent both of them airborne, flying twenty feet through the air. Raun slammed up against the wall and then slid down it as he fell to the floor. When Dave went flying through the air, he was tumbling end over end before being slammed into the wall head first. After the intense impact, Dave was lying there on the floor fading in and out of consciousness as Raun quickly jumped to his feet and started screaming madly into the room, “Show yourself! Are you scared that I’m stronger than you?”

The shadow gave no response as the cool draft passed by once more, the room temperature returned to normal and they found themselves back in the ominous stone silence. Raun picked up the flashlight, gun, dagger and bag from the floor before rushing over to where Dave had landed, lying uncomfortably lopsided against the wall. “Are you alright?” Raun asked as he started to help straighten him out..

In no more than a whisper, Dave mumbled, “Yeah, I just need a little nap.” He was immediately out like a light.

Raun tried repeatedly to wake him, but his efforts yielded no progress. Realizing this, the only thing he could do was let him sleep it off, Raun decided it would be safer in the corner of the room. This way, he could stand guard and be able to see everything around him in all directions as he waited for Dave to wake up. He laid everything on Dave's chest, grabbed him by the wrists and lifted up his head as he began to drag him across the room into the corner. When he finally got to where he felt they were safe, he sat down, laid Dave's head across his lap and got comfortable. He turned off the flashlight to conserve the dying battery and now stood guard in the dark armed with the gun. Taking a bottle of water out of their bag, he tried getting Dave to take a drink to no avail. Instead, he just cleaned him off the best he could as he waited for Dave to wake up.

Dave suddenly found himself standing in the center of that rickety old bridge. He stood there looking over the edge as he held onto the rope handrail with both hands tightly clinched. Desperately wanting to turn his attention away from the endless canyon below, he looked back down the bridge toward the cabin. The woods and sky were pitch black., not a single trace of light existed, especially since the moon didn't feel obligated to make its presence known. The silence was deafening and the entire surrounding wilderness was as still as a mighty oak standing atop a windless world.

As he turned his head to look down the bridge in the other direction, he was in shock. The woods and the sky were brightly lit with the heavenly midday sun. The trees danced ever so gracefully as the cool breeze taunted the leaves. The woods were alive with an abundance of wildlife for as far as the eye could see.

After seeing this, for some reason he again looked to the bottom of the canyon. Right before his eyes, the canyon ignited and turned into a raging inferno that stretched for miles in each direction. As it followed the curves of the canyon, it resembled the image of a giant snake that had been set ablaze with fire.

He stood motionless in the midst of all the confusing images that surrounded him. He could barely grasp what was happening or why, but his mind was racing. As he stood there lost in his thoughts, he instinctively knew that if he were to turn and head toward the light, that would mean his brother and friends would have died in vain. On the other hand, if he were to turn and go back toward the darkness, that could very well seal his own fate to be certain death.

He started to sweat as the fires below him raged and burned with intense hatred, patiently awaiting his decision. Still undecided, he slowly sat down and leaned his back against the rope handrail. He just couldn't force himself to make the choice. He sat there holding his knees to his chest with his arms wrapped around his legs. Frustrated, he laid his forehead on his knees and upper thighs as he closed his eyes. He could feel the tears forming in the corners of his eyes when his thoughts were suddenly disrupted by the squawking of a bird. He raised his head, expecting to see the same raven he remembered from the cabin. Much to his surprise, this wasn't the same bird at all. At least there was no way for him to know for sure. This one was of the same build and size, but instead of black, this one was ghost white.

"What do you want?" Dave asked in a sarcastic voice.

"Squawk," the large bird turned its head to the side as if it understood Dave's question.

"Jeez, it's almost like you understand me," Dave said, thinking the white raven was sincerely trying to answer him. The raven squawked once more, but before it had a chance to do it a second time, the annoying noise turned into softly spoken words of a soothing voice that appeared to be coming directly from the white raven.

"Once you've located all of the stones, the shadow will be forced to reveal himself for the final confrontation.

Squawk!" The voice changed back into the sound of the bird as the white raven began to flutter its wings, taking flight. Dave just watched in awe as the bird flew away, following it with his eyes as it graciously followed the path of the twisting curves of the burning canyon below.

As the bird disappeared into the horizon, he forced himself to stand up. He still wasn't sure whether he was hallucinating, or if he had really just carried on a conversation with a raven. He just stood there for a moment, shaking his head as he tried to make sense out of this confusion. As his eyes tried to regain focus, he looked back toward the dark side of the bridge. The deadly stillness and deafening silence caused another cold chill to race down his spine. He took in a deep breath and glanced back toward the side of the bridge with the light and patiently watched an eagle glide gracefully on the strong wind currents as it soared high above the tall evergreens.

The raging fires below seemed to react to every thought that entered his mind. They burned more and more intensely as he began to speak out loud to himself. "Jeff, Allen, Raun, this is for you and I'm gonna give it my best," he said, trying to convince himself that he wasn't committing suicide as he walked down the bridge toward the dark side of the canyon. He made it all the way to the other side and as soon as he stepped off the bridge with one foot, it all stopped.

PART FIVE

The Moment Of Silence

Incoherent, Dave struggled as he tried to open his tired eyes. Dave couldn't figure out how he was back inside the cabin, but he was completely aware of his surroundings now. He couldn't grasp the fact that he had been dreaming, especially since he didn't even remember falling asleep.

He was laying on the floor, surrounded by complete darkness. Raun had turned on the remaining flashlight and stood it on end so it was aimed at the ceiling. The light was growing very faint because the batteries were almost entirely drained. Dave continued to lay there with his head resting on his thigh when Raun calmly asked, "Are you alright?"

"Yeah," he quietly answered, "I think so. I'm not tore up too bad, am I?"

"Na," Raun replied, "that cat only made a couple of puncture wounds in your shoulder. They're kind of deep, but it pierced you clean and didn't rip you wide open."

"It sure feels like it did," Dave stated.

"Actually, I was more worried that you might have broken your neck when you hit the wall, you hit it hard."

"Well, you're a real dip shit if that's the case, moving me around with a neck injury wasn't that good of an idea, didn't they teach you anything in health class?" Dave asked.

"Yeah, but I had to get us over here in the corner of the room, that way I wouldn't have to watch out in so many directions."

"I see your point, " Dave agreed.

"Besides, I had no idea of how long you would be out for and I was just happy that you were still breathing."

With a puzzled look on his face, Dave asked. "How long was I out for?"

"A good couple hours, I guess," Raun answered.

"Did I miss anything? Or did any more of those mutated cats show up?" Dave was wondering.

"No," Raun replied. "It's been quiet, almost too quiet. I've just been sitting here on full alert wondering when and if you were going to wake up and what I would do if you didn't?"

"What did you decide?" Dave had to ask.

"Nothing really, I just kept hoping we wouldn't get attacked again while you were sleeping."

"Really," Dave agreed, "I can see how that could have been a problem." There was a moment of silence between them as Dave continued resting his head on Raun's lap.

"I just don't know how we're gonna beat him," Raun whispered, not helping as he sounded pessimistic

"Wait a minute!" Dave shouted as he sat right up and started to massage his sore shoulder. "I had a dream!"

"Really," Raun exclaimed, "'like the one I had?"

"No," Dave chirped back at Raun. "Totally different, it was about another raven, only this one was white!"

"What happened? What was it about?" Raun asked, anxiously rattling off questions.

"Well, let me think for a second, I was on that raggedly old bridge," he paused, "I was all by myself, totally lost in my thoughts with no idea of what to do next."

"You mean just like we are now?" Raun suggested.

"No! We're not," Dave insisted, "I do know, listen, the raven had a voice."

"What?" Raun asked. "Was it was the shadow?"

"No. It was different, it seemed friendly and helpful."

Raun interrupted, "What did it say?"

"Stop interrupting me and I'll tell your jabber jaw

ass," Dave demanded.

"Alright," Raun agreed. "I'll shut up, just tell me."

"It told me that once we have all of the stones, the shadow creature will be forced to reveal himself for the final confrontation."

"The final confrontation?" Raun repeated with a puzzled look on his face.

"I guess that's when we'll send him back to hell where he belongs," Dave insisted, trying to sound hopeful.

"Or it's when we'll get killed," Raun amended Dave's interpretation.

"Either way, this nightmare will finally be over," Dave reaffirmed.

"Is that it? Is that all it said?" Raun asked curiously.

"That's all I can make out of it, how 'bout you?" Dave answered with a question.

"Hell, I don't know, it was your dream," Raun said, pointing out the obvious.

Dave agreed, "I guess your right."

"Just remember," Raun added, "dreams are hard to interpret, so it could have meant anything."

"But it's kinda like the one you had," Dave pleaded, "right?"

"Yeah, well, kinda, but mine didn't involve a talking raven. Besides, you did whack your head against that wall pretty hard."

"Oh!" Dave shouted as he slowly climbed up to his feet. "So now you think I'm crazy? You're the one turning into a lizard and yet you're calling me crazy over a talking bird."

"No," Raun replied, as he too was now standing up. "I'm just saying that we have to be ready for anything."

"Whatever!" Dave shouted. "I'm taking heed to the warning and I don't care if it comes from a talking raven or your lizard looking ass."

"Fine," Raun reluctantly agreed with Dave's sarcasm. "Let's just find these stones. We have to stop that freak before he kills us and destroys the whole damn world."

Dave agreed, "I know that's right."

"You feel up to it yet?" Raun asked.

"Oh yeah," Dave replied. "My head's pounding, my ribs and shoulder are sore as hell. I don't think you have any aspirin, do you?" he added hopefully.

"No," Raun said, "I'm turning into a lizard, not a pharmacy. Here, drink some water"

"Thanks," he replied, taking a large gulp from the water bottle. Then he finished his thought, "Well it was worth asking, but yeah, I'm about as ready as I can be. Let's go make this piece of shit pay for killing our brothers."

"Then let's do this," Raun agreed.

Still standing there, Raun bent down and picked up all their things off the floor. He handed the gun and flashlight to Dave and he informed him, "I think you should know, there's only one bullet left in the gun."

With a confused look on his face, Dave asked, "But I thought it held quite a few?"

"It does," Raun replied. "But you made Swiss cheese out of that last cat."

"I guess that means we'll just have to save this one for a special occasion," Dave remarked.

"I agree with that, just make sure you don't miss."

"I ain't missed yet," Dave reminded him.

"Yeah," Raun agreed, "but usually you crack under pressure."

"Bite me! I ought to crack you under some pressure," Dave said as he raised the gun, acting as if he was about to bash Raun over the head.

"Chill out," Raun replied. "Let's just get these stones and get this over with."

"Your right," Dave apologized. "I'm sorry."

A new door had appeared on the far side of the room at some point during all of the commotion. As they started making their way toward it, Dave stopped when they came across Jeff's mangled body laying on the floor. Raun was following behind Dave when he too suddenly stopped. Dave knelt down, placed his hand on Jeff's chest and grabbed a hold of his brother's cold fingers with his other hand. Tears started to form in his eyes as he squeezed his dead brother's hand. "I'm gonna make him pay for this, I promise, be with us bro, I love ya," Dave continued on with his moment of silence for several more seconds, then he stood up. Holding on to the gun with his right hand, he wiped the tears from his eyes with the back of his hand. Raun had been standing there as they had their moment of remembrance. When Dave was finished, Raun continued to silently follow his lead as they resumed heading toward the door on the far wall.

When they arrived at the door, Raun briefly looked Dave in the eyes before he grabbed hold of the door handle and attempted to turn the knob. Much to their surprise, the door was actually locked. "Let me try," Dave suggested.

Raun stepped aside expecting Dave to grab hold of the handle. Instead, he backed up a few steps and lunged forward, slamming his good shoulder into the door just above the latch. "Ouch!" he cried out. The door didn't budge at all, but that was the exact moment in time when Dave realized that he was more than just a little banged up. Several of his ribs were actually broken and not just bruised like he had originally thought. His whole body felt like it had gone through an entire war. Standing there in pain, he didn't have enough hands to try massaging all the areas that were causing his paid. Raun gently placed his claw on Dave's shoulder and said, "Here, let me get it."

"How can we be sure that we're even done in this room?" Dave asked.

"I know we're done with this room," Raun stated. "If there was another stone in here, I'd be able to sense it."

"You'd know better than I would," Dave remarked as he stepped aside, letting him try the door.

Dave stepped to the side as Raun crouched down. With Dave now out of the way, Raun closed his eyes as he sprung forward like a frog. Dave just watched, looking at him like he was crazy. When his shoulder hit the door, it didn't budge, but the whole door frame separated from the wall, toppling over like a domino as Raun came crashing down on top of it. "Holy shit!" Dave shouted. "You've gotten a lot stronger."

"Yeah, I've noticed quite a few other changes too, besides my appearance," Raun said as he climbed to his feet. "And I think once we get these last two stones, I'll become even stronger."

"Probably so," Dave agreed, "but will you be strong enough to beat him?"

"I hope so," Raun replied. "but we won't know until we find them, so let's get moving."

"I'm ready when you are," Dave retorted.

"Come on then, but we better stay on our toes since he definitely doesn't want us to find these last two stones, he's going to do everything he can to try stopping us."

Standing nervously in the doorway, Dave shined the flashlight around the interior of the room. They were bewildered by how small this room was in comparison to the rest of the cabin. They had a strong feeling they were being watched and that they weren't alone in here. Since the room was so small, they didn't understand their strange feeling of uncertainty. The room resembled a kitchenette, it was a combination of a small kitchen and a breakfast nook. In the far right corner of the room was a smaller wood burning stove and on their right, running the full length of the wall, was a massive amount of cabinets for a room this tiny. The counter top was wooden and as smooth as a piece of glass. Directly in front of them was a small picnic table that had been painted a dull yellow color. To their left there was an icebox, followed by a closed door tucked behind it.

Beginning to search the room, it didn't take them long before they had gone through all of the cabinets and drawers. For the most part they were empty, with the exception of several miscellaneous pieces of antiquated kitchenware. They checked the empty candle holder sitting on the table and the wood burning stove. Dave even grabbed the picnic table and slid it out several feet, looking behind and under it. This way he would be able to stand on it as he checked the interior of the chandelier, but it too yielded no results. The room appeared to be barren of the stone, their hopes of finding it were rapidly diminishing right before their eyes.

Dave was getting tired and irritated from playing all these games he didn't fully understand. He looked over to Raun in dismay, "It's not in here, we're never gonna find them."

"I think you're right," Raun agreed, catching Dave off guard as he agreed with him.

"What? That we're never gonna find them?" Dave asked, still in a state of disbelief over Raun's agreeing with him.

“No, they are here somewhere,” Raun reassured him. “I just don’t think they’re in this room. I’m almost positive that I can sense their presence and I just don’t feel it in here.”

“I hope you’re right, because if not, this search could really become hopeless,” Dave was pointing out the facts.

“We’re close, but they’re definitely not in here. Yup! I’m sure of it,” Raun said as that red glow ominously passed over his eyes once again.

“Well, come on then. We’re just wasting our time in here,” Dave pointed out.

“This way,” Raun suggested as he started to make his way over to the other door in the room.

Dave followed his lead and when they arrived at the door, Raun reached out with his free claw to open the door and was relieved to find that it wasn’t locked. He twisted the handle and pushed the door open, allowing Dave to lead the way since he was armed with the flashlight and gun.

As Dave stepped inside, he began to scan over the room with the light. Pausing for a second, he said, “It’s a bedroom, but I don’t see anything dangerous, come on.”

PART SIX
Revelation Of Terror

They stepped into the bedroom, directly in front of them with the headboard up against the far wall was an antique canopy bed made of solid mahogany. The dusty semi-transparent drapes were all pulled back and they were able to clearly see that no one had been in that bed in a very long time. The bed was made ever so perfectly with the comforter and both pillows covered in the same thick coat of dust that blanketed most of the cabin.

Located on the left side of the room in the center of the wall was a small closet with no door and a wide variety of clothes hanging inside. On their right was a large dresser that matched the décor of the bed. Perched on top of it was a large rectangular mirror, they could barely even see their reflection in it due to the thick film of dust and grime that had coated it over the years.

On each side of the headboard was a small night stand with the heads of black bears centered and mounted to the wall hanging above them. Sitting on top of each night stand was a candlestick holder made of tarnished silver, each one holding a long narrow black candle that looked as if they had never been lit. As Dave shined the light on the stand located on the left side of the bed, he noticed that the night stand on the right side of the bed wasn't a night stand at all, it was a small two drawer filing cabinet. That struck them as odd, something inside them was screaming that the next stone would soon be in their hands.

Dave led the way as they headed toward the filing cabinet. When he tried to open it, he quickly learned that the drawer was locked. Determined, he gave it a quick couple of yanks, but the locking mechanism wouldn't give way to his persistence. "I've got an idea, let me see the dagger for a sec," Dave suggested.

Dave set the gun down on top of the cabinet next to the candle as Raun handed it to him. Using both hands, he managed to wedge the tip of the dagger into the tiny opening and with a forceful motion, he was able to pop the lock. He pulled the dagger out and handed it to Raun before pulling the drawer open.

After only a quick passing glance, they were sure the stone wasn't located in this drawer. The only thing in there was a plain manila folder. Curious, Dave picked it up and opened it. Thumbing his way through the stack of papers he noticed the majority of them were written in the same language as the notepad they had found earlier, presumably German. When he arrived at the end of the stack, he located a strange paper that was faded, but written in English and it appeared to be some kind of memo. It stated that Eric Aben was to be hosting a meeting on May 23rd and to make sure that all proper arrangements be made to ensure the meeting would go unnoticed and it was signed by Rudolph Hess.

"This guy was a big shot with the Nazi's," Dave stated. "And look at this," he added, pulling out a photograph of who they guessed was Dr. Eric Aben. He was standing at a podium, presumably in Germany, shaking hands with Adolph Hitler himself as he stood there posing with several other high ranking officers of the Third Reich.

"Big deal," Raun remarked, "that doesn't help us find the next stone, just check the other drawer."

"Alright already, hold your horses," Dave replied as he put the photograph back inside the file before placing the whole thing back in the cabinet, shutting the drawer. "Quit being so impatient," Dave added as he crouched down and opened the bottom drawer. It wasn't even opened all the way when they caught a glimpse of the stone. Lying right in front of them, there it was sitting on top of a perfectly folded Nazi flag. As Dave reached down into the drawer, he caught a glimpse of something out of the corner of his eye through the grime covered mirror. Moving ever so slowly, it was one of those mutated cat creatures in the process of trying to sneak up on them from behind.

Raun had obviously saw it too. Immediately, they both turned around as the cat let out a ferocious roar and leapt toward them. Instinctively, Raun raised up his arms trying to fend off the surprise attack. In the process of his instinctive reaction, Raun accidentally drove the dagger directly into the cat's body. As the blade pierced its chest cavity, the cat let out a hissing shriek of immense pain as it slammed into Raun. He was knocked backwards and slammed forcefully into Dave. After crashing into the cabinet, Dave quickly climbed to his feet. He noticed immediately that the cat was trying to regain control over its equilibrium, as it lay on top of Raun's chest. It was quivering as it snarled and growled while bleeding profusely all over Raun. Without giving it a second thought, Dave rushed to Raun's aid and assisted him as they together somehow managed to roll the massive cat's body off of him without getting bit.

With the cat now lying on the floor dying at Raun's side, Dave turned around and picked the gun up off the floor from where he'd dropped it during the surprise attack and bashed the cat on top of its skull. Knocked unconscious, the cat collapsed limply the remainder of the way onto the floor. "Are you alright?" Dave asked concerned.

"Yeah," Raun replied, "I'm just glad you got that bleeding ass mutation off me."

As Dave helped Raun climb back to his feet he said, "Damn! How many of these things are there?"

"I don't know," Raun answered the question before suggesting, "my guess would be about the same number as the amount of people that came up missing back in the day. Think about it, they're all part human."

They stood there, awkwardly still for a moment as the thought of that cryptic image washed over their minds. Then in an attempt to vent his frustration a little, Dave kicked the unconscious dying cat in the ribs a couple of quick times. Feeling confident the cat was incapacitated, Dave bent down and picked up the small blue stone from next to its front paw. "So, you think you're ready for this?" Raun asked holding out his claw, anticipating Dave handing him the stone.

As Dave dropped the gem into his claw, he replied, "Yeah," pausing for a brief moment, "I mean, I'm as ready as I'm gonna get, ya know?"

"I know," Raun replied as he stood there examining the stone. He lifted his arm, bringing the dagger to his mid section. Bringing his free hand to the dagger, he dropped the stone into one of the remaining slots in the handle.

Once again, both the stones and Raun's eyes flashed bright blue for several seconds. All of his facial features cringed as every muscle in his body seemed to tense up. Fighting for control of his body, he raised up his arm so the tip of the dagger was pointing toward the ceiling. "One more stone!" he screamed out as a bright blue bolt of lightning discharged from the tip of the dagger. It blew a hole ten feet in diameter right through the ceiling, exposing the dark night sky in which even the thick overcast had a bluish tint to it.

Dave turned his attention away from the gigantic hole in the ceiling and back to Raun as he shouted, "Hell yeah, I can almost feel the power now!" He exaggerated his words as he over pronounced the sentence. With his eyes and the stones returning to normal, he lowered the dagger.

"Okay," Dave said slowly, "now you're starting to scare me."

"I just wish I could fight him right now," Raun stated, feeling flushed with power.

"Don't worry, we'll be doing that soon enough," Dave replied.

"It's just, these stones," Raun tried to explain. "They bring me such a feeling of power, I can't wait 'til we get the next one, then I'm sure I'll be able to beat him."

"So how the hell did you do that?" Dave paused, "you know, with the lightning?"

"I'm not sure," Raun replied. "I just felt this enormous energy building up inside me, I just knew that I had to release it somehow. I raised my arm and let it flow out through the dagger."

"Well, can you do it again?" Dave asked curiously.

"I think I can, but I see your point, we should find out for sure," Raun agreed.

"Good," Dave retorted, "cause somehow, I just don't think our one bullet and that little dagger are gonna be enough to beat this freak."

"This definitely increases our odds," Raun agreed.

"Since I almost used our last bullet when that cat dove on you, we need this to work," Dave pointed out.

"I was actually surprised you didn't. I wasn't sure if you saw that it dove right onto the dagger before you fell down," Raun added.

"I saw that," Dave stated, taking a seat on the ancient bed, "so, can you do it again or what?"

"I told you I'm almost positive I can," Raun said, starting to get an attitude with Dave's persistence.

"We need to be sure. It might just have happened

because you put the stone in place," Dave reaffirmed.

"I guess it won't hurt to give it a try, if it'll make you happy," Raun caved in to Dave's wishes.

"It will," Dave stated, "because if you can, that makes this about the equivalent of a BB gun," brandishing the 9mm pistol.

"Well, what should I try it on?" Raun asked.

"I don't know, how 'bout that cat? See! I knew they had to have some kind of purpose. But hold on," Dave demanded, "let me get the hell out the way first."

"That's probably not a bad idea," Raun agreed.

Dave got up off the bed and headed over to the doorway. With Dave now standing behind Raun, he raised his arm and aimed the dagger at the cat. Standing there in silence, it only took a couple of seconds worth of concentration before another blue lightning bolt discharged from the tip of the dagger. The cat's body twitched and shook as it absorbed a massive amount of electricity. The intense heat from the blast caused the cats body to briefly catch fire and all they could smell was singed hair and burning flesh.

Suddenly saddened, the whole scenario reminded Dave all too much of how Allen had died. He just couldn't shake the awful image of Allen's charred remains lying on the floor in front of him. Since Raun didn't say anything, Dave figured that he shouldn't either. He knew this whole situation was an emotional nightmare and there was no way to judge Raun for how he chose to deal with all they've been through.

The blast itself wasn't as powerful as the one that blew the roof open, but they were satisfied that they at least had some kind of control over the powers it contained. As Raun lowered the dagger, he turned around to face Dave. "I wonder why it wasn't as strong as the first one?" Dave curiously asked.

"I think the dagger needs the last stone to reach its full power potential," Raun replied. "I do know one thing for sure."

"What's that?" Dave asked.

"I can feel them."

"Feel what?" Dave demanded.

"Where the stones are located," Raun stated, not understanding why Dave didn't know what he was talking about.

"That's great!" Dave shouted. "I thought we were gonna have to search this place forever."

"Don't get all excited just yet," Raun suggested, trying to slow Dave down a little. "I've got some bad news."

"What do you mean bad news?" Dave repeated.

"I know where the last stone is," Raun stated.

"That's great news! Did your brain quit working? That's what we're looking for."

"No," Raun paused, "you don't understand, it's not here."

"What do you mean it's not here?" Dave demanded in a panicked tone of voice. "Where the hell is it?"

Raun started to pace nervously around the room for several moments before he turned back to face Dave and said, "You're not gonna believe this, but the last stone is located under that rickety bridge, it's stuffed in a knothole."

"You've gotta be shitting me," Dave said doubtfully, sincerely hoping that Raun wasn't being serious.

"Not at all," Raun reaffirmed.

"Let me guess," Dave suggested, "it's in that new board, the one in the middle."

"We have a winner," Raun said sarcastically.

"Ha. Ha. Real funny," Dave replied. "I just knew there

was something suspicious about that board," he added as he sat back down on the edge of the bed. Raun followed suit, and they both sat there in silence for a few moments as they tried to gather their thoughts.

After the silence, Dave asked, "How the hell are we supposed to get it out from under the bridge?"

With a puzzled look on his face, Raun suggested, "Well, we can try pulling up the board."

Terrified by that thought alone, Dave asked, "Are you nuts? That thing is barely holding itself together! I don't even want to think about what would happen if we started picking it apart."

"Do you have a better idea?" Raun asked.

"Why don't we just lean over the side and try popping it out," Dave suggested.

"Hell no," Raun replied. "What if it pops out and we can't catch it, then it'll fall to the bottom of the canyon and probably shatter. Then where would we be?"

"We just can't let that happen," Dave stated as if it were that simple. "I guess we'll just have to wait and see what it looks like when we get out there."

"What if crawling under the bridge is the only way we can get it?" Raun calmly asked.

"No way, are you out of your mind?" Dave shouted, adding sarcastically, "I think you inherited the brains of a salamander when you started getting all those scales."

Raun turned around and walked right up to Dave, he lifted his arms and shoved his claws right in Dave's face as he said, "But with my claws, climbing across the underbelly should be a snap?

"Fine, then you go right ahead with your bad self," Dave retorted, thinking Raun had totally lost his mind.

"I will, but there's another problem."

"What now?" Dave asked.

"There's something else about that board on the bridge," Raun stated.

"Oh yeah, what's that? How could this possibly get any worse or weirder for that matter?" Dave rattled off a series of questions as he started to hyperventilate.

"That's as far as I can go. Once I cross that point," Raun paused briefly, then continued, "I'm considered home and with his end of the contract fulfilled, the deal is complete and he will have full control of the star. That will give him the power to kill you, me and who knows what else."

"This is nuts and crawling under the bridge, that's just a bad idea," Dave stated as he began to pace again.

"Then what are we supposed to do? We have to get the stone," Raun demanded.

"I don't know," Dave replied. "I can see it now. If you try climbing under that bridge, you ain't gonna have to worry 'bout the shadow killing you. You're gonna go plummeting to your death just trying to get the damn thing."

"I'm glad to see you have so much faith in me," Raun said sarcastically.

"I do," Dave pleaded. "It's just that one little slip and you'll be falling for days. I mean, I know this whole situation is nuts, but that's suicide."

"Maybe," Raun agreed, "but it might be the only way!" Raun stated as he stood up from where he was sitting on the bed and now followed behind Dave as they both paced around the small room. Shouting, Raun continued, "Besides, if we don't get the stone, we're as good as dead already!"

"Good point," Dave hesitantly agreed. "Let's just hope that once we get out there we can figure out an easier way to get it."

"Don't get me wrong, I don't wanna do it either, but

for some reason, I just know that it's gonna have to be done that way."

"Well, we'll just have to see what happens but that's definitely our last resort," Dave demanded.

"I agree," Raun said. "Hey! Let me have your belt."

Dave stood there with the look of confusion etched into his face as he asked, "Why? You're not even wearing pants anymore."

"That way I can slide the dagger through it, this things heavy, ya know?"

"Whatever," Dave replied as he stood there shaking his head.

Dave was fortunate that his pants fit him well enough that he didn't even really need a belt. After he finished pulling the belt through the loops, he handed it over to Raun and said, "Now all we have to do is find our way out of this shape shifting cabin without running into any more of those mutated cats."

"Really, that should be a task," Raun agreed. "But at least now we don't have to waste any time looking for the stones."

"Not to mention, you know how to use the dagger," Dave added.

They knew they had to proceed with extreme caution. There was no way to know how many more of those cats they were destined to run into so they had to remain on full alert. What scared them even more was the recurring thought of what other kind of surprises the shadow might have in store for them as they continued on their journey.

PART SEVEN

Surge Of Power

As they started to slowly make their way through the immense labyrinth of rooms, Dave realized they had managed to find themselves standing back inside the trophy room. With this sudden realization, his slow walk turned into a full speed run as he headed toward the other side of the room. As Raun sluggishly followed behind him, he realized that Dave was heading to the spot where his brother's mangled body still lay dead on the floor in a huge pool of dried blood. Raun slowed down as Dave reached the body to give him a little space.

Standing at Jeff's side, he dropped to his knees. He set the gun, bag and flashlight down on the floor before grabbing up his brothers stiff arm. He took the hand and sandwiched it tightly between both of his own, tears started to stream down his face as he began pleading to his brothers dead body, "Soon we will have the last stone, I will make him pay for this, I promise."

Dave suddenly felt Raun's claw resting on his shoulder. Tightly, he closed his eyes and took in a deep breath as Raun began to speak out into the void, presumably to Jeff. "This last stone is going to take everything out of us, so wish us luck my friend."

As Raun's words trailed off, Dave opened his eyes, stood up and turned to face Raun. They held the fearful stare for a brief moment before Dave wiped the tears from his eyes with the front of his shirt. He then bent down, picking the gun, bag and flashlight off the floor. Standing back upright, he noticed something out of the corner of his eye, it was that soft blue glimmer flashing through Raun's eyes once again.

Dave made nothing of it. He figured that with Raun's body changing form right before his eyes and the strange powers he was inheriting, the blue glow must have been some kind of show of emotions. Raun knew Dave had seen the blue glow pass over his eyes. He could tell by the startled look on Dave's face. Trying to break the shocked expression, Raun suggested, "Let's go get this creep. I'm ready for him now."

Dave just nodded his head in acknowledgment as they started making their way over to the doorway leading out of this creepy room. As soon as Dave pulled the door open, they immediately recognized the room they were about to walk into. "It's the room with the table," Raun proclaimed.

"How the hell did we end up in here again?" Dave asked.

"I don't know," Raun replied, "but at least now I know where we are."

"Me to, come on," Dave agreed as he started leading the way out of the room through the other door. Practically running through the library and into the dining room, Raun noticed that Dave was holding onto the right side of his rib cage again.

"Are you alright?" Raun asked concerned.

"Yeah, I'll be fine," Dave replied. "I just can't run very effectively," he paused briefly, struggling to catch his breath. "It's just when I get winded, my ribs start to bother me."

"That's alright, we ain't gonna do any running from that freak anyway," Raun stated, trying to comfort him.

Now that they had stopped running for a second, they found themselves standing in the dining room. That itself astounded them, they couldn't believe they had actually found it, especially in the same condition as when they first discovered this place.

"I know that's right," Dave agreed.

"But you have to let me know if I'm moving to fast

for you," Raun insisted, "I keep forgetting that I can do stuff that you can't, not to mention you're all busted up."

Dave suddenly copped an attitude and began to shout, "I might have a cut here and a break there and you might have all of those powers but when all of this goes back to normal, I'm gonna beat your ass like never before."

"Maybe so," Raun said, taking the defensive, "but for now, let's just remain focused on getting this last stone and ending this."

"And sending this shadow freak back to hell where he belongs," Dave added.

Dave had finally regained control over his erratic breathing. Now, at a slightly slower pace, Dave led the way as they walked around the dining room table. They headed over toward the main door, hoping it would lead them out of the cabin. Standing there for a moment, they waited to open the front door, Dave asked, "I wonder if he's gonna try that switching the rooms around again, ya know, putting us back inside when we know damn well we're outside?"

"Na, he knows I can block all that out now," Raun replied. "He was just taking advantage of us mentally before I realized I could counteract all his little mind games."

With that said, Dave grabbed hold of the door handle and pulled it open. As they stepped onto the front porch, they gently closed the door behind them. Outside, they both took in a deep breath of fresh air and let out a huge sigh of relief as they had finally escaped the foul odor they had seemingly grown accustomed to. The smell of the air alone told them they were actually outside this time.

Much to their surprise, it was still dark outside. They couldn't believe it, since it felt as if they'd been inside that cabin forever, losing all sense of time. Glancing around at the night sky, they quickly realized it hadn't changed a bit. The thick, lingering overcast looked as if it hadn't moved an inch since they'd originally entered the cabin. Only one spot of the sky was still clear. It was the same spot they were able to see through the opening that had been blown through the roof, revealing just a sliver of the moon with a single lonely star hanging offset just below it.

"Do you hear that?" Dave asked.

"No," Raun replied, "hear what?"

"Nothing, there's not a sound out here," Dave stated.

"That's a good thing, right?" Raun asked puzzled.

"No!" Dave demanded. "That just shows you how evil this place really is."

"I know," Raun agreed. "I don't know why we didn't listen to the silent warning of the woods and just go back."

"I'll tell you why!" Dave paused, "Allen was just so determined to check this place out and I knew better! I should have put up more of a fight to prevent us from coming out here," Dave continued blaming himself.

"Why didn't you?" Raun curiously asked.

"I didn't wanna listen to him cry about it," Dave replied. "Besides, it would've just given him something else to bitch about and frankly I just didn't wanna hear it."

"I know what you mean," Raun agreed.

"And let me tell you this," Dave stated, "if I get killed now, I'm gonna beat his ass so bad in the next life he'll wish he could die all over again, just to get away from me."

"Then let's get this done," Raun suggested.

They stepped off the porch and back into the field of overgrown grass. Making their way down the trail, they found themselves trembling inside. It seemed the farther they got away from the cabin, the more they started to feel like they were at least slightly in control of their own fate, even being fully aware the worst was yet to come. Ever so cautiously, they continued heading down the not so familiar path. Feeling like they were making good time, they'd just passed through the thick patch of fog from earlier. To the best of their memory, they figured they were about halfway to the bridge when they both suddenly came to an abrupt stop. Paralyzed, they both began scanning the environment area around them. After several intense seconds of looking in every direction, they made eye contact. “We’re not alone out here,” Raun whispered. “Something is watching us.”

“I know,” Dave agreed, “I can feel it too. I thought the farther we got away from that place, the better I’d feel, but it’s like we just can’t get away from him.”

“This is nuts, it’s like he’s everywhere,” Raun paused. “Let’s just get this last stone and bring all of this craziness to an end.”

Dave agreed, they cautiously resumed making their way down the winding trail toward the bridge. It didn’t take long before they were standing at the cliffs edge. They found themselves gazing down into the dark canyon, knowing in their heart this bridge shouldn’t even still be here after all this time. All of a sudden they heard the loud snapping sound of a twig breaking behind them. Quickly they both turned around to face the opposite direction, only to learn that another cat had snuck up on their flank and launched a surprise attack. They had no time to react, by the time they realized what was happening, the cat was already airborne, diving toward Raun.

With the dagger still holstered in his belt, he raised his arms in an attempt to fend off the attack. There was an ear shattering sound as the cat latched onto his forearm. The crunching sound alone told you that his hand had been severed from his arm. Dark blue blood began spiriting in all directions as Raun was tackled to the ground by this enormous cat. Raun was screaming bloody murder as he and the cat wrestled dangerously close to the edge of the cliff.

Dave was fully aware that if he didn't intervene now, they would both soon tumble over the cliffs edge and fall to their deaths at the bottom of the canyon. Acting as quickly as he possibly could, he moved in on the cat and Raun. He aimed the gun sideways, pointing it directly at the cats head so the bullet wouldn't penetrate through the cat and into Raun. He pulled the trigger and the cats head exploded, liquefying into a disgusting slurry. Blood and brains started to rain down onto Raun's body, but that was only for a split second since the force of the blast threw the cats body over the cliffs edge.

Dave stepped to the edge, until it was consumed by the darkness, he watched as the cat's limp body tumbled and bounced its way down the steep, rocky side of the cliff. Although he couldn't see it, he was able to hear it as it presumably splattered on impact with the canyon floor.

Raun jumped to his feet, his wrist continuing to discharge the heavy flow of deep blue blood. He pulled the dagger out of his belt with his remaining claw and held it over his head. Aiming it at the sky, he began shouting in another language, but the last of his words were in English and Dave was able to understand him as he yelled, "I need you now!"

Suddenly, the clouds above them began rumbling violently and the winds picked up to nearly hurricane speeds. Dave struggled as he fought hard against the winds, trying desperately to get far enough away from the cliffs edge before being forced over the rim. Raun's eyes abruptly flashed and remained a vibrant, glowing shade of bright blue. From three separate points in the rolling clouds above, three individual bolts of lightning arced out, forming an upside down pyramid with the points all connecting to the tip of the dagger.

Dave couldn't believe Raun didn't get electrocuted in the sudden discharge. When the flow of electricity finally dissipated, Raun was left standing as he held the dagger over his head with the entire blade still glowing bright orange. Dave wasn't sure of whether it was from the heat induced by the lightning, or from the raw power of the dagger and the mysterious stones. Either way, what happened next was hard for Dave to comprehend. Raun lowered his arm and touched the tip of the glowing blade to his bleeding severed wrist. His blood and skin began to sizzle, searing the wound closed. Dave couldn't even fathom the immense pain Raun must have been going through. The smell of the burning flesh was hard to stomach, but Dave knew that if Raun hadn't done what he did, he would have bled to death in a matter of minutes.

Dave was frozen in place, watching helplessly as Raun stood there staring at the nub that now constituted his entire left arm. With the dagger hanging down at his right side, the blade slowly returned to its normal color. The winds had completely died off and the clouds seemed to have stopped dead in their tracks as if someone had pushed the pause button on a DVR.

With no words spoken between them, Dave followed Raun as he stepped over to the edge of the canyon. Despite their best efforts, they could barely see the cat's dead body at the bottom of the canyon through the vast perpetual darkness. Dave placed his hand on Raun's scaly shoulder, looked down to his wrist and mumbled in a defeated tone, "I don't think we're gonna make it."

"Come on Dave, we can't just give up now," Raun pleaded.

"How the hell are we supposed to do this?" Dave shouted, "Its pitch black out here and I can't even see my hand in front of my face."

Offended by Dave's thoughtless remark, "At least you still have both of them!" Raun shouted back at him as he shoved the burnt nub into Dave's face.

"I'm sorry," Dave apologized. "I know I shouldn't complain, it just seems like we're prolonging our inevitable deaths."

"We'll be alright," Raun tried to reassure him. "We just need to retrieve this last stone and bring all of this chaos to an end."

"You know that's right, I can't wait for this to be over," Dave agreed, "But are you gonna be able to fight that creep with only one hand? Because I don't know how much help I'm gonna be?"

"What do you mean by that?" Raun asked perplexed.

"The flashlight broke, I dropped it when that cat attacked us, the gun's empty and I'm all beat to shit," Dave explained, feeling utterly defeated.

They stood there in silence as Dave's words washed over them like an endless wave that finally breached the shore. The reality of their whole situation was more than depressing, the chances of them coming out on top were growing slimmer by the second.

Raun finally broke the silence as he suggested, "We're gonna have to rely on the stones for their strength. Besides, I don't think that gun would have worked on him anyway."

"After what happened to Allen, you're probably right," Dave reluctantly agreed, "but it sure did come in handy against those cats."

"Ain't that the truth," Raun said as he started to grin nervously. "I just hope we don't run into anymore of them since you're unarmed and I'm shorthanded," cracking a tasteless joke on himself as he held up his nub.

Dave forced himself to laugh a little, even though he really wasn't amused. Somehow this just didn't seem to him like the appropriate time for wise cracks. Trying not to offend or even respond to Raun's sarcasm, he asked. "So are you ready for this?"

"Oh yeah," Raun stated. "I feel like bait just standing here surrounded by the fresh sent of blood."

Deciding it was time, they stepped over to where the bridge met the canyon wall. "Well, here we are, the last stone is finally within our grasp."

"Yeah," Dave agreed, showing his apparent lack of enthusiasm. "Don't you think it's kinda strange the shadow has been so quiet lately?"

"What do you mean?" Raun asked.

"I mean, think about it. He's only sent one cat after us since we've left the cabin," Dave was trying to explain.

"Maybe he's not as powerful this far away from the cabin, we know that I can only go so far," Raun suggested.

"But we've both felt like he's been watching us ever since we left that place," Dave stated. "And what about that last cat?"

"I don't know," Raun replied, "but let's just get this last stone and get the ball rolling, I'm getting real tired of all this."

Completely off the subject, Dave asked, "I wonder if he's gonna appear as soon as we have the stone in our possession, or will it happen when we put it into the dagger?"

"That's a good question," Raun stated. "I don't think we'll know the answer until its happening."

PART EIGHT
The Beginning Of The End

Standing at the edge of the bridge, they couldn't help from looking down into the dark abyss, unable to even see the canyon floor. Adding to the long odds already stacked against them, a slight breeze had started to pick up. It was nothing strong, but was just enough to cause the bridge to rock and sway ever so slightly. "Come on," Raun suggested, leading the way out onto the bridge. After several steps, Raun turned around and reminded Dave, "Don't forget, I can only go half way."

"I know, I didn't forget," Dave replied.

The bridge creaked and swayed in response to even the slightest movements as they headed across. Nearing the halfway point Raun stated, "I was right, it's here, I can feel it."

"I knew something wasn't right about that board, I just knew it," Dave reiterated

Since Raun couldn't go past the halfway point of the bridge, Dave wondered why he'd taken the lead. Without an inch to spare, Dave somehow managed to step around him, taking the lead. Now standing on the other side of the board, they stood there facing each other. "Come on, take a look underneath and tell me if you can see it," Raun demanded.

"Alright already, just make sure you keep your weight on the back of my legs so I don't fall over the side of this death trap."

Raun nodded his head in agreement as he scooted back a little, allowing Dave some room to get into position. Cautiously, Dave laid down across the bridge so his legs and head were each hanging off opposing sides of the bridge. Raun straddled his legs over his back and sat down acting as a counterweight. Dave leaned forward in a difficult attempt to bend under the bridge. Using his fingers, he began feeling around on the board, after only a few seconds, he hollard up to Raun, "I found it!"

"Can you get it?" Raun asked hopefully.

"Hold on, no, I can't get it. It seems to be stuck in a knothole pretty deep."

"Can you dig it out with the dagger?"

"Yeah, probably, but if I try to get it like this, it's probably going to fall to the bottom of the canyon because I can't see how deep it is or when it's about to break free."

"Then we need to figure out another way," Raun stated. "We need this stone too badly to take a risky chance that might let it fall and shatter on the rocks below."

"Come on, help me back up," Dave demanded. "I'm starting to feel a little queasy and it looks a hell of a lot farther down to the bottom from this angle."

Raun struggled with only the use of one hand as he tried assisting Dave back up onto the bridge. With Dave now standing safe and sound back on the bridge, they both knelt down with the board centered between them. Raun grabbed a hold of each side of the plank and tried pulling up on it with several quick jarring yanks. That action didn't accomplish anything except for shaking the whole rickety bridge to the point of nearly tossing them both over the sides.

Frustrated, Raun pulled the dagger out of his belt and without thinking, he began trying to saw through the rope. "Are you nuts? What the hell are you doing?" Dave screamed at Raun.

"I was just gonna cut the rope on one side so we can pull the board up," Raun tried to explain.

"Are you out of your rabid ass mind? Haven't you noticed that there's only one rope on each side holding this death trap together?"

"I didn't really give it much thought, we just need this stone," Raun tried justifying his actions.

"Well, if we cut either one of those ropes, the whole bridge will dump sideways as the bottom falls out from beneath our feet, and exactly where do you think we'd end up?" Dave couldn't believe he actually had to explain this.

"I guess you're right," Raun agreed. "That was kinda stupid."

"Kinda stupid?" Dave reiterated "That's giving yourself a lot of credit. That's like cutting down a tree limb you're sitting on, its suicide."

"Well in the cartoons the tree falls away and the limb stays put," Raun was comically still trying to justify his thoughtless actions.

"This ain't a cartoon and that's crazy," Dave stated.

"Alright already!" Raun shouted. "I don't know what I was thinking but somehow we've gotta get this last stone."

"Then what do we do now?" Dave asked.

"I really hoped it wouldn't come to this," Raun hesitantly replied, "but one of us is going to have to cross the bridge from underneath and grab the stone as you go by."

"What the hell do you mean, as I go by?" Dave demanded. "I can't do that! Are you crazy? I'll die for sure."

"Originally, when I thought we might have to do it that way, I figured I'd be the one to do it," Raun stated, holding up what used to be his other hand. "But it don't look like that's gonna be possible."

Dave could tell by the desperate look on Raun's face combined with the process of elimination, it would have to be him that traversed the belly of the bridge. "I really don't think I can do this," Dave pleaded.

"You have to do it," Raun insisted. "You're our only

hope."

"I don't know Raun, this is freaking nuts."

"But you can make it, I know you can," Raun tried to convince him.

"I sure hope so," Dave reluctantly accepted the facts. "But if I don't, you'll be the only one left. Then what are you gonna do?"

"I'll just have to stay out here and be a thorn in his side, never letting him be able to kill me."

"Yeah, but you'll be trapped for eternity, as a lizard, with only three limbs," Dave stuttered, still trying to grasp their forlorn situation.

"We just can't let that happen then, can we?" Raun stated, ignoring Dave's remark.

"Not if I can help it," Dave replied, trying to remain hopeful

"Then are you ready?" Raun asked.

"I guess I'm about as ready as I can get for a suicide mission. Let me have the dagger and my belt back."

"Alright," Raun agreed, "I'll give them to you as soon as we're safe back on the cliff."

They stood up from where they were kneeling down and started making their way back across the bridge. While they were walking, Raun reminded him of the obvious, "You have to be real careful not to drop the dagger or the stone."

"Glad to see you're so worried about me falling," Dave remarked.

"Oh that's a given," Raun replied. "I didn't say it because I know your not gonna fall. And as long as you know that, you'll be fine."

"Thanks, but you never were real good in the support department," Dave commented.

When they stepped off the bridge and back onto the safety of the cliff side, Raun handed Dave the dagger and the belt. When Dave finished putting on the belt, he slid the dagger into place at his side, adjusting it so the dagger wouldn't fall out as he climbed across. Reaching into the bag, he pulled out the length of rope they commandeered earlier and looped it over his shoulder diagonally

Reluctantly, Dave started making his way toward the edge with Raun following closely behind. Standing at the rim, Raun abruptly called out, "Hey!"

"What? Did you see something?" Dave asked as he turned around.

"Whatever you do, make sure you give me the stone and dagger separately," Raun added.

"Why's that?" Dave curiously asked.

"I," Raun paused, apparently searching for the words he needed to finish his sentence, "I just don't want the shadow revealing himself while you're still under the bridge."

"I thought we didn't know when he'd show up? Once we have it or when it's in the dagger?" Dave asked.

"We don't," Raun replied, "but I'm pretty sure it won't be until it's in place."

"You have a good point," Dave agreed. "If he shows up while I'm stuck under the bridge, this would be a little too easy for him."

"Yeah, you'd be a sitting duck," Raun agreed.

"So what are you gonna do? Wait here or chance it on the other side?" Dave asked.

"Waiting on the other side is not an option, that makes us both vulnerable."

"So your just gonna wait here?" Dave asked puzzled.

"No, I'm gonna walk above you as you cross underneath, then you can just hand the dagger and stone up to me once you get it out, that way you won't have to worry about dropping them."

"No freaking way!" Dave shouted, surprised by the absurdity of that ridiculous idea. "That thing is enough of a death trap on its own. It sways and bounces if you even look at it the wrong. Besides, it's gonna be moving enough just with me crawling under it."

"Alright," Raun acceded to Dave's logic.

"So you can either wait on this side or that side. But if you even think about stepping on that bridge while I'm under it, I'll kill you myself."

"Alright, chill out. I see your point."

"I'm gonna make it and I won't drop either one of them," Dave proclaimed, radiating a level of confidence Raun didn't know he had in him.

"I'd better stay on this side then," Raun suggested. "I really shouldn't cross the halfway point until we're sure I can. I would hate for him to fulfill the contract before we even get a chance to fight him."

"Well, I'd better get moving then," Dave anxiously suggested. "You just make sure you keep your eyes open and let me know if you see anything, I mean anything!"

Nervously Dave continued readjusting the belt, dagger and rope as Raun nodded his head in acknowledgment. When he was finally comfortable with how it felt, he bent down and took off his shoes and socks knowing he had to do this barefoot. There was absolutely no way around it, some of the boards were so close together, it would be impossible for him to fit his foot between the planks with his shoes on. Standing upright when he finished, Raun placed his remaining claw firmly on Dave's shoulder, spinning him so they faced each other and gave him a hug as he said, "You can do it, I know you can. Just remember, were doing it for Jeff and Allen."

"I got it, don't worry," Dave replied, worried himself.

With that said, Raun made his way back to the edge of the trail where he sat down on a dead tree that had fallen. Dave reluctantly positioned himself at the base of the bridge as he prepared to make the epic fifty foot journey across the underbelly of the bridge. Fearful, he awkwardly started trying to position himself under the bridge. Not helping his concentration, Raun added one last piece of advice, "Don't let us down bro, this is our last chance at bringing an end to all this craziness."

"I know," Dave replied, still awkwardly trying to position himself underneath the bridge, "no pressure, thanks."

It appeared that getting into position underneath was starting to prove harder then crossing was going to be. Luckily, after a couple close missteps at the edge, he'd finally got himself mounted safely in place. Deep in concentration, Dave started making his suicidal crawl under this scary skeleton of sticks and twine. One foot, one hand, one foot, one hand. Each time before he made his next risky movement, he made absolutely sure that he had three of his limbs locked firmly in place before moving the fourth limb forward. Progressing slowly and carefully, the farther out he got, the more the bridge seemed to violently react to even his slightest of movements. Totally immersed in a state of deep thought and concentration, he forced himself to ignore whatever Raun was trying to yell from the cliff side With the wind whipping loudly in his ears, he was unable to make out the words well enough to understand them regardless Even if it was some kind of warning, it would do him no good, he was trapped and this task needed his undivided attention if he was to defy gravity and succeed.

Dave kept his eyes relentlessly focused on the boards above him, mainly because he refused to glance down. In addition to all of his injuries, he had muscles in his body starting to ache that he wasn't even aware he had. Already growing tired, he knew he had to hurry. With his body starting to ache and rapidly becoming numb, he tried unsuccessfully to block out the pain. With no other choice available, he had to fight failure and keep moving forward against the odds. Being too far into this crazy escapade to turn back, he knew letting go and giving up was not an option. He was well aware of the facts, if he didn't complete the task soon, it would only be a matter of time before his strength would finally give way and he would go plummeting to his death in the rocky canyon below. Trying not to think of the morbid alternative, his mind continued to race as he pondered two questions that kept repeating themselves in his head with no immediate clear answer. How long it was going to take and how hard removing the stone from the knothole would be?

One hand, one foot, one hand, one foot, was the motion he continued as he headed for the center of the bridge. His mind was burned like a wildfire as negative thoughts were starting to overpower his will to succeed. With his hopes diminishing rapidly, he was suddenly overcome by the sight of the stone just above his face. He was simply amazed that he could see the stone embedded in the board above him and the fact that he had made it, the whole situation seemed surreal. He patiently crawled forward two more planks, enabling himself a better position with the stone stationed directly above his chest.

In a desperate attempt to try securing himself to the bridge, he readjusted himself by curling his fingers and toes, wedging them tightly into the spaces between the boards. Since his left shoulder was where he had been bitten by the cat creature, he adjusted his grip predominately using his stronger right hand. Confident he was locked firmly in place for the moment, he reached across his stomach with his left hand and removed the rope hanging over his shoulder. Starting to panic, he could feel his grip start to loosen as his strength began to dissipate at a rapid rate. Desperately not wanting to fall, he tried to hurry as he carefully wrapped the rope around his back before giving the loose end a quick toss over the bridge above. Luckily, he succeeded on the first try and quickly fed the rope through two of the planks before wrapping it around his waist. This created a sling to assist in holding up the weight of his body while attempting to remove the final stone. He managed to complete the slipknot, securing himself to the bridge just as he began to lose his grip and the ability to hold himself up.

Frightened by how close he just came to falling to his death, he was at least temporarily able to breath a sigh of relief as his strained muscles enjoyed the brief chance to rest and recuperate before the dreaded return trip.

Wanting to complete this ridiculous undertaking and get out from under this bridge he focused on the task at hand. Unfortunately, even from this unique position, he was unable to free the gem with his fingers alone. With no other option, he removed the dagger from its restraint in his belt and gently placed it on his chest so he could readjust his grip once more.

Secured to the bridge, he knew the rope wasn't a perfect harness and with his battered body, it was extremely uncomfortable to say the least. His weight seemed to be putting pressure on his broken ribs. Tolerable or not, the pain was well worth the added help it gave in supporting the majority of his weight. Taking in one last deep breath, he grabbed the dagger off his chest and started to perform mock surgery on the plank.

Wedging the tip of the dagger deep into the knothole, he attempted to wiggle the stone free. After several seconds of chipping away at the wood with the blade, he could see the stone was starting to loosen and ready to break free. Setting the dagger back on his stomach, he tried stuffing his pinky finger into the tight cleft. Struggling, he tried to curl his finger behind the stone to give it a nudge, when suddenly it popped out. Catching him off guard, he tried hard to catch it by quickly closing his palm, but he missed. Heart racing, he began to panic before he realized it had landed safely in the dip of his pigeon chest. He couldn't believe he didn't feel it hit, but with his adrenaline pumping so hard, he probably could have been hit by a bus and not felt it. Taking in another deep breath, he tried to calm himself down as he carefully plucked the stone from the divot in his chest.

With the stone gripped tightly in his hand, he was awestruck that he had even come this far. With his mind starting to wander, he nervously wondered if the shadow would inconveniently choose now to make his presence known. After placing the stone in his mouth to ensure he wouldn't drop it, he gracefully grabbed the dagger off his chest with his left arm and in one quick swipe, he severed the rope. Disconnected from the bridge, the rope swiftly fell to the canyon floor. No longer supported by the makeshift sling, he was almost overwhelmed by his own weight and relentless gravity. Knowing he had to move quickly if he wanted to complete his mission, he slid the dagger back through his belt and once it was secure, he started the second leg of his journey across the bottom of the bridge. One hand, one foot, one hand, one foot. The tedious and treacherous task was progressing ever so slowly when it was suddenly interrupted mid stride. The mysterious white raven from his dream had ominously reappeared, landing on the plank directly above his head.

Dave could barely see it through the dark spaces between the boards, but he could hear it plain as day as it made its loud squawking sounds. Trying hard not to break his concentration, he ignored it at first and continued to move swiftly across the belly of the bridge. Walking above him, the bird followed his progress gently hopping from plank to plank. Suddenly, the distracting squawks transformed into the familiar, soft, friendly voice from his dream.

"Nothing is as it seems, the completed dagger is all he wants." Then the calm soothing voice returned back into the annoying squawks as the raven fluttered its wings and took flight. Dave turned his head to the right and followed the bird with his eyes. Taking a moment to himself as he watched it fly ever so gracefully, following the curves of the canyon before it too was absorbed into the darkness. As the bird disappeared he resumed his death defying crawl across the canyon.

Growing more exhausted by the second, he knew he had to pick up the pace or fail. His mind was racing faster than ever before, barely even considering the ever important placement of his hands and feet. He tried desperately to make some semblance of sense out of what the dove had told him. "It just doesn't make any sense," Dave said out loud to himself, "none of this makes any sense." Pondering the never ending stream of thoughts running through his head, Dave suddenly realized that he had run out of planks to grab a hold of. Turning his head to the side, he finally glanced down and was ecstatic to see the ground only inches away from his back. He spit the stone out of his mouth. "Yes! I did it!" he screamed as he let go of the bridge, allowing himself to fall onto the ground.

He winced at the pain, but only for a brief moment, the pain felt good as it reminded him he was alive after thinking he surely would fall to his death on this journey. He slowly rolled out from underneath the bridge, picked up the stone and climbed to his feet. Then immediately, he dropped back down to his knees, leaned forward and kissed the ground once more for good measure.

When Dave stood up, his back was facing the other side of the canyon where Raun was patiently waiting for his return. He picked the gem up off of the ground and wiped the dirt off with his blood stained shirt, Dave then retracted the dagger from his belt with his free hand. He stood there momentarily as a prisoner of his own thoughts while examining the two pieces. Fearing what is to come, he was fully aware that the items he held in the palms of his hands promised to bring fourth the beginning of the end.

"Hey! Come on, hurry!" Raun shouted from across the canyon.

PART NINE

Paranoia, Confusion & Reality

Ignoring Raun's plea, Dave stood there completely motionless as he tried to gather his thoughts and put everything into some kind of perspective. Placing the dagger back at his right side, he held the stone in his other hand with his fist tightly clenched around it. He knew he had to force himself to face the true grim reality. Doing so, he turned around and started walking down the bridge, only to discover that Raun had already started doing the same, coming toward him. They were now both a quarter of the way across with about a twenty foot gap between them. As this distance was rapidly closing, Raun shouted, "Do you have it?"

"Yeah," Dave hollered back.

"See! I knew it, I told you that you could do it," Raun said, congratulating him before he asked, "you didn't put the stone in place yet, did you?"

"No, it's right here," Dave replied, holding out his open palm, exposing the stone. As Dave glanced down into his palm, he noticed something odd, this stone wasn't acting like any of the others they had located previously. This one was giving off its mysterious blue glow even prior to being placed in the dagger. Dave thought this was very peculiar, but what bothered him even more, was the fact that it continued getting brighter the closer he got to Raun, the dagger and the other stones.

The gap between them had reduced itself to only a few feet when Raun held out both hands and demanded, "Let me have them."

It appeared that Dave was about to hand him the dagger and stone when he made a swift and sudden decision. In one motion, he dropped the remaining stone into the remaining hole on the dagger and raised it up over his head. Raun had a wide-eyed look of fear etched into his face from the sheer surprise of Dave's swift action.

"Nooo!" Raun cried out in a sharp ear piercing shriek.

Dave forcefully lowered the dagger, dragging the blade diagonally across Raun's shirt. Blue sparks exploded outward from his chest as the blade slashed through his outer garments and deep into the cavity of his chest. Dave was anything but surprised as the whole first set of stones were suddenly revealed.

The stones were no longer housed in a large bulky tablet. The book and gems appeared to have been transformed into a silver medallion. It held the same strange design as the engravings they found on the table back in the cabin, only in a more compact form. This made it possible for him to conceal and carry them with him without being detected. It hung around his neck dangling from a black leather strap and still held the shape of an upside down star. The star itself was held together by two solid silver rings that connected at the pentagrams points and were woven with silver strands through the middle to hold the center stone in place.

With bright blue sparks continuing to discharge from Raun's chest, the whole dark area of the canyon was now extremely well lit by the sparks from the massive electrical discharge. Raun's body started flashing back and fourth between the images of Raun, the lizard and the cryptic shadow, like a hologram slowly losing power. The whole scene was reminiscent of being back inside the cabin when Raun struggled to regain control over the rooms physical appearance. After several seconds of intense and blinding chaos, the surrounding images finally stabilized and revealed the shadow as a full reptile. Wearing his black hooded robe he once again had two hands. Even now, with all the intense blue light, there was only darkness where his face should have been and his eyes were as red as the fires of hell.

Getting hard to keep their balance, the bridge was rocking and swaying with every sudden movement. The shadow regained his balance after being caught off guard by Dave's sudden attack. With another fierce blast of electricity, he used his left hand and abruptly stopped the flow of blood from pouring out through the deep gash across his chest. With his wound seared shut, he then raised both his arms and aimed his claws at Dave. Another massive flow of electricity shot out through the tips of his fingers. Panic stricken, Dave jumped several feet backwards and somehow managed to raise the dagger and luckily blocked off the attack. He wasn't even aware of how he did it, but somehow, the blade of the dagger found itself in just the right spot to fend off the full effect of the powerful discharge. His body trembled with fear as he felt the dagger absorbing the blast.

With the attack blocked, the fierce flow of electricity suddenly stopped. Dave spun the dagger around in the palm of his hand so the tip was pointing down and raised it up over his head as he stepped forward. Forcefully, he lowered the dagger and drove the blade down through Raun's shoulder and deep into his chest. The tip of the blade ripped through his insides and punctured his heart. The shadow cried out in agonizing pain as Dave withdrew the dagger from his latest wound. The creature was gushing blood from multiple lacerations as the canyon below them suddenly ignited into a blazing inferno. The flames stretched out for miles in both directions and seemed to mirror the shadow's anger and rage.

After taking the near fatal plunge from Dave, the shadow reached out in an attempt to grab him, only to give Dave prime opportunity to swipe the blade clear across the creature's throat. Blood erupted out of the shadow's neck, squirting and spurting out in every direction as it sprayed all over Dave's face and clothes. After suffering the fatal blow, the creatures body slowly collapsed and now lay on the bridge dying. The flames below continued to rage as if they were awaiting something else.

Confident the creature was no longer a threat, Dave leaned forward and slid the tip of the dagger under the leather strap. Still keeping his distance, he used the dagger and lifted up the star and slid the medallion up over the creatures head. During that process, the hood receded from the creatures head, revealing the fact that the creature had only darkness where his face should have been.

As Dave examined the medallion, he realized the center stone had fallen out and was lying on the shadows bloody chest. He leaned forward and picked up the stone. When he stood back up, he examined it for a few seconds before carefully placing it in his front pocket. Standing there in silence, he glared down at the defeated faceless creature.

Holding the dagger and star in each of his hands, he desperately wanted all of this to come to an end. He placed his foot on the creatures shoulder and rolled him off of the bridge into the fiery abyss burning below. As the body disappeared into the fire, the flames roared up twenty feet above the bridge as if someone had dumped a million gallons of gas into the canyon. With the bridge engulfed in flames, the fire burned violently for about ten seconds without singeing so much as a hair on Dave's body, or a single strand of the rope that held this ancient contraption together.

The blazing inferno suddenly disappeared as the sun popped up over the horizon to break the new dawn and overpower the perpetual darkness of the entire area. Dave stood there astounded in disbelief that this nightmare was finally over. Still trying to grasp reality, he took in a deep breath before glancing over the side of the bridge.

When he looked down, he didn't understand how the shadow's body had vanished without a trace. How could that be he wondered? None of this made any sense, especially when the body of the half-breed cat still laid there on the canyon's floor. The cat's body was twisted and mangled, with the shadow no where to be found. And as strange as that was, what bothered him even more was the fact that the cat's body was laying only thirty feet away from a large puddle. How the puddle was even still there was unfathomable. Not even the patchy vegetation had been harmed by the blazing inferno that raged and consumed the whole valley only moments ago.

Confused, deep in his own thoughts, Dave struggled as he forced the medallion into his back pocket. He happened to glance down at the blade of the dagger and was disgusted. He never really could tolerate the sight of blood, but this eternal night seemed to have numbed his nerves. He ran the blade of the dagger across the thigh of his tattered jeans twice, attempting to remove the dripping blood from the stained steel of the weapon. Satisfied, he began walking down the bridge toward the trail leading home. Tears filled his eyes as the reality of so many losses finally started to sink in. Up until now, he didn't even realize how close he had actually came to losing his own life on several occasions. With his adrenaline winding down, it was only now that he realized how badly banged up he was.

He was an emotional wreck. Trying to hold back the inevitable tears as he continued to walk. Immediately when he stepped off the bridge he began to hallucinate. He was sure Raun's voice just called out to him. Due to his mental state, he ignored it and continued on his way. Then he heard it again, this time it was louder and clearer than before. He forced himself to turn around and acknowledge the fact that he had entirely lost his mind. Upon turning around, he was shocked at the sight of Raun running across the bridge toward him. He was carrying Dave's shoes and the duffel bag that he'd left behind as he yelled, "Dave! Dave! Wait up!"

Dave glanced down to his feet, he had forgotten that he'd taken off his shoes and left them on the other side. Regardless, he turned around and started running down the flimsy bridge toward Raun. They were both over any fears they once had about this rickety contraption. When they met in the middle, they embraced in a huge hug neither of them thought they would ever feel again.

At first Dave was leery that this could possibly be another trick. After quickly examining the facts in his head, he came to the conclusion that this could not possibly be another impostor. Everything seemed to have returned back to normal. "Are you alright?" Dave asked, no longer in control or able to hold back his tears.

"Yeah," Raun shouted, "I'm fine!" He too had tears in his eyes.

"I thought you were dead," Dave stated.

"No," Raun replied. "I've been trapped inside that room with the table the whole time. He took away all the doors."

"Why didn't he kill you?" Dave asked.

"He planned on it," Raun began to explain. "In order for him to disguise himself as me, he had to keep me alive."

"Why?" Dave asked.

"The stones only give him the ability to hold the image of active DNA."

"Then why was he turning into a lizard?" Dave had to know.

"Right before he died, he was in the process of trying to combine his DNA with that of a lizard."

"I thought you said that he would only be able to hold living images?" Dave questioned the contradictory statements.

"True," Raun replied, "but when my blood got on the tablet, the dried blood mixed with mine and the pattern got all screwed up."

"That's nuts," Dave stated.

"This whole situation is nuts," Raun repeated.

"What about Jeff and Allen?" Dave asked hopefully.

"They're dead," Raun whispered as tears intensified in both of their eyes.

"This is unreal, I can't believe all this happened," Dave said sobbing.

After a few moments, they were able to regain their control over their emotions. That's when Raun had to ask, "How did you know that he wasn't me?"

Before Dave answered, he bent down and slipped on his shoes and placed the dagger into the empty duffel bag, leaving the star and loose stone in his pockets. Raun then followed Dave's lead as they started making their way off the bridge. That's when Dave decided to explain his wild and uncertain actions. "Just a few little things gave him away," Dave started to explain as they walked.

"You must've been pretty sure," Raun stated, "unless you were actually trying to kill me."

"No, it wasn't anything like that," Dave replied. "I was almost positive when we left the cabin."

"How's that?" Raun asked.

"I stopped to say good bye to Jeff and he never even mentioned Allen."

"That's all you had to go on and you tried to kill me?" Raun interrupted, not believing what he was hearing.

"Just listen," Dave demanded. "I blew it off at first

because I didn't really know how to deal with all this myself. But the more I listened to what he had to say, I realized that he was more worried about the stones than our lives."

"Still!" Raun shouted. "That ain't much more then a guess."

"I know," Dave tried to continue. "I wasn't actually sure until a white raven showed up while I was crawling under the bridge."

"Under the bridge, are you nuts?" Raun repeated.

"That's a long story, I'll tell you that one later. Anyway, the raven told me that nothing is as it seems and that the completed dagger is all he wants."

"That's a little better," Raun said.

"I know, that's when I finally added two and two together and came up with four."

"I didn't know you could add," Raun chuckled.

"Shut up and let me finish," Dave replied. "Anyway, I thought back and realized that the shadow was only a ghost until we gave him the stone that projected the image of man onto the ceiling. That's why he wasn't able to impersonate you until then, right?"

"That's right," Raun agreed, "but it had to be me because it was my blood that was waking the beast, even then, that only gave him power over our minds while I was trapped," the tone of Raun's voice was increasing as his frustrations grew.

"I know!" Dave interrupted. "You were still in there! You just couldn't move, talk or be seen?"

"How did you know that?" Raun asked as they had started heading into the trail.

"He told us," Dave replied. "He just conveniently left out the part about you still being there and the fact that he was with us."

"He must have been trying to avoid getting caught in a lie," Raun suggested.

"Either that or he's got no imagination," Dave agreed. "Ya know what else tipped me off?"

"What?" Raun asked curiously.

"Once he showed up as you, Jeff and me always had to be the one to grab everything first and somehow give it to him, even if he was the one to find it," Dave said, not understanding why it took him so long to realize that.

"That's because all of that stuff had to be given to him. If it wasn't for that, he'd have never needed us," Raun stated.

"So I was right," Dave said out loud, mainly to himself. "That's why he faked that last attack by that cat thing." Dave couldn't perceive before how elaborate this game of trickery had become, it all seemed so surreal.

"What?" Raun shouted, "he had himself attacked by one of those cats?"

"Actually, he did it several times," Dave stated. "He even had the shadow speak to us one time before he tossed us across the room. But that was probably part of his plan to help convince me that he was you."

"I'll bet it almost worked too, didn't it?"

"It did," Dave agreed. "I can't believe what a scam that was. He was even supposed to be the one to scale the bridge and get the last stone."

"How was he gonna do that?" Raun didn't understand.

"Of course, that was before that last cat attacked us and ripped off his hand," Dave said as he slightly chuckled at how obvious all this was in hindsight.

"That's one way to get out of it," Raun agreed.

"Really," Dave agreed, "once that happened, there was no way that he could have done it with one hand and that's how I ended up under the bridge."

"Well, it's a good thing you figured out everything when you did," Raun stated. "Once he had his hands on the dagger and the star it would have been over."

"Why's that?" Dave asked.

"He wouldn't have been confined to this area. He'd have been free to go wherever he wanted."

"So that's why he didn't want to get too far away from this area," Dave stated.

"He told you?" Raun asked.

"He claimed if he went past the half way point of the bridge, the shadow would be able to kill him."

"That's one way to hide your own boundaries," Raun agreed.

"Anyway, how did you get out of the cabin?" Dave asked curiously.

"Actually," Raun paused, "I finally found a hidden exit when a door showed up out of no where."

"You couldn't find it on your own?"

"Trust me, I tried," Raun said, "but with no light it seemed hopeless and I'd all but given up."

"I thought you had a flashlight?" Dave asked with a confused look on his face.

"I did," Raun replied, "but the batteries died."

"I swear," Dave said as he began shaking his head, "if Allen had half a brain, he'd still be alive."

"I was kinda surprised he brought four of them," Raun added.

"I'd of rather had one that worked right," Dave said as they could now see the entrance to the trails only twenty feet away. That alone was a beautiful sight they never thought they'd see again.

“And you were right,” Raun said out of the blue.

“About what?” Dave asked.

“I did stop and see Jeff and Allen before I came looking for you,” Raun replied.

“See!” Dave shouted. “I knew, I knew you better then that.”

CHAPTER FOUR
AGRESSIONS & DISBELIEF

As they stepped out of the trails and onto the dirt road, they were nearly run over by a sheriff's car that just happened to be passing by at a speed they would have pulled someone else over for going. They were barely able to see the brake lights through the massive dust cloud it left behind as it passed. Dave and Raun stood there and waited as the car turned around and started making its way back to where they were standing. As the car pulled up next to them, they realized that the officer driving it was none other then Raun's uncle, Nick Balden.

The car hadn't even come to a complete stop when Nick slammed it into park and jumped out of it as he began to shout, "Are you two alright? Jeez! Look at you. What happened? Your parents are worried sick! And we've had the whole town out looking for you."

"We were just messing around in the trails and we found the cabin," Dave exclaimed.

"What cabin?" Nick asked. "The one from the myth?"

"Yeah," Dave confirmed.

"How did you find it?" Nick asked. "No one ever found it! In fact, those stories have never been proven true."

"They are!" Raun stated, "and they're even worse than anyone knows."

"Where are your brothers at?" Nick finally got around to asking.

They both lifted their heads with tears in their eyes as they simultaneously replied, "They're both dead."

Nick was standing there in shock as he tried taking in the information they just provided. Forcing himself back to reality, he unlatched his police radio from the side of his utility belt and called into the station. "This is 139. Come in dispatch, over."

"Go ahead 139, over," A woman's voice replied.

"I'm on 24th near Warwick. I need paramedics and someone from the homicide division ASAP. Over."

"What's your status 139? Over."

"I have two of the missing boys, Raun Stevens and Dave Healy," Nick paused, "their telling me the other two are dead."

"Roger that, anything else? Over."

"Get Shane out here right away and have the boys parents go to Leslie Memorial. Over."

"Got it, over and out," she replied. Then the radio went silent for a moment before they all heard her request for 142 to report in to dispatch.

As Nick reconnected his radio to his utility belt, he doubtfully insinuated, "So you're telling me an age-old legend killed your brothers and tried to kill you?"

"I know it sounds crazy, but it's true," Dave pleaded.

"I believe you," Nick reluctantly said. Trying to reassure himself, he asked, "Why would you guys lie to me? So this maniac is still alive and out there or what?"

"I don't think he's been alive for a long time," Dave suggested as he handed Nick the bag with the dagger in it, then he pulled the star and loose stone from his jeans pockets and handed them to him as he added, "but he's dead now."

Nick briefly examined the star and stone before he placed them on the hood of his car. He then unzipped the bag, when he looked inside he couldn't believe what he was looking at. As much as he wanted to believe the kids story, he knew that he couldn't take the blood stained dagger out of the bag. This was still most likely a murder investigation and taking the dagger out of the bag without taking the proper precautions could destroy evidence and fingerprints. He zipped the bag closed and led the kids to the rear of the car. He opened the door and had them sit in the back seat. Once they were inside, Nick closed the door and climbed into the front seat closing the door behind him.

There was complete silence for several seconds before Nick started to say, “I remember my dad telling me stories back when I was your age, but I always thought he was just trying to scare me into not staying out too late and that he'd made them up.”

“So did we,” Raun insisted, “we never thought we’d be the ones to actually find that place.”

“I’m gonna have both your parents meet you at the hospital and I’m gonna have to ask you guys some more questions later. But for now, I just wanna get you guys checked out. You don’t look real good.”

“You going out to the cabin?” Raun asked his uncle.

“Yeah,” Nick said. “Don’t worry, I’ll take care of everything and get it all figured out. So exactly where is this cabin?”

Dave and Raun both pointed to the entrance of the trails as Dave said, “You gotta take the trail to the left of the hill. It’s got a big rusted chain blocking it off. Then you go all the way past the rope bridge and it’s about a hundred yards on your left.”

“It’s just past the patch of fog, you can’t miss it,” Raun added.

He no more then finished his sentence when they could all hear the sounds of rapidly approaching sirens. Nick stepped out of the car and opened the rear door for them. As they climbed out, an ambulance pulled up and parked behind Nick. Still a mile or so down the road, there was another squad car approaching.

With the three of them standing there, Nick unhooked his radio once again and called in to the station. "This is 139, paramedics and back up are arriving as we speak. I'm sending the two minors to Leslie Memorial and we'll proceed with our investigation as soon as homicide arrives, over."

"This is dispatch, roger that, over."

"139, over and out."

When Nick replaced his radio onto his belt, he looked at both the boys sympathetically as he told them, "I'm sending you guys to the hospital now. Your parents should be there soon and I'll come check on you in a little bit."

Dave and Raun both nodded their heads in agreement as the two paramedics ran over toward them carrying their medical supply bags. The taller of the two medics had short dark hair. Nick had known John Brandons for the last three years. They met in a course on CPR that John was teaching to all the area precincts. The shorter guy was kind of stocky with long blonde hair and blue eyes, Tony Brown, he started tending to the kids right away as John got the details from Nick. "Are these the only two? I thought there were four kids missing?" John asked Nick, sincerely concerned.

"Yeah, for right now anyway," Nick said, letting it be known that it bothered him that they'd only found two of the boys. "The other two are presumed dead, but we haven't located their bodies yet," he finished with a tear in his eye.

"Sorry to hear that," John said, trying to comfort him a little. "Should I radio in for another unit?"

"Don't bother, I'll call it in as soon as we locate them. I'm still holding onto hope of finding them alive," Nick stated. "You're taking them to Leslie Memorial, right?"

"Yeah, they already know we're en-route. They're trying to locate the parents as we speak," John replied.

Officer Shane Marys was Nick's partner. They'd

known each other for years, both of them had transferred here at the same time. He'd just arrived on the scene and was getting out of his car as Nick gave both Dave and Raun a hug before they were carefully escorted to the ambulance by the paramedics. “I’ll see you guy’s in a couple of hours,” Nick said to them.

“Alright,” Raun agreed as Dave rudely cut him off.

“Make sure you have that stuff destroyed! It’s pure evil!”

With a confused and concerned look on his face, Nick replied. “Don’t worry, I’ll take care of it and I’ll be seeing ya in a little bit.”

The kids were now in the back of the ambulance with John. When Tony climbed into the driver’s seat, he looked back and asked, “You guy’s ready?” Turning on the sirens.

With the ambulance pulling off of the scene, Officer Marys was now standing across from Nick as he leaned against the drivers side front quarter panel of his squad car. The bag containing the dagger was still closed, but the star and loose stone were in plain view laying on the hood. To Shane the sad look of confusion on his friends face was more than apparent. As much as he hated the idea of sharing in the pain his partner was feeling, Shane was well aware that Nick didn’t have any answers yet, but he had to ask, “What the hell is going on here? And what’s all that shit?” Shane added as he pointed at everything lying on the hood.

“I don’t know,” Nick hesitated, “but I have a bad feeling, I think when we find the other two boys, there gonna be dead.”

“Those two didn’t look that good themselves,” Shane added.

“I know,” Nick agreed, as he pointed to the artifacts lying on his hood, adding, “they gave me all this stuff and said they'd found Eric Aben's cabin and that he was still alive, until they killed him."

"But that's just a myth," Shane insisted.

"They swear it's the truth and they say he caused their whole situation."

"That's completely insane!" Shane shouted. "You can't honestly tell me you believe that story, do you?"

"They said that his ghost killed their brothers and tried to kill them. Aside from how beat down they looked, they claimed to have won," Nick explained.

"Listen to yourself," Shane demanded. "Would you believe this story if I were telling it to you?"

"Probably not," Nick agreed, "but you should have heard these kids. They seemed so sure about what they were saying."

"Alright," Shane said, showing his frustration. "Let's say I believe ya, now what the hell are these?" Shane asked as he leaned forward and picked the star up off the hood of the car.

"I'm not sure," Nick replied. "They just told me they're evil. Then they begged me to have them destroyed."

"Come on Nick, these kids can't expect us to believe this ridicules story. They're just old folk tales and they've never been proven."

"I know," Nick agreed once again. "It's just that they seemed so sure of themselves and I really don't think my nephew would lie to me, he wasn't brought up like that!"

Shane set the star back down on the hood and unzipped the duffel bag. He was baffled by what he was looking at inside the bag. He reached into his back pocket and pulled out two pair of latex gloves. Shaking his head, he handed a pair to Nick and they both began putting them on as Shane suggested, "Sometimes kids do this weird kind of stuff because they want attention."

"Yeah, but not this time," Nick demanded. "I wish you could have got a good look at those kids. I mean, some of their wounds looked horrible. Dave's shoulder looked like raw hamburger meat for Christ's sake."

"I did get a quick look as they walked past me," Shane insisted.

"Just look at all the blood in my backseat," Nick added.

"It is a lot," Shane agreed as he peered in through the window. "It's gonna take you all afternoon to clean that up."

"I know, that's why I rushed them off to the hospital so quick. I didn't want them dying in my car," Nick stated, showing his sincere concern for the boys well being.

"Were gonna have to talk to them soon, we definitely need some more information out of them," Shane said.

"They know, I told them we'd be over to see them in a little bit. I just wanted to get them checked out," Nick reaffirmed.

With latex gloves on, Shane reached into the bag and pulled out the blood stained dagger and asked, "So where did they get these? They look ancient and they're probably worth a fortune."

"I know, just look at the size of those gems," Nick agreed. "Not to mention they're both made out of solid silver and pewter."

Shane set the dagger back down inside the bag as they both heard the wailing sound of another siren approaching. Hearing the sound, they both turned their heads to look as a black unmarked Plymouth pulled up and parked behind Shane. As the car came to a stop, the driver's side door popped open. Instantly, Nick and Shane gazed at each other with a disappointed look on their face.

Krista Rose was the short haired blonde climbing out of the driver's side as her partner remained in the car calling in their location. Shane lightly stomped his foot on the ground as he quietly shouted, "Damn! Why the hell did they have to send her?"

"I think she's a curse someone placed on you," Nick said sarcastically.

"I'm telling you," Shane replied, "I just can't get away from that bitch."

Shane and Krista had just gotten out of a serious relationship that had taken a severe wrong turn down a one way street. Their engagement broke off just over a year ago and when Shane asked her for the huge diamond back that he had to mortgage his house to purchase, it mysteriously came up missing in their last big fight. Shane held onto a growing resentment for this woman, yet she seemed inescapable. He was still making payments on the ring because the infamous fight occurred before he was able to get the ring appraised and covered on his insurance policy.

The bitterness between them was more than mutually shared. Now-a-days it had escalated to the point where they both hated even being in the same room with one another. Making occasionally seeing each other at work awkward to say the least and when the occasion did arise that they were forced to work with each other, those days were the worst. Even though they worked for separate departments, they were still both police officers and situations did arise. Just like now, all they could do was bite their lips and deal with the situation as best they could.

They didn't recognize Krista's new partner. In fact, they didn't even actually notice him until he got out of the car and started walking toward them. He had dark brown hair and a medium build. To Nick and Shane he didn't even look old enough to have graduated the academy, let alone be a homicide detective. All they could do was presume he was still a rookie under Krista's supervision. "Nick, Shane," Krista politely acknowledged their presence as she walked up.

"Morning Krista," Nick replied.

"This is Steve Duncan, my new protégé," Krista stated as she pointed to her partner, finally climbing out of the car.

"What did ya do, break up with your last partner and send him to the poor house?" Shane commented, putting Krista's character on display for Steve to see.

"He's on vacation," Krista defended. "Not that it's any of your business."

"This isn't the time, nor the place," Nick interjected, trying to change the subject, feeling awkwardly in the middle.

"So what's the situation?" Steve asked, trying to remain professional and get out of this melodramatic situation where you could cut the tension with a knife.

"Really," Krista added, also wanting out of a bad spot.

"We're not exactly sure yet," Nick hesitantly replied.

"Tell us what ya know so far," Steve suggested.

"Well," Nick started to explain, "I sent the two minors to Leslie Memorial. They claim their two brothers were killed by the ghost of Eric Aben."

"A ghost," Krista repeated, unable to believe what she was hearing.

"The one minor," Nick continued, trying to remain professional. "Dave Healy, was torn up pretty bad, so I at least believe them that something crazy was going on out here."

Shane's frustration with the whole situation had caused him to nervously pace back and fourth as he began to shout, "I don't care what them kids say! I refuse to accept the fact that some fifty year old myth is behind this."

"Do you two goof balls even have a body yet?" Krista interrupted.

"Well, no, not exactly," Nick's words trailed off with embarrassment.

"Then why did you radio in so presumptively for a homicide investigation?" Steve asked.

Shane looked over to Nick with doubt in his eyes, frustrated and hating the fact that they really looked like a couple local yokels. Then he turned his eyes on Steve and then back on Krista as he replied, "They're just a couple of little kids. So I do believe them at least about their brothers being dead. Why would they lie about something like that?"

Nick stepped in between the two ticking time bombs and calmly stated, "Look, two of these boys are my nephews and my sister didn't raise any liars."

With a disgusted look on her face, Krista shook her head and said, "Listen you guys, both of you know this isn't proper procedure. You don't call in for a homicide investigation until you have a body."

"I know," Nick agreed, pleading, "it's family."

Krista abruptly cut him off, making it known that she was going to continue, "But since we're here and two of these boys are your nephews," poking her finger into Nick's chest, "we'll get this checked out real quick. That way, we can all get back to more desirable company."

"I couldn't agree more," Shane stated, slightly puffing out his chest.

"So what kind of real facts are we actually working with here?" Steve asked.

Shane looked over to Nick and repeated, "Really then, what would those facts be, Mr. Ghostbuster? I'm kind of lacking in the information department myself."

"To tell ya guys the truth, I really don't know much,"

Nick replied, "but here's what I do know. The four boys have been missing since sometime after school three days ago. That's the last place and time they'd been seen. Neither of their parents were home when they got out of school, but when we talked to them they said there was no way they could tell if they had ever been home and left again."

"How did you find them?" Krista asked.

"I was just cruising down Warwick here and I spotted the two of them coming out of the trails," Nick responded, "before I was even able to get out of my car and approach them, I could already see that Dave was covered in blood. Then when I asked where their brothers were, they told me they were killed by this legend we have here."

"So you're telling me that we have an actual living ghost?" Krista remarked, trying to hold back her laughter.

"No, they claimed they killed it," Nick said, trying not to sound as crazy as this story implied.

"I can't believe this town," Krista said as she could no longer hold in her laughter. "These people are still telling this story? Its fifty years old and it's fake! You see," she said as she looked at her partner, "this is why I can't live in a small town like this. These people have nothing to do. Do ya?" she asked as she glanced back and forth between Nick and Shane.

"There's nothing wrong with life in a small town!" Shane barked at Krista. "I love it, it's just not for everyone and apparently it's not for you."

"This town is lame," Krista replied. "You guys keep telling the same story, over and over again just so the tourists will have something to remember this shit hole for," she paused momentarily, "are you guys ever gonna grow up and face reality?"

Nick had finally heard enough of her big city jive and cut her off as he demanded, "Stop interrupting me and let me finish."

Krista was startled by Nick's sudden assertiveness, but managed to reply, "Damn, you're just as mentally unstable as he is," pointing to Shane.

Shane didn't take too lightly to Krista's remark and snapped, "Just shut your trap and let him finish so we can all get back to what we're supposed to be doing"

"I really don't know all that much more," Nick reluctantly replied. He paused, creating an awkward moment of silence. "They just said that the cabin where all this happened is located down the trail on the left," he finally added as he pointed to the entrance to the trails.

"You can't be serious?" Krista asked.

"This is what they told me," Nick insisted. "They said on the high side of the trail, there was a path that had been blocked off by a rusted chain barricade. They also said that it's about a hundred yards past the rope bridge, oh yeah, and just past the patch of fog."

"Like there's still gonna be fog there," Krista added doubtfully.

"I'm just relaying the message," Nick stated. Then as he pointed to the artifacts lying on his hood, he said, "That's all they told me. Then they handed me the duffel bag with all this stuff in it and he pulled the loose stone out of his pocket."

As they all stood there with their full attention focused on the artifacts, Krista asked, "Where did they get all this stuff?"

"Really," Steve said, pausing briefly before adding, "looks like something someone stole out of a museum, there ain't been no museum robberies, have there?"

Nick just shrugged his shoulders as he replied, "I don't know, they only told me that this stuff needed to be destroyed."

The three of them stood there staring at Nick with the intense look of confusion collectively burned into their faces. Trying to break up another awkward moment, Nick said, "I don't understand any of it either. All I know is, there is a whole lot of information missing and we'd better get started if we're gonna piece this puzzle together."

When the state police homicide unit arrived on the scene, Krista automatically became lead officer in charge of the investigation. Nick and Shane didn't like the idea of her calling the shots, but that was the privilege of her position. "Shane," Krista called out, "since you're not related to either of the kids, I want you to go to the hospital and see what kind of information you can get from them."

"I need to be there too, for my sister," Nick pleaded.

"That's fine," Krista agreed, as she pointed to the duffel bag she added, "but first I want you to take these artifacts over to the Sacred Heart."

"Why?" Nick curiously asked.

Krista replied "Just see if Reverend Soncrainte can make any sense out of what they are or where they came from?" She paused for a brief moment before continuing, "Steve and I will go and check out this cabin. We'll let you guys know as soon as we know something and keep me posted on anything you find out that might prove to be useful."

With that said, they all dispersed and proceeded to accomplish their assigned tasks at hand.

PART TWO
The Hospital

The ambulance pulled into the hospital's emergency entrance, John Brandons opened the back door. He helped Raun and Dave out of the vehicle, then escorted them as they entered the hospital. When John closed the rear door of the ambulance, Tony pulled over onto the side of the hospital and parked. As John and the kids walked over to the admissions desk, the young lady working behind the counter greeted them gleefully.

She was around twenty-five years old, tall and slender with long brown hair. Her eyes were a shade of emerald green neither of the boys had ever seen before. She was the most beautiful woman they had ever saw, but their hearts were quickly broken as they noticed the eye contact between her and John. "Ah, Renae, how ya doing this lovely morning?" John said.

"I'm fine," she replied. "What do we have here?"

John looked at the boys and said, "This is Renae guys, she's gonna take good care of you."

Raun and Dave both smiled, blushing as they said, "Hello."

John turned his attention back to Renae and started to explain as he pointed, "Well, this is Raun. He appears to be fine other then a few little nicks and bruises. And this is Dave, he's not as fortunate. He has a sprained ankle and says he was bitten by a mountain lion."

"Oh my god, mountain lions?" she asked, before adding, " you poor thing."

"It wasn't that..." Dave started to explain before John cut him off.

"You can tell her later, we just need to get you guys

through all this real quick so we can get ya looked at," John apologized to Dave and continued explaining the situation to Renae. "He does have several deep lacerations and bruising on his shoulder, they needed serious attention hours ago."

"Let me have a look you," Renae said as she gently pulled Dave's shirt off of his shoulder. "Ouch," she added.

They looked like they needed some stitches a while ago," John stated, "but at least the blood has dried them closed for now. I also think a couple of his ribs are either broken or bruised, he's gonna need an x-ray to know for sure. Aside from all that, I think he's gonna live," he added as he rubbed his hand on top of Dave's head, embarrassing him slightly.

"Alright guy's, come with me," she insisted as she rested her hand on Dave's good shoulder. As the three of them began walking down the hall, Renae turned her head to look behind her, giving John a flirtatious wink as she pointed at him and spoke in a provocative tone, "I'll see you, later on tonight."

John stood there, momentarily paralyzed by her voice, watching obsessively as she walked down the hallway. She was just about to turn the corner when he was finally able to break his trance like state, "Hey! Renae."

"Yeah?" she replied, turning her head to face him.

"I forgot, I have to work late tonight. Can I just meet you at the bowling alley, say, around seven?" John asked.

"That'll be fine, but try not to be late. The league starts at seven thirty," Renae responded. Then she looked to the boys and pointed to an examining room down the hall to the left and said, "Why don't you guys go and have a seat in there, I'll be right with ya in a moment."

Dave and Raun both agreed and made their way into the examining room. Renae headed back down the hallway and spoke to John for a few more minutes. When they were all finished, John headed out of the hospital through the emergency entrance and back toward the ambulance. Renae headed back to her desk in the triage area, grabbed a stack of files and disappeared into one of the back offices.

Dave tried to get comfortable on the examining table to the best of his ability. Up until now, he hadn't even realized how much pain he was actually in. While they were both bored and waiting, Raun kept him entertained as he sat on the doctors small mushroom stool and began to impatiently spin around in circles as they discussed all they had been through.

PART THREE
Mysterious Body

Steve and Krista had made it quite a ways down the dark and winding trail. They weren't sure of exactly what they were looking for, but according to the kid's story, they had supposedly located this cabin that had remained elusive for over fifty years. They were both fully aware that the whole town legend was based on the assumption that this place did in fact exist, though it had never been proven. The fact that it was never found is what gave the story its romantic affect on the tourists and the town. Assuming there had to be at least some aspect of truth to the wild tale these kids supposedly swore by, they continued to walk down the trail.

Steve still felt a little uncomfortable around Krista after the awkward introduction to her ex and his friend. He wasn't prepared, nor was he expecting the tension to be so high, even though Krista had warned him on the way over. As they continued to walk through the darkness, Steve finally found something he was willing to mention. "Look!" he shouted. "Up ahead, it's a clearing in the darkness. That must be where that rope bridge is?"

"That must mean we're going down the right trail," Krista stated. She'd been slightly unsure at first, due to the many different paths they could have chosen near the entrance.

"That's a good thing, right?" Steve asked redundantly.

"Wow, look at that, I didn't know there were any of these still in use around here," Krista said, pointing ahead.

"Me neither," Steve agreed.

Arriving at the bridge, they couldn't believe their eyes. Even more so, they couldn't believe those kids had enough balls to cross this rickety death trap. Krista looked at

Steve with her sparkling, sapphire blue eyes and quietly asked, "Do you think this thing will hold us?"

"I don't know, but I sure hope so," Steve reluctantly replied. "We've got to cross it. I guess I'll go first." Hoping to impress his boss, not to mention his being attracted to her. Krista did not dispute his offer of going first. Truth be told, neither of them wanted to go across at all, but they silently kept that to themselves. With Steve leading the way, Krista followed closely behind. They were no more then a few steps out onto the bridge when they noticed the wind had picked up in intensity. It was frighteningly obvious that the farther they progressed, the more the entire bridge started to rock, shake and sway. With them now suspended high above the canyon floor, their fear was starting to get the better of them.

Trying desperately to hide his morbid fear of heights from Krista, Steve refused to look down and kept his undivided attention focused on the other side of the cliff. The erratic movements of the bridge were making them both queasy, it felt like they were trying to walk across the surface of the ocean in the middle of a storm. They were nearing the halfway point and it was nearly impossible to hear anything with the wind whipping fiercely in their ears.

Krista called out to Steve, "Hey! What's that? Down there, at the bottom of the canyon."

"Where?" Steve asked, trying not to take his eyes off the tree directly in front of him where he had intently focused his eyes the whole way across.

"Over there," she replied as she pointed off the right side of the bridge.

"You're determined to make me look down, aren't you?" Steve asked, trying not to indicate his level of fear.

"I thought I was supposed to be the fragile little girl here," Krista said sarcastically. "You're not scared of heights, are ya?"

"No," Steve replied, "I just don't like them."

Somehow, Steve managed to make his legs stop with their relentless forward motion, it was as if they had a mind of their own and were racing to get off of this bridge. Tightly, he grabbed a hold of the rope handrail. Virtually closing his eyes, he forced himself to look over the edge. When he finally managed to force his eyelids the rest of the way open, he shouted back to her without turning around, "It's a body!"

"Is it one of those boys?" Krista asked, unable to tell.

"I can't tell from here," Steve replied. "Looks like there's a bunch of vultures down there on it."

"Let's get down there," Krista demanded.

"Alright, I'm moving," Steve stated as he looked for the strength to make his legs respond to his wishes.

Both Steve and Krista feared the worst. There was no way they could possibly identify the body from this distance, especially with it being covered with the flesh eating birds. The unpleasant visual image of hungry vultures eating one of the boy's bodies temporarily sidetracked his mind from his intense fear of heights. They were now moving at a faster pace than they had even realized. In no time at all, they'd made it all the way across the bridge. "See, that wasn't so bad," Krista said sarcastically as she patted Steve on the shoulder like he was a child.

"Yeah, whatever," Steve replied, feeling defeated and embarrassed

"Come on, this way," Krista suggested as she now took the lead onto a narrow pathway located just to the right of the bridge. The trail was mostly overgrown with tall grass and would have gone completely unnoticed if the weeds wouldn't have started dying off due to the rapidly approaching change of season. The concealed narrow path was made up entirely of loose gravel and dirt. Forcing their way through the thick patch of grass, they couldn't believe how steep the incline was on this dangerous trail. It felt almost suicidal just attempting to go down it, but given the situation, they knew they had no other option.

Steve led the way as they started heading down the treacherous path. They were no more then a few steps into their route when they were overcome by gravity and their speed began to rapidly increase against their will. There was no turning back, they were committed to this forward motion and it took all of their concentration to avoid letting their legs give way beneath them. Dreading the thought, neither of them wanted to be the first one to go tumbling the remainder of the way down the steep incline.

Half way down, Steve heard a strange rumbling noise that seemed to be getting louder by the moment. Still running uncontrollably forward, he somehow managed to turn his head and look behind them. Thankful he wasn't the only one having a hard time keeping his footing as they neared the bottom, but he was shocked by image he saw. A massive avalanche of loose gravel, dirt and rocks were racing down behind them. The landslide was not large enough to be of any danger to them, but it was enough to trigger a whole new train of thoughts racing through his mind. No longer concerned with embarrassing himself in front of his beautiful partner, he was more concerned with how they were going to make it back up this mountainous slope. He knew going back up was going to be a whole different story with gravity working against them. Thinking quietly to himself, he decided he'd let her lead when they headed back up so he could at least enjoy the view during their struggles.

PART FOUR
The Surgery Room

Back at the hospital, Renae had just come back into the room where Dave and Raun were waiting. She walked over to them and said, "Both of your parents are here," she paused briefly as she looked at Dave and added, "but we need to take you upstairs first, we gotta see what we can do about that shoulder."

"What about me, can I go see mine?" Raun asked, showing his excitement, "can I go see my mom now?"

"They'll be in here in a few minutes, they're just taking care of some paperwork. The doctor needs to see you too though, that way we can make sure you're as alright as you say you are."

With Dave now sitting up in his hospital bed, Renae walked over and assisted him in climbing down. "Come with me, we're gonna go upstairs and get you all stitched up," she said in her soft voice as she began to lead Dave toward the door.

Raun immediately grew impatient and anxiously followed them over to the door. Having a huge crush on Renae, he watched her as they exited the room. Standing in the doorway, he followed her movements with his eyes until they turned the corner and were no longer visible. Bored, he returned to the mushroom stool and resumed spinning in circles as he waited for his parents to arrive.

Renae continued to lead Dave as they walked down toward the end of the hallway where the elevators were located. They waited for several moments for the doors to open, then they headed up to the second floor. When the door to the elevator opened, they stepped off and proceeded down the corridor past several exam rooms before entering one.

Above the door was a big black sign that read "**SURGERY ROOM B.**"

As they stepped into the room Renae said, "Why don't you take off your shirt and hop up on the bed?" Dave did what she asked. He was just sitting there watching her as she took out all different types of medical supplies from the large cabinet and set them on the counter. Dave took off his blood soaked shirt and set it down on the small table next to the bed. Sitting there bored, Dave began to examine his wounds for himself, this was really the first opportunity he had to see the damage. When Renae was finished setting up the supplies, she walked back over to him and began to carefully examine his shoulder for herself. Satisfied she had a better understanding of the injury to his shoulder, she then took two fingers and began to examine his rib cage. It didn't take her long before she found a spot that needed some attention.

"I'm so sorry Dave but it feels like a couple of these are broken."

"I figured that," Dave replied.

"Don't worry, we'll get ya all fixed up as good as new," she added. Then she turned around and headed back over to the supply cabinet, grabbed a paper gown, hospital slippers and handed them to him as she asked, "Why don't ya change into these for me while I go and grab the doctor?" With that said she left the room and closed the door behind her.

Dave struggled as he painfully began to change into the hospital gown Renae had given to him. He thought the gown looked totally ridiculous. It wasn't anything more then an overgrown pajama shirt with no back and impossible to tie. He didn't realize how long this minor task had taken him, but he was just finishing tying the back when someone knocked on the door. "Are you dressed yet?" a man's dry voice asked.

"Yeah," Dave replied, "come on in."

Renae walked into the room first, she was followed by the doctor. He was a short Korean man, about five feet six inches tall. He had short dark hair and brown eyes with a clean shaven face, so smooth it didn't look like hair even grew there. He was in his early thirties and was presumably single since there was no wedding band on his hand. "Hi Dave, I'm Dr. Lee and you already know Renae."

"Right," Dave agreed as he nodded his head.

"So how are we doing this morning?" Dr. Lee asked.

"Not too good," Dave replied sarcastically. "If I was doing alright, I wouldn't be here seeing you."

"I guess that's a good point," the doctor agreed with an expressionless look on his face. Dave just assumed this man had never heard a joke before. "Let me have a look at that shoulder," the doctor said, ignoring Dave's snarky remark.

The doctor leaned forward and slid the gown off of Dave's shoulder. With the injuries now in plain view, he began to examine them as he explained to Renae what he was thinking and she stood at the cabinet writing down notes as he spoke. "Most of these are gonna need to be reopened and these here are going to need some dissolving stitches inside too," the doctor explained. "You said that you were bitten by a mountain lion?" the doctor asked, now speaking to Dave.

"It was kind of a mountain lion," Dave tried to explain. "Ya see, it was half human, I mean. Its lower body looked human, but it was covered with fur. But the head and shoulders were definitely a mountain lion's! And it ran on its hind legs." Even Dave could hear how crazy this story sounded as he was telling it.

"Is that right? Sounds like you were attacked by Bigfoot," the doctor proclaimed in a tone clearly expressing his skepticism of any truthfulness to this tall tale.

"It wasn't Bigfoot!" Dave demanded, offended by the doctors total disbelief in his dramatic tale of survival. "It was a human and mountain lion mutation!"

"How come you didn't come in right after this happened?" the doctor curiously asked, still speaking in a smug tone.

"Because we had to kill the ghost first, that's who those cat things belonged to!" Dave shouted at the doctor. "He killed my brother and my best friend!"

"At least he didn't kill you two good looking guys," Renae said, trying to calm Dave down by flirting a little.

"He tried and he came pretty close too!" Dave told her, assuming she at least believed him.

"Yeah," the doctor added, noticing what Renae was trying to do. "Listen Dave, we're gonna put you to sleep for a little while, that way it won't be as painful for you when we reopen these wounds. We have to do it that way so we can clean out the infection real good and close them up correctly."

"Is it gonna hurt?" Dave wondered out loud.

"You'll be a little sore when you first wake up, but it shouldn't be that bad and it will feel better than it does now."

"What about my ribs and ankle?" Dave asked.

"We'll take some x-rays while you're asleep. But for now, your shoulder is our main concern," the doctor told him.

"When ya wake up you'll be as good as new," Renae added.

"When can I see my mom?" Dave asked Renae as the doctor walked out of the room.

"As soon as you wake up you'll be able to see her, I promise."

"How long will I be asleep?" Dave asked.

"Just a couple of hours," Renae said. "Besides, you look like you could use the rest."

"I guess you're right, I'm kinda tired."

"Then I'll see you in a couple of hours, why don't you just lay back and get comfortable for me," Renae suggested.

Dave laid down and adjusted his position so he was comfortable, Renae pulled over an IV machine and placed it next to the bed. She turned it on and grabbed a new needle out of the package in the drawer next to the bed. When she got the machine all set up she grabbed hold of Dave's arm and poked the needle into his vein. "This is Demerol and Valium. It will help with the pain and will make sure you sleep real good," she explained. "I want you to count backwards from one hundred," she instructed him and gave him a quick pat on the head.

Dave didn't feel anything special about this stuff at first, except where she poked the needle into his arm. He did what she asked and started to count backwards from one hundred. He only made it to eighty seven before he could no longer hold his eyes open and he slowly let them fall shut. He'd stopped counting out of sheer exhaustion but was sure that he was still awake, he just continued to lay there trying not to move.

PART FIVE

Denial Of The Truth

Shane Marys had just pulled into the hospital parking lot. He placed the shifter in park, turned off the car, grabbed a hold of the CB handle on the dash and called back into the station, "This is 142. Come in dispatch, over."

"This is dispatch. Go ahead 142, over," a woman's voice replied.

"I just arrived at Leslie Memorial. Have you heard back from 139 or the state police yet? Over."

"That's a negative 142. Would you like me to patch you through to one of them? Over."

"Negative, just put them through as soon as they radio in. Over and out."

Shane reattached the radio to the dash mount as he took off his seat belt and opened the car door. Climbing out of his car he somehow managed to drop his keys. After picking them up, he closed the door and started walking toward the emergency entrance of the hospital. When he neared the entrance, the glass double doors opened automatically and he stepped inside and headed toward the triage desk. The nurse sitting behind the desk was busy working on her computer and didn't even notice that he had walked in.

"Excuse me," Shane interrupted her.

Turning her attention away from her computer, "I'm sorry," she apologized and smiled as she was taken by Shane's charm.

"The two young boys that just came here, have their parents arrived yet?" Shane asked politely.

"Yeah," she replied as she pointed across the lobby to where she was sitting. "She's right over there."

Shane turned his head to look in the direction of where

she was pointing. Immediately he noticed a woman sitting in the corner of the waiting room all alone. She looked like she had been crying intensely and Shane was positive this was the woman he needed to speak with. Turning his attention back to the nurse he asked, "What about the Stevens? Are they here yet?"

"Mr. And Mrs. Stevens are with Raun in room 117," she pointed down the hallway to her left and added, "I think the doctor is seeing him right now, but I'm sure he wouldn't mind if you were present."

"How come Mrs. Healy isn't with Dave?" Shane asked curiously.

"Right now he's in surgery. It's going to be a little while before anyone can see him."

"Thank you," Shane quietly said. "You've been a lot of help. I'll be with Mrs. Healy for a few moments before I go back to room 117, right?" Shane asked to double check the room number.

"117, that's right," she replied with a smile on her face. As Shane walked away she resumed pecking away on the keyboard of her computer.

With Shane making his way across the waiting room, Mrs. Healy was yet to even notice a police officer had entered the hospital. She sat there hunched over, her elbows resting on her knees and she was utterly submersed in her own world of crying and emotional despair. Shane was in the process of sitting down next to her when she finally noticed he was even there. As soon as she lifted her head, Shane introduced himself. "I'm officer Marys, but please call me Shane."

She sniffled and wiped her nose with a large wet wad of tissue she had lying on her lap. "I'm Ann, Dave and Jeff's mother," she stated, continuing to wipe her nose. Politely, Shane waited as she continued trying to pull herself together.

After a few moments of waiting, he realized that this was probably the best that she was going to get, so he forced himself to speak.

“Well Ann, we have a very unique and strange situation developing here, and to be honest with you, I’m afraid that I just don’t have any answers for you yet. In fact, we’re not even sure of what all the questions are.”

“They say that my baby and Allen are dead,” she mumbled and then as she hopefully waited for him to correct her, she again started to cry.

“Calm down, Ann,” Shane sympathized as she leaned her head into his shoulder and started crying harder. “We don’t even know if that’s true yet,” he added against his better judgment as he tried to comfort her.

Quickly, she lifted her head off of his shoulder and looked at him with teary, hopeful eyes and asked, “Really, they might not be dead?”

“Nothing has been confirmed as of yet, but we have the state police working with us on this investigation already. I’ll keep you posted on any of our progress. For now, all we can do is keep our fingers crossed and hope for the best.”

“I know,” she said with a glimmer of hope still lingering in her eyes. “Dave and Raun are our only source of information so far, right? And their story doesn't make a whole lot of sense.”

“You’re definitely right about that,” Shane agreed.

“But you’ll tell me as soon as you know something, right?” she sobbed.

“I will, I promise,” Shane replied, “in fact, why don’t you come with me right now while I go and talk to Raun? That way we can both get to the bottom of this together.”

“I’d like that,” Ann appreciated Shane’s offer, especially because she didn’t like waiting in the lobby all alone. “Besides, they say I won’t be able to see Dave for a few hours and I shouldn’t be out here alone worrying myself to death,” she added.

“Especially when you’re not even sure of what to be worried about,” Shane said. “Come on, lets go.”

With that said, Shane stood up from where he was sitting and held out his hand offering to help Mrs. Healy to her feet. Not noticing his hand, she stood up on her own and grabbed her purse off the chair next to where she'd been sitting. Trying to pull herself together, she attempted to wipe the tears from her eyes and then they started walking across the waiting room. Following the nurses directions, they walked through the automatic doors and headed down the hallway toward room 117.

When they arrived at the room, the door was open. Inside, they could see Raun sitting on the bed talking with his parents as they sat in a couple of chairs sitting next to his bed. As they stood there in the hallway, a nurse began to exit the room, she was about to close the door behind her until she noticed them standing there. “Can we go in and see Raun Stevens now?” Shane politely asked.

“Yeah, I don’t see why not,” the nurse cordially responded, “he’s in there with his parents. The doctor just finished looking him over and he should be back in a few moments.”

“How is he? Is he alright?” Mrs. Healy asked.

“He seems fine,” the nurse answered, “physically, but we’re going to run some more tests in a little while.”

“Can we talk to him for a sec?” Shane asked again.

“Yeah, sure,” she replied, “but these kids aren’t making a whole lot of sense. The doctor wants to run a drug test on them, the story their telling seems way too far fetched to even resemble any truth. Aside from that, he seems fine.”

PART SIX
The Body

Steve and Krista had finally made it to the bottom of the rock slide. Neither of them could believe how steep the canyon wall actually was, it had deceived them both. Staying close to the canyon wall, they proceeded to walk back toward the bridge since the trail had led them away from where they wanted to be. When they got in closer to the body, they were still unable to get a good look at exactly what it was. It was barely even visible through the massive crowd of hungry vultures devouring its flesh right before their eyes.

The vultures had noticed the arrival of Steve and Krista, although they were barely even concerned. Steve knew the vultures were not going to walk away from their meal real easily, so he pulled his 9mm Glock from his holster. He warned Krista as he racked a round into the chamber, raised his arm into the air and fired a shot. The birds scattered, but didn't flee too far away from the carcass. They were flapping their wings and squawking at them as if they felt they had been robbed of their lunch.

With the birds now clear of their visual, they stood there staring at the mostly devoured carcass. "What the hell is that?" Krista asked with a confused look on her face.

"I have no idea," Steve replied as they continued inching their way closer to the body. "But it looks like it's some sort of animal."

"At least it wasn't one of them kids," Krista remarked.

"That things huge, what do ya think it is?" Steve asked, admitting he was clueless.

"It's hard to tell, them vultures sure did tear it up though."

"Do ya think it's a Sasquatch?" Steve asked.

"I don't think so," Krista said doubtfully, "but we'll get the ranger to come out here and check it out as soon as we find out what's going on with these kids."

"Good idea," Steve agreed. "We have enough to deal with right now. We'll deal with our crazy myth and let the Forest Service deal with this one. "

They were relieved the body didn't belong to one of the missing boys. At they same time, they knew they had to leave this matter to the park ranger so they could get on with their task at hand. They both turned away from the disgusting looking carcass and headed back toward the dreaded path leading up the canyon wall.

When they made it to the bottom of the trail, they no more then made their first attempt when Steve realized that he was right. Try after try, they both kept their frustrations to themselves as they struggled to make it back up the steep incline. When they finally did make it back to the top of the loose gravel path, they continued following the directions Nick had given them and headed back down the trail toward the cabin.

After walking for what seemed like hours, they were sure they had made a wrong turn since they had yet to find the cabin, or even this mysterious patch of fog they had been informed they were sure to encounter. They were just about to give up and start backtracking, when suddenly they stumbled into a clearing. After coming out of the darkness of the dense trail, their eyes finally adjusted to the light in the clearing and they realized they had found it. They stood there in disbelief and wondered to themselves if this was the actual place where all the tails of past and present horrors had originated from, including the towns infamous legend.

Even though they'd headed down this path in search of this supposed mysterious cabin, they were mainly following procedure and didn't actually expect to find anything. Looking at it, they were both shocked that this place did in fact exist. What baffled them even more, was how it had remained so illusive for so many years and that it was found by a group of kids. Both of them had already made up their minds that these kids had made up this whole story in some kind of sick attempt to gain attention.

"Do ya think this is really the place?" Steve asked.

"Yeah, I guess," Krista replied. "I can't imagine another run down creepy cabin being out here."

"I have to say that I agree with you. Should we call in for another unit?"

Krista stopped dead in her tracks for a second as if she was in deep thought before replying, "No, not yet, let's see if we find their bodies or something first. We don't wanna look like a couple of small town idiots too."

With that said, they resumed walking though the grassy clearing toward the strange cabin.

PART SEVEN

Fear Of The Unknown

When Nick Balden arrived at Sacred Heart on the opposite side of the town, Pastor Austin Soncrainte was just finishing up with his morning services. The church goers were exiting the chapel and Nick greeted the ones he knew as he made his way through the parking lot and into the church.

The church wasn't much more then a big open area with several offices located toward the back of the building. As Nick walked down the aisle way through the middle of the church, he was surrounded by rows and rows of pews on both sides of him. Right away, he noticed Pastor Soncrainte standing by his office door and that he seemed to be immersed in reading some papers he held in his hand. As the pastor stepped into his office, he still hadn't noticed that Nick had entered the temple and was heading toward him.

Nick made his way to the back of the church and toward the pastor's office and when he arrived, the door to the was still open. Standing patiently in the doorway, he knocked softly as he tried to gain the pastor's attention. He looked up from the pile of papers scattered about his desk and saw Nick standing there in uniform as he held onto the duffel bag. They had known each other for years now and Nick had been going to this church since he moved into this town. "Nick, come on in and have a seat," the pastor said as he welcomed his friend inside.

"Thank you father," Nick politely replied as he entered the room and sat down in a chair across from him, sitting at his desk.

"What can I do for you on this glorious morning?"

"Actually," Nick said, having a hard time trying to figure out exactly how to word what he needed to ask, "I've got a curious situation and I was wondering if you might be able to help?"

"I'll give it my best," Austin replied. "That's all the good Lord expects out of all of us."

"Ya see," Nick started to explain as he set the duffel bag on the pastor's desk. "We've located two of the missing boys."

"Oh that's wonderful," Austin interrupted.

"But the story they tell, it seems a little far fetched," Nick stated.

"Please continue," Austin patiently insisted as Nick had obviously intrigued him.

Nick reached up onto the desk and unzipped the bag. He handed a pair of latex gloves to the pastor before he put on a pair of his own. Austin was well aware of the reasoning behind the gloves and mentioned nothing of it. He knew if it wasn't absolutely necessary, Nick wouldn't have bothered giving a pair to him as well. They both calmly struggled to get the gloves on as Nick continued to explain the situation, "The two boys we located are Dave Healy and Raun Stevens."

"Are they alright?" Austin asked genuinely concerned, but knowing he shouldn't have interrupted again.

"They're fine, but the story they're telling," Nick paused briefly, "their saying Eric Aben killed their brothers and tried to kill them."

"That's just a myth," Austin insisted with a puzzled look of concern and fear wearing long on his face.

"That's what I thought," Nick stated. "But we did some checking and there's something strange about all this, the records show that some weird stuff did happen fifty years ago. What's really bizarre is these four boys disappeared exactly fifty years to the day of the last disappearance."

"That is kind of eerie," Austin replied as he began to

scratch at his chin, still wearing the glove on his hand.

"It gets a lot weirder," Nick stated, reaching down into the bag and pulling out the dagger. He set it down on the desk before he reached back into the bag and pulled out the pentagram shaped necklace. After setting that piece down, he reached into the bag one last time and pulled out the loose stone that mimicked the shape of a large diamond.

"Where did you get all this?" Austin curiously asked, beginning to examine the engravings on the medallion as Nick took the bag off his desk and set it on the floor next to his feet. "Let me see that loose stone," he added, truly perplexed.

"I have no idea where they got it," Nick replied as he passed the stone to Austin. "It all looks like it belongs in a museum if ya ask me."

"It looks like this stone fell out of the medallion," Austin suggested.

"That's the way they were when they gave them to me," Nick insisted, "and all they told me about them was that they're evil and they needed to be destroyed."

"I don't doubt that, people are evil, " Austin agreed, "although this pentagram represents my competition."

"I figured that much," Nick chuckled a little, then added, "that's why I came to see you. So what do you think all these engravings mean?"

"I'm really not sure," Austin paused, "I've seen them somewhere before, I just don't remember where?"

"I wonder how this got broke," Nick asked as he picked up the loose stone and the medallion.

"I'm not so sure you should..." Austin started to suggest, but let his words trail off as Nick dropped the stone into place in the empty slot on the medallion.

Both Austin and Nick's hearts felt faint from fear as the medallion abruptly came to life with its light show. The stones began to flash, giving off their singular bursts of red light as they projected their symbolic images onto the ceiling. The medallion completed its first rotation, then it went dormant for a second. Simultaneously, all five of the red stones flashed and lit up the room in its entirety. The stones briefly returned to their latent state before they once again started to flash individually. The star appeared to be spinning as the pulses of light began to rapidly increase in their frequency and speed until it just stayed illuminated.

Mystified and panic stricken, Nick desperately wanted to make the medallion stop doing whatever it was that he had initiated. In an act of sheer desperation, Nick grabbed the dagger off of the desk and tried to grab the medallion to look for a way to shut it off. The moment he touched it, he cried out in pain, severely injuring his hand with first degree burns. With the artifact immobilized on top of the desk, the awful smell of melted flesh permeated throughout the room. In another fearful attempt to remove the stone from the artifact, he ignored his intense pain and wedged the tip of the dagger into the diamond shape slot atop of the strange gem. Trying desperately to forcefully pry it out of the center, the stone wouldn't budge. In the failed attempt, the tip of the dagger remained interlocked with the stone as Nick twisted his wrist counterclockwise still trying to pop it out. Having no success in removing the stone, it did manage to spin in place and he felt as if he had unlocked a latch. There was a sudden explosion of light, blinded, all they could hear were thousands of screaming voices crying out in agony and painful tones that were intolerable to listen to and caused a physical pain in their ears.

PART EIGHT
The Gateway Opens

Steve and Krista had made their way into the eerie, mysterious cabin. From the moment they first stepped inside, they immediately recognized the smell of decomposed flesh. After they had been in there for a little while, they couldn't believe they hadn't yet found even one body, especially for as strong as the smell was throughout the entire cabin. After searching through the first few rooms of the cabin, they came to the puzzling conclusion that there had to be more to the story those kids had explained to Nick. They still were nowhere near accepting their story as fact and were winding up with more questions than answers as they continued their search. They didn't understand how the cabins interior could be so small when the place looked so much larger from the outside. When they were satisfied with their brief preliminary search of the living room, dining room and the strange room with the pentagram painted on the floor that contained the out of place triangular table, they decided there had to be a hidden entrance into another part of this cabin somewhere.

They were baffled by the elusiveness of this more than obvious secret entrance. In an effort to speed up the search, they decided to split up. Steve continued to search the dining room as Krista made her way back into the vast emptiness of the room with the table. Caught off guard, they both nearly jumped out of their shoes as the double doors abruptly slammed shut with no apparent cause, trapping Krista inside the room.

On either side of the access, both Krista and Steve ran to the door and tried desperately to force it open, but all of their best efforts were to no avail, causing a panic Krista was trying desperately to escape the room that now held her captive. The focus of her full attention was quickly transferred as she suddenly found herself captivated by a triangular beam of light radiating outward from the tables surface. How it held the shape of a prism as it connected from the table to the ceiling was beyond her comprehension.

Trying to grasp what was going on around her, she aimed her flashlight into the beam of light only to have the bulb explode in her hand, stranding her in the perpetual darkness that had consumed the rest of the room. Startled by the sudden explosion in her hand, she jumped and dropped the flashlight to the floor. Just then, the table and the beam of light began to rotate in opposite directions.

She briefly screamed frightfully before she was able to force herself to regain at least some control over her body. She turned around and again tried to force the door open to enable her wanting escape. She could hear Steve struggling on the other side as he pounded and relentlessly beat on the door, trying intensely to pry it open.

"Step to your left of the door!" she shouted to Steve through the wall.

"Got cha!" Steve replied as he did what she asked.

Krista withdrew her service pistol from its holster hanging at her side, loaded the chamber and fired a round directly into the locking mechanism. The shot rang out, echoing throughout the room as all four walls suddenly ignited into a blazing inferno. The intense heat and fierce flames forced her away from the walls and closer into the center of the room against her better judgment. With the flames raging on, she now feared the prospect of being burned alive while trapped inside this inescapable prison.

The fire was rapidly consuming most of the available oxygen in the room, making it difficult for her to breath. With the heat continuing to intensify, the fire suddenly reached its flash point and spontaneously ignited her hair and clothing. Screaming and crying in a frenzy of intense pain, she was being scorched to death. Oddly, as the flames burned wildly, they seemed to have no effect on any part of the cabin, except Krista. Panicking, she began ripping off her outer garments that were ablaze and used her undershirt to try and attempt putting out her hair. Luckily, she managed to succeed just as the table and beam of light had completed their opposite rotations. The beam of light abruptly vanished as the table began to descend down into the floor. By this point, Krista was hysterical, half naked and barely able to comprehend all that was going on around her. When the table finished its strange decent into the floor, the missing wooden floorboards appeared out of nowhere and sealed the hole closed and the giant red pentagram painted on the floor ignited into flames.

The temperature of the room was still increasing at an alarming rate. Steve could tell this even barred from the other side of the door. With panic taking over all of his common sense and training, he reached out for the handle in another desperate attempt at trying to gain access to the room. Quickly, he pulled his hand away from the handle as he received an intense burn on the insides of his fingers and his palm. Completely in shock, he was unable to scream. Holding his hand in front of his face, he watched as the blisters formed right before his eyes. He couldn't focus on anything, all he could hear were the sounds of Krista's delirious cries coming from the other side of the door and there was nothing that he could do about it.

With the walls still engulfed by flames, a bolt of lightning frightened her further as it penetrated through the ceiling and struck the burning pentagram right next to her. She screamed out at the top of her lungs, but the sound was over powered by the deafening crack of thunder that immediately followed. Blinded by the light, her legs gave way beneath her and she collapsed to the floor. Cupping her ears, she tried to regain her equilibrium as she attempted to climb back to her feet. When her eyes were starting to come back into focus, she couldn't believe what she was seeing. Dozens of small trolls were leaping out of the fiery hole that had become of the pentagram. It was like she was trapped in hell with no escape in sight.

The trolls were about three feet tall and unlike any creature she had ever saw before. They were surprisingly stocky and walked upright, barely bending their knees. Their facial appearance resembled a combination of a hyena and a wildebeest with warts the size of golf balls protruding from every patch of visible skin. Long grayish fur covered their entire bodies and long manes hung sparsely from their chins reflecting a bluish tint. With wild thin hair barely coating their heads, they had two small horns protruding from the top. Their short arms bore a natural weaponry of long scalpel like claws on the tips of each of their three fingers. Scariest yet, their jaws were muscularly structured with six inch fangs that looked razor sharp and strong enough to crush human bones.

Laying on the ground still in a state of shock, Krista completely broke down and lost it when she spotted these monstrous creatures climbing out of the fiery abyss. As the trolls started heading toward her, she tried desperately to climb to her feet and run away, but she was trapped inside this bizarre flaming room. Using her pistol, she tried to defend herself, but her success was minimal. For everyone of these creatures she managed to kill, a half dozen more made their way into the room through the open gateway.

When she fired her last shot, it was only a matter of time before she was finally subdued and several of the trolls managed to pin her to the floor. Within seconds, her whole body was covered with trolls like a pact of wild wolves as they began to devour her corpse. In a matter of seconds, there was nothing left of her body but a few small pieces of bone and a fresh blood stain on the floor where she'd died. Once they had finished making her life into their meal, the flames that had covered the walls dissipated and the trolls began to disperse out of the room. They ran right through the walls like they didn't even exist and scattered about.

Steve had been kicking the door and trying everything he could possibly think of in his failed attempt to force the door open. All he wanted to do was aid his partner, when suddenly these small gruesome looking trolls burst into the dining room through the walls, immediately noticing his presence, they began heading toward him. Immediately, he turned around and took off in a mad dash out of the cabin and down the trail. Scared and unsure if what he was seeing was real or some kind of hallucination, he tried desperately to avoid being caught by these tiny ghouls.

The storm clouds overhead grew rapidly as the dark clouds spread out and engulfed the entire town under the threat of a sudden thunderstorm. This umbrella of overcast forced an unnatural midday darkness that blanketed the whole horizon for as far as the eye could see. The only light exhibited came from the close and frequent flashes of violent lightning, followed immediately by the explosive sounds of deafening thunder.

The open gateway continued to grow more active as it unleashed its fury in masses of trolls, demons, translucent entities, disfigured animals and partially mutilated humans. As the hideous looking creatures continued to escape from the confines of hell, the intense fire at the base of the gateway burned with a furious rage like no other.

Steve was running for his life as he made his way down the twists and turns of this confusing trail. Scared to death, he was desperately trying to escape from the massive onslaught of strange creatures he knew were following close behind him. He couldn't actually see them through the darkness, but he knew they were there, he could hear them. By the time he'd made it all the way back to the bridge, it was starting to rain.

Still fearing heights and this unstable bridge, he was well aware that he had to keep moving forward or suffer the consequences of the monsters trailing close behind. At a slightly slower pace than he preferred, he started to make his way across. He thought that he'd gained some distance in his get away from the grotesque little trolls, but he wasn't even half way across when he suddenly felt the bridge begin to shake violently. Turning his head to look behind him, he was barely able to see through the intense darkness, but he was able to make out that the trolls were using their razor sharp claws to saw through the ropes that held the bridge suspended above the rocky canyon below.

He felt like his heart had suddenly dropped to his knees and he was instantly over his fear of heights and the bridge. Without giving it a second thought, he took off running with everything he had in a last stitch attempt to make it the rest of the way across. Suddenly, mid-stride, he felt the bridge give way as it came out from underneath him. Stumbling as he fell forward, he was flying diagonally through the air and somehow managed to grab hold of one of the planks. Holding onto the bridge was only a temporary solution. The bridge had been severed at the other end and Steve was now swinging through the air like Tarzan on a vine. He knew that his number was up, he was heading for the wall on the opposing side of the canyon at an alarming speed and nothing short of a miracle could save him now. Reaching terminal velocity, he slammed into the rocky wall full force, looking like a bag of meat had exploded as it hit. Most of the bones in his body were crushed instantly, causing him to lose his grip that he had on the plank. Falling about fifty feet, he was dead well before he ever hit the canyon floor.

With the gateway wide open and continuing to rage, countless demons and other entities, including the shadow had been unleashed upon the living world. With the shadow loose and wanting revenge, he exited the cabin and started heading down the trail. Following his lead was an ever expanding army of demons in search of the star and dagger. Once he possessed these objects, they would be unstoppable. Then him and his army of demons would rule the living world for all of eternity.

CHAPTER FIVE
THE STORM HITS THE TOWN

As officer Shane Marys and Mrs. Healy walked into the room, Mrs. Stevens said, “Ann, are you alright? You poor dear,” as she stood up from her chair next to Raun’s bed and ran over to Ann, embracing her in a heartfelt hug.

“I guess I’m alright,” Ann replied, “I just wish we could figure out what is going on here, I am so worried.”

Continuing on in their crying embrace, Shane spoke softly as he introduced himself, “I’m officer Marys, but please, call me Shane.”

While Ann and Pat were still hugging, Pat’s husband Mike had pulled over some extra chairs for Shane and Ann to sit down in. Mike introduced himself to Shane, then as Ann and Pat finally finished their hug, they all sat down and made themselves comfortable. In a soft, yet disturbed voice, “I’m Pat and this is my husband Mike,” she said as she wiped her tears from her eyes.

“Hello,” Mike said again, not having the heart to point out the fact that he had already introduced himself while she was locked in the long hug with Ann.

“And of course, this is Raun,” Pat continued, pointing to Raun, now sitting up in bed wearing a hospital gown.

“How are you feeling?” Shane sincerely asked.

“I’m alright,” Raun answered, “I guess I’m a little sore and tired, but I’m not injured if that’s what you mean.”

“That’s good that you’re not hurt. I was just wondering if you could tell me, along with everyone else exactly what’s going on here. Your parents and I are really anxious to start putting this puzzle together,” Shane said.

As soon as Shane finished his sentence, every one of them jumped out of their seats as the loud crack of thunder rang out, a bolt of lightning had struck a tree in the front part of the hospital's property. "Go ahead babe," Mrs. Stevens said. "I'm just gonna close the window." She then got out of her chair and proceeded to close the window since the sudden heavy rain was blowing in. After she closed it, she turned back around and headed back to her chair. She looked to her husband and in a soft, awkward voice she stated, "I don't remember them saying anything about rain today?"

Mike had a confused look on his face as he shrugged his shoulders and said, "It must have just blown in from the coast, you know how the weather is here in the valley."

"I know," she replied, "I just hope all of the windows are closed at home and in the car. It's coming down pretty hard out there."

"A little rain ain't gonna hurt nothing," Mike said as Pat sat back down in her seat.

When his mom had returned to her seat, Raun said, "Well, let me start at the beginning, but don't stop me until I get finished because at times this is gonna sound a little bit crazy, alright?"

Before Raun even got a chance to get started, Renae entered the room and approached Mrs. Healy and informed her, "They're finishing operating on Dave as we speak, so you can go upstairs and see him whenever you're ready. But he had to be sedated, so he'll be asleep for a little while yet. I just figured that you might want to go now."

"Thank you so much, you're a doll," Mrs. Healy replied. "Will you take me up there?"

Renae smiled as she said, "Sure, come on."

She told everyone that she'd be back in a little while. They understood and watched as her and Renae walked out of the room. Once they left, Raun had everyone's undivided attention as he began to explain their ordeal.

PART TWO

The Raven Returns

With Dave lying on the operating table, he was unable to move, still as he never thought was possible. His whole body was numb and he could not move a single muscle if his life depended on it. It was only seconds after Renae plugged the medication into his IV that he no longer had any idea of what was going on around him. He didn't even have enough strength to hold his eyes open, all he could see was a bright light penetrating through his eyelids. He assumed this light must have been located directly above him since an occasional shadow would pass over in front of it and change the intensity.

He wasn't even sure of whether he was actually asleep or still awake. He spent all of his energy trying to figure this out as he faded in and out of consciousness. By now he was trying desperately to open his eyes and bring an end to this perpetual darkness he felt trapped inside of. After what he thought to be only a matter of a couple seconds, he was finally able to force his eyes open. His vision was blurry and his whole state of mind seemed extremely cloudy. In fact, the whole room seemed distant and hazy to him.

Laying there, he still wasn't yet able to move any part of his body with the exception of his eyes. He was in a state of momentary confusion as he realized he was no longer in the same room he thought he was in only a moment ago. As his eyes slowly began adjusting to his new surroundings, he realized that he was all alone and hooked up to some type of vitals machine. He laid there motionless for a moment as he tried to muster up the strength to sit up. After making another unsuccessful attempt, he realized a few things. One was that he had a plastic brace wrapped around his rib cage and gauze covered his entire shoulder. As a bright bolt of lightning flashed outside of the open window, he noticed the rain was pouring in and there was nothing he could do about it since he was unable to move. Still feeling light headed, he decided to just close his eyes and try falling back to sleep. After no more than closing his eyes, he did in fact fall asleep. Almost immediately, he started to dream.

As Dave entered his dream like state, once again he wasn't even aware that he was sleeping. Still fuzzy from the sedation, he had little comprehension of what was going on around him. Making it hard to differentiate between the dream and what was real. Lying there, he was forced to open his eyes as he heard the erratic squawking sound of the familiar raven. Recognizing the sound from his experience on the bridge earlier, he was quick to open his eyes and to try locating the source of the sound.

As the fog in his head was starting to clear, he now realized that he was in a recovery room. Lying down on his back in the hospital bed, he tried to locate the source of the sound by only using his eyes. He was positive it was the same sound the raven made earlier, but he wasn't sure if he imagined it or not.

His eyes came into focus finally adjusting to the lighting of the room. Struggling slightly, he lifted up his head and somehow managed to prop it up with the pillow using his good arm. Looking around, he realized that he was in a private suite and that the room was cookie cutter and virtually barren. The only items in the room were the bed he was lying on, a large white medicine chest, the vitals machine he was hooked up to and two small night stands, located one on each side of the bed. To the right of his bed was an open door that led to the bathroom, to the left of that on the same wall was the closed door that led out to the hallway.

Dave suddenly stopped examining the room as he heard the piercing squawking sound ringing in his ears. Turning his head and attention to face the wall at the foot of his bed, there it was. He was positive it was the same white raven as it sat perched on the open window sill. Squawking several more, times, it then began to flutter its wings and took flight across the room, landing on the blue vital machine located next to his bed. This was when Dave first realized how intense the rain was coming down outside in the midst of the massive electrical storm. The raven continued to make the squawking sounds as it shifted its head from side to side as if it was looking around to make sure they were alone.

"Why are you back?" Dave curiously asked, not expecting to get a response.

The raven shifted its head back and fourth several more times before it answered in that familiar comforting voice Dave swore was coming directly from the bird. "The waking of the beast has begun. The gateway has been opened and a great multitude of evil spirits have already been unleashed, now walking among the living."

"What!" Dave shouted. "But we killed that freak! And the center stone was removed from the star." Dave couldn't believe what he was hearing.

"The stone has been replaced and the gateway was accidentally opened. Many of demons have already started to destroy this world and many more will continue to arrive unless the gateway is closed."

In a shaken and frightened voice Dave asked, "What do I have to do?"

"You must retrieve the dagger and star before he does," the raven responded.

"He who?" Dave asked, completely confused.

"The beast has once again risen."

"But what do I do?" Dave repeated.

"You are the only one that can defeat him. The restoration of balance between good and evil is in your hands."

"What if I can't do it?" Dave pleaded.

"You must, and you will," the raven replied.

Suddenly everything went dark and then Dave opened his eyes only to realize that he had been asleep and was just dreaming. What woke him up frightened him even more then the cabin or the dream, his mother was crying as she screamed his name, "Dave! Dave! Wake up!"

PART THREE
Chaos & Destruction

Raun was sitting up on the bed just finishing up his story to everyone in the room, with the exception of Mrs. Healy. The look on Shane and his parents faces was that of total disbelief. Nevertheless, Shane continued to take down notes throughout the entire story, although he was not looking forward to turning in the report to the Lieutenant. He was certain that he would be institutionalized into the sanitarium right along side these boys. Just wasting the paper on writing this insanity down was reason enough to be committed in his eyes. Before Raun was even able to finish telling his story, Shane stood up to answer his police radio. It had gone off four times in less then a minute's time.

"142, come in 142, over," Amber, the lady from dispatch called out over the radio.

"This is 142, go ahead, over," Shane replied.

"We need you to come back in and report to the station immediately, 139 and 144 are not responding to their radios. We have power failure all over town and the phone lines just went dead. Before that happened, I received reports of about twenty fires, fifteen accidents, sightings of ghosts, walking dead, rabid mountain lions and just total chaos breaking out all over the town and that's just in the last few minutes, over," Amber rattled off in a matter of seconds through her panic stricken voice.

"I'm on my way, over and out," Shane responded as he suddenly realized the Stevens had overheard every word she'd said.

Mrs. Stevens already looked petrified just from listening to Raun's story, but as Shane glanced over to the look on her face, he truly didn't know what to tell her. "I have to go for right now, but I'll be back," Shane insisted. "I'm sure you understand," Shane's words were drowned out as the loud crack of thunder and lightning rang out, striking something nearby. It was immediately followed by the sound of a loud explosion that had to have come from somewhere inside the hospital. The power started to flicker on and off, the fire alarm started to ring out of control and the sprinkler system kicked on and began saturating the entire building.

Shane ran over to the window and looked out into the parking lot. He could see over thirty fires spread out over the horizon off in the distance toward the town. With his eyes finally starting to process what he was witnessing, reality sank into his head and he noticed something chilling in the reflection of the windows of the cars in the parking lot. The whole rooftop of the hospital had also caught fire. Shane quickly turned around and shouted to the Stevens, "Come on! Let's get out of here!"

Raun's fear was instantly amplified as he could sense the desperation in Shane's latest demand. He quickly jumped out of the bed and forced on his shoes without tying them. Frightened, they all made their way over to the door that had them closed off in the room. When Shane pulled it open, he was pleased to see the fire wasn't an issue yet. Although, a massive panic was breaking out throughout the entire hospital, with people running and screaming in every direction. As he took a closer look, he realized the fire wasn't the cause of this outbreak of panic. There were ghosts and small troll looking creatures chasing people and trashing the hospital. When he focused his eyes and looked down the hallway to the left, he could barely still tell it was Renae's body lying lifeless on the floor, as it was being devoured by seven of the little fury gruesome looking trolls. With her body lying on the floor in a pool of blood, the evil little trolls continued slashing at her carcass with their razor sharp claws and biting out huge chunks of flesh with their monstrous fangs.

"Come on, follow me, I think we can make it if we go right now," Shane stated, then he took off running down the hallway heading for the lobby where the emergency entrance was located. The Stevens took off running too, following right behind him. When they arrived in the waiting room, they were in pure shock over the raw gore they were witnessing all around them.

There were dead doctors, nurses and half dressed patients lying all over the floor with their body parts ripped off and scattered about the room. When they made it to the glass double door entrance, they found the doors no longer opened on their own since the hospital was only running on emergency back up power. Trapped there and starting to panic, they were noticed by two badly decomposed skeletons standing behind the triage desk. The two creatures began to laugh wickedly at them as they abandoned what they were doing and started heading over to the entrance where the four of them stood frozen in place. As the morbid skeletons got closer, their demonic laugh got progressively louder. Shane forced himself to break free from his trance like state of shock and turned around and kicked the doors open as he shouted, "Come on! Let's go! Let's go!"

As the doors flung open, Shane ran into the vestibule and kicked open the second set of doors. With their confines of the hospital broken, they took off running and screaming as they headed out into the parking lot. The rain was pouring down on them and the lightning was pecking away at their surroundings, igniting fires everywhere it touched, as the loud rumbles of thunder continued to echo throughout the valley.

When they finally came to a halt in the middle of the parking lot, they looked behind them and were relieved to see the grotesque skeletons didn't follow them all the way out of the building. It wasn't until now that they realized how bad the storm was they were now standing in the middle of. Even worse than they thought, they finally realized the intensity of the chaos going on all around them. It wasn't just limited to the inside of the hospital, it was happening in the parking lot and all around them for as far as the eye could see.

Standing there in the unnatural midday darkness, the only light they were receiving came from the frequent flashes of violent lightning, the dozens of small fires and the hospital that was hellishly ablaze behind them. Despite the fact that the heavy rains were flooding the streets, it was doing nothing to tame the wild fires that had broken out everywhere. Boom! All of them jumped several feet as lightning struck the propane tank at the house neighboring the hospital, causing it to explode violently on contact.

PART FOUR
Reality Sets In

"David! David! Wake up!" his mother continued screaming as she shook him vigorously in a panicked attempt to wake him up. Finally, he opened his heavy eyelids and immediately noticed the hysterical look on his mothers face as she was crying and screaming in the same strained breath. The power was now out throughout the hospital and the rooms were steadily filling up with smoke.

The fire alarm continued raging on and they were being saturated by hundreds of gallons of water that poured out of the sprinkler system like an indoor monsoon. It didn't take Dave long to realize they needed to get out of there right away. He yanked the IV out of his arm and tore the patches off of his chest that were monitoring his vitals. He climbed out of the bed posthaste, wearing only his underwear, slippers and his hospital gown.

In a rush, they made their way over to the door. As she pulled it opened, they were almost overwhelmed by the smoke that started billowing into the room. They could barely see the raging inferno through the thick cloud of black smoke. Both ends of the hallway, including the nurse's station, were engulfed in flames, unabated by the sprinkler system and leaving them trapped in this second story room with no place to go. "There's no way out! We're trapped!" his mother shouted in a panicked tone.

"The window, quick, come on mom, we gotta hurry!" Dave suggested.

"What? But we're on the second floor," she tried to rationalize with him.

"Come on ma, it's that or we'll be burned alive," Dave reminded her of their surreal reality. Dave hobbled over to the window with the help of his mother since he was still barely able to stand on his own. The medication he was on still had a firm lingering grip on his body, but the adrenalin pumping through his veins was enough to make him immune to the pain he should have been in but managed to forget all about.

They stood in front of the window, what they were looking at was nothing short of total chaos and mayhem. For as far as their eyes could see, the entire landscape was being dominated by fires and explosions, while the storm over head was unleashing its full fury on the town. The flooding rains were mixed with golf ball sized hailstones and the fierce lightning was like nothing the town had ever saw before.

Dave cocked his good arm back and then blasted the screen with all the strength he could muster. The screen went flying out of the window and Dave hopped up onto the ledge. Sitting there with his legs dangling out over the wall, the hurricane like winds were blowing the large chunks of hail right in through the now opened window. "Dave, no. You're gonna break your neck," his mother pleaded.

"And staying in here is a better idea?" Dave shouted back to her as he pointed to the smoke steadily filling the room they were trapped in. "At least this way we have a chance," Dave added. They were both starting to cough painfully as they stuck their heads out of the window in an attempt to gain some fresh breathable air. With the room now entirely filled with smoke and the door that separated them from the burning hospital now set ablaze, they knew they had no choice.

Panic stricken, crying and gasping for air, she continued trying to reason with Dave, "Someone will rescue us, they must be on their way by now."

"Come on mom, look outside. All hell is breaking loose and ain't nobody coming!"

"David..." her words trailed off as he pushed himself off the ledge. He landed feet first, then he fell forward and rolled several feet across the soaking wet lawn that couldn't even be considered a lawn anymore. It was more like a six inch deep mud pit which helped cushion his landing. He climbed back up to his feet and turned to face his mother as she was standing in the second story window of the blazing hospital.

"Mom, mom, come on!" Dave continued shouting hysterically up to her.

Dave stood there and watched as his mother reluctantly climbed out onto the ledge. With her legs now hanging over the wall he noticed that she'd turned her head to face back into the room. Suddenly he could hear the sound of his mothers screaming voice. She was crying out in pain as she was obviously pushed off of the ledge. Dave watched in horror as his mother fall from the window, the whole event seemed to be happening in slow motion. Her body flipped and tumbled, Dave somehow managed to make eye contact with her for a brief second before she hit the ground. She was not prepared for her jump and there was no room for her to compensate for the landing. With a loud crunching sound, she hit head first with her back toward the sky, as the weight of her body came crashing down inward on herself. Dave was only twenty feet from where she had landed and he could here the disheartening sound of the multitude of bones snapping throughout her body.

Dave ran to her side and quickly learned that she had died upon impact. When he arrived there he collapsed to his knees and buried his head into her shoulder. Closing his eyes tightly, he tried to ignore the sight of her left leg being folded the wrong way and her spinal cord sticking out of the front of her throat.

Dave knew this wasn't the time or the place to mourn his mother's death. He was fully aware that if he didn't move on and do what needed to be done, there would be nothing left at all for anyone to morn or be saddened over. He forced himself to stop crying. When he was finally able to open his eyes, he looked back up to the window she had just fallen from only to see two small trolls standing on the windowsill. They were pointing at him as they laughed hysterically like two rabid hyenas. The one on the right side of the ledge used its razor sharp claws and slashed at the curtain and they watched as pieces of the shredded curtain fell to the ground. Then the two trolls hopped back down off of the ledge and disappeared back into the blazing inferno the hospital had become.

Dave again looked at his dead mother lying at his feet in front of him. Distraught, he picked up her right hand and kissed it as he thought to himself that he needed to avenge her death. He knew what needed to be done and that he needed to hurry or he too would soon suffer the same fate.

PART FIVE

Running For Cover

With Shane and the Stevens standing in the center of the parking lot, they were absolutely hysterical and in total disbelief as the storm was pummeling them with large hail and freezing cold rain. They continued to glance around at their unreal surroundings that truly resembled the end of the world. Standing there puzzled, Shane finally spoke and broke the awkward silence that had eerily befallen them, "You guys go find a safe place and stay there until we figure out what the hell is going on here!."

"How long will that be?" Mrs. Stevens asked. "How will we know when it's safe?"

"I don't know," Shane shouted as he threw his arms up in the air out of frustration. "I guess when everything settles down, just make your way to the station and we'll go from there. I'm heading there now to see what I can find out. You guys be careful."

Shane took off running across the parking lot toward his squad car, the Stevens did the same thing as they headed in the opposite direction toward their vehicle. They were half way there when out of nowhere there was another massive explosion coming from the hospital. All three of them were abruptly knocked down by the intense blast as the whole east wing of the hospital exploded in a violent display. Fragments of glass, brick and other debris went flying through the air like deadly projectiles.

Laying face down in a giant puddle on the blacktop, they covered their heads with their hands and tightly squeezed their eyelids closed as tight as possible, trying to shield their eyes from the massive fireball. On top of the intense rain and hail, the shower of rubble from the massive explosion was pouring down all around them. After a few seconds had passed by, they opened their eyes just in time to see the giant mushroom cloud of fire and smoke rising from where the east wing of the hospital used to be. They were praying they were far enough away from ground zero, but as they laid hoping the worst was over, they suddenly felt the massive heat blast pass over the top of them.

With large chunks of the building continuing to rain down all around them, they all cringed as the loud sound of something large crashed and landed right next to where they were laying. After the shock of the large object hitting that close wore off, Raun and Mrs. Stevens opened their eyes to a sight they were not expecting to see. Mr. Stevens had been killed, crushed instantly by a large piece of an x-ray machine and ominously sitting on top of the machine was a grotesque, slightly transparent living skeleton with fiery red eyes and whose clothes had been mostly burned off.

Mrs. Stevens screamed, Raun screamed, then oddly the skeleton screamed in a high pitched tone that slowly turned into the most unforgettable obnoxious laugh they had ever heard. Raun and his mother both immediately jumped to their feet and took off running across the parking lot. Raun didn't even know where they were running too, he was just following his mother since he'd came here in the back of an ambulance. The skeleton hopped off of the giant piece of machinery as it held a scalpel intently in its bony hand, without hesitation, it began to chase after them. The parking lot was a complete wreck. It was now full of chaotically smashed, mangled and burning cars that had been left behind and destroyed in everyone's panicked attempt to flee this insanity.

Continuing their mad dash toward their Explorer, the skeleton chasing them would have caught them if the doors have been locked. Raun jumped in through the driver's side door first, followed immediately by his mother. She managed to pull the door shut just in time as the skeleton slammed into the side of the vehicle. The creature was pissed off and started to beat on the windows relentlessly. After the fourth hit, it finally succeeded and spider webbed the windshield. Raun and his mother were both screaming and panicking as she frantically looked for her keys in the garbage can she called her purse. "Come on mom, hurry up!"

At last, she found them. Forcefully, she slammed the key into the ignition as the skeleton continued trying to force its way through the shattered glass as it continued letting out intense high pitched squeals. She turned the key and luckily the explorer started just as the driver's side window shattered, exploding inward and covering them with glass. The creature grabbed a hold of her blouse with its right hand. In its left, it raised the scalpel over its head as it was getting ready to strike. Mrs. Stevens screamed as lightning struck a tree only thirty feet in front of them, she slammed the shifter into reverse and floored the accelerator.

The tires screeched as the explorer took off in reverse. The skeleton had a firm grip on her shirt, but the sudden movement of the vehicle caused the creatures arm to separate from its shoulder as its body was flung and sent into a spin before it fell to the ground after losing its balance. They nearly received a whiplash as they slammed into and rode right up the hood of a Camaro that was parked behind them. Without letting the crash faze her, she dropped the shifter down into drive and gently resumed pressing down on the accelerator. As the explorer slowly climbed off of the hood of the Camaro, she went out of her way to run over the skeleton that was just now starting to climb back to its feet from where it had bent sent crashing to the ground. The explorer bounced twice as the front then rear wheels passed over its body. Mrs.

Stevens began to slowly maneuver her way out of the chaotic parking lot, ripping the creatures arm off of her blouse and tossing it out the shattered window.

PART SIX

Hopes Of A Ride

Dave finally regained his composure after been knocked down by the sudden blast that took place at the other end of the hospital. Saddened over the loss of his mother, he stood up and started to make his next move when he noticed the Stevens' explorer chaotically weaving its way out of the parking lot. Dave took off running as fast as he could, given his condition, trying desperately to catch up to them. Dave maneuvered his way through the six inch deep mud that used to be the lawn and continued to run after them, holding onto his rib cage as he shouted, "Stop, stop, wait for me!"

To his dismay, his cries for help went unnoticed as the explorer was pulling out of the parking lot. In a last minute act of desperation, Dave picked up a large stone and hurled it toward them. He watched anxiously as it sailed through the air, but he lost hope as it fell far short of gaining their attention. Frustrated, he resumed running after them in an apparent useless attempt at trying to catch up with a moving vehicle. On the positive side of his fruitless attempt, he was glad to finally be putting some distance between himself and the blazing hospital.

When he made it to the main road, he realized that being away from the hospital didn't make him feel any better. The chaos behind him had spread and plagued the whole town and there seemed to be no escaping it. The torrential rains and frequent flashes of lightning and thunder seemed to rumble right through his body. He was freezing cold and in more pain than he could have ever imagined. Yet he knew that he was the only hope of bringing this morbid chaos to an end.

Since his mother had woken him up before the raven had a chance to tell him what he needed to do next and where the dagger and star were located, Dave stood at the main road aimlessly wondering where he needed to go next. Standing there in a state of incessant confusion, his luck finally took a turn for the better. He noticed a sheriff's car heading directly toward him through the monsoon. This sight was more than a relief to him, it's the first car he'd seen other then the Stevens' that hadn't yet been smashed or caught fire. Standing in the middle of the road as the car approached, he waved his hands vigorously trying to make sure that he was noticed. He was praying to god that the car would get here before one of the demonic creatures running around here would take notice of him standing defenseless in the middle of the street.

PART SEVEN
Deadly Silence

When Shane pulled into the police station's parking lot, he still couldn't get over the horrible sights he had seen all throughout the town on the way here. The whole town was on fire, if it hadn't already burned to the ground. There were dead bodies everywhere, with ghosts and strange looking animals running wild in every direction. Mass destruction was wide spread throughout the entire town, he couldn't fathom why revelations had come to be and chose their town as the epicenter. The only living person Shane had came across on his way back to the station was devoured by some kind of disfigured mountain lion right before his eyes. He couldn't get the thought and graphic imagery out of his mind, this must be the end of the world as he knew it. Frightened to the bone, he knew that he was doomed. It was only be a matter of time before he would be killed by one of the many different creatures he'd seen destroying the town since this massive outbreak of armageddon started.

Looking around the parking lot, he quickly realized there were no other patrol cars parked here. He thought this to be odd since there were usually always at least four others aside from the ones him and his partner drove. Assuming a few volunteers had been called in due to the massive chaos, he didn't make to much of it. He recognized the only two remaining vehicles left in the parking lot, one was the blue mustang that Amber, the dispatcher drove, the other was a red Chevy pickup that Brandon and the cleaning crew drove.

The place looked virtually abandoned, the power was out and the backup generator hadn't kicked on yet for some odd reason. Amazed the building was even still standing after what he'd seen throughout the town, he was scared as he sat there wondering what to do next. Setting aside all of his fears and common sense, he knew that he had to go into the building. He pulled up his car as close to the front door as humanly possible, put the car into park and turned off the ignition. In a last stitch effort, he grabbed the CB handle off the dash unit and desperately tried to reach someone, anyone.

"This 142, come in dispatch, over." He was getting no response. He tried several more times and still got nothing in return. Having no luck, he tried changing the channel, but found nothing except radio silence. "This is 142, come in 139, over." Once again he got no response. He was starting to panic as the reality sank in that he might be the last living living person on the planet. Desperate, he threw the formality out the window as he tried again, "Nick! Come in Nick! Anyone! Is anyone out there? This is the police, can anyone hear me?"

With the silence from the radio and the sound of his own heartbeat, he just sat nervously in his patrol car for a few seconds and listened to the torrential rain pour down all around him. Managing to slightly pull himself together, he decided that he needed to go in and check inside the station to see if anyone was still alive. Even if no one had survived, he knew that he needed to get in there and grab some heavier artillery. He did not have the ability to deal with this chaos without access to the police arsenal.

Realizing that he wasn't going to be able to reach anyone to come and assist him, he reattached the CB to the dash unit, opened the car door and stepped out into the monsoon. Slamming the door shut behind him, he took off running toward the steps, slowing down once he was under the poor shelter the awning provided against the hard rain. Standing in front of the first set of glass double doors, he unhooked the flashlight from his utility belt, turned it on and shined it into the dark abandoned lobby. Unsure of whether to be joyous or distraught, he couldn't see anyone, dead or alive. The entire place seemed devoid of life and there was no movement inside whatsoever.

Slowly, he pulled open the first set of glass doors and stepped into the breezeway. He felt like he was in a giant fishbowl as he vulnerably stood motionless between the two sets of glass double doors. Unsure of what to expect once he got inside, he withdrew his 9mm Glock from its holster, racked a round into the chamber and stood ready for anything as he prepared to enter the dreaded lobby.

Cautiously, he stepped inside and began scanning the room with his flashlight, the silence was deafening and something he'd never heard before in here. Continuing to waved his gun and flashlight around the room as he quietly called out, "Hello? Is anyone here?"

The only sound he was able to hear was the soft reverberating echo of his own voice. The lobby was empty and the information desk had been vacated, yet nothing looked out of place or disturbed by any account. It looked like the whole place had just abruptly abandoned ship when all of this craziness started. Regardless of what must have happened, Shane proceeded to make his way across the lobby toward the back offices and the dispatch room. All the while, he couldn't get over the intense feeling of being watched.

When he made it to the hallway leading to the back of the station, the first door he came across was the one leading to the records office, it was closed. He slowly grabbed a hold of the handle, took in a deep breath and then in one quick motion, he turned the knob and flung the door wide open. Immediately, he began to scan over the room with his gun and flashlight. He didn't see anything out of the ordinary and the room looked virtually untouched. Thinking in hind sight, his forceful method of opening the door probably wasn't the smartest choice he could have made. The loud echoing noise of the door slamming into the wall would have undoubtedly alerted anyone here to his presence.

Standing in the doorway still regretting his course of actions, he swore that he had seen something scurry across the floor and head into the dispatch room, but he wasn't sure. He'd only caught a glimpse of it out of the corner of his eye. "Who goes there?" Shane shouted out into the void. "This is the police! I demand you show yourself!"

Realizing that whoever or whatever wasn't going to abide by his demand, Shane started to make his way down the hallway toward the dispatch room. The door to the room was partially open and he stopped several feet before reaching the doorway. Pausing for a minute, he took in a deep breath and then jumped in front of the entry aiming his gun and flashlight into the room as he yelled, "Freeze!"

Frantically scanning the room for whatever he thought he'd just saw, but all he found was Amber and Brandon's dead bodies lying in front of her desk in a giant pool of blood. With his senses overwhelmed by the horrific sight, he lapsed in judgment momentarily and forgot that he'd followed something into the room as he ran over to where their bodies were lying. Almost puking as he examined the gory scene, he immediately noticed the huge ripped out chunks of flesh and severed bones. Their bodies were barely recognizable and looked as if they had been half eaten.

He was in a total state of shock as he quietly mumbled to himself, "What the hell is going on here? This can't be happening." He paused for only a brief second before getting the surreal answer to his own question. "Hey, what the, stop!" He managed to squeeze off two shots before he was wrestled to the floor by a swarm of little trolls. Trying to fend off the attack, Shane was kicking and screaming as the trolls were biting and slashing him to pieces with their razor sharp claws and fangs.

His success was minimal at best as he tried to fight off the pack of wild creatures and climb back up to his feet. After suffering massive injuries, he managed to make it half way to his feet before the creatures overpowered him and pinned him to the floor. As he went down, they proceeded to rip him to shreds and started to eat him alive. He died a painful and miserable death and in a matter of only a few minutes, his body was nothing more than another unrecognizable bloody corpse, missing most of its flesh as it lied there on the floor next to Amber and Brandon's bodies.

PART EIGHT

The Final Confrontation

Nick spotted and instantly recognized Dave as he stood there in the middle of the street, obviously deliriously screaming and waving his arms in a desperate attempt to get noticed. As he pulled over to pick up him up, his mind was wandering and he couldn't comprehend the murderous rage this massive amount of strange creatures, demons and spirits were inflicting upon this once peaceful town. The electrical storm alone, seemed more than enough to have destroyed the whole community The town itself looked like a destroyed battlefield with fires raging everywhere and lighting up the whole horizon. They had lost power, the phone lines had been severed and all the static electricity from the lightning rendered the police radios absolutely useless.

Nick was out of ammo and injured, his leg was slashed wide open earlier in a frivolous attempt to save a helpless woman from a grizzly death. She had been killed by a translucent purple entity that seemed to melt the flesh of anything it came into contact with.

When Dave climbed into the car, he wasn't at all surprised by the intense look of pain and fear on Nick's face. Although Dave was in desperate need of a mentally stable adult telling him not to worry and that everything was going to be alright, he accepted the fact he wasn't going to hear that here or anywhere else unless he did what needed to be done.

"What the hell is going on here?" Nick demanded. "What did you kids do?"

"Nothing," Dave replied as Nick began weaving his way through the cluttered maze of wreaked and burning cars. They had been abandoned when demons commandeered the town as everyone tried making their frantic escape in a mass exodus from the hospital, now they just clogged the roads.

"Don't nothing me!" Nick shouted at Dave as he was finally in an open stretch of road and able to increase his speed as they headed out of town.

"I told you to have those things destroyed! Now look what you did, look at this mess!" Dave shouted back at Nick.

"How was I supposed to know this was going to happen?" Nick asked in a crude tone.

"I told you they're evil! Where are they at?" Dave tried taking charge and was now asking the questions.

"Why? What is all this?" Nick retorted.

"I need them, it's the only way to stop all of this craziness."

"How?" Nick asked as he continued driving like a madman in his brazen attempt to try out running this chaos that seemed to be spreading faster than he could drive.

"Never mind that! I don't have time to explain," Dave insisted. "Now where is the star and dagger? I need them. It's the only way to end this!"

"The star is at the church, in the pastor's office. It burned me every time I tried to pick it up after we put the stone in the center," Nick tried to explain.

"The dagger? Where's the dagger at?" Dave asked in a panicked tone.

"Under your seat," Nick answered as Dave reached under the seat pulling out the dagger. Looking at it more closely than he had before, he noticed that each of the three stones locked in the hilt held a darkened image. Upon closer examination, he realized that each stone had the number six in the center. As if he didn't already know the scenario, he immediately recognized the triple six as the mark of the beast.

"We have to get back to the church!" Dave demanded, realizing that Nick was steadily heading out of town in the opposite direction of the town, church and the cabin.

"No way," Nick stated, "I'm getting the hell..."

"Look out!" Dave shouted as he pointed out of the windshield at an elderly woman standing in the middle of the road, directly in front of them. Nick slammed on the brakes and swerved as he tried to avoid hitting her, but lost control of the car due to the slippery road conditions the torrential rains inflicted upon the valley.

With the car spinning out of control, they slammed into a ditch on the side of the road. Both Nick and Dave managed to brace themselves for the impact, but from the second the car stopped, they knew they were stuck and there was no way they were going to be able to get it out without a wrecker.

Slowly climbing out of the shelter of the car and back into the monsoon, Dave was holding onto the dagger as they made their way up the slippery, muddy ditch. Even though they were both injured, not only from the wreak but from all they had been through, Nick's police instincts forced him to run toward the woman to see if she was alright. As soon as Nick was standing in front of her, she noticed that Dave was holding onto the dagger.

Her appearance suddenly changed from the casually dressed elderly woman into the shadow creature from the cabin wearing his black hooded robe with no visual face, only the fiery, red beady eyes. The shadow abruptly reached out with his claw and grabbed Nick by the throat and lifted him several feet off the ground. In fear for his life, Nick screamed at the top of his lungs. The shadow made a sudden twisting motion with his wrist and snapped Nick's spinal cord at the base of his neck. Holding him there elevated for several seconds, he then flung his arm in a sideways motion and tossed his limp lifeless body to the ground like a piece of trash.

“I’m gonna send you back to hell!” Dave shouted from across the street.

“Give me the dagger,” the shadow demanded in an angry deep dark voice.

“Never!” Dave replied.

“Then I’ll just have to kill you and take it,” the shadow replied as it took off running toward the town.

Dave knew instantly that he made a mistake and missed his best opportunity by not fighting the creature right here and now. He could only assume the shadow left because without the dagger or the star in his possession, his powers were minimal at best.

Dave ran over to Nick’s body only to confirm his suspicion, that he had been killed instantly. His heart ached in pain from all of the senseless death and turmoil that had plagued the town. Dave now knew where the star shaped medallion was located and that gave him a slight advantage over the shadow. Unfortunately, the shadow had already started making his way back into the town. With Dave stranded and already injured, that easily took away his slight advantage.

Dave assumed he knew the town better than the shadow and figured if he cut through the subdivisions, he might be able to beat the creature back to the church. As he took off into the subdivision, he was hopping fences when he realized this was still going to take him too much time. He needed at least a half hour to get there this way and the shadow was still likely to beat him there. He couldn’t let that happen, he needed to come up with a plan and he needed to do it quickly.

Hurdling over yet another fence, he suddenly got an idea. He was in the backyard of a house that had a swing set, this led him to the conclusion that whoever lived here must have children. With a little luck, they would be the right age and own a bike. He walked over to the garage and grabbed the handle, fortunately it was unlocked.

Before he was able to pull the door open, he nearly jumped out of his skin as another bolt of lightning struck the mammoth tree in the neighbor's yard and severed off a huge branch from its trunk. As it came crashing down, it happened to land on the sidewall of the above ground swimming pool and crushed it, releasing a knee high tidal wave that ripped across the already flooded yard. Already soaked, Dave kept his focus on the task at hand.

When he pulled the door open all he could see was darkness at first, but his eyes slowly adjusted the blinding flash of lightning. The garage itself was mostly empty, but the entire back wall was lined with boxes, stacked neatly all the way to the ceiling. With his luck continuing to hold up, the place had exactly what he was looking for. Leaning fortuitously against the right side wall were two ten speed bikes and a brand new BMX, similar to his own.

He walked over to the bikes and raised the kick stand of the BMX, turned it around and headed toward the front gate, quietly pushing the stolen bike. When he made it to the gate, he gently leaned the bike up against the house. The rain had started to lighten up just a little, but lightning continued to rage and ripple violently across the sky.

He walked over to the latch and tried rigorously to lift it up, but as he looked more closely, he realized there was a small padlock holding it firmly in place. Quietly he said to himself in a mumble, "Why can't anything just be simple? And what the hell is the point of locking the gate if your just gonna leave the garage wide open?"

He grudgingly walked back over to the bike, grabbed

it and rolled it up to the gate. Giving it everything he had, he moaned out in pain as he struggled to lift the bike over the fence. Against all odds, he somehow managed to complete the arduous task and gently set the bike down on the other side of the gate. Once it touched the ground on the other side, he let it fall over slowly away from the fence.

With his ankle sprained and foot swollen, he needed a quick way out of this backyard without having to climb the fence the traditional way. He thought if he could just step back a few feet from the fence, he could use this added distance to gain a little extra speed and leap clear over the fence, avoiding the climb altogether. All he had to do was run, grab the top rail of the fence with both hands and toss his legs to the side and allow his momentum to fling them across. This would allow him to clear the fence without having to use his sore foot to climb. The only down side was, in order to avoid the intense pain of the landing, he just had to make sure he landed solely on his good foot.

As he sprinted forward, he grabbed a hold of the top of the fence with his hands and attempted to swing his legs over the top like he envisioned. Unfortunately, as soon as the fence was bearing all of his weight combined with the momentum, both sections of the fence just toppled over forward with him still perched on top and crash landed on the bike. Feeling stupid and adding to the pain his dilapidated body was already in, he shouted, "Damn! What a piece of shit! I'd swear, if I didn't have bad luck I wouldn't have any at all."

Humiliated, he slowly climbed back to his feet and walked over to the fence post against the house and found two more of those little cheep padlocks in place and busted where the hinges should have been. "No wonder it was locked," he again said to himself. "The damn locks are the only thing holding this piece of shit together."

Now walking on top of the fence where he'd originally planned to land, he stepped off and began lifting it off the bike. When he finally got it upright, he gave it one last fateful push and let it fall over in the opposite direction, finally achieving success in his not so simple solution. He picked up the bike, sat on it and began coasting down the driveway.

Finally acquiring a mode of transportation, he felt his options weren't as limited as they were only moments ago. Although, knowing he was short on time, he figured it'd be much quicker to cut through the subdivision rather than taking the main drag. Additionally, taking this off beat route through the neighborhoods would give him an added advantage of slipping through the cracks and possibly beating the shadow. Not to mention, it didn't look nearly as dangerous, trashed or overrun with demons like the rest of the chaos he had witnessed all over town.

Given his condition, he began peddling down the street with everything he had. All the while he was trying to conserve what little strength he had just in case something would try to stop him prior to reaching the church. Soaking wet and wearing only what he'd left the hospital in, he was now being pounded on by large chunks of hail that happened to reappear as the rains once again picked up. Continuing to ride, everything was quiet for the majority of the way, just him against the storm. For right now, his biggest fear was that of being struck by the incessant lightning that continued to ravage the landscape and ignite fires with no remorse

Virginia Avenue was the back street in the subdivision that led directly to the back of the church. Turning down the homestretch, he just happened to glance behind him and noticed that he was being followed. Immediately, he knew exactly what was giving chase, he'd recognized the morbid abomination from previous encounters at the cabin. Running straight down the middle of the street in a mad dash after him, one of those twisted looking half-breed mountain lions was only about two blocks behind and the gap between them was rapidly closing.

Dave knew he didn't stand a chance of out running the cat, it was capable of far greater speeds then Dave could possibly peddle, especially given his condition. Since cats are predators and hunters, he knew trying to lose it would be like trying to reroute a stream to flow uphill. Even if it were possible, it would take too much time and this was a luxury he just didn't have. His mind was racing and Dave knew he had to make a decision, keep going and try to out run it, or stay and try fighting it. With no idea of what he was going to run into when he made it to the church, he didn't want to leave anything extra right on his tail, his only viable option was to stay and deal with this nuisance of a cat right now.

To test out his theory, he stayed exactly dead center in the middle of the road acting as determined as the cat to have this kamikaze head on collision. After a couple of seconds, Dave veered abruptly over to the right side of the street, getting as close to the parked cars as he possibly could. Just as he suspected, the feline brained cat mimicked his sudden movements. Testing his theory once more just to be absolutely sure of his plans possibility for success, he shot expeditiously over to the other side of the road on a steep angle. Dave just grinned, as the cat again followed suit just as he suspected it would. Now utterly positive this cat was suicidal, it was clear that it was fully intent and definitely determined to crash full force into him. Dave was gaining in confidence that this mutant cat was totally unsuspecting of his ultimate and devious plan. With the distance between them rapidly decreasing, Dave could now see in his minds eye exactly where this unavoidable collision was destined to take place.

He made a last second adjustment to his speed and moved the point of impact ever so slightly to occur where he wanted it to be.

With the impending collision rapidly approaching, they were converging at a ridicules speed. Dave stayed his course on the right side of the street, hugging the parked cars tightly. The cat followed his opposing lead, staying directly in front of him as they continued on their dramatic collision course. Dave continued on this heading until there was only about a fifteen foot gap closing between them. Abruptly, Dave kicked his plan into action and made a direct sharp turn. Hitting his brakes and sliding out his rear wheel, he skidded across the concrete at a ninety degree angle. Shifting his weight, he was able to cut instantly to the other side of the street just as he passed a full sized black Chevy van parked in the street.

Dave didn't account for how much speed he would lose as he cut sharply across the street. Barely going fast enough, he nicked the rear bumper with his peddle as he passed the van, knocking him slightly off balance. Oblivious to the plan plotted against it or the fact that it was rapidly falling apart, the doltish cat mimicked the sudden change in Dave's trajectory. As it crossed over the middle of the street, it leapt into the air and took flight. With its body fully extended and claws out, it let out a ferocious roar as headed directly toward him. Dave had timed it almost perfectly and was just about where he wanted to be. The cat barely missed Dave as he'd just passed by the back of the van and cut onto the lawn. The near collision was so close, Dave could actually feel the movement of the air as the cat passed behind him and all he could hear was a loud crashing sound. By missing Dave in the attack, the cat slammed into the back of the van head first with all of its weight and speed, amplifying the brunt force of the impact. It let out a loud, painful sounding yelp as it fell to the ground like a ton of bricks after knocking itself unconscious.

Dave had just missed the collision with the van and barely avoided losing out to the ferocious cat. As he glided across the muddy lawn after his sharp cut away, his front tire hit the curb of the approach to the driveway, twisting his handlebars right out of his hands. He was knocked too far off balance to salvage and regain control of his jump as he launched into the air. When he awkwardly landed, the front tire sank deep into the saturated muddy lawn, stopping the bikes forward motion dead in its tracks. As the bike flipped over forward, passing its own front wheel in an endo, it tossed Dave right over the handle bars. He went flying through the air before he landed doing a face plant in the mud and slid several more feet before he finally came to a complete stop. Laying there, he felt victorious and defeated at the same time. He knew hitting the bumper of the van with his peddle is what nearly did him in.

Quickly, Dave jumped up to his feet and wiped off most of the excess mud. Picking up the dagger and what remained of his pride, he ran back over to the bike. Giving a solid yank, he managed to pull the bike out of the mud. He gave a quick glance back over to the cat as he climbed onto the bike. He wasn't sure of whether it was dead or if it had just knocked itself out, but either way, he wasn't about to go check. All that mattered to him now was getting back to the church before the shadow. He resumed riding down the street as he headed for the church and it only took about a block before the rain had washed off the remainder of the mud.

With his heart racing and his hospital gown holding more water than he ever imagined possible, he started to wonder to himself if he was even going to make it to the church, let alone have enough strength to beat the shadow should a confrontation arise. Regardless of these unwanted and negative thoughts forcing their way into his mind, he tried desperately to maintain hope that he would be the first one to arrive at the church. Knowing that if he were to be that fortunate, he might be able to bring all this chaos to an end, virtually unopposed. Even if he still had to fight the shadow, he was positive that if he had both the dagger and medallion in his possession, this would greatly increase his chances of being able to come out victorious. Especially since the shadow made it more than obvious earlier that he didn't want a confrontation when Dave was armed with the dagger and the star was still located in town and out of reach.

As he neared the end of the street and the town came into view, he was horrified by the level of mass destruction that had nearly abolished the town in its entirety. There wasn't a single living soul for as far as the eye could see. The whole town had been repopulated in mass with evil spirits, ghosts, entities and little brown trolls that seemed to be trying to destroy the destruction.

As Dave arrived at the church, he was surprised, it was one of the few buildings that had yet to catch fire or be totally destroyed. He set the bike down in the front next to the bushes and proceeded in through the front entrance. The church was also without power, but the light from the nearby fires penetrated through the giant stained glass windows and managed to light the place up. As he stepped inside, he left the door open behind him, unsure why. Standing in the vestibule of the congregation room, he was surrounded entirely by empty pews. The church had been completely vacated, no people, no ghosts, nothing, just a vast amount of eerie silence. Dave thought this to be strange given the condition of everything else in the town. What bothered him even more was that it was really warm inside the church and yet it wasn't on fire, at least that he was aware of. Trying to make some sense out of all this insanity, he just stood there in a state of momentary confusion when suddenly he heard a voice call out to him. "Dave," the familiar voice called out to him from the office located in the back of the church.

"Pastor Soncrainte, am I glad to see you," Dave replied as he started walking toward him.

"Are you alright?" he asked showing a genuine concern for his well being.

"I'm fine, has he been here? Where's the star?" Dave asked as he continued his approach.

"Who?" the pastor asked curiously.

"The shadow, where's the star?" Dave demanded as he began to lose his patience.

"I hid it in the safe. Don't worry you're safe here," the pastor insisted.

Puzzled, Dave froze in his tracks as he suddenly recalled the exact words Nick had spoke in the car and it kept repeating quietly in his head. "It burned me every time I tried to pick it up after we put the stone in the center."

"What's wrong? Come over here," the pastor was pleading to Dave as he was now walking backwards down the isle.

"You're not Pastor Soncrainte! You're him!" Dave shouted. "You're him! You're trying to trick me!"

"What are you talking about? That's just crazy, come here."

"No!" Dave shouted again, "Never!"

An awkward silence fell over the church as Dave stood there paralyzed by the intense thoughts running wild through his mind. Suddenly, the door he had entered through slammed shut behind him and every window in the church suddenly shattered. Dave had to move forward slightly to avoid being struck by the falling pieces of stained glass. The image of the pastor slowly began to change back to the faceless image Dave knew all too well as the shadow.

Trying to gain the upper hand by means of intimidation, the shadow stood there about halfway up the isle holding open his black robe. He had his claw firmly gripped on the star shaped medallion as it dangled several inches off of his chest. Blatantly flaunting it as he made sure Dave knew that he already had it.

"Now I know you didn't think you were just gonna walk in here, grab this and close the gate, did you?" the shadow asked before releasing his sadistic laugh that normally sent a chill down Dave's spine.

Dave raised the dagger and aimed the tip toward the shadow as he shouted, "Give me the star! Now!"

"Never! You gonna kill me and take it? Now where have I heard that before?" the shadow remarked sarcastically referring to their earlier confrontation back at the cabin.

"Give me the star!" Dave repeated, showing no fear.

"Why don't you just give me the key and we can rule together?" the shadow suggested as he stepped out of the aisle way and into the pews.

Dave finally broke free from the tunnel vision of anger and rage he felt growing toward the shadow, only to watch as he pulled a large machete out of the real Pastor Soncrainte's chest as he lay on the floor in between the pews. Dave was now able to notice his surroundings and became suddenly aware the whole church was full of all the creatures of chaos that had destroyed the town. The sheer number was unfathomable as they seem to have formed a large audience to witness the event that would inevitably seal their fate. The shadow stepped back into the aisle stating, "Even your myths state that I will rise to finish what I started."

"Not if I have anything to do about it," Dave retorted.

"Then you have chosen your fate," the shadow replied, "and now you must die."

With the machete in hand, he turned his claw like hands so his palms were facing the sky. The fury of the storm outside took on an even more angry state of rage. The violent cracks of lightning and thunder seemed to be coming in an almost continuous flow. His red eyes flashed as bright as the fires of hell themselves as his robe was being rippled by a fierce wind that seemed to only blow on him, with no apparent source. The ground beneath their feet began to shake violently with the raw force of ten major earthquakes all happening simultaneously.

Dave raised the dagger up over his head and started to run down the trembling aisle way as he charged fearlessly toward the shadow. The creature dropped down to one knee and raised the machete up over his head as he fended off the onslaught. As their weapons collided and locked in a test of power and endurance, a bolt of lightning ripped through the ceiling, striking and destroying the podium located just behind the shadow. Aided by the deafening thunderous distraction, the creature forced his locked arm upwards and Dave was nearly knocked off balance due to the shadows strength combined with the shifting earth. The creature spun around in a complete circle as he stood back to his feet in one fluid motion. Trying to take advantage of Dave's discombobulated state, he followed through by executing a forward slashing motion.

Dave had picked up on the counter attack right away. Luckily, he had regained enough of his balance to enable him to jump backwards just in time to prevent his insides from being exposed. When the shadow's swing missed, using all the momentum he could muster, he exposed his backside to his attacker and Dave seized on this opportunity, lunging forward and driving the dagger into his back, sliding all the way through his chest.

"No!" the shadow cried out in pain as he leaned away from Dave in a desperate attempt to try removing the foreign object from his body. The shadow managed to free himself from the penetration, raised up the machete and spun back around in a final attempt to regain control. Dave grabbed his arm out of mid air by the wrist and nullified the attack. Momentarily holding the shadow motionless, he raised up the dagger and brought it down forcefully as he slashed the blade across the creature's throat once again. Blue blood started gushing out of the creature's open neck and its body suddenly went limp, falling to the floor.

Seconds after the shadow hit the floor, the earthquakes came to an abrupt stop and the storm outside grew excessively quiet. All of the creatures that had filled the church only seconds before scattered in all directions. Dave bent down to grab the star medallion off of the shadows bloody corpse. As he lifted the leather strap up over the creatures partially severed head, the hood that shielded his darkened face from being visible slid back and fell off.

Dave was astonished by what he saw. The true face of the creature behind this all was none other then his friend Allen. His face was pale and his eyes were so cold that Dave couldn't even begin to understand it. Baffled by this strange discovery, Dave stood upright again with a puzzled look on his face, wondering what it was that he was supposed to do next. Standing there in momentary confusion, the white raven flew in through the broken stained glass window and perched itself on a pew to the left of him.

"Is it over?" Dave asked.

"Yes," the Raven replied in its soft gentle tone.

"What do I do now?"

"Insert the dagger into the center stone and turn it clockwise, that will set everything right again," the Raven instructed.

Pausing briefly, Dave did as the bird suggested. The storm outside once again started to rage, but this time there was no lightning or thunder, only the fierce howling of a wind that sounded strong enough to be part of a hurricane.

Back on the trails, the ground shook violently as a colossal section of earth spontaneously erupted in a powerful blast. Dirt, gravel and debris were ejected hundreds of feet in every direction as the terrain ripped wide open, closely resembling the shape of a lightning bolt. The gash itself was approximately five feet wide, twenty feet long and glowed intently with a deep crimson hue.

The surrounding storm continued to advance and intensify with gale force winds. The apex of the storm was centered directly over the opening and began to form a funnel cloud. When the tornado fully developed, its vortex plunged several feet beneath the surface through the portals massive opening.

With its maneuverability confined to the size and shape of the aperture, it began swaying erratically, violently bouncing back and fourth between the inner sidewalls of the fissure. Anchored to the bottom and reaching for the sky, the funnel turned dark gray and augmented as if it was trying to escape to no avail.

Fierce gusts of wind whipped towards the epicenter from every direction. Despite desperate attempts in resisting, the gale force winds aggregated creatures near and far. Haphazardly, creatures began being plucked mid stride from places all over town, soaring chaotically through the air and inescapably toward the vortex. Drawn in by the intense cyclone, as the monsters reached the event horizon, they seemed to pause, tethered momentarily, before being plunged forthwith, instantly vaporizing as they disappeared deep beneath the surface of the fiery pit.

With the storm peaking in ferocity, the cabin began to disintegrate. The abomination itself was ripped to shreds by the tempest. Piece by piece, all of its contents began to slowly vanish into the storm. Absorbed by the whirlwind and forced through the gateway, the last remaining fragments slipped beneath the surface and disappeared into the abyss.

With the final traces of this abomination rendered moot, the storm front began loosing steam as the gateway started to collapse in on itself like a black hole. The winds started to dissipated and the evil gateway began to close. The gash in the earth started to heal itself, fusing at both ends simultaneously as they encroached towards the middle. The torn ground continued pulling itself together, inch by inch before vanishing completely into a pinpoint of light as everything in the surrounding area became abruptly silent.

PART NINE
Uncertain Of Reality

"David!" his mother shouted. "David! Wake up!" As Dave suddenly opened his eyes, he discovered that he was laying on his own bed in the room he shared with his brother.

"What?" he said in total disbelief, sounding a little snippy.

"Don't what me. Get up, you're gonna be late for school again," she said. As his mother walked out of the room, he quickly sat up and noticed he was soaked in sweat. Turning his head, he looked to his right and saw his brother sleeping soundly in the other twin bed.

Confused beyond belief, he sat there quietly as he examined his body for all of the injuries he was sure he would find. Under his own breath he asked himself, "Was it all a dream? It couldn't have been, it was so long and I remember it all so vividly."

When he climbed out of his bed, he was wearing only his boxer shorts. He took off running to the other side of the room and started to frantically shake his brother in an attempt to wake him up, "Jeff! Jeff! Wake up, are you alright?"

"Yeah, what the hell is a matter with you? I'm tired and I ain't gotta get up for another half hour, so leave me alone," Jeff demanded as he rolled over and pulled his pillow over his head.

Puzzled, Dave stood there and shook his head. He was sure that he was losing his mind. He couldn't stop thinking to himself that there was no way that couldn't have all been real. Frustrated, he decided to get ready for school in an attempt to avoid being late. He grabbed his jeans off of his dresser and slowly finagled them on. Dave decided that he needed a few more seconds to regain control of his thoughts. He opened his dresser drawer and grabbed his pack of cigarettes out from underneath his socks, pulled one out and set the pack on top of his dresser. Then he reached into his pocket for a light and suddenly found himself staring at the all black matchbook with no writing on it from the cabin. When he opened up the cover, only one match was gone.

The End